CAPTIVE SOULS

ANNE MALCOM

Cover Design: TRC Designs
Editing: KimBookJunkie
Proofreading: All Encompassing Books

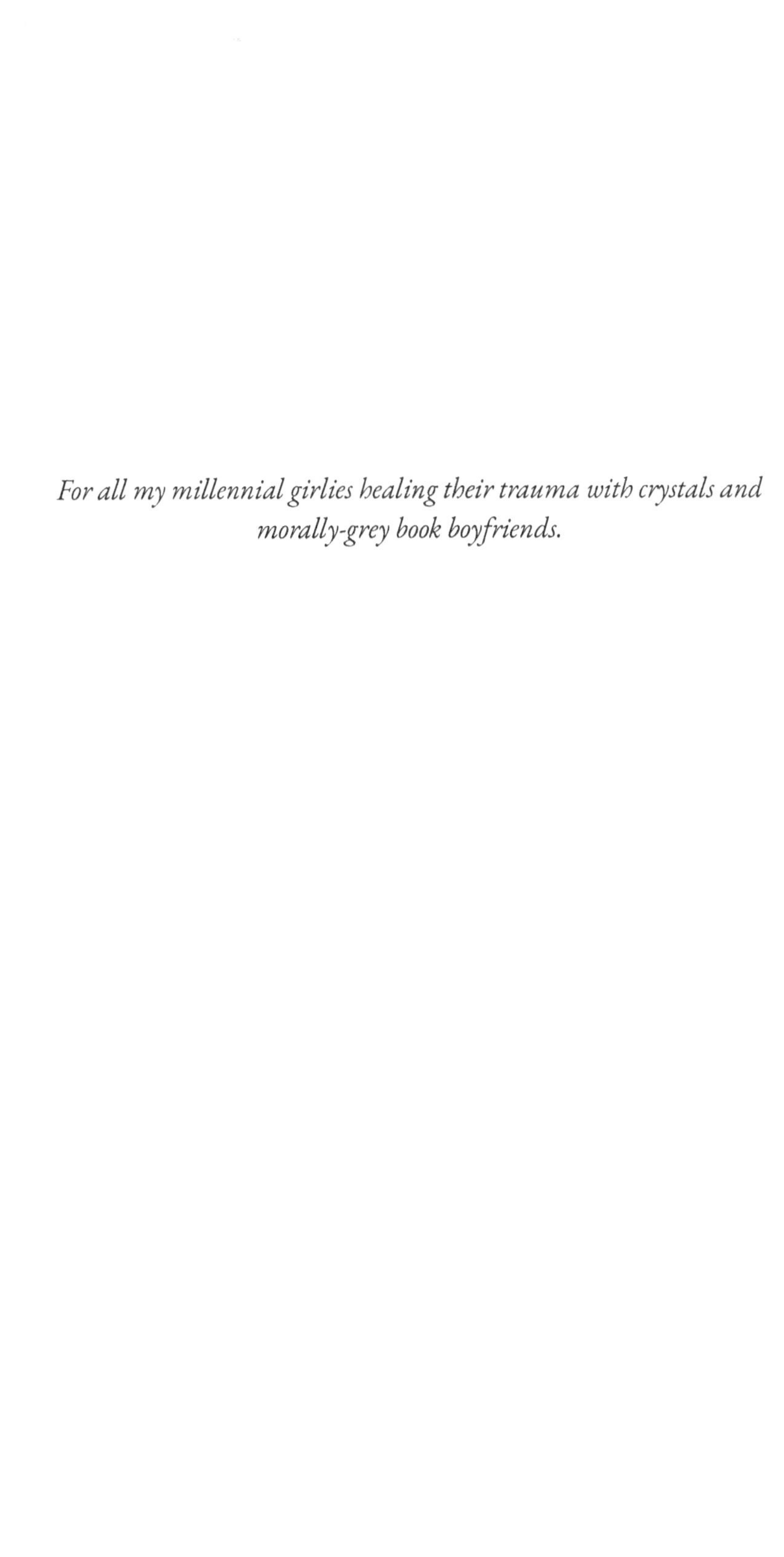

For all my millennial girlies healing their trauma with crystals and morally-grey book boyfriends.

ONE

KNOX

The room I stood in reeked of expensive cigars and bespoke aftershave.

My body craved the scent of iron. Blood.

Soon.

The man in front of me was a necessary evil, one who thought controlled me. I'd let him believe that as long as he served a purpose—offering me an endless supply of victims.

"I need you to catch someone for me."

"Catch?" I repeated, even though I'd heard him just fine.

He nodded once, steepling his fingers as his elbows rested on the oak desk between us. "*Catch*."

I was standing in front of him. He'd offered me a chair, as he did every time I was in this room. And as always, I stood. My posture didn't change, my expression stayed the same—blank, uninterested. But Stone knew me as well as anyone could truly know me. Which meant he understood that I was questioning his request.

He leaned back in his chair, smiling. "When I say catch, I mean alive. And she stays that way until you hand her over to me."

I felt the dynamics of our relationship shift as I processed this request. "You want me to *catch, not kill,* a woman?" I wasn't one to ask rhetorical questions, but this ventured far outside our regular formula. Stone and I had enjoyed a stable, predictable and mutually beneficial relationship over the years. I enjoyed stability. Predictable. Controlling all the variables.

He thought that I worked for him. His rabid, dangerous dog who obeyed his every command and never stretched the leash.

Maybe he thought it was because I was loyal to him or because he paid me well or because I was scared of him.

None of that was true.

Without a leash, I was scared of myself.

His leash kept the world safe from monsters like me.

"Catch, not kill," Stone said for the third time. "And keep her safe. Whole."

Irritation bloomed in my gut, yet I didn't show it, giving him a flat stare. "You want me to babysit. I don't babysit. And I do not keep people safe." It annoyed me that he even asked this of me. He was stretching the limits of what I would tolerate.

Stone chuckled. He did that, laughed often and easily. He had a decade on my forty years with creases in his face to show it. The creases did not just signify his age but the variety of expressions this man wore, plenty of them smiles.

He was tall but not overly so, fit but not cut with muscle. His hair was cropped close to his head, a sensible cut. He was always clean-shaven. He wore exquisitely tailored suits, one of the only shows of his wealth. Otherwise, he looked like any other middle-aged banker.

He did not look like the don of one of the most dangerous and lethal organized crime syndicates in the country.

Most of the time, he looked and acted like the American archetype of the 'fun uncle.'

I'd seen him peel the skin off someone who'd betrayed him

without breaking a sweat. You'd be very unwise to let his demeanor lower your guard or think you could best him.

More than one Made Man had been stupid enough to try to steal power from him. I'd killed them myself.

That was my job, after all.

Killing.

He did it when he needed to get the point across, but mostly he didn't like getting his hands dirty. Literally or figuratively.

Hence our mutually beneficial relationship.

"I know this job may seem beneath you." He stroked his chin. "But rest assured, there is no one else in my organization I want in charge of this. Of her."

"Her?" I questioned again. Women were unusual but not unheard of in my role. And the way he spoke of this woman was different. Possessive. My instincts prickled with warning bells.

His smile turned predatory. "Yes. My future wife."

I didn't let my surprise show. Stone liked women. He always had them around. Young, shallow, stupid, unaware of how dangerous he was, blinded by his wealth. He used them then discarded them. Alive, luckily. But a little wiser to what the world truly was.

"It's time," he told me, as if I'd questioned him. "For me to settle down, make a family."

Again, I didn't react, but the idea of this man inflicting himself on a child was vaguely sickening to me. And for me to say that meant something.

"And your wife needs..." I stare off unsure of what my role was to be in this charade, though I could take an educated guess as to why he was involving me. It did not speak of a mutually consenting courtship.

"She needs some *convincing* that marrying me is the best and safest decision for her." He spoke carefully, reasonably, as if what he was saying was completely sane. To him, it was. "I need you to break her."

He needed me to scare the shit out of her and let her know that death was the only way to get out of this marriage.

Should I have deemed this deplorable? Absolutely. If I had morals, I'd walk out of the room, refusing such a mission.

If she had to be persuaded to say yes, this woman, his *bride*, was probably not someone who had chosen this life.

That should go against my code.

Criminals had codes, fucked-up belief systems that gave justification for what they did. That helped them sleep at night, deluded themselves into thinking they were heroes of their own stories. They didn't touch innocents, women.

No one in life was innocent.

And women could be murderers, criminals just as well, if not better, than men could.

I hadn't killed one that wasn't deserving, but that didn't mean I had a code. It just meant I hadn't happened upon an innocent woman I was ordered to kill.

I didn't delude myself into thinking I was a hero. I knew exactly what I was.

"Don't kill her, hurt her or fuck her." Stone's eyes twinkled. "Not that I have to worry about the latter with you."

My teeth gnashed together as my blood suddenly turned to acid. I stayed placid outwardly. Stone knew me as well as anyone could, which wasn't at all. But he did notice things, and he obviously had me followed or watched closely enough to know that I didn't fuck. Women or men. He'd offered, plenty of times, both women and men, seemingly nonjudgmental of my sexual orientation—he just wanted me to have one. If I fucked someone, had an appetite for something, it was something he could use to control me, manipulate me. But I didn't take any of his offers, uninterested in the variety of people he'd either threatened or paid to throw themselves at me.

He'd eventually given up on trying to make me fuck something.

He'd considered that a weakness, my lack of sexual appetite, assuming it must mean there was something wrong with my manhood.

Probably why he chose me for this particular task. I wasn't a threat.

Not that he thought, at least.

I was always a threat.

He watched me carefully, eyes narrowing. "Is there a problem?" There was a challenge in his question. He was daring me to refuse. Not that I'd face repercussions. It would be a show of weakness for me to refuse.

I didn't trouble myself with archaic shows of masculinity and mind games within this world. I didn't need either to show who I was. I could easily say no to this. Stone would likely try to punish me in some kind of way, but he wouldn't succeed. No one could hurt me or punish me as profoundly as I did to myself.

This was the fork in the road, one that I'd been waiting for. I'd known Stone would eventually challenge the boundaries of this relationship, ask things of me that I didn't want to do. Kill... That's all I wanted. None of these benign tasks that made things messy.

It was time for me to part ways. This was a sign. For me to disappear into the ether and find a new path.

"No," I said slowly. "There's no problem."

In a split second, I decided against walking down a different path. Disappearing at this juncture in my life would be complicated. One job outside the norm, one job to continue to delude Stone into thinking his leash was unbreakable... Then it would be back to regular scheduled programming.

I didn't see any reason to make him stop believing I was anything but his loyal beast.

Four days later, I was in Central Park, following my target.

If I was the kind of person to smile, I would've grinned at the dark irony of her heading into a dense part of the park, me following her, her clothed in red.

Like some kind of fucking fairy tale. The monster following her into the woods.

Except this wasn't a fairy tale. And she wasn't going to triumphantly defeat me. Or outsmart me.

Piper Matthews was doomed the second I laid eyes on her.

PIPER

I didn't mean to get involved with the mob.

To be fair, I didn't think anyone really *meant* to get involved with the mob.

Sure, there were the select few who watched *The Sopranos* and decided that's exactly what they wanted out of their life then dove headfirst into the world of organized crime. But I'd bet that most people tried their hardest to avoid it, beyond enjoying arguably one of the best television series to be written.

I was one of the latter people.

My sister, unfortunately, was one of the former.

She did not want to be a 'Made Man'—was it still a Made Man if the person in question was a woman? Did they even let women fill that role? I'm guessing not, since the patriarchy was still going strong, but maybe the mob was progressive. She did, however, get tangled up in the 'romance' of what it would be like to be with a morally- gray man who looked tough and didn't live by the word of federal law. An outlaw. The ultimate bad boy in an Armani suit.

Yes, all of this was *romantic* to her, and she got swept up with the wrong man.

Trouble ensued, as it tended to do with my sister.

I tried to come to her rescue, as I always had and always would with my sister.

Usually, I was a dab hand at dealing with trouble.

Not this time. Not only did I not get her off the mob's radar, but I somehow got myself in the crosshairs of the don of the mob. The don being the big boss. And though he seemed polite enough in the scant interactions I had with him, I was under no illusions that one got to the top of a ruthless, international crime syndicate by being *nice*.

I knew he was a murderer, among other things. And that did not charm me.

It sickened me.

His suits, his shiny, Botoxed skin, the manicured hands, the smiles that never reached his eyes... All of it.

He wasn't unattractive, but he turned my stomach, nonetheless.

I didn't let this show. Though I might not have been practiced at moving around in the criminal underworld, I'd been in the dating scene since I was eighteen, so I understood that even the 'safest' of men could turn deadly if they were rejected.

As I'd been trying to do, all while slowly coming to the realization that if I didn't want to be involved with this gross murderer, I would either have to learn how to fight off him and his underlings for the rest of time, go to the police, or disappear.

I was competent at defending myself, no slouch at all. I didn't own one, but I knew how to operate a weapon. Though I understood that I wouldn't be a match for men who literally killed for a living. And again, my knowledge of the mob was based solely on my love for *The Sopranos*, but I understood that going to the police in any capacity was likely a death sentence, especially since I had no actual evidence of anyone breaking the law, merely them grossing me out with unwanted advances.

Therefore, disappear it was. Disappear from the job I loved, the friends I'd made, the home I'd finally settled into and the cat who had just recently decided he might tolerate me. Not to mention I'd have to figure out a way to bring my sister with me. Most likely I'd have to chloroform her because she wouldn't go willingly. And even then, if I did manage to convince her we couldn't come back to New York, she would probably make some slip-ups when it came to disappearing from your old identity so that killers couldn't find you and punish you for running.

It was somewhat of a conundrum. And though I'd done a lot for my sister, I would do almost anything for her, I didn't think I could date—and maybe marry, if he was to be believed—a crime boss.

With all of this chaos swimming through my mind, I'd understandably been distracted during my run this morning.

Running in Central Park at six in the morning wasn't exactly a dangerous pastime; there were plenty of other people around. But as a woman doing it alone, it was risky. Made even riskier when you were on the radar of a mob boss who you very politely rebuked. Multiple times. And he just kept coming.

Half of me was expecting it. Some kind of attack, or at least an intimidating man in a leather jacket coming to tell me what might happen if I did not accept Stone's not-so-decent proposal.

What I didn't expect was the man in a bespoke suit, looking like midnight against the sunrise, standing directly in my path.

I knew immediately he was there for me.

I'd done all the things women were supposed to do. I ran differing routes at differing times, never making my routine predictable, trying to make myself less vulnerable. There was no way he could've possibly predicted where I could've been running. Yet there he was, standing in my path. Evidence that no matter what precautions you took, being a woman existing in a world of men was a dangerous thing in and of itself.

I could've gone around him; there was a wide enough berth for me to do so. And I was in gear equipped to run while he was wearing loafers that wouldn't do well in a chase. Theoretically, I could've gotten away from him.

But some part of me knew, just by laying eyes on him, that he'd catch me eventually. A part of me was tired, exhausted by living in this state of fight-or-flight, waiting for this to happen. I was relieved, in a way. The parts of me that weren't utterly and completely terrified, that was.

Nausea swirled through my gut as the music from my earphones continued playing. Not loud enough for me to be defenseless from the world around me, though.

I still heard the far-off city sounds, traffic, sirens, other people in the park. But somehow, on this stretch of path, there was only me and this man.

The Midnight Man.

He was gorgeous. With the sharp, angular bone structure of a model, high cheekbones, severe jaw, broad shoulders, shiny black hair that bordered his face exquisitely.

Eyes so blue they were like hardened sapphires.

He seemed like a work of art. A truly gorgeous villain had walked off the pages of a book. An immensely odd thing to notice about the man who was going to be my murderer at the very worst and threaten me at the very best. But I couldn't not notice it. The sweat on my body turned to ice as my instincts recognized him as a deadly predator.

My chest rose and fell rapidly as my body screamed at me to run as fast as I could from this man. I could make it to my apartment before he did—if more of his people weren't waiting there. I had a go bag, I could leave. But I had no idea where my sister was, and no way would she be answering her phone at six in the morning. That meant if I couldn't find her, I'd have to leave her. Not an option.

I came to a stop a healthy distance away from him—even though a healthy distance away from this man would likely be Rhode Island. My heart thrummed, my breath coming in quick pants. I didn't dare take my attention away from him even though the prolonged eye contact felt sticky, heavy and uncomfortable.

He watched me for longer than I expected, remaining silent. His gaze froze me down to the bone, my lips trembling from the force of it. I'd never been in the presence of someone like this. Not even Stone, my would-be suitor, had this kind of coldness about him.

I was suddenly aware of my clothing, or lack thereof. In my attempts at keeping myself safe from stalkers, rapists and the Italian mob, I listened to music at a low volume and varied my route, but I didn't cover myself from head to toe. I ran five miles a day, and though it was spring, I got hot. I started with a windbreaker on, but about halfway through, I slung it around my waist, leaving me in only a bright red, cropped sports bra and matching leggings.

I knew my skin was likely flushed with that same red, my cheeks warm, and the hair that had escaped from my ponytail was sticking to the sides of my face.

Though it bothered me plenty that men stared at my exposed skin like they had a right to, I'd never let it get to me like it did now. I had a wild urge to cover every soft spot, every vulnerable piece of flesh from this man's gaze.

But I was frozen in place, waiting. Unmoving, paralyzed by the knowledge that nothing I could cover myself with would make me invulnerable to a creature like this.

I might as well have served myself up on a silver platter.

There was no expression on the man's face. Nothing I could glean. It was empty, a handsome, menacing mask of nothingness.

"You need to come with me," was what he said when he finally spoke.

My body shivered upon hearing his voice.

It was deep. Quieter than I expected. Barely above a whisper, but it had a resonance to it, an authority that made me want to obey him.

I licked my lips, suddenly absolutely parched, my throat burning.

When his eyes followed the motion, I clamped my mouth shut.

I could disagree. Yell. Try to reason with him. But something told me all of those things would fail, and I'd eventually be going with him anyway. And I might or might not be unconscious.

I didn't run.

I said one word.

"Okay."

And though I was a millennial who liked all things witchy, I didn't consider myself a psychic in any kind of way. Nonetheless, I knew deep in my bones that that single word, that submission, would change the trajectory—and maybe the length—of my entire life.

Two

Piper

The kidnapping itself was rather anticlimactic. I followed the man to a black SUV, getting in the front seat after a moment of confusion. Was this like a rideshare where I was expected to ride in the back? The front felt intimate, consenting, yet the back was far too vulnerable for my liking. I didn't quite know the etiquette of an abduction.

Not that it mattered where I sat in the end, since he didn't even spare me a glance. I ended up in the front, even though the nearness to this man made my muscles stretch to their limits with tension.

The interior of the SUV was impeccable. It smelled like new car and ... something else. Woodsy, masculine. Him.

Appealing.

Absolutely abhorrent and unhinged of me to notice my maybe murderer was sexy and smelled nice. But I couldn't help but think that.

He drove to my apartment building on the Lower East Side, which I was only able to afford because a great aunt we barely knew had owned it and lived in it until she died and bequeathed it to me and my sister. It was worth millions now. We could've sold it

—God knew we needed the money. But I would never. That place was the one sign that the universe hadn't damned us completely. We'd been given it when we had no other home, no family, nothing.

It was a symbol of hope. We'd turned it into a home, even if Daisy had moved out and it was now just me and a moody cat.

And where would I go? Even the millions I would've made couldn't buy me anything comparable in the city, and leaving the city seemed absolutely unthinkable. It was my home. I'd forced it to be that way because I didn't have the strength to go back to the one other place in the world that made my heart sing.

I was overrun with the 'what ifs'—what if I had made a fiscally responsible decision and sold this place when we got it, getting me and Daisy out of the city and somewhere … safe? I wouldn't be getting kidnapped right now and Daisy wouldn't be...

"Where is my sister?" I demanded, turning in my seat as we somehow got an impossible parking spot right out front of my building.

When his eyes darted to me, there was nothing in them. Nothing human or empathetic. It was terrifying, like I was looking into a black hole. "Unharmed," he said. "And she'll stay that way as long as you comply."

The threat wasn't overt. It didn't need to be. This man just existing, breathing, staring at me was a threat.

"Comply with what?" I bit down on my bottom lip. I knew that this was obviously some sort of intimidation tactic in order for me to surrender to Stone, but I didn't understand any of it. And even with this man beside me, even with the pure terror he instilled in me, it wasn't enough to make me submit.

Instead of answering, he handed me a vibrating phone.

The name *Stone* flashed on the screen.

My hand wasn't shaking when I took it—I was proud of that.

I pressed answer on the screen but didn't say anything. How

exactly was I supposed to greet the crime boss who didn't take no for an answer?

"Piper," he drawled. "I hope you're well."

The sound of his voice made my empty stomach turn. The forced politeness was ridiculous. As if this was all normal. Sane.

My spine straightened as I forced myself to ignore the man beside me, who I knew was watching me. Instead, I looked out into the busy New York street, at the people going about their lives as if mine wasn't imploding in the cab of an SUV.

"Well?" I repeated on a cold laugh. "I wouldn't consider me being forced from my run and my sister's life being threatened as *well*."

"He hasn't touched you, has he?" was Stone's cool, biting response.

Still, I didn't look at him, my kidnapper, the man whose gaze was as heavy as a hundred city buses. "No, your lapdog has not touched me." The air in the cab seemed to chill, my bones practically chattering.

A pause. "Good." I could almost see him nodding.

"What is this, Stone?" I clenched my hands around the phone, wanting to crush it in my palm. "What's your game plan here?"

"I'm going to give you a little ... vacation," he said pleasantly.

My heart continued to pound. "Vacation?"

"Yes, you work too hard, and I know you haven't taken one in years. Not since Turks and Caicos in 2017."

The hair on my arms stood at hearing how much information he had, just how much digging he'd done on me. I wasn't a dark or sordid person, but my past had its fair share of skeletons, and all could have been used against me.

"Yes, but I went to Turks and Caicos with my friend Hailey, not a six-foot-something brute who looks like he strangles puppies for fun." My sharp tone was entirely put on. Inside, I was trembling and crying and screaming.

My windpipe constricted at the sound of Stone's laughter. "He will not hurt you, you have my word."

"Excuse me if your word means jack shit to me," I snapped. Being a smart ass to the crime boss having you kidnapped wasn't smart but I didn't want to go quietly either. My life was quickly careening into something too strange and terrifying to be real. I couldn't just *let* it happen.

Even if I had the horrifying certainty that I had absolutely no control here. No way to escape.

"I understand," Stone replied calmly, with no hint of a temper. Though I assumed he had one. You didn't become a crime boss by being mild mannered or kind. I'd do well to remember that.

"You live a busy life, Piper," he continued. "You work very hard, take care of others, are constantly on the move. I understand that doesn't give you the time for the consideration that my proposal requires."

My lungs seized.

"I may have a bit of a shitty memory, but I'd remember a proposal." I remembered the flowers, the gifts, the letters. But no proposal.

"Uh," he grunted. "Not exactly romantic, I'll admit, but it is not a reflection on how the rest of your life will be."

"The rest of my life?" My heartbeat was a hummingbird, and an anvil settled in my throat.

"It'll be a good life, I assure you." I heard tapping, like he was working on the computer while ruining my life. "You won't have to work. You'll be able to move out of that apartment of yours, and I'll ensure you have the best of everything."

"I *have* a good life." My mouth tasted sour. "I like my life. And I apologize for the obvious sting it is to your ego, but I want my life to be lived without your … attention." I tried for yet another one of my gentle but crystal-clear rebukes I'd been giving since it became obvious Stone wanted me.

It was a complex dance to have to do, to reject a dangerous man. Well, to reject a man in general. All rejected men were dangerous in the right circumstances. Protect his ego, make it seem like you're doing him a favor but don't insult him. Otherwise, your life would be in danger.

"I know you think that now." He didn't sound even slightly perturbed. "But your time away will give you plenty of space to reconsider."

"I won't. Reconsider," I replied firmly. I was still clutching on to the vague hope that he'd finally get the picture, take the rejection well and let me go back to my life, no hard feelings.

"You will," he replied, just as firmly yet with no threat in his tone. He didn't need it, did he? He had someone beside me doing all the threatening. "And we'll watch over Daisy while you're gone. I know how much she means to you." He let silence fall between us so the heaviness of his words could crush my heart. Crush my hope.

My vision clouded with tears I would never let fall.

"Understand that we'll never be far," Stone continued. "I've taken the liberty of drafting an email and a text you can send to your friends and your employers about your sudden need to walk the Camino de Santiago. To go find yourself. Without the trappings of a phone or social media."

Acid burned my stomach. He knew. I didn't know how he knew, but he knew that I'd been planning to one day—when I had the time and the money and the courage—take a month off to walk across Spain.

I squeezed my eyes shut and pinched the bridge of my nose. I understood exactly what he meant. Running would result in Daisy being hurt or maybe even killed. Talking to anyone, trying to get help, same deal.

In an instant, all my fight left me. My entire life had been dedicated to taking care of my sister. Keeping her safe. No way would I do anything to put her in harm's way.

"Enjoy your trip, Piper," Stone said, taking my silence for what it was: defeat. "I look forward to seeing you upon your return."

Eyes still closed, throat searing with fury, I replied on instinct, as if he hadn't just threatened my sister moments earlier. "I wish I could say the same."

Instead of being mad about my words or the bite to my tone, he laughed again. As one might at a toddler talking back, trying to assert dominance, thinking they had some kind of agency when in reality they didn't.

Well, maybe not a toddler since I'd worked with plenty to know they were mini dictators. The reality was I had less rights and control than a two-year-old right now.

I ended the call.

Steeling myself, I handed the phone back to the man beside me, my captor. When our fingers brushed, I didn't miss his swift intake of breath from the simple contact.

Shouldn't I be the one getting all weirded out by the causal touch of a stranger, one connected to the mob boss threatening to kill me?

Yet his cool skin, smooth as porcelain, didn't make me want to jerk my hand away. Especially with his reaction. Some part of me stored this away for later. He didn't like to be touched. Or it might've been just my touch in general. Still, something to keep, maybe use. Not that storing up information would get me anywhere. Even if I outsmarted this man—which a knowing part of me said would be highly unlikely—they'd just hurt Daisy.

"Go inside." The man jerked his head to the building. "Pack a bag."

He didn't move as if he was going with me to supervise, ensure I didn't call anyone, try to escape. It was extremely cocky. Or maybe it was because he expected me to understand just how really screwed I was. There was no escape, no one to rescue me.

I was going somewhere with him, and there was no fight to be had, despite the animal inside me clawing for it. Instead, I got out of the car, walked into my building, ascended the elevator, entered my apartment and packed a bag. Within an hour, we were leaving Manhattan, the island that held my entire life.

I wondered if I'd ever see it again.

Because if I did, it meant I had been convinced to marry a monster.

And if I didn't, I was fairly certain it would mean I was dead.

I supposed it wouldn't matter then, would it?

THREE

PIPER

How had I gotten twisted into this situation?

By attending my sister's birthday party. That was it. That was my sin.

The birthday party was an apology, an attempt at groveling by her boyfriend Joey. The mobster.

Is that what we called them? Mobsters?

Not that titles really mattered at this point.

And at that point, the birthday party point, I didn't know he was in any way involved with the mob. I knew he was an asshole, because my sister had been sitting on my sofa, crying into a tub of Chunky Monkey just last week over him. I made a rule to dislike any man who made my sister cry.

Which meant I disliked all of her boyfriends.

Daisy dealt with our daddy issues by choosing men who treated her badly, under the impression that she could turn them right. Fix them. Under the impression that by doing that, she'd somehow erase our own past, posthumously turning our father into a good man.

And those men, after treating her badly, cheating on her,

standing her up, stealing from her—none of them had laid hands on her, thank God—would come crawling back. Because even assholes understood that Daisy Matthews was a catch. She was ethereal in her beauty, which had brought them in in the first place. Golden ringlets, wild around her heart-shaped, delicate face. Wide blue eyes, high cheekbones, full lips. Petite too, so even the smallest men—pun intended—felt big around her, strong. Her bones were slight; she barely had an ounce of body fat on her. She couldn't, not to be a dancer.

Ballet. She truly was a talented ballerina. Worked herself to the bone to do it too. She was just starting to see the fruits of her labor, after graduating from Juilliard—I scraped together every penny I could to get her there, but even with scholarships it was tough—she had landed a job at the prestigious Waldorf Company.

Just the way she carried herself was magical, her steps light, graceful, her body moving to silent music. Watching her dance ... transcendent.

And men, bad ones, seemed to gravitate toward her because she was good, she was pure, and she had a talent that they instinctively wanted to taint. To ruin.

I'd tried to protect her from them, tried to convince her that she deserved so much better, but that didn't work. Not on deep-seeded childhood issues. Not with her trying to find a version of our father and fix him, prove he could still be saved. That he could love her. So I just watched, my heart breaking a little more every time I saw a man chip away at her brilliance, hoping that she'd put herself on a pedestal so high that none of these men could reach her.

Joey didn't give me much hope.

Even if the birthday party he was throwing was at the exclusive Italian restaurant, Rosso, in Little Italy. I'd heard about it. How you couldn't get a reservation unless you were connected to the right people, rich or famous. I was none of those things, therefore, I had not eaten there.

I was a huge foodie, had been desperate to dine there, but that didn't mean Joey's connections charmed me. The more bells and whistles a man of Daisy's managed to pull off, the more red flags I saw.

Because a real, good man didn't need fancy restaurants, expensive gifts or trips across the world to prove he was good.

Good men didn't need to prove anything.

Well, at least that's what I figured from books, movies and secondhand accounts from friends in healthy relationships.

I had not had one. A relationship. I had my own daddy issues. Daisy treated hers by throwing herself headfirst into any kind of relationship that promised love, while I treated mine by avoiding emotional intimacy like the plague. The men I did sleep with were all boring, unthreatening and more or less vanilla.

Even I recognized that I was a little jaded, so I let Daisy drag me to the party. And yes, the glee in my younger sister's eyes helped. The hope. And selfishly, I did want to experience Rosso.

I'd tamed my hair—unlike Daisy, it did not fall delicately around my face in tight ringlets. It was frizzy, wild, chocolate waves that tumbled down my back and caused me great frustration as I tried every product on the market—within my price range—to tame it. Most of the time, I had it pulled back in a French braid. Easier for work anyway. Toddlers liked to tug on any loose strands.

But that night, I'd spent time, used a curling iron to help smooth it, rubbed product into it. I'd put on makeup—just a little mascara to frame my eyes. Unlike Daisy's, they were not a vibrant blue, a woody hazel. My face was rounder than hers. Though I ran every day, I did not train for hours like she did. Nor did I monitor my diet. So my face was fuller, my cheekbones less defined.

It was still winter, so I'd worn a skin-tight turtleneck dress that went down to mid-calf but clung to my body like a second skin. I paired it with leather, heeled boots that were my one unreasonable, outrageous purchase. Daisy was in her usual soft pastels—a cashmere wrap cardigan, light pink slacks and delicate heels.

She was glowing. Happiness made her shine. I let myself believe that maybe this was the time. More than anything, I wished that for my forever romantic, forever hopeful sister.

Joey had picked us both up in a limo—a little much, in my opinion—had flowers for Daisy, gifts. He'd showered her with physical affection—also a little too much, in my opinion—and had been overly polite and warm to me.

I'd bristled against his peacocking but hadn't let it show. It was my sister's birthday; it was about her being spoiled. She hadn't had a man make her feel special in that way. Treasured. Maybe I was just seeing red flags because I didn't know what else to look for. That's what I'd told myself at the time.

All of her friends were at the restaurant. Everyone from the studio, from school. Some of our mutual friends too. And a lot of people I didn't know. Mostly men. Joey's 'friends.' All of them were in suits, all of them carrying themselves in a certain ... way. I couldn't explain it. There was just something off about them. Even though they smiled, were perfectly polite, and some were quite handsome.

I'd come with the intention of keeping myself open to a man. It had been a while. I hadn't had sex, a connection. I craved it. But immediately upon seeing these men, my desire dried up. My warning bells sounded, honed from years of witnessing Daisy pick men just like these, years of being a single woman living in New York City. A childhood of living under the thumb of a violent man.

I had initially dismissed my thought that Joey was somehow involved with the Italian mob. I knew it was irrational to make assumptions based on my love of television shows and my general overactive imagination. Throughout life, I'd been known to create intricate scenarios in my head, get lost in daydreams and just generally believe the world to be a more fantastical place than it was. I believed in magic, practiced it in my own way, read Tarot cards for fun, and always carried a crystal with me. The amethyst ring on my finger was a mainstay, one of my only physical reminders I had of my grandmother.

I got swept up in stories, so of course, after watching a highly dramatized TV show, I would deduce that slick-looking men gathered in an Italian restaurant, wearing mid-range suits and looking ... off, for lack of a better word, would be members of the Italian mob.

The more likely reality was that they were all criminals of some variety, maybe wannabe mobsters. Not entirely harmless but not members of the mafia. I was pretty sure it didn't even exist anymore. The general party line was that organized crime's heyday had come and gone, that the world was too small for criminals to act in the ways they had before the age of smartphones and technology.

Even so, I'd steered clear of the men the entirety of the party, instead mingling with Daisy's friends from the studio, who unfortunately mentioned they'd seen less of Daisy than usual, and that she was missing practices.

My lips had pursed, my fingers clutching the stem of my glass.

I'd have to talk to her. Not there, though. Not on her birthday. I didn't like having to chastise her in general, to act like her mother. But I was the closest thing to a mother she'd ever had. I didn't resent the role, but sometimes I did just want to be the fun sister, one that didn't follow her life so closely, that didn't try to correct her mistakes.

Then again, it seemed that she was making a pretty big fucking mistake with Joey and his friends, whoever they were.

I went to the bar to get another drink—soda in a champagne glass. I couldn't be bothered with questions about sobriety.

"You're Piper."

The words were punctuated with a hand on my lower back, the pressure light but still invading and uncomfortable.

My entire body had stiffened from the unwanted contact, even though I'd had to endure plenty of it throughout my life. Some of it seemingly benign from men, other times not. Men were brought up to think they could conquer the world—history gave them every reason to believe this—and that included the women in it. It was wild that something as simple as personal space was breached constantly by men who thought they had the right.

His voice was close. Too close to my neck. It might've been attractive. Low, throaty, masculine. It had all the right ingredients, yet it felt off. Before I even looked at him, I knew the man was trouble.

I sucked in a breath, steadying myself. Not only did I need to remind myself that this was my sister's birthday party and not to make a scene, but that there were definitely some shady characters here. Offending one could be a lot worse than making a scene at a party.

I didn't have a smile on my face when I turned, but my expression was as pleasant as I could force it to be.

Me turning meant the man was no longer touching my lower back, thankfully. But it also meant that we were face-to-face, and he was standing much closer than was polite. I could smell the sharp twang of his expensive aftershave, that again should've been nice, alluring, yet there was something off, something bitter about it that made me want to recoil.

"I'm Piper," I had replied, looking at him in his murky-brown eyes, my voice sharp.

He smiled, looking me up and down in appreciation. My jaw hurt, I ground my molars together so hard.

He wasn't ugly by any means. He was significantly older than me, communicated by the lines at the corners of his eyes and the silver streaking through his ash brown hair. His forehead was shiny, though, one of the telltale signs he indulged in a little bit of Botox. Everything about him seemed shiny. His flashy watch, the bespoke suit that almost completely hid the paunch at his belly but not entirely. The gleam in his eye that counteracted the warm smile. The gleam in his eye that sent my heart hammering in my chest. It was cold. Predatory.

He was large too, much taller than me with broad shoulders. But not just in size. His presence felt large, like I had suddenly been encompassed in a cold shadow.

I repressed my shiver.

"I thought Joey got himself a good one with Daisy." The man nodded his head to where my sister was laughing, Joey's arms around her possessively as they had been all night. The casual but somehow caging embrace had set my teeth on edge.

I didn't look their way for too long, just a second. Everything told me to keep all of my attention on this man. You didn't take your eyes away from a bear when it cornered you, did you?

Somehow, inexplicably, I would've rather been cornered by a bear right then.

"But it seems that there is another prize in the Matthews family." He buttoned and unbuttoned his jacket, his long, manicured fingers moving fluidly.

His words were meant to be charming, I was sure. And along with the obvious wealth he flaunted, the air of power that threatened danger, they might've been charming to a younger, more naïve woman.

But I was not charmed.

I smiled tightly, fingering my amethyst ring on my left hand. "I'm not sure that being called a prize is the compliment you intend it to be." I was unable to be pleasant, to tread carefully even though I knew I should. My mouth tended to get away from me. Most especially when rich men referred to me as an object, one they presumed could be bought. Or stolen. "I'm a woman. Not a soft toy in an arcade game. I can't be won. Or owned." My voice was firm, bordering on hostile.

It was meant to repel this man, urge him to move on to easier prey. Less difficult. Men didn't like difficult women. They always said they wanted strong, complex partners, but they merely wanted a plaything they could control, a voice they could snuff out.

This man screamed that he wanted a docile, submissive woman who knelt at his feet and didn't dare say a word against him.

Surprisingly, he didn't sneer or frown. His face was blank for a second before he chuckled.

The sound vibrated in my bones, and not in a good way.

"Not to be won or owned," he repeated, almost to himself. "I like that." He leaned in so our bodies almost brushed. I held my breath.

"But I'll look forward to proving you wrong. You will be won. And owned."

The statement was ridiculous, considering we'd only exchanged a few words. It was overly intimate, cocky and just ... wrong.

It took everything in me not to bite out something else—obviously, my snark did not deter him, it interested him. I didn't flinch away either. There was no need to show weakness since that would likely excite him too.

I held my ground, looked him in the eyes and tried to communicate that I would not be worth his while.

After a few tense moments that felt like eons, he stepped back, straightening his suit and smiling at me. The expression was slick, satisfied, somehow victorious, as if he knew something I didn't.

"I'll be seeing you, Piper Matthews," he promised.

Then he was gone.

"Not if I see you first," I muttered.

I didn't even find out his name until later. Stone De Luca.

Admittedly a badass name.

But it didn't sway me, not even with the knowledge of his vast wealth from Daisy, who had urged me to go on the date with him after he sent a designer dress, roses and a note with a time and place to meet him.

To her, the gesture was romantic, right out of one of her romance novels.

To me, it was controlling, possessive and waved every red flag in the book.

I sent the dress back—which had Daisy almost in tears, as she worshiped at the altar of couture—with a polite note saying I was busy.

I'd hoped it was enough.

There was a little voice inside of me telling me it wasn't. That for whatever reason, this man eyed me as a prize, and that he was used to winning.

And it didn't stop. There were more lavish gifts, more invitations. Phone calls. Enough to make me sick.

And it did. I'd spent days unable to eat, sleep, my body tense, feeling as if I was essentially being stalked.

I'd done what I thought was the most logical thing in an admittedly crazy situation. I'd said yes to a dinner so I could speak to him face-to-face and gently explain that I wasn't interested.

I didn't wear the dress he sent, yet another one. But it was lovely. Blood-red, buttery fabric that I just knew would fit me like a glove. And the shoes. Red-soled, leather, delicate straps crisscrossing up my thighs. Sky high. They'd be uncomfortable. Same with the dress. Beautiful but constricting. Made to contain me.

I didn't bother to think about how he'd known my sizes. It was too scary.

Instead of the dress and heels, I'd worn black jeans, low-heeled boots and a cashmere sweater. A little underdressed for the fancy restaurant but not in an offensive manner. Just enough to make a statement.

I'd expected Stone to take it as an insult, a mark against me—it's what I'd wanted, after all. But he'd merely smiled, leaning in to kiss the side of my cheek, too close to my mouth.

I was frozen still until he pulled back.

"You'd look stunning in the dress I sent, but this is fine too." I tried not to grimace when he looked me up and down as he pulled the chair out for me.

My teeth gnashed together as I fought against the slimy feeling of his presence and the thin spike of fear shooting up my spine.

I'd done as much research as I could do on Stone De Luca. I was a kindergarten teacher with friends who were teachers, receptionists, graphic designers, stay at home moms. None of them were 'in the know.' I didn't have connections anywhere. All I had was a laptop and an internet connection.

Searching Stone's name didn't tell me who exactly he was, but the news stories about him and the businesses he owned gave me the sense that he was a dangerous man. Nothing outright saying he was a mobster, except for one journalist who had gone so far as to write a scathing piece on his control of the ports.

That journalist had gone missing two weeks after the story went to print.

I might've been a little too interested in true crime and somewhat of a sensationalist, but I knew that Stone had something to do with the disappearance.

And if I didn't tread carefully, that could be me. Every instinct I had screamed that at me. I refused to succumb to my mother's fate.

"I'm not a doll you can dress up and prop up in chairs," I informed him after he sat across from me.

Tread carefully, my inner voice reminded me.

Stone chuckled again, leaning over to pour wine from a decanter into my glass. "Ah, you are no doll. Even though you are as perfect as one," he said, the liquid sloshing as red as blood.

I kept my hands fisted in my lap.

"No one has given me quite as much trouble as you have in order to get them sitting across from me." He set the decanter down.

"I'm sure." I forced my breathing to steady. "I'll say it plainly, so we don't have miscommunication here, and so I don't waste your time. I know it's valuable to you." I had to stroke his ego, I reminded myself. "I'm not doing this to play hard to get or to make myself seem more interesting. I'm not. Interesting. I'm a kindergarten teacher who likes a boring, quiet life. This..." I waved my hand around at the restaurant, "world is not for me. And you, although very handsome and successful, are not for me either. I'm sure you can find a thousand women better suited and *willing* to sit across from you."

Stone leaned forward to grasp his wine glass, swirling the liquid around pretentiously, leaning forward to inhale, making a big song and dance before taking a demure sip.

"The wine is sublime," he declared as if I hadn't even spoken. "There are only fifty bottles in the world left." He glanced at the decanter. "Forty-nine, now." He nodded his head. "Try it."

"I'm afraid it would be wasted on me." I tried to sound polite, not moving my hands.

Engaged in a silent standoff, he stared at me then the wine glass, still smiling but now with an edge. He was trying to intimidate me into drinking. And if I were younger and hadn't been through what I'd been through, it would've worked.

I didn't like making people uncomfortable. I'd been a people pleaser all my life, starting because that was the only way to survive. But I no longer pleased people—especially men—if it resulted in harming myself. Even a little.

Once it had become clear that I wasn't going to obey his silent command, Stone blinked, another slow smile moving across his face.

"There are definitely a thousand women who I could have sitting across from me, wearing a dress, heels, drinking wine." He took a sip of his wine. "And they'd be more than willing. They'd be boring. All the same. I don't want them, Piper." He put down his wine, placing both hands on the table, leaning forward. "I want you."

There it was, plainly put. Said almost like a grumpy toddler might say it, or worse, a petulant child king. As if *want* equaled *having*.

My body tensed as what I'd been fearing had come to fruition. There was no gentle, polite way out of this. Maybe I could relent, eat dinner, have sex—*gross*—with him and show him that I was nothing special, I was easily had. He'd lose interest.

Maybe.

But then I would've sacrificed a very important piece of myself.

No way.

I pushed back my chair, standing.

"I apologize for wasting your time, for giving you the wrong idea." The false apology melted on my tongue. I had nothing to be sorry for since I most certainly didn't give him the wrong idea, and he was the one wasting my time. "But you can't have me, Mr. De Luca. I'm not something to be had, and I am, respectfully, not interested. I wish you well, and I'd appreciate it if you didn't call me again."

I turned quickly, but not before I saw a cold determination cover his features. Replaced by that quick, oily smile. It sent the world tilting for just a second before I hightailed it out of there.

I'd known that wouldn't be the last I'd see of him, known I was in trouble, but I never in a million years could've predicted where I'd end up.

In a car, going God knew where with a man who most definitely was a murderer.

Four

Piper

I had resolved to stay quiet the entire drive. My form of protest, maybe? But upon reflection after about an hour, I decided that silence was not protest but submission. I'd gone with him willingly, without a fight, which was shameful enough. I wouldn't sit there meekly, letting him think I was entirely at his mercy.

I had a voice. It was pretty much the only thing I had left at this point.

"What's your name?" It was a pertinent question to ask my kidnapper. Though was it kidnapping if I went willingly, albeit under duress? Though I didn't even know if it counted as 'under duress' since he hadn't made any outright threats. Although just his existence alone was a threat.

I sighed loudly. Great. Even if I did decide to run away at a gas station and go to the police, I'd have nothing to truly convict him of, and I'd be laughed out of the station for getting in the car with a stranger.

"You work for Stone, right?" I probed when he didn't respond to my question. "I just want to ensure that I didn't somehow just get in the car with a stalker completely unrelated to my..." What was

Stone? Definitely not a boyfriend. Not a friend. "Overly friendly with hostile undertones acquaintance who wants me to be *his* with my coerced consent." The word spewed from me in a quick babble with air quotes and nervous smiling.

I did that—babbled and smiled when nervous.

He obviously worked for Stone. He'd had him on the phone, after all, a detail that had floated out of my mind. As if I could erase Stone's very existence. I hadn't realized just how quickly my mind would fracture in a situation as unbelievable as this. My brain was already attempting to erase memories to protect me from them.

I was looking right at him. My nameless abductor, road trip buddy, Midnight Man. Parts of me didn't want to. Look at him, that was. Though he was hauntingly attractive, there was something unnerving about staring at him in such an enclosed space. The act of even speaking to him felt dangerous. But I pushed past that. Showing my fear would not do. You didn't do it with horses, and you didn't do it with mafioso enforcers or whatever his title was.

Until this point, he'd been looking straight ahead. But his head tilted enough so his eyes slid to me. It took all my effort not to plaster myself against the door and let out a little scream. I might've peed myself a little. Mostly out of fear but also because I'd been holding it since we left and was too embarrassed to ask for a bathroom break. One of the many things in this situation that didn't make sense. I should be shaking with fear, terror; embarrassment shouldn't have been anywhere in the mix.

I didn't break eye contact, even though I really, really wanted to. The weight of his gaze wasn't just terrifying, it was probing, ice barbs pricking at my skin, awakening something inside me I didn't know existed. The magnetism I felt toward this man was unexplainable. And unhinged. It had to be some kind of psychological effect from being kidnapped.

"I work for Stone," he finally said. He didn't remind me of the exchange in the car or seem at all surprised at my amnesia, holding my eyes longer than was technically safe for the driver of a motor vehicle to be averting his eyes from the road.

Though a car crash was likely the least of my worries. And inexplicably, I knew this man wouldn't crash. There was no way he would let ordinary dangers come to me. I felt safe with him. In that respect, at least. I was more than aware that I definitely wasn't safe in any other ways.

I swallowed heavily. "Good." It was an effort to keep my voice light, even.

Only because I was watching him so intently did I see the very slight twitch to his eyebrow. Before this, his face was so expressionless, it could've been made of marble.

"I wouldn't say it's *good* that I work for Stone De Luca," he remarked dryly.

My bones trembled at the tone of his voice. Fear. Yes, fear was a living being inside of me. But I couldn't deny that was the only thing I felt. There was also warmth. From the vicinity between my legs.

Unlike my sister, I did not have a bad boy infatuation.

Until now.

Not that the man beside me was a *boy*.

I had a hard time imagining he'd ever been a boy. This man had never been a defenseless, cute, squishy baby. No, he'd burst onto this earth ready to fuck shit up. Like an orc. Just a lot more handsome.

"No, it's not good," I agreed, thrumming my fingers on my thighs. "None of this is good."

Most especially my burgeoning obsession with this man, my inability to stop looking at him, cataloguing every inch of him.

"Oh, Jesus." I ran through the situation in my mind, picking at my cuticles. "I'm going to be on a segment of *60 Minutes* one day. Maybe I'll even get my own Netflix special if Daisy is dramatic enough about it ... which she will be. My colleagues will all go on. Even Trina, and she hates me. But she'll be talking about how we were best friends. How I lit up the room."

I looked back at him, his profile sharp. He didn't seem to be listening, but the sound of my own voice was better than silence.

"Have you ever noticed that murder victims always 'lit up a room?'" I made air quotes. "I mean, sure, some of them might've. But just by law of averages, they couldn't all have been angels. Even murder victims can be bitches." I toyed with a thread on my jeans. "Do you think that death does that to the people who survive it? Makes them remember people differently? Better?"

For a moment, I thought of my parents, cataloging my memories of them. Not a single one was pleasant. They were all thorny and painful.

"No," I decided. "Death doesn't do that to people. TV does. Some people lie, doing whatever it takes, to be on TV." I pause, nibbling on a dry piece of skin on my lip. "Although I do hope people lie for the airtime. I don't want to be remembered as a bitch. I'm not a bitch. But if Trina decides to make up stories about me on national TV... well, I guess I won't be around to care, will I?"

I rubbed my amethyst ring again, harder this time. I then fingered the onyx necklace I'd put on for protection as I'd hastily packed. As if lumps of rock could protect me in any way from this man beside me.

We lapsed into silence for a long while, me looking out the window, contemplating my fate and trying to best my bladder.

But there was only so long I could do that.

"I need to pee." I eventually broke the long, cold, ominous quiet.

It felt infinitely embarrassing, admitting I had bodily functions to a man who seemed to be made of stone. But it was either that or wet myself.

He didn't say anything except a slight incline of his head that I guessed was a nod.

I started to squirm in my seat as he pulled off at an exit.

Not very modest of me, nor attractive, that I was a thirty-something, childless woman who had trouble controlling her bladder. But I shouldn't have been worrying about being attractive to this man in the first place.

My hand was on the handle before he came to a full stop, seat belt unbuckled. I was about to leap out when a band circled around my wrist.

My bursting bladder was momentarily forgotten as I looked down at a large, pale hand clutching my wrist. It made mine look tiny, dainty. And I did not have dainty limbs like my sister. The grip was tight, painful. I knew that he could snap the bone in a moment, if he wanted to.

My skin exploded with sensation at the contact between us. Not all of it was unpleasant. This close I couldn't deny the ... presence he had. It blanketed me like a shadow. His eyes were even more vibrant this close, glittering.

"You know, it would be a bad idea to try anything in there." He nodded to the gas station. It was busy, one of the nicer establishments that boasted snacks and knickknacks. A place I normally would've been overjoyed to look around, buying a cheap shot glass or some sort of tacky fridge magnet or tee.

People walked in and out, parents chasing children, truck drivers clutching extra-large cups, people living normal lives that weren't under threat of their family being murdered.

"I know." I turned my head to him. "As hard as it may be for you to believe, I'm not actually worried about finding help right now that isn't in the form of a porcelain throne. And even if that weren't the case, I'm not that stupid. Now *let me go*."

My voice was cold and commanding, partly because of my overwhelming need to not wet myself in front of this man and also because I was pissed off.

He held me a beat longer, as if to show he could, that he was in control. He could hold me here and watch me pee in my pants if he wanted to. For a second, I thought he would. It's not like he was any kind of gentleman.

But thankfully, he let me go.

I didn't hesitate, darting out the door.

No matter how tempting it was to run for the state trooper I'd just seen pull up, I went to the bathroom instead.

Knox

I watched her walk into the gas station.

More accurately, I watched her ass walk into the gas station. It was the perfect size, perky, big, and I couldn't stop myself from imagining my hands on it, the way I would slap it when taking her from behind.

The thought was a foreign invader in my mind, unwelcome and unusual as I never had sexual feelings about people.

She rushed past the state trooper without so much as a glance. Granted, she was desperate to use the bathroom; she'd been squirming in her seat for a while. I imagined her skin underneath my palm, warm, soft, breakable. I had the urge to do that, break her.

My hands twitched for the knife at my ankle. The need to grab it, slice it through the skin of my arm in order to let out the poison of those thoughts. But I didn't have enough time. She'd notice. She'd notice because she looked at me. Right at me.

Very few people did that.

Three, in fact. My brother, Stone, and more recently, my brother's woman, Avery.

Everyone else on the planet, in my world and on top of it, averted their eyes. Even if they didn't know who I was, didn't understand my reputation, some primal part of human nature understood what I was. People avoided me. Gave me a wide berth on even the most crowded sidewalks.

Though I avoided crowded sidewalks and crowds in general when possible. I didn't like it, being around people. Living people, normal people. Hence why I made my living in death. My habitat was the underworld, full of scoundrels, demons and murderers. My kind.

Piper was not my kind. And being in an enclosed space with her for an hour was pure torture. She smelled of some kind of fruit. Peaches, maybe. Sweet. And despite the gravity of her situation, she had a fucking spring to her step as she walked into the gas station. The spring that only served to make her ass wiggle that much more.

She opened the door for someone heading in, smiling at the mother and small child in front of her as if she didn't have a care in the world. As if she wasn't hurtling toward some unknown location with a murderer. A monster. Me.

I had an urge, an almost overwhelming urge, to drive away, leave her here. Safe. As far away from me as possible.

But the problem was she wouldn't stay safe for long. Stone would just send someone else after her. Likely Groves.

My hands clenched the steering wheel. Stone had strict instructions not to harm Piper, but I knew that Groves would do everything he could to circumvent that order, to ensure that he hurt her, took her in any way he could.

I relished in death. Pain. But only of those who deserved it. I did not like to take people apart just to see them hurt. Didn't find joy in sullying those who didn't deserve it.

Groves did.

He would not lay a hand on Piper. He would not even glimpse her. That was a promise I made to myself, even though there was no real way to keep it.

Eventually, I'd have to hand her over to Stone, untouched, her will broken.

The thought made me want to burn down the fucking world.

PIPER

Our trip ended in the Appalachian Mountains. I'd spent a large portion of my childhood in these mountains. Some of my most treasured memories were made here. Before my father decided that he wouldn't allow me or my sister to be away from him. Ash-filled memories that were previously coated in sunshine and smelled of morning dew against the trees.

Whether he knew about my bittersweet history here remained to be seen. How much he knew about my past remained to be seen. Stone had communicated just how much he knew about me, so I assumed he'd told his minion. I shifted uncomfortably, knowing he must have at least a rudimentary understanding of my life, my past, while I knew nothing about him other than he was highly dangerous.

Dusk was falling as we drove over bumpy dirt roads, climbing higher and farther into denser vegetation with signs of civilization growing sparse. Large trees surrounded us, encasing us in their embrace as we wove up the mountain.

Though I was plenty afraid, I didn't think I was going to die. He wouldn't have gone to such an effort in order to merely kill me. That could've been done in Central Park. Although there were plenty of other things a man could take a woman to a very secluded location for that weren't killing her.

"Are you going to rape me?" I blurted, unable to handle the bubbling of that thought tearing away at my insides like acid. Was it better to know in advance? Probably not. There was no real way to prepare for rape, yet I asked the question, nonetheless.

His head whipped in my direction, the most attention he's

given me. The car even jerked a little, drifting precariously close to the edge of what was becoming a sheer drop to our right.

He righted the car quickly, eyes and head returning in the direction of the road.

His knuckles were pure white.

"No." The word was heavy, settling like a weight in my stomach.

It could've been a lie. A man who worked for Stone was likely in the practice of lying, but it didn't feel like one.

I rolled my lips against each other, my shoulders relaxing somewhat.

"Torture me?" I asked after a few more moments, the faint crunch of the tires against the dirt the only sound.

He didn't turn so dramatically this time, as if the question was less egregious, or maybe he was prepared for it.

"No." He said it quieter this time.

Though the tenor of the response was slightly different, it seemed just as sincere.

I clenched and unclenched my fists, tapping my fingers on my knees.

"No rape or torture," I repeated. "Always a plus with abductions, though this is my first time. Being abducted, that is."

He didn't respond, I didn't really expect him to. He wasn't here to engage in conversation, after all.

The sun was quickly creeping behind the curtain of the woods, making me wonder if we would still be driving when it was completely dark. Sure, I didn't know that much about my abductor —thankfully, not rapist or torturer. I had noted the manicured nails, the suit, the loafers. He worked for Stone in New York. It wasn't a stretch to deduce that he didn't have experience driving in the woods, the Appalachian Mountains. The roads weren't reliable; turns often came seemingly out of nowhere, even in full daylight. The mountains played tricks on outsiders, as if they were sentient beings, aware of intruders in their realm. I'd always thought these ancient mountains were full of magic and wonder. With talk of dangerous, otherworldly beings roaming the woods after dark, a lot of people tread carefully there. The area had never scared me, not with the father I lived with day in and day out. Compared to him, faceless monsters were welcome.

And yet there I was, driving into the wilderness with yet another monster.

Asking him about his competence driving in the conditions wouldn't be smart, and offering to drive would be even less so.

His posture was rigid, though it had been that way throughout the entire drive. He'd been awake ... how many hours now? A badass he might be, but I was almost sure he was human. Despite my overactive imagination and fantasies about some ancient vampire being enthralled by the siren song of my blood, I knew that was less than likely.

Therefore, human. One who needed sleep. And without it, reaction times were sluggish, brain performance was hindered, concentration was more difficult.

I breathed a sigh of relief when we crested the hill and turned onto what looked like a very overgrown driveway. My body jostled as we hit dips and potholes, driving farther into the woods.

The headlights illuminated the cabin we were approaching. It was wooden, small, with a dense overgrowth of weeds and wildflowers bordering it. One of the shutters on the windows was askew, the other had fallen off entirely. But the roof was intact, and it looked vaguely habitable.

Our accommodations, I assumed.

Throughout the entire experience, I had prided myself on how composed I had been. Maybe in denial was a more accurate way to describe it. But right then, seeing the end of the road, so to speak, the reality of my situation set in.

I was in the middle of the mountains, without anyone knowing where I was, without anyone looking for me or coming to save me. I was completely powerless, at the hands of a strange, frightening man. On the orders of another man who wanted to terrify me into marrying him. If I escaped or survived this captivity, I'd just be trading it for another. Till death do us part.

My death would likely come first, since I didn't think marriages based on coercion were long-lasting.

My hands began to shake, and my stomach roiled against the last few bumps in the road.

Spots danced in my vision, my breaths becoming rapid and shallow.

A panic attack. Understandable in the situation, but not ideal. Showing any kind of vulnerability in the presence of my captor could be my demise.

I tried to tell myself to calm my breathing, focus on something safe, stable. The problem being there was nothing safe nor stable in the car. Or in my life in general.

My breathing only grew more erratic as I understood just how far from home I was. How vulnerable. Worse still, these mountains used to be a home of mine yet now taunted me with what had been taken from me.

My lungs seized, no longer working. Pain speared up my arm as I came to understand that I was having a heart attack. Surely, I must've been. A feeling of doom covered me like a second skin.

Maybe a heart attack was a mercy. Nature trying to save me from an unnatural fate.

"Piper."

My name was a command more than a title.

I opened my eyes more on reflex than anything. My vision was tilted, the world moving even though the car had stopped.

Of their own volition, as if he were a gravitational pull and my eyes were planets, they found their way to him.

There was no gentleness on his face, nothing soft or comforting. He was wearing that same cold, menacing expression he had when I first laid eyes on him. That helped, somehow. The predictability of it. Stability of it. My father had always been unpredictable. One moment he'd be smiling at you with utter adoration, yet seconds later, his eyes would be clouded with rage and violence.

"Knox," he said quietly.

My eyelids fluttered. "What?" I asked, still gasping for breath yet, thankfully, not as badly.

"My name." He cleared his throat. "Knox."

Knox.

He was giving me his name. Because he saw me spiraling. Somehow, it was something to hold on to. An anchor, even though he shouldn't be that. If I were assigning metaphorical titles to the man in question, it would be a blade, a weapon, something to hurt and cut and kill.

But still, I held on to the name. It served to tether me to the earth. To sanity.

Silence thrummed between us, neither of us looking away for a long while as my heartbeat steadied, my breathing eventually slowing to an even cadence as my fists unclenched.

I was sure that I'd blink first. I'd be the one to break our stare-off.

But it was him, his body jerking as if someone had physically shaken his shoulder. My body went slack at the loss of eye contact, and my breath left me in a whoosh as he swiftly undid his seat belt and got out of the car. I jerked at the slam of his door.

My head fell back against the headrest as I took stock of my surroundings. For the foreseeable future, I was in a cabin in the woods with a man called Knox, who might not be my murderer. But he was a killer, that was for sure.

FIVE

KNOX

I'd been given little notice to prepare a suitable location for this assignment. I didn't know if that was yet another test from Stone or if he just didn't give a shit. Or he understood that I was competent enough to do what was necessary in the time afforded. Not that I gave a fuck what he thought of me.

He'd told me he wanted her broken, helpless, with nowhere to turn but him.

Privacy was my number one priority. Complete isolation with no way to escape.

No TV. No modern luxuries. Although the cabin did have running water because I wasn't that much of a masochist.

I thought I'd done a good job—that her being alone with me in woods that many people were afraid of would be enough. I hadn't thought about what *my* reaction would be to being alone with her. Prior to this, people hadn't elicited reactions from me.

Just Piper.

Watching her unravel in the car sent my skin crawling. It was difficult, watching her hyperventilate and grow smaller and paler.

I'd been avoiding her, a fruitless notion since we were in a cabin in the middle of nowhere together for the foreseeable future. My throat constricted, realizing that there was no escape from this, from her.

I longed for my knife, for the relief that would come from the warmth of blood spilling over my skin.

Soon, I promised myself. *Soon*, I promised the hungry beast inside of me.

Once night came, when she slept, then I'd get it.

For now, I focused on practical solutions, putting away the supplies I'd bought at the store, our last stop before we ascended the mountain. I expected them to last two weeks, at least. Then I'd reevaluate. Previously, I'd thought it was smart, having everything here so there was no cause for me to leave, inflicting myself on her twenty-four seven. Now I understood that was a mistake.

I'd felt her eyes as she watched me take things to and from the car. I hadn't looked at her. She had already shown she wasn't going to run, so I wasn't concerned about that. Not that there was anywhere to run to. I'd selected this location for that exact purpose.

Not even Stone knew where we were. He trusted me that much. A mistake on his part.

Not that I planned on betraying him. But it was sloppy, overconfident for him to think I'd blindly obey him. Feral beasts bowed to no master. He'd learn that one day. I'd learn that one day.

As I was unpacking, she'd first walked around the exterior of the cabin, looking at things, running her hands along the long grass, picking flowers.

That gave me pause. She was an educated, smart, sane woman who understood the gravity of her situation. I'd seen the terror in her eyes, the gut-clenching fear.

Yet she was *picking fucking flowers*.

I tried my best to get her smell from my nostrils, to forget the way her shirt shifted with her breathing, the way panic had overtaken her body as we'd pulled up, how vulnerable and scared she'd been.

Wasn't that the entire point of this? To scare her into submission?

Yet I'd brought her back from the brink. Given her my fucking name. I hadn't planned on that. I hadn't planned on having any interaction with her beyond what was completely necessary. Usually that wasn't hard for me, distancing myself from human interaction.

It was impossible not to interact with her.

Weak, I scolded myself. Weak.

I'd rectify my mistake. Leave her alone. Shut her out like I had every other human before this.

Eventually, she made her way into the cabin, inspecting the bare space, trailing her index finger along the back of the old sofa in the middle of the room, poking her head in the bathroom then peering at the bed in the corner of the room. One room and a bathroom. Intimate. Uncomfortable. I'd planned it that way. So she couldn't escape me. Resulting in me being unable to escape her.

I'd tried to ignore her, slamming the refrigerator shut as I put the last of the food in it.

But her voice, soft and throaty, punctured the silence I usually preferred. I was surprised to find myself thinking there would be no greater comfort than hearing that tenor for the rest of time.

"It's going to be dark soon. We need wood."

I stared at her.

"Wood?" she repeated when I didn't reply. "It comes from trees."

I wanted to smile. I didn't know why. Nothing made me want to smile, certainly not half-ass sarcasm. But coming from her... *Fuck*. Never in my adult life had it been hard to control my expressions, my emotions. But with her, it took all my effort to remain emotionless.

"I'm aware of the origin of wood," I replied in the tone I used with everyone. Flat. Threatening.

Her eyes glimmered with mirth she shouldn't have been feeling while alone in a cabin with me, with darkness approaching. She should've been shivering in her ridiculous fucking shoes.

I hadn't told her where we were going, what to pack for. That wasn't my job. I hadn't known what I expected her to be wearing, but definitely not a skintight pair of jeans that showed off her juicy ass, a faded Fleetwood Mac tee and leopard print sneakers. That had glitter on them. The attire wasn't conventionally sexual, but regardless, I found it infinitely appealing.

"Excuse me." She put her hand on her chest. "I didn't mean to offend."

Wrong move.

It brought my attention to her tits.

Small. Perky. Fucking perfect for her frame.

That withered thing inside of me that was desire woke up.

I struggled against the stiffening of my cock. It was a foreign feeling, more than unnerving to have no control over my own body. To experience such profound weakness.

"If you know the origin of wood, then you may understand we're in the Appalachian Mountains in spring," she said, thankfully unaware of my hard cock. "Daytime is still quite warm, but the nights will turn frigid." She looked around the room. "Especially in something like this without the updates it needs." She sucked her teeth. "I don't want to be *cold* on top of being a captive. Therefore, we need wood for that." She motioned to the fireplace. It took up a decent amount of space in the room, stained black and shrouded with cobwebs.

Though a lot of blood had pumped to my cock at that moment, I could still use my brain. She was right; we needed wood. I hadn't thought about that. I hadn't thought much about the logistics of any of this. I'd gotten food, rudimentary supplies, everything you technically needed to survive, but not the finer details.

Unlike me. Very unlike me.

Granted, my usual hunting grounds were decidedly more urban than this, but that wasn't the excuse. It was her. It had been her since the moment I saw her. She had me off-kilter. Sloppy.

Her green eyes danced with amusement, but they were also penetrating, as if they saw right through me. Into my soul. But that couldn't be true. I didn't have one of those.

"There's an axe outside," she continued.

I hadn't seen it.

Sloppy.

Very fucking sloppy.

I'd scouted the surrounding area, ensured that there was only one usable road in and out of the property, the woods dense and full of predators. Nearest neighbor was fifty miles away. I'd made certain that there was no way for her to escape, but I stupidly hadn't taken stock of things that could be used as weapons.

She was 5′5″ at best, one hundred and fifty pounds soaking wet. Her eyes were wide and innocent, though she was full of curves and substantial—she looked like she wouldn't hurt a fucking fly, let alone me. Even though I was holding her captive. Even though I was intending on breaking her like a broodmare.

But people were animals. And no matter how shapely her hips were, how soft her edges, how big her eyes, a cornered animal would attack. Always.

Part of me—that rotten, wrong, evil part of me—itched for her to fight me, to sink her fingernails into my skin, coat her hands in my blood.

"Do you know how to chop wood?" she asked, innocent as can be. But her lips were pursed in a way that made it distinctly clear she was trying to hide a smile.

It was almost as if she was ... *teasing* me.

No one, not a single person who had interacted with me, had dared tease me. Except perhaps my brother, but even he was careful with his actions around me. He protected himself, cautious with his words. Even him—the one person on this hunk of rock who saw me as something more than a killer—knew to keep his guard up around me.

Piper, despite being my literal fucking captive, was not guarding anything about herself. This woman seemed to have absolutely no self-preservation. How she'd survived all these years was anyone's guess. A trait that I should've found deplorable, not ... endearing.

"I know how to chop wood," I replied after a long silence she didn't seem to be in a rush to fill. She hadn't dropped her eyes from mine either.

Though I had lied to some of the most dangerous people in the world, had made them not so much as second-guess me, this woman seemed to see through me in a second. The tilt of her lips, the arch in her eyebrow, the overall victory glistening in her golden eyes.

I had never chopped wood in my life.

I had chopped up people, though, so I was sure it was a similar process.

"Okay, well... Even though I'm sure you'll be *excellent* at chopping wood, I really need the exercise since it doesn't seem like these accommodations feature a gym," she explained, eyes sparkling playfully.

Again, my dick twitched at the teasing in her tone, the confidence in the face of her situation, the terror and panic of before nowhere to be seen. Piper was a survivor. She wasn't weak, her strength unlike anything I'd ever seen. To cultivate a warmth inside of herself that resulted in her being able to find the will to smile in a situation as dire as this was unlike anything I had ever experienced.

She started toward the axe, but I stepped in her path.

She stopped, looking up at me. There should've been fear in her eyes. Terror. I could see shades of it now, but it mixed with that lightness that shouldn't exist in my presence. My presence alone should've snuffed out every inch of light.

"I can't let you use that axe," I informed her. My muscles were taut, the effort it took to keep my form still, my expression blank, was more than I'd ever expended in a simple interaction.

She tilted her head to regard me. "Because you think I'll try to hack you into little pieces and escape?"

I thinned my lips, answering her with a curt nod.

She laughed.

Laughed.

The sound warmed up the room that had previously felt frosty.

Her laugh cut through layers of steel and ice, penetrating right to the core of me, finding something soft and pliant, something I didn't even know I had inside me.

Her face quickly turned faux serious, presumably because she realized I hadn't so much as smiled. "I'm a little squeamish, so axe murdering is a little too grizzly for me," she said dryly. "And the process of using an axe to cut up a human being sounds overly tiring. Especially since I doubt you'd go quietly."

I struggled to keep my composure as she pointedly looked me up and down. Her eyes on me were a physical fucking thing.

Walking around each day, I felt lifeless. I knew logically that my heart was pumping blood to my limbs, my organs were functioning correctly, and I was medically alive. But despite that, I was sure I was dead inside, a sociopath. I didn't feel things the way other people did. Nothing warmed me.

Except her smile.

Her laugh.

Her simple fucking gaze on me, bringing me to life. Like I hadn't existed until she looked at me.

Whether or not she saw what she did to me was unclear. I hoped to fuck she didn't because then I'd truly be fucked.

Apparently, she saw my silence as acquiescence since she skirted around me, grabbed the axe, hauled it over her shoulder and whis-tled as she exited the cabin, presumably to chop wood.

I didn't stop her. Didn't try to reassert dominance. A huge mistake since she needed to know I was the one in charge. But I was lost. I didn't usually need to make an effort to exert dominance. I'd spent years, decades, honing myself into a weapon even the most obtuse people recognized and instantly submitted to.

Sure, I'd been challenged over the years, especially by idiots in Stone's ranks, wrongly assuming my position was his right-hand, wanting to take that from me.

Few had tried to challenge me, and those who did had perished. The stories were now infamous in the ranks, and no one had dared go against me since. Not in a long while.

Except Piper. My fucking captive.

The low thumps coming from outside told me she was chop-ping wood.

I should've ignored it. Even if she accidently chopped a finger off. That wasn't my problem. Stone hadn't specified whether she needed all of her digits, though I supposed that he'd be unhappy to find her maimed.

He was all about appearances, so he'd want a shiny, flawless wife, which I understood he could get out of Piper. Once I sucked all the vibrancy and will to live out of her.

I sighed and went to the dirty window that looked out at the overgrown yard where I'd seen a stump the previous inhabitant had used to chop wood.

The place had been abandoned for years. In the scant amount of time I'd had, I'd scouted it then done my research on the locals. I'd found someone, recently out of prison—rape and aggravated assault —and had paid him handsomely to outfit the cabin with what was needed. Then, ensuring that he hadn't had time to open his mouth about the job done, I killed him.

He'd done a subpar job—everything was still overgrown, and

the linens for the bed looked cheap and worn. But he'd obviously gotten wood to be chopped, just not chopped it himself.

Something that would've irritated me if not for the vision out the window. Piper, fluidly moving the axe up and down, a thin sheen of sweat already shining on her brow, making her chocolate-brown hair stick to her forehead.

She was not petite, not with the hills of her curves. But her body appeared delicate, not seemingly strong enough to lift the axe over her head, let alone use it to cleanly chop wood in two.

But that's what she was doing. With confidence that told me she'd done this before. I watched, fucking entranced at the window, like some voyeur.

I'd done basic research on Piper. Surface level. Her job—kindergarten teacher. Her finances—enough to pay her bills and survive in Manhattan. Barely. Her social life—friends, but none who would cause me trouble. No boyfriend.

I hadn't had time to go further into her past, medical history, childhood, like I might've. It was all necessary. Information was power. If I was going to break her, I needed to know which tools to bring, which soft spots to probe.

I'd mistakenly assumed a kindergarten teacher who had lived her entire life in New York would easily crumble in the Appalachian Mountains.

I'd been wrong.

And watching her, the way she moved, still hearing her fucking laugh echoing through the empty parts of me, I knew I was in a lot of fucking trouble.

PIPER

I was exhausted. Chopping the wood was a huge part of it. Despite my snarky comment, I was not a huge gym goer. I liked my runs.

Pounding the pavement, the burn in my legs, the high in my blood, the fresh air in my lungs.

I ran daily. Which meant I was physically fit in the cardiovascular sense, at least. But it had been a long time since I'd chopped wood. Luckily, it was like riding a bike. I'd gotten the handle of the axe, found the right angle, pressure and impact to slice the wood, but my shoulders screamed after an hour or so.

We likely didn't need as much wood as I chopped. Or I told myself I wouldn't be there long enough to need that much wood. But the only other option was to either wander around the woods or stay in the cabin with Knox.

The latter wasn't a possibility. I couldn't. His presence overwhelmed the small space, suffocating me. He scared me. A lot. Which was his intended purpose, I assumed. But more than that I was … curious about him, something inside me responded to him. The darkness seeping from him.

One thing I did not need to stoke was some kind of fucked-up Stockholm syndrome.

By the time the sun had completely set, I was soaked in sweat, the crisp air chilling me down to my marrow. The pile of wood beside me was impressive and my entire body groaned with exertion.

Not just from the chopping, but because of the tense way I'd been holding myself since seeing Knox in Central Park. My nervous system had been in a state of fight-or-flight, so it was inevitable that I would crash.

I snatched handfuls of fitful sleep during the drive, but never relaxed enough to let myself be pulled into a deep state of unconsciousness. Not with Knox a few feet from me in the car.

It took all my effort to drag myself into the cabin, dim light pouring out of it. It was force of will alone that allowed me to carry in some wood.

The small space smelled of food, Knox's back to me at the stove.

The sight made my step stutter. Well, that and the exhaustion.

It was such a benign, domestic task. A human task.

The sight shouldn't have been shocking, but it was as if I'd walked into the cabin and saw a grizzly bear holding a spatula in front of a sizzling pan.

My captor was cooking. For us, presumably. Or maybe not. Maybe his goal was to starve me. Force me to watch him eat.

Maybe that was Stone's plan to get my submission.

My stomach growled and turned at the same time.

Right then, I had resolve. Even if I'd had nothing but processed gas station snacks since ... breakfast this morning.

Despite the scant amount of substantial nutrients in me, I was certain I'd be able to withhold. That I'd be able to starve rather than relent.

But then I thought. Remembered. What starvation felt like and how vastly it differed from simple hunger.

I'd felt it once in my life, the memories were faded because of my young age, and I suppose my subconscious, trying to protect me from the horror of it.

The details were hazy, but I remembered the pain. The desperation. How I'd turned into an animal, tearing apart old cracker boxes to find stale crumbs that I would then split between Daisy and me, always giving her the larger portion.

I'd been a child then. Helpless. This would be different.

But would it? I was essentially as helpless as a child right now.

I tasted the acidic tang of bile as I considered this. The sharp taste brought me back to my body, to where I'd been standing in the middle of the room, staring at Knox, covered in sweat, holding a pile of wood. I glanced to where I should put it, if only to escape his gaze.

Apparently, he'd turned at some point as he was now looking at me. There was a flatness, a deadness in his expression that made the hair on my arms stand on end.

His eyes were deep, unyielding and ... soulless. It was like there was nothing human or soft inside of them. Yet I couldn't deny the pull I felt toward them, toward him. One that I'd told myself was a figment of my traumatized brain. I was searching for redemption in this story, in this man, that maybe if we had a connection, he wouldn't hurt me. He was watching me so intently because I was his captive, not because he felt anything toward me. I reminded myself of that.

I swallowed knives at the thought that I was stuck in a one-room cabin with him for ... however long. However long it took me to decide that marrying Stone was preferable to being here with Knox.

I quickly averted my gaze. "I'm going to have a shower." Why I felt the need to tell him this, voice it to him almost as if I was asking for permission, made me rageful. I hoped that the cabin had hot water. The chances were slim, but a girl could hope. Even if it was safe to say hope was dead there. Knox had trampled on it with his loafers.

He didn't say anything. Not even a hint of a gesture to acknowledge that I'd said anything. That further served to amplify my rage. Though I wanted to scamper off to the bathroom with my tail between my legs, I gritted my teeth and stood my ground, lifting my eyes up to once again meet that soulless stare.

I counted to ten in my head, holding it, unmoving, remaining silent. It wasn't exactly a challenge because I knew I'd lose any kind of staring or menacing competition with him. It was more of a statement. That I wouldn't wither under his gaze like a flower dying from lack of sunshine.

I might've looked like a delicate flower, but my roots were hardy, unyielding. I didn't wear my strength on my sleeve like he did, but it was there, deep under the surface.

I would survive this. Him.

It was a promise I made to myself in those ten seconds.

Then, with my head held high, chin tilted upward in defiance, I marched to the bathroom.

It was only once my clothes were stripped off and I was under the spray of water that was somehow gloriously hot when my strength started to wane.

As my muscles loosened, fatigue flooded my bloodstream.

Why did I think I could handle this?

I had to work up the strength to schedule my dental cleanings.

The water rained over me, washing away my tears.

It was the first time I'd cried since I was taken. Not that there hadn't been opportunities for me to indulge in a sob fest. Yet no matter how much I wanted to, I would not cry in front of Knox. He would not see that. He would not get that.

I gave myself a minute. A minute curled up at the bottom of the shower, stifling my sobs with my fist lest he hear them.

And once the minute was up, I was out of the shower, the biting air prickling against my skin.

My first instinct was to rush into my clothes, get comfortable, warm. But I needed to get used to discomfort. Needed to relax in the frigid environment.

So I squeezed my eyes shut and stood there, dripping on the bathmat, shivering, for another minute.

My clothes were as practical as you could get for someone like me—someone who loved color, who taught children for a living and expressed herself through clothing. The worn jeans I dragged on were covered in painted flowers, all in different colors, some fading from wear.

I put on a tight, basic tank, not bothering with a bra since I was slinging on a bright-pink, loose, knit cardigan over top.

I wanted comfortable clothes, eager for my PJs, but Knox was out there still. I couldn't be waltzing around in PJs with fruit all over them.

Not that my regular clothes served as any kind of armor. They communicated just who I was—a kindergarten teacher who didn't take life seriously, loved pink and flowers, and who was an easy murder victim.

Methodically and slowly, I towel dried my hair, trying my best to prolong the process by putting in my conditioning products, curl-taming sprays, brushing it one hundred times exactly.

Why I'd thought to bring my entire toiletry cabinet to my kidnapping was anyone's guess, but I was glad to have my creature comforts.

Eventually, I had to leave the bathroom, as much as I wanted to live in there. My stomach was informing me of how hungry I was, and the scent of dinner coming from the nearby kitchen was making my mouth water.

On bare feet, I trod on the well-worn rugs—scattered across the wood floor—to the dining table in the middle of the room. Knox was already sitting there. There were two plates on the table.

He'd cooked for me too.

Huh.

I guessed he must've wanted me alive for the moment. He wanted me alive in general. Healthy, Stone had said.

My molars ground together at the thought of it. I was basically a pig getting fattened up for slaughter. But even that wasn't enough to kill my appetite.

Though it evaporated as soon as I was brave enough to pull out the chair and sit in front of the food Knox had cooked. How I didn't recognize it by smell was confusing. My senses must've been scrambled.

I stared at the plate of meat. Charred and steaming and vaguely sickening.

There was a hunk of bread beside it, and that was it.

I looked from Knox to the meat, but he was already eating, obviously not standing on ceremony. I was surprised he was even sitting at the table with me. It implied some kind of civility that didn't exist between us.

Instead of speaking, I took a piece of bread and nibbled on the edges. Yes, I was still starving, almost deliriously so, but the smell of the meat was putting me off.

No, that wasn't it. I'd been a vegetarian for my entire adult life, and I'd never been sickened by people eating meat in front of me. I didn't have a holier-than-thou attitude about it either. If someone wanted to eat meat, I was fine with that. I didn't make my preference their problem.

So no, it wasn't the meat.

It was the predator sitting there, eating it. Blood dribbled from the middle of the steak as he speared it with his fork before putting it to his mouth.

He chewed with his mouth shut, used a knife and fork and had good table manners. Except for the fact that he was blatantly ignoring me, as he had since I walked in the door with the wood.

That should've made me thankful. Being out of this man's line of vision or attention was good for me, it was the only way I was going to survive.

Wasn't it?

What was the path to my survival? Yes, if I survived this cabin it would be great, but it would only be to pass me over to another death sentence. I'd die before being forced to marry Stone. I couldn't run without Daisy being hurt or killed.

The scant amount of bread in my mouth turned to dust.

I'd been so lost in my thoughts, everything around me had grown blurry. Even him, except now he was cut from sharp lines against everything else around him. My body felt like lead as his attention zeroed in on me. Then on the forgotten piece of bread in my hand.

"You're not eating."

I restrained a shiver over the sound of his voice in the quiet room. It was a cleaver cutting through everything.

Keeping my cool in front of him was paramount. I couldn't show my discomfort. Therefore, I looked up and held his electric, cruel gaze.

"I don't eat meat," I informed him.

His expression didn't change. He didn't stop eating either, chewing slowly as we continued to stare at each other.

"You do now," was what he said once he swallowed.

The iciness of his tone was no match for the fire I felt inside at his words.

"I get that you're under the impression that you have complete control over me since you took me against my will and have marooned me here in a cabin with you." My fists clenched under the table, my voice steel. "And you may have control over those things, but you do not have complete control. I will not submit to your every will and whim. I may be your captive, but I am not your puppet."

I considered myself an assertive person ... in more of a passive way. I'd never really rocked the boat with friends, lovers, bosses. I shied away from conflict as a survival instinct since I knew what happened when life turned ugly. If there was any situation where I should've shied away from conflict, it was in that cabin in the middle of nowhere with a monster, yet I didn't. I held on to what little was left of my agency, and I refused to let it go.

Though I was proud of my little speech, how strong and unyielding I'd sounded, Knox didn't seem the slightest bit impressed. Or even mad.

Though the contours of his face stayed the same, I could've sworn he seemed ... amused.

That only served to stoke the fire of my fury further.

But before I could do or say anything more, his utensils were on his plate, his chair was out from under the table, and the scrape of wood against the floor entered my ears.

I was moving.

Caged in by him. His hands were on either side of my chair, his thumbs almost brushing my thighs. His body surrounded me, his heady, masculine scent, face inches from mine.

My entire body tensed, and my head throbbed with terror.

He'd never stopped being dangerous or deadly. Even when doing something as benign as eating. I'd figured he'd stop being deadly when his heart ceased beating. But part of me had gotten used to it. Or gotten used to the undercurrent of fear I felt in his presence.

But his entire energy had changed. This was not a passive undercurrent of fear he was eliciting. It was heart-stopping terror as his eyes held mine hostage.

Luckily, I had just emptied my bladder because if I hadn't, I might've wet myself.

My eyes roved over his face, pale, high cheekbones, sharp jaw. His dark brow was heavy with a tiny whisper of a scar at the edge of his eyes, the one mar in the perfect features of his face. His eyes were glaciers, ice blue with a solid azure ring around them. Riveting, interesting, unique.

Knox leaned in even closer. For one insane moment, I thought he might kiss me.

It should've roiled my belly with disgust; instead, my heart merely thundered as my palms started to sweat. I squirmed for reasons other than discomfort, instantly forcing myself to ignore that. This was not the time nor the place to inspect my body's highly inappropriate reactions to my kidnapper.

But he didn't kiss me. His head shifted, barely brushing my cheek with his hair as his lips hovered over my ears. Though he was so close I could feel his energy imprinting onto mine, hindering my breathing, my heartbeat and ability to stay calm, he wasn't actually touching me.

He seemed to be very careful to ensure that.

"In this cabin, in these woods, you are my *everything*." His whispered words were both a blade and a weight settling against my shoulders with their certainty. "You are my captive. My puppet. My toy. My pet. Your survival depends on me." He paused, and I could feel his warm breath on my ear. It should've been icy cold for all the chill in his tone.

Yet heat surged through me.

Along with fury. Contempt. My hands bit into my thighs, digging into my jeans and the flesh beneath. Why didn't I lash out at him with those hands? Rake my hands through that unmarked skin? Even though it looked to be made of stone, he was human. If cut, he'd bleed.

But I stayed where I was, an insect under his microscope.

"Your mental state depends on whether I feel like breaking you or not." His voice was featherlight as his eyes seared through my very soul. "Which I will. It's up to me how many pieces you shatter into."

The silence that cloaked us was thicker than the starless night outside.

He hovered there for longer than was comfortable, bearable, before he finally straightened.

I'd hoped the way I stared at him conveyed the level of my hatred, hatred for his presence, his lack of a fucking heart. The fear he instilled in me. The paralyzing terror I'd promised myself a man would never elicit in me again.

"I know it's a human survival instinct to deceive yourself into thinking you have control over your actions, surroundings or survival, Ms. Matthews. Most of the time, it's just delusion with free will scattered sporadically. But none of that exists here." He sat back down in his chair, casually resuming his meal as if he hadn't just essentially threatened my life and mental health.

"Eat." He stabbed the dead flesh with his fork, his eyes containing more intensity, more emotion, than I'd yet to see in them. "Or starve."

A challenge. Posed as if he didn't care if I withered away to nothing but a skeleton right in front of his eyes. My survival mattered that little to him. *I* mattered that little to him. He was a monster, dehumanizing me, turning me into nothing more than a ... pet. Reliant on him for everything, down to food and water.

My teeth gnashed together until my jaw hurt.

A man's pet I wasn't.

I stood up and left the room without touching another bite, storming into the bathroom, slamming the door and sinking against it before dropping onto the floor.

The bathroom door didn't have a lock. No privacy. No barriers from him. Not that I thought a lock would stop him anyway. An illusion of safety was all it would be. I needed to rid myself of all illusions.

I was not safe with Knox. That much was painfully clear.

He wasn't going to rape or torture me; I took him at his word on that—as naïve or stupid as that might be. I also took him at his word that he was going to break me.

Prior to that day, I would've said no man had that power, dumbly confident in my inner strength.

Yet right then, sitting on the bathroom floor, hyperventilating, never feeling more alone or hopeless, I knew Knox was going to ruin me.

It was just a matter of time.

And how many pieces he'd leave me in depended on how cruel he truly was.

Six

Knox

I knew she was a vegetarian. Though my research into Piper Matthews was nowhere near as in depth as I would've liked, I'd gathered what information I could from her social media page.

She didn't eat meat, she loved Taylor Swift, she ran every morning, she drank lattes at the same coffee shop every day, her favorite book was some fantasy title I'd never heard of but had inexplicably purchased and brought with me. And, she believed in the power of crystals, as if hunks of rock were useful as anything more than paperweights.

I couldn't fathom the amount of shit people shared about themselves on the internet, desperate to have someone, anyone, know them. As if they didn't realize that in the right hands, that was the key to their ruin.

Benign personal information was the key to breaking her. While doing my supply run, the majority of what I purchased were meat products, very little vegetables or grains. That was intentional. She'd initially stick to her morals, the belief system she'd held as a marker of her identity. Then she'd get hungry. Eventually, she'd sacrifice who she was in order to survive.

And that would chisel off a little of her self-worth. Self-respect.

We had just over a month. Ideally, I would've had longer to draw out the process, have it be more subtle, but we didn't have time. And now that I was stuck in a cabin with her, a month seemed like it might break *me*.

Such thoughts were obviously a sign of my mind finally fracturing. Madness was the only viable explanation for these feelings. Some five-foot-nothing civilian who smelled of peaches did not have the power to break me.

No one did.

Only me.

Only I had that power. And it was happening. All of my sins—committed in the name of survival, to feed that ravenous darkness inside of me—were finally eating at me. There would never be enough death, blood or depravity to keep me sane. I'd known that for a while.

Bad timing more than anything else.

But that didn't mean I wouldn't accomplish my goal. That I wouldn't rip apart Piper and ensure she'd be begging to be taken to Stone.

Maybe my madness would help in doing just that. Or perhaps I'd bring us both down.

———

I hadn't slept in days.

There had been too much to do. To prepare. I'd snatched a couple of hours here and there. I only slept a handful of hours on any given night anyway. Nightmares slithered in if I slept too deeply and for too long.

But this was less than even I was used to. I'd settled onto the sofa, hoping my body might shut down. Though I didn't think it was possible for me to lapse into unconsciousness, knowing that Piper was in the same room as me. She was sleeping; I could hear the soft sighs coming from her, her body still.

When her breathing settled, and I stopped seeing any movement in the bed, I got up.

I wasn't prone to making bad decisions. Every choice I made was calculated, precise, all possible consequences weighed.

Going anywhere near Piper for the purpose of doing anything other than breaking her will was a unilaterally bad decision.

My iron-clad control abandoned me as I stepped on soundless feet to stand at her bedside.

She'd yanked the covers up to her chest and was still clutching them in her sleep. She was tense, protecting herself, even in sleep. A normal person, a good person, might've felt a stab of guilt at that.

Then again, a good person never would've taken her captive in the first place.

My eyes traced the curves and ridges of her face. Her high cheekbones, her delicate nose, the gentle flaring of her nostrils as she inhaled. Her long lashes framed exquisite espresso and gold-flecked eyes.

Her rosebud lips were swollen, as if she'd been chewing on them all night. The arch at the top of her lip was enchanting. I wanted it wrapped around my dick.

Wanted *her* wrapped around my dick.

I'd always known I was sick, but not this sick. Not capable of watching my captive sleep with my cock hard, seconds away from coming all over her just by *thinking* about her.

It was shameful. Fucking creepy.

Yet I'd stayed there for an age, watching her chest move, memorizing the ridges of her face, cock standing at attention, refusing to sate my need. I didn't do that. Didn't give myself pleasure I didn't deserve. Primarily because when I was done, I felt dirtier than before, and the call of the knife was louder, the need to cut through the filth undeniable.

By the time I finally forced my feet to walk back to the sofa, I'd given in to the call of the steel, exhaling as the familiar bite of pain eased the tension. But not enough. Nowhere near enough as it had in the past. Madness was truly near, then. If the one thing I could always rely upon had abandoned me. Wired and frustrated, I stared at the ceiling for hours before sheer exhaustion finally took me.

I was contemplating my fate. A month in this cabin with her. My control was already frayed, damn near destroyed, after one fucking night.

The urge to run was palpable.

But running meant defeat.

Running meant my death.

I had to stay. And I'd keep my hands off her.

She was Stone's. I'd deliver her to him, willing and ready to be his wife. No matter how sick the prospect made me.

I'd fracture this beautiful woman because I could. Because I had to. Because she already had too much power over me.

And I'd vowed to myself years ago, that no one would have that ever again.

Piper

Despite the situation, my gnawing hunger and my overwrought nervous system, I slept like the dead.

Clearly, my body's exhaustion trumped my mind's turmoil. For one night anyway. How I could shut down and be vulnerable and unconscious in the same room as the bastard sitting on the couch was beyond me.

Survival.

My body was wired to do that. And in order to survive, I needed strength. I needed sustenance.

One cursory glance in the small fridge and freezer showed me it was packed to the gills with meat, butter and a handful of vegetables. Same with the small pantry. Some bread, grains, but very little.

The next morning, I'd mindfully chewed on the bread and an apple. Somehow, he'd known. He'd known that I didn't eat meat, ensuring that I would have barely enough food to keep me alive, let alone strong enough to fight back.

It was chilling, to be under the same roof as someone who was purely there to break my will. To batter me so completely that I would 'willingly' marry a monster. Stone could've easily forced me with a gun aimed point-blank to my sister's head. I would've done it too. To protect Daisy. It would've been a fuck of a lot simpler than all of this.

Although he was a criminal piece of shit, he somehow considered himself civilized. His ego wouldn't allow him to simply force me to marry him. He wanted to bring about the illusion of consent, whether that was for appearances or for his own warped mind, I didn't know.

My hunger wasn't sated by my meager breakfast, but it sufficed for the moment. I had to ration. It was all I had for the foreseeable future, and I was entirely dependent on Knox for all of my sustenance and safety.

A sobering and horrifying thought.

That's what had me putting on my running gear in the bathroom—while Knox was presumably sleeping on the sofa. I didn't look too closely at the large, prone form.

Although I was tempted. Sleep seemed like an impossible bodily function for him. Sleep left you too vulnerable.

There was nothing vulnerable about this man. Nothing soft, human. Nothing to cut into.

Not that I would. I'd eyed the unused steak knife he'd put in front of me at the table for about 2.5 seconds. Stabbing someone with a steak knife would do little. Unless by miracle you hit an artery or were willing to continuously stab. And that's on someone who wasn't fighting back.

Knox wouldn't need to fight back. He was watching me so carefully, I'd have the knife out of my hand before it was even halfway through the air.

And even if by some miracle I did kill or incapacitate him... Then what? There was nowhere to run to.

I doubted that Knox did anything without a lot of thought. The meat. The sharp axe. All of it was a taunt. That he could give me a weapon on a silver platter, yet I was unable to use it. Even if I had the stomach for it, I couldn't fight him, kill him.

On that thought, I shoved on my running shoes—purposely not looking in the direction of the sofa in case he was awake and watching me—then crept out the door.

I couldn't kill him.

But I could run.

I felt him in the woods around me before I saw him. A slash of black against the crisp-green foliage and trees. A yawning black hole of death amidst the glorious life of the mountains.

He wasn't wearing a suit. He'd abandoned that like a snake shedding its skin.

But he was still clad in black. A form-fitting sweatshirt, even though the morning was unseasonably warm. I'd shed my layers immediately, the long-sleeved tee I'd donned tied in a tight knot around my waist leaving me in only a sports bra.

His long pants were expensive, practical and spotless. Same with the black boots. He wore them well, even if I had the inkling this was the first time he'd worn gear like it.

The inky curtain of his hair was messier today, as if he'd been running his hands through it, falling across his face and highlighting his flawless, ivory skin. His eyes were dark and predatory as I came to a stop, raking over every inch of me.

I'd previously been sweating, flushed from the exertion of running on uneven terrain without the appropriate amount of fuel in my body.

My throat closed up with his attention on my bare skin. A flashback to when we first met. Was it really only yesterday when I'd been running through Central Park?

Like I had then, I resisted the urge to cover myself up, to protect my exposed skin from his gaze.

I didn't know how he got there, how he tracked me, in the woods, at least a mile from the cabin. Not the city boy that he was. Maybe he was supernatural. Maybe he tracked me by scent. Smelling my blood. My fear.

I believed in all of that. In things that couldn't be explained by science. I believed intuition was a form of divination, that souls called to one another, that auras communicated the true nature of people.

Knox was challenging those beliefs. His aura was dark, thorny, dangerous. Yet his soul called to mine in a way I couldn't explain.

He wasn't leaning anywhere, just standing in the middle of what couldn't really be called a trail, more like a break in the woods.

I'd followed my instincts through the woods, running where the ground was most forgiving, lapsing into memories of my childhood, tearing through the trees and over ground carpeted with pine needles like the ones outside my grandmother's house. Though her old property had been sold, abandoned, hundreds of miles away, I yearned for it. To be running back to a cozy house with freshly-made biscuits cooling on the counter, scrambled eggs from the chickens she kept. Thick cuts of juicy bacon from her neighbor who kept pigs. That's what turned me into a vegetarian. I'd petted those pigs, named them.

My grandmother, an Appalachian woman through and

through, was soft in many ways but hard when it came to life and death and sustenance. She cared for animals, loved her cat Frank and her hound Lewis, but she'd never hesitated to kill when she needed to.

My grandmother didn't agree or understand my vegetarianism but had accepted it. Just as she had accepted everything from those she loved. Even when accepting that my mother loved my father and would be leaving the mountains for the city lost her her daughter.

"What are you doing?"

Knox's flat voice jerked me out of my stupor. I was standing in the middle of the woods, half-dressed, panting and sweaty, staring at a killer.

"Running." My voice was a little breathless but not weak. Weakness had no place in these woods, in front of this man.

Knox didn't respond, he just stared.

"Not running from *you*," I stipulated, unable to weather the stare. "I'm running. Like I do every day. I was planning on coming back."

Again, Knox didn't speak as the woods gently hummed between us.

"Running. Here," he said flatly. He didn't look around, keeping his gaze firmly on me.

I felt one hundred pounds heavier under the weight of his gaze. I had an urge to shift on my feet, but I couldn't signal my discomfort.

"Yes, here." My tone was sharp. Challenging.

His jaw twitched. Barely, but I saw it. Only because I was determined to scrutinize him with the same intensity as he was looking at me.

"These woods are not Central Park, Piper," he gritted out. "There are predators here."

"I'm well aware that there are predators in these woods," I raised a brow, my meaning clear. He was my predator. "And I'd rather face off with any of the animals in these woods than some of the men that lurk in Central Park, waiting for a woman to let her guard down."

Though his expression didn't change, not even a miniscule jaw twitch, I could feel his anger, his fury. A flock of birds even fled from a nearby tree.

Even though I believed in forms of magic, I convinced myself it had to be a coincidence.

"If you're not smart enough to fear the wildlife—"

"I'm smart enough to know what to fear and what to respect," I huffed.

The run was enough to rejuvenate me. Even if it depleted the physical energy reserves that I needed, I still fully possessed my mental faculties.

Again, I could feel a burst of enraged energy coming from Knox's general direction.

He wasn't used to being interrupted. I had the sense he was used to commanding a room, with underlings cowering beneath him in fear.

I wasn't going to cower. It would be my destruction. My instincts told me that much.

After not so much as blinking, Knox drew in a visible breath. He was a fearsome creature. Like some kind of devil walking the woods. Though I sensed that even Satan would fear him.

"If you do not fear the animals, you're still running in unfamiliar terrain. You could get lost."

I didn't mistake those words for concern. If he was concerned with me in any way, he wouldn't have taken me here in the first place.

"You found me," I shrugged, my tone as sharp as a blade.

He nodded. "I'll always find you."

My skin raised with gooseflesh at the promise in his words. It was terrifying. And exciting. Comforting.

Comforting? The fact that my captor would always find me? My mind was obviously fraying at the seams. I thought I'd last at least twenty-four hours... The reality of how brittle my mind truly was, was frightening.

"Well what's the issue, then?" I folded my arms in front of me. "Even if I'm some damsel in distress, lost in the woods, you'll come rescue me."

Again, there was a long pause while he gave me that unyielding stare that turned my limbs to jelly and my skin ablaze. "You are not a damsel in distress," he eventually replied. "And I'm not someone who rescues damsels. I kill them."

I forced my expression to remain unaffected. He was trying to scare me. I wasn't going to give him the satisfaction of seeing that it worked.

He stayed stock-still, as he had the entire time. It was unnatural for a person to stand like that, without any kind of physical tic, shifting of their weight, needing to scratch an itch, clenching their fists. He had complete control over every inch of his body. It was a finely-tuned weapon, that much was clear. "You wouldn't want to deal with the consequences of me having to find you if you get lost."

A threat.

"I'm not lost." A flat-out lie. I wasn't lost in these woods. But in life? Yeah, I'd never been more lost in my life.

His silence conveyed his disbelief. In his eyes, I was a damsel. If I wasn't a damsel, I wouldn't be here, would I? I would've found a way to escape Stone's attention, to outsmart him. Defeat him.

I read books about women overcoming all odds, slaying dragons or riding them then laying waste to entire regimes. Yet there I was, face-to-face with a monstrosity I was powerless against.

"Fine." I turned on my heel, even though it went against all my survival

instincts to give him my back.

I started running.

"Try to keep up. And don't break an ankle on a protruding tree root," I called over my shoulder, willing him to do just that.

The crackling of detritus behind me was the only thing that told me he was running behind me. That was it, though. The initial crunch of boots against the forest floor, then … nothing. I listened for him with an experienced ear, but I couldn't hear him. He moved through the brush like a hunter. Impossible. Even me, someone accustomed to these woods made small missteps, making my presence known.

Even though he made no sound, I didn't need to turn to know he was behind me. I felt him. The hairs on the nape of my neck were raised in fear.

My heart slammed against my breastbone as I pushed my already burning legs to go faster. I kept mind of the roots, rocks, the uneven terrain. Even nature was primed to test you to see if you could survive there.

The woods flashed by; my previously cold body warmed up, more sweat running down my skin, my pulse pounding in my ears.

It was an eternity and a second when the small cabin came into view. I let out a fractured breath of relief, of victory.

This had been what I wanted, wasn't it? To prove to Knox that I was no damsel in distress. To prove to myself that I wasn't afraid of him. I turned, panting with a self-satisfied smile, planning on gloating.

Until I saw the expression on Knox's face.

There was no longer cold calculation holding his features captive. No, there was a wild animal, a demon glowing behind his ferocious eyes.

Reflexively, I scuttled back, almost tripping on the uneven ground of the cobbled walk to the cabin.

Knox advanced, prowling toward me like a feral animal. And the animal inside of me responded with a singular instinct—to run.

The door to the cabin hit my back hard, stopping my retreat.

Just as I was about to dart to the left to run toward the overgrown garden, Knox's arms caged me in. His palms rested on the wood of the door as he leaned forward, his face inches from mine but not touching me.

Still, my body trembled. Fear was a physical, tangible thing inside of me, squeezing at my throat.

He didn't speak immediately; he just stood there, hovering close to my face, eyes locked onto mine, pupils dilated, his entire being a threat to my very existence.

My heart must've been beating because I didn't drop dead there and then, but my lungs shrank. Not from the run but from the pressure that was burgeoning inside my body, the very air being sucked from them.

"Don't *ever* run from me again." Knox's voice was featherlight. But there was a tension there, as if he was about to snap. The pulsating cords in his neck told me that he was having trouble holding himself back.

I couldn't tear my gaze from him.

Nor could I speak.

I just stood there in the cage of his arms, breathing rapidly like the prey I was. Like a scared rabbit. It didn't seem out of the question that I was going to have a heart attack from terror.

"Piper." My name was like the crack of a whip I swore I could feel tearing apart my skin.

All I could do was blink at him.

"If you value your life, I need you to tell me you won't ever fucking run from me again."

It struck me that I'd never heard him curse before. I got the sense he didn't do it often, only when needed. The four-letter word was spoken in a velvet tone, but it cut like that same whip.

I was scared. I don't think I'd ever been more scared in my entire life. But not just that. I was filled with shame and disgust about it, but there was a wetness between my thighs. And it was not my bladder releasing.

It was from desire. My clit pulsated in response to the violence emanating from Knox. Because I would've bet my life on it—my life that could very well be in jeopardy right then—that he was feeling some kind of desire right then too. Yes, he was a predator. But he was also a male predator. Some primitive chase and mate instinct.

Mate. Rut. Fuck.

Filthy carnal words for an act I previously considered sacred, something I only did with people I respected. I certainly didn't love or respect this barbarian.

But I wanted him.

It was undeniable.

Still, my mouth couldn't open. Wouldn't open.

"Speak," he demanded.

I flinched. Again, the command was a weapon. Used to wound, to make me bleed on the inside. To make me cower.

And despite my terror—and yes, my shameful craving—I didn't submit. Wouldn't.

He was there to break me. And this was just the beginning. A hairline crack, a harbinger of further destruction.

I jutted my chin upward, my teeth grinding together with force that made me worry they might shatter.

"No."

He didn't even flinch. But I swear, the weight of his gaze became even heavier. The air felt thicker.

"Excuse me?" he asked quietly.

"No," I repeated. "I will not tell you that I won't run from you again because I'm not a liar. And because I'm not a liar, I will make you a promise." I sucked in a deep breath. "Once it's safe for my sister, I will run from you. And you can make chase, try to catch me, but you won't. Eventually, you won't have any power over me."

Like I had last night, I felt proud that I was able to stand up to what was the most terrifying creature I'd come across in my life. Even if I understood that he wouldn't let me get away with this. That this wasn't a victory. It just wasn't submission.

He proved me right seconds later, leaning in closer. Still not touching, my body betrayed me, arching forward ever so slightly toward him. As if we were opposing magnets, drawn to each other while repelling each other at the same time.

He went rigid as he noted my body's movement, then he straightened so our bodies didn't even brush.

"If I so choose, Piper, I will always have power over you. So you better pray to whatever gods you worship that I do not choose that."

He let the words linger for a second, still as a statue with his gaze scalding my eyes. And there was a moment, a moment when I must've been delusional with fear because I was sure that he was going to kiss me.

And what was worse, and infinitely more delusional, was that I was getting ready to kiss him back.

Thankfully, there was one shred of mercy left for me in the universe.

Knox rolled back onto his heels then stalked back into the woods like the wild animal he was. I watched the foliage swallow him up, still pressed against the door, unable to control my breathing.

"Pray to whatever gods you worship that I do not choose that."

The words echoed throughout the quiet clearing.

I wasn't a deeply religious person, spiritual for sure, but even I knew that the moment Knox came into my life, the gods—and even my treasured goddesses—had abandoned me.

Only the devil remained.

SEVEN

KNOX

I almost tore off her clothes and took her right there against the door. Covered in sweat and terror. The fear in her yes—the fright—equal parts disturbed me and turned me the fuck on. My cock pressed painfully against the zipper of my pants, demanding to be used, demanding to claim her.

Rape.

That would've been rape. To take a petrified woman.

I'd done a lot of deplorable, unforgivable things in my life, but never that. Never would I abuse someone like that. I killed plenty of people without remorse.

But I learned at a young age there are worse things than death.

And I may be a devil in many respects, but never that kind of devil. Never would I sentence a person to hell without the mercy of death.

Shame.

The unfamiliar, uncomfortable emotion coated me as I prowled through the woods.

Shame at just how fucking close I'd been to losing control.

Me.

But was she *completely* unwilling?

She despised me. Feared me.

But I saw something else beyond hatred and fright in her eyes. I saw lust.

The gold in her eyes turned molten. Was the flush in her cheeks solely from the run, the hitch in her breath caused by just fear and physical exertion? The way her rosebud lips had parted, her long eyelashes fluttering...

But I couldn't trust my eyes. Not with my traitorous cock telling them lies. A cock that had never once influenced my decisions.

I rubbed at my eyes, the brush crumbling under my feet.

Fuck, I needed a coffee.

But I didn't since Piper was a 'caffeine addict' as declared on social media. I was going to strip her of all of her vices, comforts. Withdrawal from substances even as seemingly benign as caffeine could help break a person.

Under the right circumstances.

I'd been confident that I had all of the right ingredients to break Piper. I just hadn't accounted for my hunger for her. Hadn't thought that she might possess all the right weapons to break me. An easy, lyrical laughter, a soft exterior hiding a will of stone beneath.

"Fuck!" I roared, slamming my fist against a tree, disturbing the silence of the woods.

Blood trickled from a cut in my knuckle.

Though I relished the pain, the relief that came from tearing open my skin, this mark was a problem.

It was not easily hidden, masked. It was somewhere that would declare my lack of control. Lack of power.

I thought about my initial feeling, waking up to find Piper gone. To discover I'd slept through her moving around the cabin. Leaving.

She could've taken the opportunity to kill me in my sleep. That's what I would've done in her position.

But not everyone was like me. Not everyone killed easier than breathing, became a living nightmare to escape their own demons and needed to split their skin open to feel anything.

Not everyone was a monster.

Somehow, Piper was gentle. In this cruel world, she hadn't been beaten down, embittered. Not even with the proof that goodness was not rewarded. It was only coveted by men like Stone, destroyed by men like me.

That wasn't what captivated me about her, though. It was the fire that burned through that gentleness. She wasn't weak. That defiant tilt of her chin, the way she overcame her fear of me. The confidence of her gait as she tore through unforgiving woods. Her sense of direction in a place that almost turned me around. Her chopping fucking wood.

I stared at my blood staining a tree that had likely been standing longer than I'd been alive, in woods that were older than our civilized country.

Civilized.

That's something I wasn't. Something I'd never be. A demon in a suit, masquerading as a human but not quite pulling it off.

We were different species. I needed to remind myself of that.

I did not deserve an ounce of pleasure or happiness the prospect of her promised.

And she did not deserve the lifetime of ruin I promised.

Then again, her life was already ruined with or without me.

Piper

The temperature was impressive, given how remote the cabin was, but even the scalding-hot shower couldn't cure me, couldn't chase away the chill nesting in my neurons. I'd investigated the hot water source—a large propane tank slightly removed from the house. I wanted to ask Knox about the plumbing, the running water. My guess would be some kind of gravity fed system from a nearby creek, or maybe a well. But no way was I making conversation with Knox after what happened.

It was selfish of me to take such a long and hot shower since the propane would eventually run out. But I didn't give a shit about Knox's hot showers. I probably should've at the very least thought about future me needing showers, but I wasn't able to think practically right then.

I'd scrubbed myself raw, as if I could get the power of his gaze off my skin. It wasn't on my skin, though; it was imprinted in my cells.

Despite the warmth of the shower, the body heat generated from the run and the rapidly warming spring morning, my teeth chattered.

I'd put on a long-sleeved shirt, a cardigan and leggings, trying to let my hair air dry outside in the sun while again nibbling on an apple and some bread.

My body was crying out for coffee, but a half-desperate search of the cupboards showed there was none to be had.

That further solidified my theory that Knox was some kind of robot or vampire. There was no way he could be human if he didn't operate on caffeine. Especially considering the lack of sleep he'd had. And I assumed chasing, kidnapping and terrifying people took up a lot of energy.

Drugs, then, if he was indeed human. It had to be stimulants. I'd seen behind the curtain, discovering that many successful people were on some kind of drug to keep them up, to get them up, to bring them down.

Although I didn't see the signs of addiction in him. That didn't mean much; addicts were experts at lying, hiding their true selves.

But Knox wasn't hiding his true self. He was showing what a

monster he was without shame, regret. He wanted me to see it. Be scared.

And though I was plenty scared, I couldn't give in to that fear. This was only the beginning, after all. This was a month of living with the devil, and I was going to use it as training to survive being married to whatever Stone was.

Training to end him.

Because I'd figured there was truly no escape. Nothing that wouldn't risk my sister. I'd let him think Knox broke me. And while I was here, I'd watch Knox. His cruelty, brutality, hoping it would rub off on me. It basically leached from his skin, so it should.

And most importantly, I would ignore any and all attraction I had to the man. It must've been some kind of mirage, some trickster magic of the Appalachian woods that had me feeling it.

I was definitely not attracted to him.

No.

I was fascinated by him. Because on the surface, he seemed like my destruction, but if I played things right, he might just be my salvation.

He'd teach me to be the villain I'd need to be.

Because I was beginning to understand that life wasn't like my books. A woman didn't need to slay dragons nor ride them. No, she needed to *become* a dragon, breathe fire on all men who considered her conquerable.

ONE DAY LATER

I didn't see Knox for the entirety of the day after our ... altercation, if that's what you'd call it. I'd hidden inside the cabin, bracing for him to come in the door, hurt me ... or make good on that shadow of prurience I'd told myself I had imagined.

I'd shuffled and dealt my cards, the spread changing except one Tarot card.

The Devil.

It came time after time.

It was too weird, even for me.

The Devil card was, granted, a misunderstood card. It didn't hold its roots in the classic religious connotations of the term. Not to me anyway.

The Devil represented a darker side of us all, one we rarely brought to light, one we ignored, shunned or reviled. It was the ugly little voice in our heads saying jealous things, self-deprecating things, or wanting things that were deplorable. Destructive.

It warned against taking the path of instant gratification because it was often the path of destruction.

Even without a Tarot card, I understood that giving in to any kind of carnal desire I felt for Knox would lead me to ruin.

And yet...

I'd always felt an affinity for that card. Especially given the battles I'd fought in the past. It had brought shadows to light, understanding them so I could release their hold.

The Devil was also about sexuality. About being unashamed about cravings that society scorned or shunned—providing everything was consensual and everyone was of age. But again, this card represented how exploring such things was walking on a narrow path. If not with someone safe and respectful, pain and devastation would ensue.

Again, this was all too chilling and much too accurate for my situation, even for me. Rattled, I'd buried the cards in my bag then stared at the wall until I couldn't stare anymore.

I was not a person to sit idle. So I'd tidied. Cleaned. Straightened up the rustic cabin as best I could.

The furnishings were sparse, linens mostly threadbare, but the table was made of solid wood, the rug covering smooth wooden floors. In the tiny linen cabinet I'd discovered old lace curtains that had once hung on the windows. This place had fallen into disrepair, but it was built well, to withstand. And small touches like the lace curtains, the fading paint on the shutters, the rugs, the overgrown garden, told me that at one point, people had lived here and been proud to call it home.

Now this was little more than a cage. But I could rectify that. Turn it into something a little better, do the previous owners a favor. I was relieved to have a task, to do something other than gaze at the door, waiting for Knox to return.

When Knox finally came in, I instantly retreated to the bathroom, telling myself I was there to clean it, not escape him. I mentally said that as I scrubbed behind the toilet with an old toothbrush I found in the back of the cabinet.

When I emerged, he was once again cooking, the telltale smell of meat wafting through the cabin. Disgusted, I'd pursed my lips, stomped into the cabin to snatch a piece of quickly staling bread, careful not to look at him before retreating outside to eat before going to bed.

I didn't fall asleep for a long time. Couldn't. Not with him there. It was barely possible to breathe through the thick air.

Eventually, my body succumbed, the exertion of the run, the adrenaline and the scant amount of food I'd consumed exhausting me. I woke early again, donning running clothes. Knox didn't chase me that time.

Which was good, I reminded myself.

I especially reminded myself that the little urge inside of me didn't exist. The urge that wanted to be chased, wanted that fear and desire mixing inside of me, wanted to go back to yesterday, to the most alive I'd ever felt in my three decades walking the earth.

The plan was to talk to him as little as possible. Give him the silent treatment, be an overall bitch to him. I didn't consider myself a bitch and didn't think it was an okay thing to be—though too many women were labeled that way by men for merely being assertive and not fawning all over them—but I thought etiquette dictated that you could be a bitch to the man holding you hostage.

Again, that had been the plan. But I wasn't practiced at being a bitch. So I kind of forgot my plan. I didn't forget about my captivity, mind you. Just the vow I'd made to myself. I liked being alone, was happy with books, cooking, being in nature, meditating, reading Tarot, tending to my small herb garden on our rooftop.

But it was hard to do a lot of those things in a small, one-room cabin with a statuesque man quietly emanating various degrees of menace.

It made me uneasy. And very scared.

But I didn't want to show my fear. Something told me that he was used to that, Knox.

I assumed he had plenty of people submitting to his will, his commands, doing everything in their power to avoid him. And yes, ancient survival instincts and general common sense were telling me to keep as far away from him as possible and to keep our interactions to a bare minimum.

But there was something more than common sense, something borne out of my penchant for romance books and affinity for the villain as opposed to the hero. *Beauty and the Beast* was my favorite Disney movie, after all. I liked the beast, I liked that he could've ripped Belle apart at any moment. And aside from the fact that it would've made the movie a lot less child-friendly, it wouldn't be as appealing to young girls.

We want to tame the beast. We want to know its talons could rip us apart, but instead, they stroke our skin. That their teeth could chew our flesh, but instead, their lips go to our most intimate and vulnerable of places...

"Here." I kind of yelled the word as I placed a steaming mug of tea in front of Knox. In the short time we'd been in each other's company, I'd noted that he drank it often. Not coffee—we didn't have any coffee. Tea. An interesting choice for a man like him.

Tea, a delicate, mindful drink that required care, ritual. Or at least the way I drank it.

I'd likely put too much thought into it, since there wasn't anything else to drink but tea. It could've been borne from necessity, nothing else.

He looked up from the book he'd been reading, the battered paperback so worn the title wasn't legible. I'd tried to crane my head to find it in the interior, but I never got close enough to it—to him—and he didn't leave it lying around.

It was likely *How to Dismember and Dispose of a Body in Less Than Twenty Minutes.*

He closed it as I got close, not marking where he'd left off. I didn't see him look to memorize the page number either.

Interesting.

His entire form stiffened as I leaned close to place the tea in front of him.

"It's not coffee." I stepped back, circling my fingers around my own warm mug, inhaling the steam as it came out. "Obviously. You know that, since you didn't buy coffee. If I didn't already think so due to you working for Stone and kidnapping me and everything, I would've pegged you as a psychopath for that alone."

It was an attempt at a dark joke. To break the tension between us. Why I thought that breaking the tension with my kidnapper was a good idea was anyone's guess.

Knox, quite unsurprisingly, didn't smile at that. It wasn't funny. Especially because he likely *was* a psychopath.

Then again, weren't psychopaths highly charismatic, able to blend in, act like humans?

Knox wasn't trying to act as if he was anything but a stone-cold killer. He was going out of his way to communicate that.

I took a deep breath then sipped my tea, looking out at the woods. They always seemed to stare back. I knew that made a lot of people afraid of this portion of Northern America, but it had always comforted me. Being looked upon by something wild, unpredictable, ancient.

"We're going to be stuck together for a month. At least," I continued my attempt to create some kind of dialogue between us. My plan of being a bitch and giving him the cold shoulder going up in flames. More flies with honey and all that. "I figure even you can't talk in veiled threats and bad guy speech for that long. And we're the only company we have. So..." I nodded to the tea. "An olive branch. One that you could reciprocate by, you know, going to the closest town to buy me something that isn't dead animal. Not that I judge your eating habits. You do you." I tucked my hair behind my ear with a free hand, not having felt this awkward since I was thirteen, trying to talk to a boy I liked.

Granted, he hadn't kidnapped me, been over six feet, radiating menace from his pores, but he'd felt just as scary at the time.

And it hadn't gone well. He'd been one of the cooler kids, and I'd taken a while to grow into my features. I always wore clothes that were slightly too small—even on my skinny frame—and blatantly cheap. It was clear we were poor, and things like socioeconomic status was fair game back then.

It had scared me off talking to boys for a long while. Then I grew boobs, and my features fit my face a little better. The boys did most of the talking, though. Not that they said anything worth listening to.

Knox had barely blinked during my babble session, nor had his features softened at all.

"You know, if the wind changes, your face will stay that way," I joked lamely. "Or maybe it already has, and that's why you're always so..." I tried to school my features into his menacing expression but likely didn't pull it off.

I'd been aiming to crack him a little by being a bit silly. But there wasn't so much as a hairline fracture. He likely thought I was a ridiculous person.

That was fine. The goal was to have him thinking of me as a person instead of a job, a victim.

He looked from me to the tea.

Then, with the utmost patience and grace, he wrapped his hand around the tea, lifted it carefully and slowly, then hurled it at the wall. It shattered and splashes of hot water caught my face.

I flinched. Though I wanted to scream, scuttle away in terror, it took all of my self-control to stay in place; my mouth tasted of copper as I bit my lip hard enough to draw blood.

His chair screeched as he stood. He didn't move toward me as I expected him to do. Part of his routine—getting in my face, using his size to intimidate me and threaten me. Though he stayed where he was, the distance between us didn't help my blood pressure any.

"We won't need to be here for a month," he sneered, eyeing me as if I were little more than a gnat buzzing around his face. "You'll break long before that."

Then he walked out.

My shaking hand lifted to sip my tea. I was trying to pretend I wasn't rattled, while my teeth literally chattered against the rim of the mug.

"No, I won't," I called to his back.

But even I didn't believe me.

Eight

One Week Later

PIPER

My lungs were crying out for mercy.

Same with my thighs. My hamstrings were taut, feeling as if they might just snap at any moment. The growling in my stomach had stopped, replaced by a gnawing, seemingly endless emptiness. All I thought about was food. I'd scoured the woods already, looking for edible plants. There were none. Or my brain had forgotten how to distinguish food from poison. Soon, I wouldn't care. Soon, I'd be stuffing any plant into my mouth, willing to risk death just to stop the pain.

Every night, I sat at the dinner table with Knox as he ate juicy cuts of meat that smelled better and better every time. He always put some on my plate. I didn't have to sit there, he didn't force me at gunpoint. He didn't do anything to me at gunpoint. He wasn't holding me hostage against my will.

Although he wasn't cutting me with a blade, his stare, his presence, was just as sharp. My body was constantly in a state of fight-or-flight, unable to rest properly.

The days were long. Not just because I got up at dawn to run in the woods. Knox didn't follow me like he had that first morning, but his eyes did from the moment I got out of bed.

I did my best to ignore him, even though my entire body hummed with fear and desire and hatred.

Yes, I hated him. For being so calm, for being so unflappable. So resistant to my charm, immune to anger. Even when he'd hurled the mug at the wall, he hadn't done it out of fury. He'd done it calmly. To make a point. That was so much worse.

The shards of it still remained where they fell. No way was I cleaning up his mess, and he didn't strike me as someone who would either. Well, that was a lie. He did the dishes from every meal. Everything in the cabin was kept spotless.

But the shards remained. A reminder.

My body was weakening. There was no fresh fruit left, even though I'd tried to ration. The bread that remained was stale and hard. And with the calories I was burning from pure fear, from running, pulling weeds in the area that could roughly be called a garden, from chopping wood, it was nowhere near enough fuel for my body.

Running was stupid. Expending energy I didn't have. But I had to. There had to be some way to release the adrenaline, to feel like myself. Running had always been my therapy. My one solace. Escape.

I wouldn't let him take it from me. Even as my body failed me.

Black spots danced in my vision, and I rapidly tried to blink them away. I was only a couple hundred yards from the cabin.

I'd make it. Couldn't a person last for like months without food? I had water. And it's not like I was technically starving. People in L.A. ate less than I did and managed to star in movies and walked catwalks.

Dramatic. I was being dramatic by thinking the trees were turning sideways. There was no way I was going to pass out.

Then the trees moved jerkily, the ground rushed toward my face and with a loud thump. With a flash of pain came blessed darkness and thankfully, no more hunger.

"Fuck."

The single, four-letter word filtered through my groggy brain, mixing with the gnawing, urgent hunger that had become a part of me like a barnacle against a reef.

It was hard to think around it, even in my half-conscious state.

That was likely why I heard emotion in that single, four-letter word. Emotion that sounded incredibly like worry laced with an edge of panic.

I must've conjured that, though, in my desperation to have someone care for me.

Before I could register his closeness, Knox's arms were wrapped around me and I was up off the ground. The movement made my almost empty stomach lurch as I fought to hold on to the meager nutrients I'd ingested that morning.

Plus, vomiting on Knox would be kind of embarrassing.

I somehow managed to steady my nausea, even as we started moving. He held me close to his chest, his arms like a band, absorbing the impact of his steps so he barely jostled me.

He smelled of pine and the ocean. Again, something I must've made up. And warmth I felt against his chest. That couldn't have been possible; he was a human block of ice.

He didn't speak, so all I heard was the low thump of his heartbeat. It was nice. Calming. It beckoned me back to the darkness.

"Piper, don't you—"

Again with the urgent, worried and commanding tone. But even he couldn't call me back from this blackness.

Fortunately.

KNOX

Her runs lasted forty-five minutes to an hour.

The past few days they'd been closer to forty-five.

Because she was hungry. Weak. Expending too much energy by running through rough terrain followed by spending the day in the garden, pulling weeds, chopping wood. Doing anything but being still, reserving her energy.

It was driving me fucking crazy. Seeing her pick at food that was barely enough to keep her alive, let alone fuel her body for the constant movement throughout the day. A lot of people—most people, actually—would spend their time in captivity curled up in a ball. Sleeping. Escaping their reality. She had books. I knew that because I'd looked through her suitcase during one of her runs. And she had flashes of colorful clothes, lacy underwear that had made my cock weep at the sight of them. I slept with a pair of her pink panties curled in my fist at night.

It was fucking creepy, crossed a line even I thought I wouldn't cross. Stealing panties like a fucking sex offender. But I couldn't stop myself.

It was sick. That my thoughts were solely counting how many calories she was consuming, expending, calculating when exactly she'd succumb to the consequences of malnutrition and mild starvation.

Her cheeks were already hollow, dark circles ringing her eyes, even though she collapsed into a dreamless, exhausted sleep for over ten hours a night. Her frame was shrinking, clothing that fit her like a second skin a week ago beginning to hang off her.

Yet she still ran.

And chopped wood.

Hacked away at the overgrowth surrounding the cabin with rusty shears she'd found fuck knows where.

She'd managed to repair the shutters. She was ... sprucing up the place where I was holding her captive, and I had no idea what the fuck to do with that.

I'd been expecting some kind of mental break. It usually happened a lot sooner than people anticipated. People fantasized how long they might survive in deadly situations. Self-aggrandized about their mental and physical strength. But when taken from familiar surroundings, creature comforts, and forced into survival mode, people generally withered within days.

Not Piper. She was waning, yes. But not withering. Even though she was showing a physical toll, her eyes were bright with life. Stubbornness. She sat at the table with me every night, head held high, nibbling at what food she could tolerate while staring defiantly at the plate of meat that must've been appealing to her animal nature, desperate to survive.

Her principles were stronger than her baser nature. Not many people existed like that. Certainly not in my world.

She was a flower, none of the bloom fading despite the lack of care and attention she received.

It impressed me plenty. But it didn't weaken my resolve. The stronger she showed me she was, the more desperate I became to be the one who broke her. Then she'd be mine somehow. Even after I handed her off to Stone, part of her would always be mine.

When she'd been gone for fifty minutes, I started looking for her. I wasn't a tracker by any means, but I knew I could find her wherever she was in these vast woods.

It didn't take me long.

She was sprawled facedown in the dirt, unconscious. Blood trickled from a wound in her head.

Such images were not shocking to me. Blood. An unconscious person. Yet my heart rate increased, my breathing became shallower, and the tips of my fingers prickled with something.

Though new voices inside of me that made me uncomfortable

urged me to run to her, I purposefully slowed down my gait. Approached her unhurriedly. As if I didn't care. I didn't.

I didn't care about Piper beyond the pieces I broke her into.

The few seconds it took to get to her side, kneel, to put my fingers to her pulse felt like an eon.

It was there. Sluggish, almost concerningly so, but she had a pulse. Her skin was still warm, and I failed to stop myself from breathing in the scent of her shampoo mixed with the bitter yet not unpleasant twang of her sweat.

Even in her prone state, I wanted to lick the perspiration off the side of her head, to taste it. I wanted to run my fingers through the stream of blood from her forehead, coat myself in it.

There wasn't time for me to indulge in my increasingly strange yearnings. There was never a time for that. I had a task. To break her. But not kill her. I was doing my job, I told myself as I picked her up.

She was light. Too fucking light considering her stature a week ago. She let out a tiny sound and nestled her head into my chest, proving she was wholly without survival instinct. She should've been battling out of my arms, even in her semi-conscious state. Yet she was as helpless and fragile as a fucking baby.

I kept my eyes on her as her eyelids fluttered then groggily tried to focus on me. The image of her mud-stained, blood-smeared, gaunt face was more beautiful to me than I could describe.

But her awareness and consciousness only lasted for a handful of seconds. I watched as the force of her exhaustion, malnutrition, dragged her back down again.

"Piper, don't you dare pass out on me again."

Even as I commanded her to stay, she left.

And she took part of my sanity with her. Part of my soul lapsing into the darkness with her.

PIPER

Something warm brushed against my forehead. Not the same warmth of the chest I'd been pressed against. Nothing was warm like that.

This was softer, wetter.

A washcloth, I deduced without opening my eyes.

My head throbbed painfully, so I assumed that opening my eyes to the reality of the situation would only make it worse. I decided to keep them closed a little while longer. Damn, they were heavy, impossibly heavy. Even if I wanted to, I didn't know if I had the strength to open them.

There was a crushing, unyielding weight over my whole body. My limbs were heavy, and my stomach was excruciatingly empty.

Though I felt sluggish and out of it, my hunger was visceral.

The warmth at my head disappeared, replaced by a sharp sting.

My eyes popped open as I let out a hiss of pain, unable to move myself because I was too weak.

I was met with an icy, intense gaze.

Knox.

Inches from my face, watching me with a practiced concentration, cold expression in place.

"Hold still," he ordered as I tried to wiggle. "I need to clean this."

More pain at my head, eliciting another hiss between my teeth.

I glanced down at the coffee table. There was a bowl of water with a washcloth in it, the washcloth was stained crimson. My blood. I'd hit my head on my way down, obviously, which might have been the reason for losing consciousness. Or the mild starvation. Or the trauma of the past week.

I held still, considering the sequence of events, gritting my teeth as Knox cleaned my wound.

Then it struck me.

He was cleaning my wound. He had carried me in the gentle cocoon of his embrace after I fell. Which meant he'd come looking for me. Then he'd washed my blood.

My eyes traveled to follow the journey of his hands into a first aid kit.

"Doesn't need stitches," he told me, focusing on my head and not my curious gaze.

He was speaking too. Volunteering information when he could've just stayed silent. I hadn't asked any questions. I was too shocked, tired, sore and hungry to do that yet.

He was speaking. Why? Did the silence make him nervous? Surely not.

And had I imagined the concern on his face as I'd briefly woken up.

Could he … *care* about me?

I was considering this as he put butterfly bandages on my forehead. His fingers were gentle and cool, my body reveling in the caretaking touch from such a violent man.

He leaned back as if to create distance. "Stone wouldn't like you if you were … damaged."

Cold water washed over me.

I flinched away from him, pushing myself upright on the sofa, bracing myself as the room tilted much like the woods had. My head pounded, my stomach lurched, and I saw stars.

"Well, I should've fallen harder, then." I sounded too weak for my liking. "I'd rather disfigure myself for life than be pleasing to that monster."

I considered that as a very real, albeit drastic option. Do something to myself to make me unappealing to a sick fuck who liked his victims to be pretty. Would that save me?

The vain part of me recoiled at the prospect, but only for a moment. I didn't treasure surface beauty. I wanted freedom and would be more than willing to sacrifice for that, though it sickened me that that's what I might be pushed to do.

Hurt myself so I wasn't pleasing to a man so he wouldn't want me. I'd been so sure that the world had moved on from such brutality, having never considered the possibility that mutilation would be required to keep me safe from men. But times hadn't changed as much as I'd thought. The tyrants just moved further into the shadows, like Knox, or got better at disguising themselves as men, like Stone.

Knox had been inspecting me the entire time I mulled this over. Like I was an insect under a magnifying glass, and he was considering whether to set me on fire or not.

"You would do it," he nodded, as if he were reading my mind. "You would scar yourself for life if it meant getting out of this."

"In a heartbeat."

"But you're extraordinarily beautiful."

My throat went dry.

It wasn't said as a compliment. He said it as if it was a statement, an indisputable fact. The sky was blue, grass was green, and I was extraordinarily beautiful.

I wasn't falsely modest; I knew that my features had arranged themselves into a way that wasn't abhorrent. But I wouldn't go so far as to call myself *extraordinarily beautiful*.

And though he uttered it in his same cruel, lifeless tone, the words shook my insides.

I swallowed, trying to hide whatever effect he had over me, my head still throbbing.

"Looks don't mean anything to me if they're going to be a collar a man thinks he can hold around my neck."

Still, Knox inspected me. "Even scarred, disfigured, you'd still be gorgeous. It wouldn't save you. It would be a mistake. And messy. Don't do it."

He got up and walked in the direction of the kitchen. My eyes didn't follow him. I just stared at the space he previously occupied, feeling numb to the conversation we'd just had. The dichotomy of his gentle touch, confusing words and ice-cold demeanor.

There was a clang in the kitchen, the whistle of a boiling kettle, yet I still remained motionless.

It was in part due to weakness and the fragility of my stomach. I might've had a concussion, and I was exhausted. It felt like there was no passage of time.

Then Knox was back.

With a steaming plate and mug.

"I'm not going to eat that." I flicked my wrist toward the plate. I couldn't see the contents, but I assumed it would be meat since it was all that was left.

My gnawing hunger urged me to snatch it, eat it with my bare hands, keep myself alive by abandoning my principles, markers of my identity. I could get those back when I was free.

But I'd never be free if I submitted to Knox.

Despite the power of those thoughts—my finger even twitched —I held fast.

Knox didn't say anything, he just placed the plate and the mug on the coffee table in front of me.

I blinked down at the bowl.

It was a heaping portion of rice topped with beans of some kind. No sign of meat. My mouth watered. Again, the instinct to jump on the food was overwhelming.

Instead, with all the willpower I possessed, I looked up at Knox.

"You've had food for me this entire time," I deduced slowly. There was no way I'd just missed a bag of rice and a can of beans. When you were as hungry as I was, looking for food became a constant thing you did with desperation. Food was a background thought throughout the day, hunger a part of my being.

"You've been watching me slowly starve knowing there was food that I could eat," I realized out loud.

Not even an ounce of guilt crossed Knox's expression.

"You enjoyed it," I hissed. "Watching me hurt. Watching me starve."

No reaction.

My cheeks heated from my hatred toward him. And his fucking games.

"Can you hurl wrath at me and eat at the same time?" he asked mildly.

I ground my teeth together, furious, starving, confused. I wanted to hurl the plate at the wall, just like he had with my mug of tea. It would be the thing to do, to establish my strength, dominance, to show him that he couldn't break me.

But I needed to survive too. And therefore, I had to make the choice between a show of strength or possibly looking weak in order to help me stay strong.

I gave him one last scowl before leaning forward to grasp the plate, my movements stilted and wobbly.

He didn't offer to help as I fumbled with the fork with numb hands, he just watched.

Knowing that he was eyeing my every movement, I didn't shove the fork in my mouth like an animal as I was desperate to do. With forced casualness, I leaned back on the sofa, slowly bringing the fork to my mouth as if I hadn't been surviving on handfuls of fruit and bread for a week.

I bit back the moan that built at the back of my throat once the food hit my mouth. It was good. Anything would've tasted good at that point. It was well made, the rice buttery and perfectly cooked, the beans dynamic with flavorful spice and herbs.

I swallowed with relief and delight.

"Good girl."

My entire body jolted at the praise coming from Knox's mouth as he watched me swallow.

I looked at him, my entire body having a visceral reaction to the words. Heat, warmth pooled in my core, my nipples pebbling.

It must've been my head injury because suddenly Knox did not look cold and cruel; he looked hungry, ravenous ... for me.

My hand holding the fork shook as I battled against my own hunger.

"I. Am. Not. Your. Good. Girl." I spat the words out as if they were made of gravel. They were that heavy to speak too, not entirely truthful.

I wanted with all my independent, feminine fury for them to be true. But in my darker heart, I questioned it.

The hunger that I might've imagined left Knox's face.

"Keep telling yourself that." There was a slightly arrogant yet sexy drawl to his normally lifeless tone. "When I come back, that plate will be empty."

And then he left the cabin. Left me with food I didn't want to eat on principle and feelings that were absolutely depraved.

Yet I finished the bowl. I damn near licked the bowl. I finished the tea too. And, although there was no logical reason for me to even think of doing it, I lay back down on the sofa.

It was where he slept. It smelled of him. The scent enveloped me.

Pine and salt and darkness. As if darkness had a smell. It did, though. Rich and deep and enchanting. Forbidden.

He slept there. I wondered what he dreamed about. Did monsters dream? Did his sins build up and sit on his chest like a kettlebell? Or did he sleep peacefully? Without regret.

Or, I wondered, did he dream of me like I dreamed of him?

Without knowing I was doing it, my hands went to my leggings, slipping beneath the tight fabric and finding my panties.

I toyed with them, biting my lip, knowing what I was doing was impressively fucked-up, knowing that Knox could walk back in at any moment.

But I didn't care.

Not enough to stop.

My fingers went to where I was aching, where his words had stroked me. My teeth sank into the flesh of my lip, drawing blood as I circled my own clit, thinking of Knox's hands. Imagining him coming in here and finding me like this, pressing me down on this sofa that smelled of him, ripping off my leggings then violently thrusting into me, bordering on painfully.

I writhed against the sofa as I imagined him pounding, his fingertips biting into my hips, filling me. Losing control with me. Claiming me.

My orgasm found me hard and quick, lost in a fantasy that was completely taboo.

My limbs were rigid from the way my body tensed against the overwhelming pleasure, and though I tried to silence it, a moan left my mouth.

Knox could hear me. Could walk in right now.

But wasn't that what I wanted? Wasn't that what made my orgasm that much more intense?

As I came down, my breathing was heavy, my shame weighing on me like a lead apron, unable to fully take root because of how good I felt.

The reality was heavier still.

I wanted Knox.

My cruel captor.

The man who would not save me from the devil, but eventually, once broken, he'd deliver me to him.

Despite all of that, my body yearned for him stronger than it had any substance on the planet.

Curling into the sofa, stomach full and soul tattered, I lapsed into a troubled sleep.

KNOX

I couldn't believe what I'd seen. It had taken every ounce of control honed over years and years not to go in there and finish her myself.

Not to yank her leggings off and bury myself in her cunt.

I'd walked into the cabin expecting to find Piper glaring daggers into me. That's why I'd come back, wasn't it? Because I craved her anger like it was my lifeforce. More so when she was strong enough to wield it.

Yeah, I had been hiding the food. Because I was trying to break her. Not kill her. It had been insurance I didn't think I'd have to use.

It took a human around a month to entirely starve, give or take, but that had some long-lasting and messy effects, so I hadn't intended to drag it on that long. Hadn't thought I'd need to.

But seeing her eyes close, seeing her trying to hide just how fucking starving she was… Yeah, I needed to. I wanted to cook every one of her meals for her to see her body react like that.

I'd come back in to ensure that she had eaten it. I was almost certain she was smart enough to give herself the energy she required, but she was also stubborn as fuck, so I wouldn't have been entirely surprised if she'd left something in the bowl to challenge me.

If she had, I'd planned on punishing her, relishing the thought.

What I hadn't expected was to walk in, find her reclined on the sofa, eyes closed and writhing in ecstasy as she made herself come.

It had stopped me dead in my tracks to see that. She was so far gone she didn't know I was there, watching her. I'd never been so captivated in my life. My cock was straining in my pants so hard it was almost painful. The need to stroke it overwhelming. If I so much as brushed it, I felt like I'd spill in my fucking pants like a teenager. Not that I got the chance to have any regular sexual experiences as a teenager. Never did I have a feeling of need or desire without it being tainted with shame.

With the silent gait of a predator, I backed up from where I came, never taking my eyes from her.

I wanted to stay. Fuck, did I want to stay. Close enough to hear the crescendo of her shallow breaths, smell the scent of her in the air. But staying meant that I ran the risk of interfering, marring a moment that was nothing less than absolute perfection.

I made it to the door, skulking out of sight at the edge of the window, watching her finish. Because all I was good for was being a voyeur, witnessing her experience this pleasure while denying my own.

There was nothing there for me.

Yet I wanted it all.

NINE
PIPER

I woke to loud banging in the kitchen. It felt wrong, ringing against the tenderness of my skull. Fully rousing from my slumber, my limbs burned with an urgent aching, likely from the surge of chemicals and fear hormones that I'd been pushing into them to keep them going, crashing now that I was at my weakest, showing me how severely I'd been abusing my body.

It was dark outside.

The passage of time was murky to me, but I'd begun my run in the morning. I didn't know how long I'd been unconscious initially, but it couldn't have been that long. Then ...

Shame washed over me.

After Knox and I had had that strange conversation where I could've sworn I saw emotion, desire on his attractive face, he'd left. And I'd ... pleasured myself on this very sofa. Where he slept.

After I'd almost killed myself from running miles with no nutrition. After Knox had almost starved me, all while having food that could've avoided the entire situation.

Humiliation ate away at my already aching muscles. It was one thing to be attracted to my captor—something I'd need years of therapy to work through—but it was quite another thing to act on it.

No, I didn't throw myself at him, but the act of pleasuring myself, thinking of him in a spot where he could've walked in at any moment—*wanting* him to walk in at any moment—that was going too far.

My mind flashed back to The Devil card and its urging me to embrace my shadows, my sexuality, but also reminding me that doing so could destroy me.

The clanging sounds continued as my indignity spiraled.

He was in the kitchen, that much was clear.

How long he'd been in there was anyone's guess.

A burst of horror squeezed my lungs.

What if he'd come in when I was…?

No. Even with my extremely questionable survival instincts and my dulled senses from injury and masturbation, I would've noticed a killer in my midst.

Surely.

No. He hadn't seen me.

But I'd done it. And I absolutely couldn't do it again.

Masturbation was healthy and normal; I believed every adult should regularly indulge in self-love, using whatever fantasies got them going. But that should be done in the privacy of their own home, not in a cabin in the woods while being held hostage until they agreed to marry a murderous mob boss.

A pang of panic and thick homesickness clutched my stomach.

Would I ever be home again? In my warm, chaotic, messy apartment that held all of my memories, an entire life that I'd treasured?

Never in my life had I felt so hopeless. And that was saying something since I'd lived a far from charmed life.

But I'd always, always had hope. Even if it was just a small shred of it shining in the darkness.

In the cabin, despite the soft lamplight in the corner, there was only bleakness and despair.

I angrily wiped away the single tear trailing down my cheek.

It took a lot of effort, both mental and physical, to get myself up off the sofa. My legs were shockingly unsteady, as if I'd been lying in a coma for weeks instead of napping the day away.

My bladder urged to be emptied, so I made my way toward the bathroom, planning on ignoring Knox completely. For the rest of our time together.

A dark form emerged in my path just before the bathroom door.

Since I'd been so intently *not* focusing on him, he'd been able to catch me off guard.

Coward that I was, I couldn't lift my eyes to look at him in the face. Not out of fear. Out of shame. I was convinced I was wearing some kind of brand, a scarlet letter from what I'd done on his makeshift bed, and he'd be able to see it, figure out what I'd done.

Then he'd find a way to use that to break me.

That was his sole intention, after all.

He wasn't interested in me. There was no way he felt the spark between us. In order to feel a spark, you had to be capable of warmth. Possess human emotion. Neither of those applied to him. Whatever vision I'd had of him was conjured by my mind, having watched too many movies, read too many books, had too many fanciful notions about the inherent goodness of the human race. I'd spent my time around kindergarteners, letting the purity of their innocence sink in to remind me that everyone had been a child once, that everyone deserved a chance at redemption.

Not Knox.

"You shouldn't be up."

His cold tone slithered against my clammy skin, cooling it. Caressing it.

"You shouldn't be telling me what to do," I told his chest.

It was a nice chest. He was wearing yet another of his high-quality, outdoor shirts. Black. Long sleeves again. It hit me that I'd never seen his arms exposed, even on the overly warm days we'd been having. He always donned black, long-sleeved shirts. Though he never showed that he was uncomfortably hot. It made sense since he was cold as ice.

"You need to go back and sit down." As usual, his voice told me he was unencumbered by my snark.

Why would he be? He was used to far more than snark.

I was forever reminded that I didn't have the tools to go up against him.

"Again, I'm not doing what you tell me to," I snapped, folding my arms across my chest and glaring at his defined pecs.

My fingertips itched with the need to rip at it, pull his skin apart, make him bleed.

"I'll carry you back there if I need to." The threat was barely audible yet uttered in an ironclad tone.

Finally, I found the courage to glare at him in the eyes. The expression on his face trapped the air in my windpipe. It was as blank as his tone... at first glance. But I could've sworn there was something different about the way he was looking at me.

I couldn't put my finger on what it was, though. The slight flaring of the nostrils, the tenseness of his shoulders, the way his vein pulsated in his neck.

Did it speak of fury?

Or something else?

"You try to lay a finger on me, I'll claw your face off," I promised. "Mark that pretty skin of yours."

I used *pretty* on purpose. Men like him—toxic, alpha types— would see pretty as a direct affront to their masculinity.

Instead of reacting the way I expected, the corner of his mouth twitched in what could almost be described as a smirk.

"I'm not afraid of your marks on my skin, Piper."

There! A flash of heat. Want. I was sure of it.

My intestines plunged toward the floor, and that wantonness I thought I'd assuaged came back with the heat of a thousand suns.

I struggled to keep my composure. What would he do if I jumped on him right now? If I plastered my lips on his and climbed him like a tree? It was so taboo, so wrong, so tempting to give in to base desires when there was no one watching, where I felt free from the shackles of any civilized arrangements.

That's why I was there, wasn't it? Stripped away from all semblances of appearance that our world operated under law and order. That I was safe.

It had been proven. I was not safe. Not even while running in broad daylight. Not while attending my sister's birthday party.

And wasn't I sick of living with that fear? Running from it? Yet when that fear was embodied in Knox, I wanted to sink into it, indulge in it.

Then my bladder alerted me to other baser needs my body required.

Thankfully.

"I need to pee." I was still looking into lifeless eyes that mercifully couldn't read my mind.

Knox blinked at my words but didn't step aside. He just stood there. Staring. I resisted the urge to shift my weight from foot to foot.

My bladder clenched uncomfortably, but I resolved to stand my ground. I wasn't going to beg him to move, nor was I going to release my bladder in front of him—even though the need was quite urgent.

There it was, another power play. Him showing he was in charge of my every need, that he could stop me from the basic act of relieving myself with dignity. More white-hot hatred melted away whatever insane salacity I was feeling moments ago. The rapidly changing, visceral feelings were giving me heartburn.

I was not prone to wild mood swings or emotions. I left that to my sister. My job was to be around a bunch of unregulated kinder-garteners all day. And though I was paid to teach them, those children really just needed a stable, emotionally regulated adult in order to feel safe. I prided myself on having that ability—not born from my job but certainly honed by it. I'd forced myself to be emotionally stable amidst a terribly unsettling home life. I'd had to when I took it upon myself to take care of my sister, show her that chaos was not everywhere. That peace existed.

Yet there, in the cabin, Knox teased the chaotic darkness out of me with an expert hand. In his presence, peace was nothing but a concept floating in the wind.

Finally, fortunately, he stepped aside.

Again, I resisted the urge to run to the toilet.

Straightening my spine, I looked him square in the face. "You are not as powerful as you think you are." I was completely bluffing and likely laughable to him, but I needed something borderline threatening to say.

Then I calmly walked the handful of steps to the bathroom, noisily closing the door behind me.

Knox

I'd been physically unable to move while staring at her. Her features were etched with need. Now that I knew what she looked like at the peak of orgasm, I could recognize small markers. The way her plump lips separated, the way her cheeks flushed with color, the spark in her eyes. Her small hands clenching and unclenching. All of it told me she was again thinking of whatever she had been thinking about earlier.

Me, perhaps?

By process of deduction, it was *me* who was eliciting this response in her.

I was no stranger to women finding me attractive. I knew, upon first glance, I could be construed that way. But when given more than a first glance, women usually found what was lurking underneath. The uncanny valley effect kicked in. They couldn't put their finger on it, but their instincts told them that I wasn't quite human and that they needed to run.

A small few did not listen to instinct, were romanced by the idea that I was inhuman, thanks to idiotic popular culture of women romanticizing killers. But I soon set that straight. There was nothing romantic about me.

No one had seen my true nature, the demon beneath, and found anything attractive about that wretched, evil beast.

There was obviously some trauma at play. Stockholm syndrome. Or Piper was shockingly calculated and much more adept at fooling me than I'd ever imagined. Which, if that was the case, only made her more fucking attractive.

But my instincts told me that it wasn't an act. That Piper was having a visceral reaction to me that she was fighting with her own body.

I knew this only because I was fighting against my molecules, every cell in my body telling me to claim her.

Not just to claim her but to … *take care of her.*

I'd never taken care of anyone in my life. Never wanted to. Hadn't even cared about anyone beyond my brother. And the way I showed that was by keeping my distance, only appearing when he needed a villain.

Piper didn't need a villain. She needed a hero. One to save her from me. But there was no one walking this earth strong enough to go to battle against me.

Except herself. She was the only one who could save herself from me.

Once Piper was in the bathroom, I returned to the stove. She'd devoured the plate of rice and beans earlier, and it had been hours since she ate that. She needed more calories.

She needed her health if she was going to fight. Fight me.

Because I was starting to understand that I wasn't strong enough to fight against her.

And if she gave up, we were both doomed.

Piper

I decided to take a shower after relieving myself. I was still coated in dried sweat from the run, from desire, plus dirt and blood. I needed to wash it all away. Magic it away. And water cleansed. I could close my eyes and will it to. For the water to wash away the things that didn't serve me. Enchantments I was under that weren't safe.

The warm spray did nothing for my tense muscles, and it was only after I got in that I realized I hadn't brought in clean clothes.

The cabin had a washing machine and a clothing line I had planned on using since I was down to one last pair of clean under-wear—though I could've sworn I should've had two. But I'd packed under duress, so it's not like I was a reliable narrator when it came to cataloguing my underthings.

I could've put my dirty clothes and underwear on, but I already felt dirty enough, even after my shower. I'd been unable to instill it with any magic.

I wanted my clean clothes, and the towel I wrapped around my naked body covered me more than some of the dresses I'd worn before. And if I was honest with myself, some naughty, devious part of me liked the idea of walking out there in a towel. Testing Knox, coaxing that intensity out of him. And out of me.

My hatred of him and his cruelty weren't enough to make me stop wanting him. He was playing games, wasn't he? In order to break me. He was starving me when food was within reach. His very presence was a game.

And he was starving too. Starving for me. I'd seen it in his small lapses in control. And I got an inkling that he wasn't the kind of man to feel a hunger like this. That whatever was between us was novel to him too.

Turnabout was fair play.

So taking a deep breath while giving myself a mental pep talk, I walked out of the bathroom with the towel wrapped around me.

The towel itself wasn't a thick, large bath sheet like I was used to. The one indulgence in my life was expensive linens and towels.

This was a cheap towel, barely large enough to cover my torso and butt. But it did. Barely. It helped that the butt in question had shrunk somewhat during the past week.

Regardless, I was still exposing a lot of skin, and it was the suggestion that I was entirely naked under the thin piece of fabric that I hoped would serve to do something to the man made of stone and darkness.

Walking through the main room of the cabin, I didn't look at him. I made it my mission to walk slowly, confidently, as if doing this wasn't making my stomach pitch and my skin prickle with nerves and excitement.

My romantic life had always been very vanilla, very civilized, no games, no hard to get, no fuckboys. I specifically chose men who called when they said they would, had manners and didn't play games with me. Who wouldn't threaten or stalk me when I broke things off. Although it was increasingly hard to pinpoint which man would do that. Up until that point, I'd been lucky with the men I chose.

Safe.

Boring.

That's what I thought my kink was. I'd lived my formative years under the whims of an unstable and violent man, never knowing if he was going to hug me or hurt me.

The uncertainty and the constant state of fight-or-flight was what I was healing by going for the safe men.

Or so I'd thought.

I'd deprived myself, starved certain parts of myself that I kept hidden. Because despite all the wrought emotions around my current situation, the core part of me was ... excited as I walked through the room with my captor, naked and wet.

Though I hadn't peeked in his direction, I swore he was looking at me. I could feel the weight of his gaze and the physical brunt of it even though I'd never truly 'felt' someone looking at me.

Maybe I wouldn't be able to feel a regular person gazing at me, but when that person was Knox, it was as if I could feel his very thoughts about me.

It took everything I had not to peer in the direction of the kitchen, where all sounds of cooking had ceased.

Instead, I went to my bag, bending at the hip instead of crouching down to get my clothes and underwear.

That hadn't been in the previous plan. Yes, I'd wanted to tease him. I'd wanted to establish some kind of sexual, feminine power, but I hadn't intended on flashing *that* sexual, feminine power.

But it was what my body commanded. The dark, lustful voice inside of me that had been silenced without my even knowing it.

And without self-consciousness or doubt, I just did it.

Bared my naked pussy to him.

I didn't imagine the swift intake of breath I heard from across the room.

He had been watching me.

My hunch was proved by the sound of his gasp. The sound of him losing control, the tightly wound man coming undone at the appearance of a vagina.

He wasn't the first, nor would he be the last. I smiled to myself in victory as I grabbed my clothes, straightened and turned.

Then I let out my own swift intake of breath.

He was still standing, watching me. He was holding a knife. He'd obviously been in the middle of cutting something for dinner. But Knox, all in black, clutching the knife while staring at me like he'd stepped out of a nightmare stole the air from my lungs.

Except the expression on his face... It was not just deadly. It was the picture of masculine need unlike anything I'd ever glimpsed in my life. I'd stood naked in front of men, lovers. Had felt their appreciation for my form, sure.

But nothing like the way Knox was looking at me.

It wasn't like he wanted to worship me.

It was like he wanted to *ruin* me.

My breathing quickened as I clutched at my clothes, instantly regretting my decision, chastising my previous boldness.

The moment lasted longer than it should've. Much longer. It was charged with an uncertain energy. What would happen next? The silence in the room seemed to boom with tension. I could hear his breathing. Fractured. Unsteady. Nothing that denoted his trademark control.

Knox was still holding the knife. He was a killer, he wasn't quite hinged, that was clear. And I was pushing him. Pushing him toward an edge I didn't even understand. I thought he simply desired me, and the 'worst' possible outcome of my teasing him was him acting on that desire.

Even though that's what that secret part of me craved all along.

I'd never considered just how fucked-up Knox might've been. That I could be coaxing a wild animal out of its cage, not knowing whether it was going to fuck me or kill me.

Knox didn't seem like he knew whether he was going to fuck me or kill me either.

For a long moment, my life hung in the balance. I swore I felt it. The whisper of death that could come at the hands of a man I both despised and craved. And insanely, I wanted to risk it. I wanted to drop the towel and invite him closer.

I was seconds away from doing it, caught up in the madness of the moment, a wild animal of my own unleashed and eager to play.

Milliseconds before I did it, Knox moved.

Not toward me like I'd expected.

No, back to the kitchen. He walked slowly, his steps measured and rigid, as if he were made of stone or metal. His gestures were almost robotic as he chopped whatever he was using the knife for. But I knew the clang of the knife against the cutting board was harder than it needed to be, as if he were letting out just a whisper of the violence he possessed.

The violence I was courting. Willingly.

Anxiety bubbling inside of me, I rushed to the bathroom to dress, flattening myself against the door the moment I closed it.

My heart was galloping against my heaving chest, my breathing as rapid as if I'd run a marathon.

My nipples were peaked, my core throbbing with need even though I'd realized what a mistake that was. My mind understood the stakes, my body did not. Or maybe it did, and that's what made it respond in such a way. A way that felt panic-inducing, like I couldn't trust what I might do moment to moment. Like another version of me was taking control over my body and I was powerless to stop her.

That version urged me to find relief between my legs. To do it loudly, loudly enough for Knox to hear.

My fingers itched to do that.

But I fisted my hand.

"No," I whispered out loud to myself. It couldn't have been healthy, talking to another version of myself. But it wasn't healthy trying to seduce a psychopath either, so I was obviously fucked either way.

No pun intended.

With great difficulty, I dressed. And as I was doing it, I folded up that interaction. I did it tightly and with precision I'd learned from years of therapy. I put it far in the back of my mind then closed the door.

It was the only way I could walk back into the room with him without shrinking in embarrassment. And unfortunately, I couldn't very well stay in this bathroom all night.

I had to go back out there as if I wasn't profoundly affected by our moment. As if I didn't feel changed forever.

———

I hadn't wanted to talk to him during dinner, but giving the silent treatment had never really been my thing. Whenever I'd fought with men in the past, I had always promised myself a period of stonewalling—before I learned in therapy how toxic such a thing was—yet always, always lasted less than an hour, unable to hold on to a grudge, desperate to repair the chasm between us and desperate to be wanted. Desperate to be in a healthy relationship, feel safe and secure. Not that I'd ever really had a relationship. I always ran before things got too serious.

In the cabin with Knox, it was actually a good thing to engage in toxic behavior, fighting fire with fire and all that. I was not under any pressure to feel safe and secure with him, such a thing was impossible. There was no relationship to preserve, to nurture.

Therefore, the charged silence should've been my victory. I could feel it, like a crackle in the air, the sexual tension I'd poked at. His grip on his cutlery was tight, his shoulders taut and his movements stilted, as if he was forcing himself to be still and calm.

Yes, I'd affected him.

Points to me. To what end, I didn't know. Weaken him in order to manipulate him into saving me? No, I wasn't that calculated, and Knox wasn't the kind of man who would save me. Ever.

Did I just want to torture him a little? Or did I really want to act on this forbidden carnality?

If I was asked out loud, by an outside party who was witnessing this, I would obviously say the former. It was only fair to use whatever wiles I had to torture my captor. But in my heart of hearts, I knew that wasn't entirely the case. I wanted him. My darker side, the side of me that had been starved and denied, was only growing stronger, hungrier in his presence. I'd been so sure my childhood had beaten out any allure dangerous men might've had. But instead, I'd just stifled those feelings and ignored them, only for them to come bursting out of my captive soul.

Which was what I was battling with as I forced the food into my mouth. I needed the calories. I had a lot of strength to replenish. And it was good. Flavorful. He had a talent in the kitchen, especially while working with canned food and dried spices.

A little tidbit of information which was at odds with the image of him being a cold psychopath. But then again, just because someone was a psychopath didn't mean that they couldn't also be a good cook.

Not only was I battling the arousal I felt in the air but I was simultaneously struggling with the act of eating the food he prepared under his watchful eye. If his intention was to simply fatten me back up like a pig to the slaughter, he could've dumped a tin of beans in front of me and commanded me to eat.

I would've done it too, now that I'd brushed against the familiar feel of starvation, after hovering much too close to the abyss of death. Would I have eaten meat if he had forced it upon me after waking up? I didn't want to answer that question.

He could've done it, served it up to me and taken the win by breaking me just a little. Instead, he'd made me the beans, tended to my injuries.

And now he was doing it again.

Mulling over all of that took up a decent amount of time from dinner. But I was not an overly interior person. I wasn't used to going so long without speaking. I worked with children all day who constantly asked questions, helping them develop their language skills. There was barely ever a moment when I was silent.

When I was at home alone, I was usually speaking to my sister or singing to music. Otherwise, I was out with friends.

Silence was not a familiar companion of mine.

"How did you come to work for Stone?" I asked, looking up from my plate.

I could've asked a safer question, his favorite movie or color, perhaps. Pretending we were on a bad first date, skirting past the elephant in the room. But that wasn't possible for me. The elephant was not an elephant but a huge, black shadow, corporal and oppressing, stifling the life from me.

"I'm curious as to what happens in a person's life to result in them working for a mob boss, doing his dirty work," I continued, no bite to my tone.

Half of me didn't expect an answer. Knox didn't have the same trouble keeping silence intact as I did. He seemed to despise the human practice of conversation. Or at least with me. Though I found it hard to envision him discussing normal things with anyone.

"Why did something have to happen in my life?" he asked, his voice smooth as silk. "Can't I just be evil?"

His response caught me off guard. There was no teasing or sarcasm in it, just a note of truth. Did he truly consider himself to be evil? And if he did, then I doubted he truly was. Evil people weren't aware of their wretchedness. More often, they were puffed up with their own importance or convinced they were the hero.

I put down my knife and fork to answer his question.

"No." He shook his head before I had the chance to. "You eat and talk."

I pursed my lips against the command, tempted to fight against it. But the prospect of conversation with him was more important than holding on to the façade of my sovereignty in this situation.

Dutifully, I loaded up my fork with tomatoey lentils and rice then put it in my mouth. I felt Knox's eyes on me the entire time.

It felt intimate, the way he watched me eat. Possessive.

"No one can just be evil," I wiped my mouth with a napkin. "Maybe a small portion of the population, but I think that's a farce more than anything. Evil, if such a thing exists, is made. Created. Situations continually push someone into less and less desirable circumstances until they commit more heinous acts, justifying them until they don't feel the need to do that anymore because they consider their acts to be a reflection of who they are now instead of things they do." The words spilled out of me, things I'd been marinating on my entire life while desperate to find explanations to my parents' behavior.

Knox had been impassively, coldly watching me before I spoke, but something in his eyes changed when I finished. His jaw slackened just a little, and the force of his attention no longer felt entirely cold and predatory.

Then he recovered, his mask slipping back on.

That's what I was becoming sure it was. A mask. There was a human underneath there. Who'd endured trauma. A human with wants. Needs.

Me. I was one of his needs.

I felt somewhat powerful that this seemingly controlled man was beginning to unravel out of want for me. Or perhaps that was a story I was telling myself.

"You have too much sympathy for assholes," he said matter-of-factly. Coldly. "They don't deserve it."

I tilted my head to regard him. "Or maybe they need it most of all."

He didn't reply. I didn't expect him to.

"What prompted you to work for Stone?" I repeated my question, a daring thing to do as I felt myself dancing with his cruelty, bracing for the verbal snap of it. I waited for a threat, a reminder of my place in the world as his helpless captive.

I watched him consume a mouthful of food. He was polite in

how he ate, had good table manners. Chewed with a closed mouth, the column of his throat moving pleasingly as he swallowed. My gaze dipped down to his chest, following the movement.

"I went to work for Stone because I wanted to." At the sound of his words, my eyes snapped up to his. Dark, endless. "He didn't trick me, blackmail me or control me into my role. Nor am I a mindless goon following orders out of fear. I'll work for him for as long as this role aligns with my needs."

"What are your needs?" I asked without thinking. An innate instinct in me wanted to know them so I could meet them. I wanted to take care of this man. Save him. No reason for this existed beyond the inescapable thread tightening between us. He was giving me proverbial crumbs to prove it existed, yet I was feasting on them.

His gaze never let go of mine. "Death," he said simply. "I need to kill people, Piper, in order to survive. There is no justifying my acts. And despite what your armchair analysis says, I am my acts. I kill because I am a killer. There is nothing deeper than that."

He was trying to scare me.

And it was working.

But I'd known he was a killer for a long time. It was impossible not to know that after just gazing upon the man. Something instinctual told you what he was.

Yes, hearing him say it out loud was unnerving, but not as much as it should've been.

He'd said it in large part because he believed it. He was sure of what he was. There was conviction in his tone, grim resignation etched into every one of his features. But he also wanted to push me backward, back into our defined roles of captor and captive.

Instead, I pressed on.

"I think there is a lot more depth to you than just that," I countered, my voice quiet, almost a whisper.

I held my breath, waiting for him to breathe fire. But he leaned forward imperceptivity. In our dynamic, the simple change in his posture was as mighty as a mountain moving.

"Why?" he asked, his low tone mirroring mine.

When I chewed my lip, his gaze followed the motion, hunger clouding his vision, pupils dilating slightly.

"I don't know," I shrugged. "Because I can see it."

The air between us changed. I swore it did. I could feel our roles warping, transforming. I was no longer his captor, a job, some abstract person that he was to break then deliver to his boss for a lifetime of torture.

I was a person to him. And maybe ... I was something more. Of that I was certain.

He grasped my wrist.

The speed in which his hand moved was almost unnatural. I hadn't been prepared for it. The conversation had been intense, but he was guarded, keeping his distance.

The man from moments ago was gone.

"You think you can unnerve me with a pretty cunt, Piper?" Despite the obvious violence of his grip and the crass words, his tone remained measured. His thumb stroked my wrist, right above my thundering pulse point. "You think that'll save you? Throwing yourself at me? It won't. This is the only warning you get. The next time you flash that at me, I won't be restrained. I'll take you in all the ways you're begging for, and you'll be so far beyond saving you'll regret it."

When he let my hand go, it felt so heavy it clanked onto my plate with the clutter of my silverware.

He went back to eating as if he hadn't just said all of those earth-shattering, threatening, despisable yet somehow intensely delicious things.

There wasn't a tremble to a single one of his fingers. Whereas my entire hand fumbled as I tried to mimic him by going back to my meal to prove that he hadn't unnerved me.

That he hadn't made me want to rip all of my clothes off, present myself to him in a dare to take me.

Swallowing food that was suddenly tasteless, I ate the rest of the meal in silence, unable to trust my instincts, my needs, the very air around me.

Knox was breaking me.

Just not in the way he'd intended.

Ten

Piper

I needed a distraction. I'd gone temporarily mad last night. Which was fine. One was allowed to go a little bit mad in situations like that.

Yes, I showed off my pussy to a monster, but it's okay. Act like it never happened.

Act like you didn't see that raw, almost ugly yet picturesque hunger on his face.

I could do it. I could eat and sleep in the same space as him for an indefinite amount of time until I was delivered to Stone.

Yeah, I could totally do that.

That's what I'd convinced myself during the long hours it took me to find sleep. Knox wasn't in the room. He'd gone outside after doing the dinner dishes, with me sitting at the table, watching him with a muffled ringing in my ears.

I didn't know what he was doing out there. It was long dark, and the air had a nip to it. He hadn't put on a jacket when he left, I'd noted that. He'd be cold.

Why I was worrying about him being cold was beyond me. He

deserved it. He deserved to get his fingers fall off from frostbite and worse.

Yet I'd tossed and turned after stoking the fire and almost got up to find him, to hand him his coat. The caretaker in me could not be killed by threats. Not yet at least.

Eventually, I'd fallen into a fitful sleep, restless and dreaming of Knox. Of him hurting me. Of him being in bed with me. Of the world burning.

Cheerful things.

The next morning, I'd jumped out of bed with the intention of ignoring him and going for a run. But as I'd left the bathroom, fully dressed this time, he was up.

"You're eating before you're running," he said, back to me at the stove.

I stopped in my tracks at his voice. As though last night had never happened.

That was his goal then too.

Fine, I could do that.

It was for the best.

I considered ignoring him completely and just running out the door, grasping on to whatever tenuous free will I had remaining.

But my body was still weak. There was a heaviness to my limbs, and there was still a cavernous emptiness in my stomach, growling at me to replace calories, to store as many as I could.

Gritting my teeth, I sat down at the table, hating that I was relying on Knox to feed me. Sure, I could've shouldered my way into the kitchen, insisted on cooking my own food. But that would've meant having to get close to him.

No, sitting at the table glowering in denial served me much better.

It wasn't long before another steaming plate was put in front of me, beside it a mug of tea.

"More beans, great," I said sarcastically, even though it went against the manners instilled in me by my grandmother to be so ungrateful.

Not that I needed to be grateful to Knox for anything.

"I'm going on a supply run today." I hadn't expected him to speak to me, his voice sending shivers up my spine. "I'll get more food."

"No meat," I said once I'd swallowed my first mouthful. Again, flavorful, delicious. Different from last night. Cinnamon and cumin married perfectly in a balance of sweet and savory.

I didn't look up at him, but there was a loaded pause. "No meat," he conceded, a defeat of his own.

My mouth turned up at the corners as I ate. Victory. It was sweet.

"If there is anything else you require ..." He put something on the table beside me.

A notepad and pen.

I stared at the innocuous items and what they represented. Autonomy. A little bit of it anyway. Was it an olive branch? Was it a shard of his shield that I'd managed to chip away at?

I mulled this over while I chewed, Knox walking away from me.

What would the power move be here? Write a long and complicated and obscure list?

No, that wouldn't work. I didn't think this new dynamic stretched so far as him going beyond the small store at the base of the mountain.

Would writing nothing at all be the bigger power move? Communicating I needed nothing from him. But that was a lie.

I chewed and swallowed the food, no longer tasting it.

This constant thinking about each decision, mannerism, how it might alter the situation was exhausting.

As if my decisions and mannerisms could alter Knox. That was like expecting water to alter stone.

Which it did.

Eventually.

After years.

Hundreds of them.

I didn't have years with him. Maybe weeks. If I was lucky. Or unlucky, depending on how you viewed the situation.

Whatever time I had left, despite the company, it was likely the last of the tenuous freedom I'd ever enjoy in my life.

I had to make lemonade, I guessed.

So I wrote a list.

KNOX

She was driving me insane.

I thought I'd done it. Scared her enough that she wouldn't approach me. That she'd avoid me like her life depended on it.

Which it did.

Her life as she knew it depended on her staying as far away from me as possible.

But then again, her life as she knew it was over whether she stayed away from me or not.

Stone had made up his mind about her. He didn't just want her. He already considered her his. And Stone didn't give up what was his. Not until he'd squeezed every ounce of life, goodness and will from it. Until it was dead.

I cracked my knuckles, sitting at the rickety outdoor table, chain-smoking.

I'd given up the habit years ago because I'd been determined not to have any vices, any weaknesses. Yet inexplicably, on the last supply trip before the mountain, I'd bought a carton of them.

I couldn't even explain to myself why I did it then. I'd ordered her to stay in the car, as a test. I left the keys in it. I'd expected her to drive off. It was the stupid option but one most empty-headed mouth breathers would've made, desperate for escape. It was the beginning of my mind games. Breaking her, showing her how truly helpless she was.

There was a tracker in the car, obviously. And I'd parked an extra vehicle less than a mile away from the store, paid some local to keep it in his garage.

The car wasn't only there for that purpose. It was a backup. In case something happened on the mountain. I couldn't say what, but I'd learned in this life that you needed backup plans, multiple escape routes and secrets.

Secrets were what kept you alive.

Though Piper had been smart up until that point—not flagging down strangers for help at multiple gas station bathroom stops—I'd reasoned the reality of her situation was setting in. She'd be getting desperate, with civilization getting more and more sparse, making way for the wilds of Appalachia.

Part of me was looking forward to it. Craving the chase. The defeat in her eyes when I caught her, proving to her that she'd never escape me. Part of me was half-hard just thinking of that.

Which was likely why I bought the fucking cigarettes.

When I came out of the store, the car was still there. As was Piper. Nothing outwardly changed about me, it never did. But inside, I was surprised.

On the surface, people might've thought her stupid to waste such a golden escape attempt.

I saw past the surface.

Piper was smart. She understood the gravity of her situation completely.

And she loved her sister.

Enough to die for her.

Because that's what going into the Appalachian Mountains with me was.

Death.

"Those will kill you."

I will not look at her.

My head craned upward to look upon her body, illuminated by the sunshine behind her. She was wearing cutoff shorts, cowboy boots stained with mud and a white tank with dirt smeared on it. Her legs were long, tanned, defined and went on for fucking ever. Her small tits were perky, aching to be shown attention. Her neck was slim, delicate, fragile. I unclenched my left hand, taking a long pull of the cigarette with the right as I imagined circling that neck with my palm, squeezing, cutting off air, bruising it as I came.

A glimpse in her hazel eyes was a bucket of ice water on my previously dead, rotted and fucked-up libido.

She was looking at the cigarette in my hand, her hands on her hips. Whether she'd noted my gaze on her body was unapparent.

"I'll be long dead before I can see the results of this." I took another drag before throwing it onto the muddy ground.

Piper blew out an exasperated sigh, leaning down to snatch the still burning butt and putting it out against the wall before holding it in her palm.

She kept it there, her palm outstretched like she was holding some kind of bug.

"Littering," she scoffed. "We don't do that. Not here." She waved her hand at the woods and mountains in wonder.

With reverence.

"We shouldn't do it anywhere," she continued. "But we do. We. Us humans. Pillaging. Destroying. Creating endlessly. Consuming endlessly. Discarding things when we're done with them as if they no longer exist." She squeezed her palm shut, looking at me. "I do that. I'm guilty of it all. It's easy to forget in the city. But here..." She gazed upward, drawing in a long breath.

I watched her chest move as she did so, my eyes traveling over the soft mounds of her breasts.

"Here," she repeated, moving her gaze back to me, but not

before I returned what I hoped was a dismissive stare. "Here I cannot see you sully it. Not even with something tiny. So..."

I found her words to be captivating. Her obvious love for those woods, those mountains. It denoted a history. One that I had not discovered. Once again, I kicked myself for my lack of meticulous research, thinking this job was going to be easy. Lapsing into a false sense of security was deadly in my world.

But we weren't in my world. The painful realization was inescapable now.

We were in hers.

And I was beginning to understand that that was deadly too.

I itched for a way to find out about her past. But I didn't have one. We were out of range for cell service—purposefully. And though I doubted anyone on Stone's team was talented enough to track me, I'd kept all my tech at my apartment. I had no need for it. Needing to call for help meant I was morally injured, and I deserved to die anyway. And I had no one to call.

Not a single way for me to dig for skeletons. Except to ask her. Talk to her. No way in fuck would I be doing that.

Silence descended between us, but I knew it wouldn't last long. Piper did not do well in silence. I'd observed that since I met her, during the drive here. She'd writhed with discomfort, unable to resist making conversation with a man she thought might possibly rape and murder her.

A ridiculous personality trait, yet one I found immensely charming.

"Here is my list," she said, handing me a piece of paper.

I took it on instinct. Her handwriting was messy, barely legible. But I could see she put little fucking hearts over the "I"s.

Tampons, food requests—gummy bears and pop rocks. What was she, seven?

"Seeds, dirt, planters?" I questioned, once I moved past the candy.

She nodded. "I'm going to start a garden."

"A garden," I repeated before I could stop myself.

"Yes, well, I can only hope I won't be here to see the fruits of my labor, no pun intended since I do in fact plan on planting strawberries." She winked. My cock twitched. "But there are only so many weeds I can wrestle with and books I can pretend to read, and it's good for the soul to get hands in the dirt. Grow things. And then maybe your next captive can bake you a strawberry pie or throw together a tomato salad."

Though I had discovered that Piper liked to joke, she was serious about this. About planting a garden.

"What?" she asked, tilting her head as if to regard the surprise I knew was painted nowhere on my expression. "You think I should rot away inside, trying to carve knives into shanks and plot my escape?"

My lips thinned in an effort not to smile. "You don't need to carve knives into anything, they're already a weapon."

Her face went blank then she nodded quickly. "Thanks for the pointer—pun intended. I'll stow that away for when I do intend to stab you. For now, it'll just be that." She gestured to the list. "And don't worry, I won't try to run while you're gone. I'm not that stupid."

Again, she was being serious. Though it was human nature to try to break out when you were in captivity, she had seemed to accept her cage without question. Because she was smart enough to understand just how imprisoned she really was.

Though it was rough terrain and a long way to any civilization, I didn't doubt Piper had the capability to escape if she really set her mind to it. She could get away from me, for a time anyway. And she likely wasn't stupid enough to alert authorities, knowing Stone had connections to everything. Which meant she'd try to run. With no funds, and no ID. Maybe she had contacts I didn't know about who could procure her fake identification, money, but I doubted it.

Even if she did have those connections, she was aware of the noose we'd placed figuratively around her sister's head.

I'd be expected to kill her sister if she did run.

The thought made my throat constrict.

Piper's sister was all she had. Everything to her. That was plain. And killing her would be inflicting a mortal wound upon Piper.

The thought of causing any harm to Piper's sister made my insides clench. A foreign reaction for me. I battled against it, denied the power she was quickly wielding over me.

She wouldn't do it. Wouldn't run. Wouldn't force my hand like that. She was going to *plant a garden.*

It was her way of keeping herself alive, intact. And the quickest way to nip that in the bud was to refuse her. The entire goal of this assignment was to pull her apart, not to give her ways to bring things to life.

Yet I took the list.

PIPER

After leaving Knox sitting outside with my list, I stomped inside, first removing my muddy boots then going to the bathroom. I was in dire need of a shower. The thin layer of dirt and grime covering my body felt good, though. Reminded me of the long, sticky summer days with my grandmother. Our hands in the soil, her raspy, patient voice telling me which plants were weeds and which weren't.

Leaning against the door to the bathroom, I squeezed my eyes shut at the onslaught of the memory, once so sweet, warm and pure, now painful and bitter upon reflection.

I missed her terribly. Like a dull ache. Aside from Daisy, she was the only true kind of unconditional love I'd experienced. Her love was not dependent on outward factors: access to mood-altering substances, how I'd acted that day, whether or not a sports team had won or lost. No, it was as constant as the sun, the moon, the stars. A guiding light.

Without it, parts of me felt cold, dead.

I unfurled my fists, opening my palm to contemplate the crushed-up butt I was still holding.

I lifted it closer to my face, inhaling the acrid smell of chemicals and tobacco. My nose should've turned up at the scent. It reminded me of dive bars and rock bottoms.

But it didn't.

That scent was mixed with the dirt on my hands, the fragrance of wildflowers and sunshine and ... Knox.

I must've been imagining that last part. The sheer force of the scent from the cigarette would drown out any other fragrance.

Yet I smelled him. Earthy. Salty. Wrong.

My feet directed me to the toilet. Flushing it down was my original plan. But as I hovered over the bowl, butt in hand, I hesitated.

This thing was nothing but trash.

But it was an indicator of Knox having a flaw. Being human.

Instead of flushing it, my hand clasped around it, keeping it for reasons unknown.

ELEVEN

PIPER

He got me everything on the list.

Not much of it was obscure, but I figured he'd simply refuse to get the candy. There was no way I could see a man like him touching bags of candy. In fact, I couldn't see a man like him being a child eating candy.

I'd put an obscene amount of thought into Knox—what his life looked like as a child, what his life looked like before all of this.

About whether he had someone who loved him, cared about him, someone he softened for.

Before the list, I didn't think he was capable of softening. That whatever happened to him had calcified any neurons capable of producing feelings. Empathy. Kindness.

Except...

The flowers.

The flowers that weren't on the list. Irises. The space needed something to brighten it up, life, but I'd decided against putting any kind of flowers on the list, thinking Knox would refuse to get them.

Which was actually the saner of the two options.

What was I thinking, decorating my cage?

Trying to turn it into something lovely?

And irises. I doubted he learned deeper meanings behind flowers and their roots in Greek mythology, but the iris denoted hope. And new beginnings.

I fought against my body's desperation to find meaning where maybe there wasn't any.

"They're perfect," I told him, holding the flowers, my soft voice conveying how taken aback I was.

He ignored me, his gestures stiff and expression cold. Why buy the flowers, then, if he was going to act as if he hated me? Maybe it was because he wasn't capable of using any other mode of communication?

Maybe the flowers were a sign of something.

Maybe they were a sign of nothing.

Maybe they were just merely a tool to have me twisting myself up inside, trying to figure him out, another tactic used to unnerve me.

I pondered over this as I worked the soil, planted those flowers.

And I watched him. Whenever I could. Whenever his intense gaze wasn't zeroed in on me, which wasn't often.

He'd watched me closely since the beginning. But something in the energy of his gaze had changed. It wasn't as absent or cold like it had been before. And I felt him, cataloguing how many bites of food I ate, assessing my gait when I returned from my run. He was ensuring my health only so that he could deliver me in good condition—is what I told myself.

Nothing more than that.

Yet I watched him back. In the small snatches of time when he wasn't looking. Watched him inhale those poisonous cigarettes. I'd long since thought they'd lost their allure and coolness, since it had been established that they caused a cancerous, undignified death.

Death. That's what I was watching Knox doing as he sucked

them down, one after the other. He was courting his death, sitting there pulling it into his lungs.

And yet he looked majestic doing it.

The king of death.

His.

Mine.

———

The garden was a good distraction. The only distraction, really. The books I'd brought could not hold my interest. It didn't help that every one of them were peppered with excellently written sex scenes that only served to further rile my unpredictable and inappropriate urges toward Knox.

He sat and chain-smoked while watching me garden for days. He didn't offer to help, not once. Didn't utter a word. Just watched me.

I did my best to pretend he wasn't there. Mostly I did my best to pretend I was able to pretend he wasn't there. In truth, there wasn't a moment when I wasn't conscious of his eyes on me. And it wasn't like it was particularly glamorous work. The warming of the days sent sweat spreading across my brow, dirt caking my hands, seeping under my fingernails. Not that I should've cared how glamorous or dirty I did or didn't look in front of Knox.

Every day when the sun set, Knox would stub out his hundredth cigarette of the day into a makeshift ashtray that had just appeared since I'd commented on the littering the first time we spoke about butts.

I'd started up a small collection of them.

His cigarette butts.

I hid them, and then I'd just hold them in the bathroom, looking at them.

Why, I didn't know.

Because I was slowly unraveling into a strange version of myself that scared me a lot but also felt more real than anything or anyone I've ever been.

Although we didn't speak much, this transformation was because of Knox. Because of the way he was terrifying me. The way he'd torn me from everything familiar and safe and put me back here, in the mountains, the only place I'd ever felt happy and at home.

When he looked at me, he wasn't just looking. It was as if he was cataloging every square inch of my skin so he could recreate me from scratch in his memory. All of my imperfections, blemishes, every inch of me was becoming his.

This was without him touching me, with us barely speaking.

It was a slow descent into madness that I could feel but couldn't stop. And I wasn't sure if I wanted to.

The reality of the situation rocked through me during every shower I took, washing off the dirt and grime from the wild area beside the cabin I'd somehow tamed into a garden.

The ground was freshly turned over, seeds planted. Weeds were cut back, tamed from taking over completely but not pulled at the root. They had just as much right to be there as anything else.

I felt a grief that I couldn't explain, looking at the muddy water going down the drain of the shower.

Another day ended.

Another day closer to the end of ... whatever this was.

And I wasn't looking forward to it. Not just because the end of this was likely the beginning of a long and very unhappy marriage— I was yet to find a solution to that particular scenario.

There was only so long, though, that this could last. That Stone would accept that I was still here, being broken.

And I wasn't.

Being broken.

Knox trying to chip away at me was a palpable, unescapable thing, something impossible not to feel in the beginning.

Which was why I felt the absence of it. He was no longer trying to break me. At least not in the way he was supposed to. Nonetheless, I felt pieces of myself falling away into the dirt as I worked in a garden in Appalachia with Knox chain-smoking a few feet away.

I dried my hair and dressed as I did every afternoon. I heard Knox in the kitchen, making dinner as he always did. No meat. Various types of dishes, flavor profiles. Granted, he was working on somewhat of a limited palate, but everything he served me was delicious. Mushroom risotto, chickpea stew, rich bean salads. Frittatas. He was making an effort not to just feed me but to ... nourish me too.

The weight I had rapidly lost was coming back on, my skin was tanning quickly in the sun.

My hair was somehow shinier than it had ever been with all sorts of expensive products, yet all I was using was some off-brand shampoo.

In short, I felt like I was almost ... glowing?

In the shadow of the darkest person I'd ever been in the presence of.

How did that make sense?

Knox

She was blooming. There was no other word for it.

When I'd first laid eyes on her, there was no denying she was gorgeous. But I hadn't noticed the shroud around her. The shadow. She coated herself in color and prints to hide it. She was still the most beautiful person I'd ever met, yet she was waning away.

Under the oppressive fear of Stone's attention.

I'd kill him for that.

For making her wane.

But doing that gave me the opportunity to watch her bloom. And I didn't deserve it. In my presence, she should've been further withering away. I didn't foster life.

Yet I couldn't deny it was happening. I couldn't take my fucking eyes off her as she worked in her garden, creating life. Her limbs were strong, all of her movements sure. Even with dirt caking her forehead from where she'd rubbed sweat, I had visions of stripping her down right in that garden, in the soil, exploring every inch of her, tasting her perspiration.

It was creepy, watching her the way I was. I knew that. She went to great pains to avoid my eyes. I made her uneasy, but I didn't unnerve her in the way I should've. I knew that because I saw how she eyed me when she thought I wasn't looking.

With hunger.

At first, I thought it must've been some kind of mountain mirage. That I was finally losing touch with reality, going insane.

It was only a matter of time. For decades, I had ripped apart people, ended lives on a daily basis. That had to rot the mind in some way.

But it wasn't in my head.

Not after the second glance. Or the third.

She wanted me. Unthinkable.

She must've lost her mind. I tried to convince myself of that, yet I knew she hadn't either.

Something about me was *alluring* to her.

And that somehow felt like one of the most pivotal accomplishments of my life. That I somehow wasn't so inhuman that someone like her could see me.

Thought I was worthy.

I'd carry that around with me, the one last shred of proof that I was human. That's all I'd take from her. I'd save the memories of her in the garden. With the dirt on her face. Her holding her hair off the nape of her neck, tilting her head upward to the sky, eyes closed, reveling in the sunlight.

Her lips would be stretched out into a lazy smile of contentment. How she could bask in the sunlight in her situation confounded me. She still found simple joys in life even as the walls of it closed in around her.

I knew she was intelligent enough to understand the severity of her situation. Fuck, she'd already almost half-starved herself to death and collapsed in the woods. She'd already seen the deviant she was sharing a space with, yet she somehow held on.

I knew that time was ticking on Stone's patience. On my restraint. That one way or another, I'd have to place her in the jaws of a shark.

PIPER

Something felt different today.

The air was colder, and the sun somehow hotter. Or maybe that was Knox's gaze, that somehow was no longer icy cold. No longer detached. There was a depth to it, a wildness to it that was tangible.

My instincts were itching, warning me that something was going to happen this evening. What, I couldn't be sure. And maybe it wasn't my instincts. More than likely it was my overactive imagination that tended to create completely unrealistic, romantic scenarios that couldn't possibly come to life.

I kept drawing cards from my deck when Knox wasn't around, and The Devil returned again and again. Same with The Lovers. It was laughable now, the way the universe was shoving this in my face. Or maybe it was my unconscious wants, my shadow showing me that it would not be ignored.

I couldn't trust my own mind, that was becoming more and more apparent. Knox made it crystal clear that I couldn't trust him.

The only person I trusted completely was also being held hostage, her under the threat of death.

The bottom was falling out of my life, yet there I was, taking extra time to style my hair and dab on some makeup after showering. As if I were going to have a date with my captor.

My wardrobe did not offer much variety, and I didn't pack to look sexy. But I'd put on my most favorite pair of jeans, worn and faded, clinging to every inch of me like a glove no matter how many times I washed them.

I put on a simple white tank and a cardigan stitched with tiny wildflowers. With my hair piled at the top of my head, I fiddled with pulling a few strands out here and there, trying to make it look effortless when really I spent five minutes making it seem that way.

I put on a thin amount of concealer, marveling at the freckles across my nose that hadn't been there before. They made me look younger. My eyes were brighter than they'd ever been as I brushed mascara on my lashes. As I dabbed blush on my cheekbones, I contemplated the woman who looked like a child who had run through the mountains, picking wildflowers with an unscathed heart, a full belly, ignorant to the horrors that awaited her.

Somehow, during my captivity, I'd found that child. And I was welcoming her back.

Was my kidnapping ... healing my inner child?

Ridiculous.

But true, nonetheless. And yes, it might've been the magic of the mountains, the way the air smelled cleaner here, the sun shone brighter, and the trees stood taller.

But mostly it was the man who was cut out of the environment like an intruder and a native all at once.

It took effort to act normal while walking out of the bathroom. Then again, I never acted 'normal' while anywhere in Knox's line of sight. Every inch of me was coiled, tense, hyperaware in his presence. That was likely why I crashed so hard every night, my body was working overtime in a constant state of survival mode.

I needed to get used to that, I supposed, since it was looking more and more likely that the rest of my life—however long that was going to be—was going to be lived like that.

Knox was leaning against the countertop beside the stove where dinner was simmering.

He wasn't doing anything, just leaning, one ankle over the over, arms crossed, eyes focused on the doorway I was emerging from. As if he'd been staring at it the entire time I'd been in the bathroom.

I didn't do what I normally did, which was refuse to look in his direction and pretend to busy myself with sorting dirty clothes, taking them to be washed or hiding behind the cover of a paperback I wasn't reading.

Instead of doing that, I met his stare. I didn't know what my expression said. I wasn't trying to challenge him like I had in the past, wasn't trying to convey some semblance of strength nor determination. Not even hatred.

Because I didn't hate him. Not anymore. My feelings for him were like a rose, full of thorns sharp enough to draw blood combined with lovely soft edges.

Maybe that's what I wore on my expression, all of my discomfort and longing for him. Whatever it was, he picked up on it. I knew that because when he stared at me, he did it like he was trying to study me, learn me so well that he could write a book on how to break me.

He didn't look away. He didn't even swallow.

We stayed like that, staring through the air that had become charged at some point.

I spoke first. He certainly wouldn't have. He seemed as if he would be content to stand there and stare at me for hours.

Which he was.

He did it all day every day.

And it was only then when I truly realized that he wasn't staring at me like a captor watching a captive. He was watching me like a man living in eternal darkness gazing at his first glimpse of sunshine, unwilling to blink lest it leave.

"What is going to happen to me?" I asked him, my voice so low I wondered if it would even carry across the distance between us.

At first, I didn't think it did. Knox didn't move a muscle, nothing to betray he'd heard me.

Clenching my jaw, I waited, even though my first instinct was to fill the silence. Knox had taught me about that, the power in the chasm between conversation, what it meant if you were willing to weather it and wait for someone to tell you what they truly thought after having time to consider.

Knox had taught me a lot of things.

That the world was dangerous, dark and full of miscreants.

That my life was as fragile as that of a butterfly's wings.

That I wasn't as strong as I thought I was.

But I wasn't weak either.

And most importantly, I was infatuated with wicked things. Wicked men.

One in particular.

"You are going to be destroyed," he answered finally, his voice rough, not calm and controlled like it had been.

I flinched at the animality in his tone. The life in it. The pure heat.

He pushed off the counter, reaching me in a handful of strides. His hand went to the back of my neck, holding me in place.

My breath caught in my throat, my heart in my toes.

I peered up at him, unable to look anywhere but into the inky abyss of his eyes. The famous quote about staring into the abyss said it stared back at you. But this one swallowed me whole.

"You will be destroyed." It came out softer this time, his thumb stroking my jaw in a gesture so impossibly tender, I hadn't thought he was capable of it.

He was holding me like I was delicate, precious, like he was scared that one wrong move would shatter me—in direct odds with what he was saying.

"Your fate was sealed the second Stone laid eyes on you," he continued. "The second he tasked me with breaking you." I stifled a gasp when he leaned closer. "But you have broken something instead..." He trailed off, swallowing words I was desperate to hear.

Him. That's what he left unsaid. What my wretched, hopeful, fucked-up heart was hoping he'd say. That I'd broken *him*.

I ached for him to give me that, to say it out loud.

But he didn't. Didn't say anything to further explain just how and when and by whom I was going to be destroyed. He just stood there, holding on to me.

Our lips were inches apart, my heart beating so fast it was about to explode. My skin felt like it was made of wasps, and my thighs were clenched together so hard that there was barely space for the wetness seeping from my pussy to escape.

I was sure that the loud bang I heard was coming from inside my head. But it wasn't. In the next breath, Knox's hands were no longer at my neck. Before I could unravel what was happening, I was shoved roughly behind him.

Then there was a loud crack—not as loud as I expected a gunshot to be. Not that I knew it was a gunshot right off the bat. Knox let out a grunt but didn't move.

My legs turned to cooked noodles as I stood behind his large form.

"Move or I'll shoot again!" a voice shrieked.

My ears were ringing from my heart pounding, the bang and the gunshot, but that didn't mean I didn't recognize the voice.

"*Daisy?*" I choked out.

Blinking rapidly, I tried to peer around Knox, but he wouldn't move.

"Piper, are you hurt? Maimed? Essentially changed or injured in a way that can never be repaired?" Daisy's voice was shrill and dramatic, but that wasn't outside of the ordinary. She had the same tone when she found a spider in the tub.

Though in that scenario, she was too afraid to even smoosh said spider, yet there she was, somehow holding a gun, waving it around and pointing it at Knox.

And she had fired that gun.

Knox was still shielding my body with his. I stared at his back. He was wearing black, as per usual, but I noticed a wetness spreading over his shoulder. My finger tentatively touched it, then I stared at my red finger pad.

"You're bleeding," I told Knox. I stared at my sister, standing in this cabin, wearing a light-pink, wraparound cashmere sweater over a unitard and leggings. She looked as if she'd just come from practice. Which would make sense if we were in Manhattan, not hundreds of miles away.

"You shot him," I informed my sister.

"I'll shoot that motherfucker again, right in the head if I need to!" she shouted.

I was trying to compute her words, her presence in this facet of my life that had previously been untouched by any markers of true reality. Her being here, whether armed or not, fractured it all, sent my past and present lives hurtling together in a crash that made my brain hurt.

Knox, having been still and silent during our exchange, proved he wasn't near death as I feared. He proved that by surging forward. Toward my sister. Who was still holding a gun in his direction, who had proven she was far too trigger happy for my liking.

It was by the grace of God—or his rebellious son, was more

likely when Knox was involved—that she didn't fire again. Likely shocked by the rapid advance of the man she'd just shot.

He ripped the gun from her hand, discharging the clip so bullets clattered noisily onto the floor. He flung the empty gun across the room then grabbed my sister by the throat with a casual violence that socked me in the gut. The same hand that had been tenderly caressing me was now assaulting my sister.

"You fired a gun, without any knowledge of how to do it, and it could've gone through me and *hit your fucking sister*," he snarled.

I'd never heard such rage leech from every fiber of a being before. Dangerous, murderous rage. Directed at my sister. The control he'd possessed during our time here was now absent, gone, permitting his true, violent nature to show.

I was across the room in seconds.

"Let her go, Knox." My voice shook as I stared at my sister, her hands clawing at her neck, helpless and dwarfed by the large man holding her.

Knox didn't comply. "She could've shot you."

"She didn't shoot me," I replied, forcing my voice to be softer now that I understood I wasn't dealing with the calm, calculated killer without a heart. I was dealing with someone else entirely. Someone who seemed to have been triggered into a blind rage at the prospect of me getting shot.

My mind didn't have any kind of reaction to that because my sister being in danger trumped everything.

Knox, for whatever reason, didn't hurt me, but clearly, that didn't mean he'd do the same for the person I cared most about in this world.

"Let my sister go, Knox," I ordered, my voice shaking.

For a horrible second, as she began to truly gasp for air, her eyes bulging, I thought he wasn't going to let her go. That he was going to snap her neck in front of me.

Thankfully, he stepped back, and I rushed to catch my sister as she collapsed in my arms, coughing violently.

My eyes found Knox, wishing I could shoot tiny knives into every inch of his skin.

He had been shot, so that was a start.

He didn't say anything, no apology in his face, no signs of guilt.

This is who he is, I reminded myself. *A man who lives with violence every day. Breathes death without coincidence.*

And I was about to *kiss* him?

The universe wasn't subtle, Daisy bursting in serving as a reminder of just how far gone I was. But not too far gone to come back.

I stroked Daisy's head until her breathing evened out, and she lifted her gaze to scowl at Knox.

"Are you okay?" she asked after looking at me. There was a slight scratch to her delicate tone that made me want to claw Knox's face off.

"I'm fine," I reassured her, still reeling over the fact that she was here. That she had shot Knox, and Knox had, in turn, almost strangled her. This was all after we almost kissed. Yeah, more than a lot to process.

"You're not fine," she scoffed, standing on her own feet but not letting go of me. "You've been in the presence of this maniac for weeks! He strangles me the second he sees me, so I hate to think what he's done to you." Her voice had a hysterical edge with a healthy dose of anger mixed in and directed at Knox.

I was relieved to hear that anger. It meant she was okay.

"You shot me before you even considered your sister being caught in the crossfire," he said evenly. "Be thankful you're still breathing."

My own breath caught at his words.

I pushed them out of my mind. I had to. What good was it to have a maniac care for you if he was willing to injure the one you loved most in some sort of fucked-up vengeful or protective mode?

"You hurt my sister again and I'll rip you to pieces," I vowed to Knox, unable to discern the specifics of how I'd carry out such a thing but knowing I'd find a way if I needed to.

Cold and calculating once more, his eyes traveled slowly over my face, presumably measuring me and my words. Then something twitched in his cheek, as if he found me almost … amusing.

Amusing. When I'd just witnessed his brutal violence against Daisy and had very sincerely threatened his life. That made me all the more furious.

"Whatever you say, Petal."

Petal? Where the heck did that pet name come from? Completely inappropriate, and it did not make me feel any type of way. It was insane to feel any type of way about a term of endearment muttered by a man who had been *strangling my sister* less than a minute ago.

Ignore him. That was the most sensible thing to do right then.

"Let's get you some water," I told Daisy in a calm voice. Instantly, I transitioned into the caretaker role that had fit me like a glove my entire life when it came to my sister. Though in that moment, it felt uncomfortable, stifling.

"And you sit your ass in that chair." Addressing Knox, I pointed to the dining room chair. "You were just shot, so I'm going to have to do something about that." What, I had no idea.

"It's a flesh wound," Knox grunted.

"Yes, a bullet. Through your flesh," I widened my eyes at him. "And it didn't go through said flesh and hit me, as you so daintily pointed out. Therefore, it is still in there."

He was watching me intently, no pain seeming to tighten his face. "Then I need a lighter and a knife."

This was the most Knox had spoken in a single exchange since we got here. And those words included describing my destruction, alluding to his own, threatening my sister, and then declaring he was going to fish a bullet out of his own skin.

"You need to sit your ass in the chair," I huffed, grabbing a glass for my sister after turning off the bubbling pot of food that smelled amazing. Moroccan stew of some sort, I guessed based on the scent of cloves and curry.

I handed Daisy the water which she seemed to take reflexively, observing me with wide eyes. She was likely just processing. She had probably mentally prepared herself to come in here and find me half-tortured. Which wasn't untrue, I just wasn't tortured in the way she expected. I looked exactly the same on the outside, but my insides were all gnarled and confused.

I reached into a cupboard I knew held an extensive first aid kit I'd been surprised to find. It made sense, due to the remoteness of the cabin and the fact that if either one of us got injured, it wasn't like the proper authorities could be called.

Daisy sipped her water and gazed around the cabin while I took stock of the supplies.

The kit had a scalpel that seemed sharp and hopefully what was needed to fish the bullet out of Knox's skin. Though I had no idea what one needed to fish out a bullet, and I didn't have a phone to google such information.

The premise seemed to be to find something sharp then ... dig.

My squeamish stomach turned at the thought of it.

"This is ... cozy," Daisy remarked, having looked around. I caught her eye right after she stared at the single bed in the room.

I had no idea which conclusions she was coming to, and I didn't care. Knox was sitting quietly in the chair, which was an amazing feat in itself. That he obeyed my order and wasn't speaking, merely watching my sister and I like a predatory cat, could've just been typical Knox behavior. Or it could've been indicative of blood loss.

Horrified, I looked to see a not small puddle of blood accumulating on the floor underneath the chair, dripping from his wound.

That was when I decided I'd address Daisy and the entire situation after I attempted to save Knox's life.

The thought struck me like a knife to the heart. Knox. Dying.

Absolutely not.

Had I imagined it in the early days? Maybe.

But logically, that wouldn't work for us. He might be our only way out of this scenario, if my thoughts about his feelings for me were correct. But then again, if they weren't, he could be our damnation.

Maybe letting him die was the smarter gamble.

I shook myself out of my trance—fixated on the puddle of blood—to find Knox staring squarely at me, watching, as if knowing I was deciding whether I was going to try to save him or not. Arrogant of me to think I was the one who could control whether he lived or died.

Knox was in charge of that. Beyond even what higher powers might or might not have existed—I wasn't sold on that, given the direction of my life and general childhood trauma.

I snatched up the supplies, laying them on the table before dousing the scalpel with alcohol and getting some gauze ready.

"Take off your shirt," I ordered Knox.

His demeanor changed. He stiffened. Clammed up. Not that you could've described him as relaxed in any sense of the word, but he was surprisingly calm after being shot. Yet after making my simple request, the tension in the air was thick and stifling.

"No."

I tilted my head to regard him. "I didn't take you for someone who worried about modesty."

My tone was dry, but I was teasing. How quickly my disdain for his violence to my sister waned. It didn't completely disappear, just bubbled lower, waiting, merging with all of my other complicated feelings about him.

He didn't respond, not even a lip twitch. He stared at me for two seconds then leaned forward to grab large scissors out of the pack, grunting as he awkwardly maneuvered his body to cut his shirt to expose his skin. Well, his skin was somewhere underneath the blood. And the bullet wound.

"You bleed red," I observed. "Who would've thought? I was sure it would be black and inky like tar."

I wasn't joking then, not entirely. But I could've sworn the edge of Knox's lip moved, just a fraction.

Ignoring the small gesture and the fiery response in the cauldron of my resentment, anger and desire toward him, I unpacked a disinfecting wipe from a package, wiping the blood away. Unsurprisingly, it only elicited a barely perceptible wince from Knox as the chemicals ate at his wound.

A dark part of me felt satisfied by the pain I was responsible for, revenge for the anguish he inflicted upon my sister.

I hadn't previously been one to preach the whole 'eye for an eye' thing, but I couldn't deny it felt a little good.

Pushing past that, I looked at the wound I'd revealed.

I'd assumed it was large, gory, gaping. But it was smaller than I expected. Neater. Leaking quite a bit of blood, though.

I rushed to press the gauze against the wound, forcing my breathing to steady.

"You're really going to try to treat him?" Daisy scoffed from behind me. She'd been silent longer than I'd expected. If I was honest, I'd almost forgotten she was there, which was unthinkable yet true.

Guilt coated me like oil as I struggled to get myself out of the tangle I'd found myself in with Knox.

"We should leave. Now," she urged.

I sighed, still pressing the gauze against the wound.

"We're not leaving," I told my sister, not looking at her. I wasn't brave enough.

I could practically feel the pouty look she was directing in my vicinity as well as her desperation to argue. Which was logical. At first glance, the most sensible thing to do was leave the bleeding psychopath alone in a cabin while we made our escape.

Though I'd thought through escape continuously, understanding that it wasn't that simple and it would likely mean both of our death warrants or a lifetime of looking over our shoulders.

I didn't have the time or energy to explain the complexities of our situation to her right then.

I expected Daisy to force me to, so she surprised me by sighing before snapping, "Fine." I heard her stomping around. "I'm going to eat, though. I'm starving."

This time I did turn to look at her, finding her standing at the stove. I raised my brow at her as she heaped food onto a plate. "You're going to eat across from the bleeding man you just shot while I try to extract the bullet from his flesh?" I clarified.

She shrugged. "I eat my dinner watching *The Walking Dead*."

"That is not the same," I muttered, but it was not the time to argue that.

My attention returned to Knox. He was lucidly watching me, eyes pinned to my body. I swallowed heavily at his gaze, realizing how close I was to him. The last time we were this close was minutes ago, when we were about to kiss. When he looked as if he was going to devour me whole. He still looked like that.

I forced myself to focus on the task at hand. Not to stare deeply into his eyes, not to examine complicated and thorny feelings, and definitely not to think about what might've happened had my sister not burst in and shot him.

"I'm going to dig the bullet out of your shoulder now," I told him, forcing confidence into my tone.

"This your first time?" he asked, and I swore it sounded like he was teasing. He couldn't possibly be. The range of emotions he'd displayed in such a short period of time was dizzying.

"This is a regular Saturday night for me," I quipped. I had no idea if it was a Saturday night. I hadn't been keeping track of the days, just the phases of the moon. "Your first time?"

He waited a long handful of seconds before replying. "In this particular scenario, yes."

I pursed my lips at the admission. "Don't worry, I'll go slow."

Silence passed between us. Somehow impossibly erotic to the point of making heat creep up my neck. In the presence of my *sister*. And with Knox bleeding to death.

What was happening to me?

Yet I couldn't let go of Knox's stare, couldn't deny that the moment was electrified by something I couldn't put my finger on. Once again, the foundation of what our dynamic was shifted underneath me, becoming more and more unstable. One wrong step and I could go tumbling into the darkness, never to be seen again.

I took a shaky breath, grasped the scalpel then readied myself to dig into Knox's skin. As if he wasn't living underneath mine already.

TWELVE

KNOX

I hadn't been shot before. Because I was good at my job. Any scars I had on my body, I'd put there myself.

I'd vowed I'd die that way. Without the marks of anyone else on my skin. Not when I had gnarled and knotted scars on my inside from someone I wish I could've killed ten times over.

Yet some fucking *ballerina* had managed to not only sneak up on me but made me bleed. Shot me.

Not because of any kind of skill on her part, but because of how completely Piper consumed me. I was sucked into her world, her orbit, so that no outside forces penetrated.

Lucky had never been a word I used to describe myself, but there wasn't anything else to explain how the bullet hadn't penetrated my heart, or worse, gone through my flesh and into Piper's.

I thought of her skin being punctured, marred, and my fists coiled.

Daisy was sitting across from me as Piper dug into my flesh for the foreign object, eating food I'd prepared for *Piper,* glaring daggers at me.

Though I didn't revel in hurting women, innocent women—

including women who looked to be as breakable as porcelain dolls and half my size—an ugly, evil part of me ached to hurt her for putting Piper in danger. Even if she had been attempting to save her.

She could've killed Piper. My vision tinged red at the thought.

The pain helped. It was the only thing keeping me lucid. That and Piper's hands on my skin, her tunneling into my body, her being the source of that pain.

Depraved fuck I was, it was turning me on. I was desperate to throw Piper down on the table and fuck her until I felt like I was glued to her fucking insides.

I had been about to do just that before her sister burst in to save the day. An apt interruption as that was a terrible idea.

Still, the roaring, famished beast inside of me, usually sated by blood, longed for her. And only her.

She bit her lip as she dug deeper. She was nervous. But determined. She had toyed with the idea of leaving me to possibly bleed out and make her escape. I'd seen a shadow fall over her eyes as she considered it. That moment of indecision made me so fucking proud of her. For feeding that dark part of herself that she'd starved for years.

I knew it existed because if it didn't, she'd hate me for the evil man I was, feel no longing for me. No compassion.

Her tongue poked out to caress her lips as she further concentrated. Pain speared through me, and pleasure mixed in. I wanted her to dig deeper. Fuck, I wanted her to wrap her palm around my heart, fingernails piercing as she squeezed with all of her might. I didn't care if it killed me if the last beat of that ruined organ would be in her hands.

A worthy death.

"Got it!" she declared, a girlish grin lighting up her face as she pried the bullet from my flesh. Luckily it was still whole, no small shards that would be impossible for her to tweeze out and might've eventually killed me.

I winced, not at the sting but at the loss of her touch. She held the small metal object between her fingers, holding it up to the light, inspecting it.

"Such a small thing to have the power to create so much damage," she mused.

I stared right at her. "I was thinking the same thing."

Her body jerked when her eyes met mine, catching the meaning of the words I shouldn't have even uttered in the first place. Most especially not with her sister within earshot.

Dangerous. I was walking a dangerous fucking line. Toying with a kind of disaster even I knew I couldn't weather.

Piper's gaze traveled to my shoulder.

"I need to stitch that," she whispered, nodding to the wound.

I nodded back.

If only it were possible to stitch the ugly wound she'd torn inside of me.

PIPER

"This is really good. Did you make it?" Daisy asked, gesturing to the couscous with her fork.

"Knox made it," I told her before returning my attention to the needle I was threading. Not before I saw the disbelieving raise of her eyebrows.

"They teach Moroccan cuisine at psychopath school?" she asked him sweetly.

He didn't answer her, but he did give her one of his patented chilling looks.

She didn't so much as flinch, which both surprised and worried me. For all of her dramatics, Daisy was a delicate person, easily hurt. Yet the look from one of the most dangerous men in the world didn't even scare her. What had she gone through since I'd been taken that gave her that shield?

"How did you even find me?" I demanded, keeping my eyes focused on the bloody hole in Knox's shoulder. My hands were steady, even though I was absolutely freaking out inside. This was a gunshot wound. I had experience with knee scrapes and 'boo boos'. But the first aid training I was required to keep up with didn't go so far as to cover how to treat a gunshot wound.

Digging in to get the bullet out had been weirdly satisfying. It must've been immensely painful, yet Knox hadn't made a move. He'd just stared at me. Before saying ... whatever the heck it was about the bullet.

It must've been about the bullet.

He couldn't possibly have been talking about me. But I couldn't deny the way he'd watched my face the entire time I'd searched for the bullet, his expression not blank but ... riveted. Hungry. Reverent.

"I put an AirTag in every one of your bags and suitcases," Daisy explained, still sitting at the table, staring at Knox with her delicate brows scrunched together.

"You put tracking devices in my suitcases?" I paused in my work for a moment to take her in. And to settle my stomach. It turned out I was squeamish with gunshot wounds.

But I couldn't vomit or pass out right then.

Daisy nodded, her curls bobbing as she did so. "I had a bad feeling. About Stone. And also, you're a terrible liar. When you said he'd finally left you alone... I didn't know what was going to happen, so I did research—mostly reading mafia romance books which are great, by the way..."

She trailed off, presumably having caught my look silently saying *now is not the time.*

"You can read them later," she added with a wave of her hand. "I didn't figure it was going to be as dramatic as all that. An obvious kidnapping, I mean. Messy. Stone is very good at pretending he's civilized, so I reasoned he'd done something to make you pack of your own accord. I knew I wouldn't be able to call the police, and trying to convince Joey to help me has been a shit show. That asshole." Her pretty face contorted into an angry scowl that I'd never seen before. Even when she was mad or sad about the latest breakup, she never had that kind of fire in her eyes.

She was hurt. It was radiating from her pores. She loved him. The dangerous man she thought she could tame. Who had betrayed her. He was essentially her captor now too, operating on Stone's orders.

Only a man you loved could make you hurt like she was.

I wanted to kill him with my bare hands. But my bare hands were currently covered with another killer's blood.

"Anyway, I knew that I would find a way to come rescue you," she continued, sniffling. "I figured I may have some help, but I've now learned that I can save someone all on my own."

"And shoot someone," Knox grunted.

Her eyes narrowed at him. "How was I to know that you'd bewitched my sister into *not* wanting me to shoot you? The last I heard about you was that you were a heartless killer that even Joey was afraid of."

"That's not saying much," Knox scoffed, gritting his teeth as I resumed my terrible job of suturing his wound.

I failed home economics in high school.

It was a testament to just how much of a pain tolerance he had that he was able to handle me sewing together his skin after being shot and after having had the bullet excavated out of his flesh without passing out or screaming.

Then again, screaming over a 'flesh wound' would've seriously messed with his badass reputation.

Daisy was still glaring at Knox. They weren't going to be friends anytime soon. Which made sense since great friendships were rarely built on the bedrock of one person shooting another or one person kidnapping the other's sister.

Great relationships weren't built on kidnapping, in other words. They were headed for disaster. Yet here I was.

"Okay, so the question of how you found my location is answered, but how did you get *here?*" I tried to lead the conversation away from thorny places, as if that were possible. "I was under the impression that you were being heavily watched by Stone's people." My heart stuttered. "What if they've been following you?" Alarm shot through my veins, and my body tensed, gaze darting for the door, expecting men to burst through it at any moment.

"They haven't," Knox's voice punctured my panicked haze.

His strong and unwavering gaze was zeroed in on me, too full for me to understand but blank at the same time.

"How do you know that?" I demanded.

"Because they would've killed Daisy if they got an inkling of what she was up to."

I flinched at the way he said it. So matter of fact. So certain. As if the prospect of her death wasn't world-shattering. It wasn't for him.

My sister. My brave, free-spirited, hopeful sister had yet again acted without thinking, with only her heart guiding her. And if she hadn't been a little less lucky, she would've been dead.

The blood on my hands was scorching them.

Daisy paled slightly at Knox's words, but her tone remained confident. "I couldn't come straightaway," she explained. "The second you ... *left.*" She scowled at Knox before continuing. "The second you left, things changed. Joey was everywhere, telling me I couldn't leave the city for my 'own safety' and urging me not to ask questions about you. As if I'd just give up on you. For once, I slowed down. Made a plan."

She smiled, looking mighty proud of herself. I was mighty proud of her too.

"I convinced the director of the company to send a bunch of us to a show in Knoxville then informed Joey that I had to go," she

said. "I don't know how it was cleared up the chain of command."
She waved her hand dismissively. "I told Joey we had a five-hour
practice today plus a costume fitting, then went straight from the
hotel room to rent a car to come here."

"And the gun?" I asked her, digesting how much she'd managed
to orchestrate. My sister, who barely knew how to set up her
insurance.

She shrugged. "It's America, and despite my political leanings
toward the opposition, it's still easy as apple pie to procure a
weapon here."

I stared at my sister, astonished by the impossible chain of
events that had come into place in order for her to make it here. To
rescue *me*.

Her gaze softened as she watched me, understanding my expression in a way only a sister could.

"You've spent all my life protecting me," she whispered. "Saving
me. You wouldn't even be in this situation if it weren't for me. It
was only fair I saved you when it counted."

My eyes welled as I finished the last stitch in Knox's shoulder,
tying it off.

"You haven't saved her." The cool slice of his sharp tone broke
through our moment. "You've only further served to endanger the
both of you." His words were delivered in his unflinching tone, but
I sensed the fury underneath.

"It is pure dumb luck you made it this far," he continued. "And
you need to leave. Now. You've got time. Barely enough of it. If
your luck holds, you can make it back in one piece."

"I'm not leaving her here with *you*," she spat, face no longer soft
and delicate but sharp and hateful, her nose scrunched and a
wrinkle between her eyes deepening with a scowl.

Knox just stared at Daisy. Her glaring at him was much like
Tinkerbell trying to kick a giant. "You try to enact whatever fairy
tales you've concocted about riding off into the sunset, it'll kill

you both. I'm not letting that happen. Nothing is happening to Piper."

His voice was still again, even. But the words contained a fierceness. A dedication. To me.

This man was a cold dragon willing to breathe fire to protect me.

Daisy looked between the two of us again, her face tense with concentration. A handful of seconds passed, then realization.

She opened her mouth, likely to vocalize something that both Knox and I had been refusing to acknowledge for some time.

"Knox is right," I spoke before she could, standing to go to the sink in order to wash the blood from my hands. "We don't have the resources or the skills to run from this. If we try right now, we'll fail. Stone will get what he wants, me. And he'll hurt you to do it."

I turned the taps on as high as they could go then squeezed my eyes shut against the scalding water.

"This cannot possibly be our only answer," Daisy whined.

I scrubbed at my hands and waited until I'd dried them before I turned to her. My fingernails still held crusted blood underneath them. I wanted to keep it there for a while. Knox's blood. On my hands.

Proof he could bleed.

That he was human.

That he had protected me with his body.

"It is the only answer, Daisy, you know that." I sighed. "Is Joey, is he ... h-hurting you?" I stumbled over the words. I hadn't considered what the true reality of this situation might've been. Perhaps Daisy had come to her senses once the ugly reality of what being tangled up with the mafia was and tried to break it off with Joey.

Daisy huffed and rolled her eyes in a way that communicated that she was annoyed, not scarred for life.

"He still insists he's in love with me," she flicked her wrist dismissively. "He wouldn't dare lay a hand on me. He gets all ragey when anyone else in the ... organization comes near me."

I clicked my tongue. I hadn't had a good first impression of Joey, yet it seemed like he was protecting Daisy. Not that I could count on that to continue.

"Okay, well you need to stick close to him. For now, at least. Until we figure this out."

"You think we're going *to figure this out*?" Her eyes went wide as saucers, hands on her hips. "This is not me making a mistake on tax returns... This is an international crime boss intent on marrying you and forcing you into submission. Joey told me everything."

I glanced in Knox's direction. He was still sitting in the chair, watching us intently, making no secret of the fact that he was listening to every word.

"We're going to figure this out," I told her firmly. In the tone I'd used so many times over our lives that I'd perfected it. Even when I was most afraid, uncertain or panicked, I'd always presented as assuring and confident to my little sister. That was my job, after all.

For once, though, she didn't look the least bit convinced.

"I need to talk to you. Without him." She violently jabbed her pointer finger in Knox's direction.

I sighed. The separation of these two was probably most sensible. It was going to be hard for Daisy to see reason—if that was indeed what I was preaching—with Knox in the vicinity ... being Knox.

"Let's go outside," I replied as I quickly served up a large portion of stew, taking it over to Knox.

"Eat," I demanded. "The last thing I need is you passing out, hitting your head and losing your memory or something." I made my voice snappy, not letting him know I was panicked by the very prospect. Of Knox forgetting his job, who he was. Of him forgetting who I was to him. If I truly was anything to him.

He didn't say anything, but he didn't get up and walk away, which was enough for me.

"Come on, Daisy," I told my sister, walking toward the door.

She was still standing by the sink, looking intently at me, then Knox, then the bowl of food that he had begun eating.

"Daisy," I urged, uncomfortable with her gaze.

She moved, slowly, looking pensive but thankfully, following me outside.

"You've fallen in love with him," Daisy half-shrieked before the door had properly shut.

I shot a horrified glance at the cabin before grabbing her by the upper arm and dragging her in the direction of the garden. I did not need Knox within earshot of this conversation.

Daisy had been protesting my grasp until her eyes fell upon the garden.

I'd worked with what I had. Most of the seeds had only just begun sprouting through the dirt, the ground worked and lush. The unexpected flowers bordering the space reached for the sun. The weeds were tamed. I'd managed to salvage some of the rotted wooden fence that served as a border. It looked pretty, peaceful, especially with the backdrop of the wilderness behind it.

Daisy's eyes widened. "I'm guessing this wasn't here when you arrived."

I shook my head, uncomfortable with the garden I'd labored over, of what it represented. It had previously been sacred, precious to me. Now with Daisy's eyes on it, I felt it was being sullied. I was protective over this garden. This cabin. My solitude with Knox.

I'd quite obviously gone over the proverbial deep end.

"Let me get this straight... In the time that I've been worried about your fate, your safety and whether you'd be equipped with all of your fingernails, you were here ... *gardening* and falling in love with a sick fuck?" Daisy's voice bordered on shrill and hysterical.

But there was also a hint of amusement. Daisy was shocked and caught off guard, but a large part of her was delighted.

She consumed romance books like Skittles, nothing too dark for her. She carried an idyllic heart around, unguarded and nonjudgmental. I'd thought it was her weakness, but maybe it was one of her greatest strengths.

"You crazy bitch," she smacked my arm. "You hide it well, you know." She tugged on my ponytail.

"Hide what?" I said, folding my arms. I knew she wasn't talking about my feelings for Knox. Try as I might, I was wearing them on my sleeve for my emotionally shrewd—if not street smart—sister to see.

"That you're a depraved little romantic, desperate for the villain just like the rest of us," she giggled. "I always thought the dating of accountants and insurance salesmen was a thin veneer over your true needs."

I gaped at her, unable to fathom what she had apparently known yet had taken me thirty-two years and a kidnapping to discover about myself.

"I know that route seems safer because of Daddy." She stroked an iris with melancholy in her gaze.

I still hated that she called our father 'Daddy' with a note of fondness that he did not deserve. But that was Daisy, loving things that didn't deserve it in the first place.

"The safe route may keep you alive, but it doesn't keep you living," she continued. "And the 'safe' route doesn't guarantee that bad people won't come stomping in to steal you anyway. That's what Stone did. You made all the right choices, and still, the wrong man ruined everything." She looked back to the cabin. "Maybe not *everything*, though. Maybe this was meant to happen all along. And maybe that man—wrong in all the ways he can be—may very well be right for you."

I refused to look at the cabin. I could practically feel the structure pulsating with life, with Knox, with the intensity of feelings contained in the small space. The layers of skin I'd shed like a snake to reveal my true self.

"Are you trying to find a silver lining in all of this?" I asked, agape. I hadn't put much thought into what outside parties might make of ... this situation, considering I'd been actively trying not to think of it that way. But deep down I'd been ashamed, scared of my wrongness, depravity, still uncomfortable with my shadows. And yet my sunshine sister didn't so much as blanch at them.

She smiled. "You always have to find the silver lining, Sis." She reached out to squeeze my hand. "I like this for you."

Shock tugged at my brows. "You like me falling for the mafioso who was supposed to break me?"

Her eyes glimmered with tears. "If he's the only one who can protect you from all the darkness you've bundled up and hidden inside of yourself."

The words hit me like bricks.

"I know you've spent your life absorbing every blow that might've hit me, taking all the ugliness on. You've gone through so much, Piper, and you've refused to let me shoulder the burden because you don't think I'm strong enough." She nodded to the cabin. "I'm thinking me shooting him, and him barely even flinching proves he's strong enough. And although I may not like him—on account of the near strangling and the ease of violence he seeps out from his very pores—I love that he did it in protection of my sister."

My vision blurred from tears of my own, ones I choked down. "You don't think he's like...?"

"Daddy?" she finished for me. She shook her head. "Daddy hurt us because he took pleasure in it. Because he didn't know how to love. He was a weak and broken man." She glanced to the cabin again, suddenly seeming too wise for her years. "He may be broken, but he's not weak."

I considered her words. Knox hadn't shown me violence, not true violence until he laid his hands on Daisy. That was not something to dismiss. It was a giant red flag, waving in my face.

Then there was my father. Beating my mother without remorse as she begged. While his small daughters watched in horror, crying and screaming.

A man capable of violence against women was my line. Always. How had that line become blurry? How could I know that Knox wouldn't do that to me, or worse, to Daisy?

My heart told me he wouldn't. Never. But my heart couldn't be trusted. No one's could. My mother's heart believed my father when he begged, when he promised it was the last time, when he poured out all the vodka.

I picked at a hangnail.

"Will you promise to be safe?" I asked my sister instead of addressing the enormity of the situation. "Keep your head down. Pretend with Joey a little longer."

Her eyes darted to the side, and her posture slumped, as if curling into herself would hide her secrets. "I'm not pretending. Not entirely."

I nodded. "I know."

How was it that both of us, different in so many ways, found ourselves in similar situations, tangled up with dangerously wrong men and unable to wrangle ourselves from their clutches? We were our mother's daughters... That chilled me. You couldn't escape your genetics. And apparently, genetics had doomed us to love wicked men.

The silence of the forest took over until a light giggle penetrated it. Daisy.

Who else would it be?

She giggled some more, genuine and light. "I really did it this time, didn't I?"

It was then that I understood her light giggle was covering something heavy, dark and thorny. Her guilt.

I cupped her cheek. "This is not your fault, Daisy. We don't lay the sins of men at our feet. We leave them where they belong." I infused my tone with iron.

She pursed her lips, nodding.

"We'll get through this," I promised. Even though it wasn't a promise I could make.

Daisy would get through this. That was nonnegotiable. Me on the other hand? That remained to be seen.

But I'd die for my sister.

In a heartbeat.

Thirteen

Piper

"How will we know that she made it back safely?" I asked Knox, staring at the woods, long silent from the crunch of the car tires.

"We won't," Knox replied in a level tone, not bothering to try to placate me.

I stared up at him. He cut such a harsh figure against the green of the woods. "Can't you call someone to check?"

He hadn't been looking down the empty road, his gaze was on me. I sensed it had been for a very long time. His mask was back in place.

"Me calling someone and 'checking' not only risks a trace on a call but also could blow any kind of cover that Daisy had. The call would put her in even more danger than she already put herself in. And that's saying something."

His jaw was rock hard, his posture tight, words clipped. It was not hard to deduce that he was pissed. At Daisy.

Anger of my own bubbled up inside of me, churning like an active volcano, the power ready to decimate anything in its path "My sister did an incredibly brave thing," I said through my teeth.

"An incredibly stupid thing." He didn't seem bothered by my volcanic fury. To him, it was probably less powerful than the flame of a match.

My hands balled into fists at my sides, resisting the urge to smack them against his body, remembering he did just get shot an hour ago.

"Doing something to try to save someone you love is not stupid."

He looked at me for a long time, long enough to dump a bucket of cold water on my hot fury. "Yes, it is, Piper." His voice was featherlight. "The only thing dumber than that is loving someone in the first place."

The air flew from my chest at the heaviness of his words. He believed them. Solidly. That love meant weakness.

"Don't you have someone like that, who you would do anything to protect?" I asked, desperate to find a heart in the cold enclave of his chest.

He stared at the trees, and I thought he wasn't going to answer me.

"My brother." He spoke so quietly, I barely heard it over the whisper of the wind against the trees.

A brother. Knox had a brother. And not just a person with whom he shared the same parents. Someone he obviously cared for, the admission of his existence seeming as if I'd wrenched it from his throat.

"And more recently, my niece," he added, voice even lower than before, his posture tighter, as if that were even possible.

I studied his profile, shocked at the admission and warm with knowing he was giving something to me. He was shedding his skin of armor and hinting at the human that lay beneath. The human who was capable of love.

He jerked his gaze back to me almost violently. His eyes were a sharp blade, cutting into me.

"But I am capable of keeping them safe," he uttered, voice sure and cold and cruel. "By staying away from them. By making sure that I can and will do anything to keep them that way. Neither you nor your sister are capable of doing the things required to keep each other alive."

He slung the words to hurt, to pile up on my shoulders and drive me into the ground with hopelessness, with terror. I knew he wanted me to be afraid because he thought that scaring me was the only way to keep me alive. Or maybe that was just wishful thinking. Maybe he wanted me to be afraid because he liked scaring me.

I chewed on my lip. "You're wrong. I would do anything possible to keep Daisy safe. I'm prepared to marry a monster in order to ensure that."

Knox's arm shot out so quickly, I barely noticed him moving until his hand was circling my neck. He squeezed enough to make it hard for me to breathe.

"You're not marrying him," he gritted out. "You'll never breathe the same air as him again. He'll never so much as lay a fucking eye on you."

I rasped against the pressure and the pain against my windpipe, Knox's hands on my skin a scalding brand. And the words... The promise in them.

He was planning on saving me. That's what lay underneath his words. He didn't deem me or Daisy capable of the depraved acts required to get out of this situation. Although having a self-professed killer declare he was going to do horrible things in order to keep me safe should've been unnerving, I felt ... safe. Even with his hand wrapped around my throat, obscuring my air flow.

The man who was tasked with breaking me had at some point decided he was going to save me instead.

With his hand around my throat, his eyes searing into me and my heart pounding in tandem with his words, I knew I was not being saved. I was damned. Because even though I might not have to marry a monster, I was tangled up in one, nonetheless.

"You can't promise that," I croaked, barely able to grind out the words with the pressure on my neck not letting up.

I should've been clawing at his hands, fighting him, hating him for only being able to touch me in violence. Just like he had my sister. Instead, I leaned into his touch. Into him.

"I can't make many promises to you, Piper." He bent forward so our mouths were almost brushing. "But I can promise you that you won't be going near him the rest of your life. And that I'll ensure that your life will be a long one. You'll die warm and wrinkled in your bed, with the memory of this being nothing but a nightmare."

The promise threaded through the air, slithered down my throat then squirreled its way somewhere deep and permanent. Not only that he'd save me but that this situation—him—would be nothing but a nightmare.

My chest heaved up and down as my breath came in short bursts.

Knox's hand was still around my throat.

For a shadow of a moment, I thought he might not let go. Thought he might just keep squeezing until the darkness at the edge of my vision crept further and further until it swallowed me up, releasing me from this world.

I was sure the thought had crossed his mind. It was clear he was fighting whatever feelings he had for me. That those feelings made him question his whole existence, made him feel weak. And men who felt weak would do anything to delude themselves into feeling strong again. Even if it meant hurting a woman. Especially if it meant hurting a woman. The moment lay in the balance, of whether he was like my father or not, whether he'd use me to feel big.

His hands released a second later. He stepped back, running his hand across his jaw in a rare gesture of unease.

I rubbed at my neck, not hating the pain, even though it served as more evidence that he could hurt me. That he was the kind of man I'd spent my life ensuring I'd never get close to.

"My father killed my mother when we were young. I was thirteen," I blurted in a hoarse voice.

This was not information I shared readily, definitely not first date kind of fodder. But the scant amount of people I had told always had varying expressions of shock, horror, pity, discomfort. It was not a nice thing to hear. You perhaps read about such things in the news or scrolled across the stories on social media, but it was rare you met someone central to the acts countless true crime documentaries covered.

But I supposed to Knox, acts of horror and depravity were commonplace, so he didn't have an outward reaction to my news.

Yet his hands balled into fists. Not something I'd seen him do. His face remained impassive, though.

"He abused her since I can remember," I continued, staring from him to the trees, unsure of why I was sharing this now, of all times. "And us. To a lesser extent, not that I think there really is a lesser extent of abuse." I sighed. "My mom didn't protect us, really. She was too broken down by then."

The memories I had of my mother were mostly sullied with violence, her bruised, begging, being hit. I couldn't even remember if she was pretty. Because all I saw was the ugliness wrought upon our life.

"The only escape we had was summers here." I smiled at the trees, seeing much further than just the ones bordering the cabin. "Not right here, but somewhere in these mountains, there was a two-story house with a wraparound porch, three rockers and a vibrant garden out front, vegetables in the back along with a chicken coop. The woods and mountains stretched as far as the eye could see."

I closed my eyes, smelling the lavender my grandmother grew by the porch, the dirt, the dew, feeling the sunshine on my face.

Opening them I saw Knox staring at me with such intensity it was hard to breathe around.

"My grandmother was my mother's mom," I explained. "And to this day, I do not know how my mother let my father batter her so completely when my grandmother had given her support, endless love and was the picture of feminine strength." I shook my head. "The eternal question of how a man can break a woman who seemingly has everything going for her."

I didn't miss the parallels there. My spine stiffened as the truth settled into my bones, and I forced myself to continue the story.

"My mother, even in the peak of her brokenness, knew how to hold on to a façade." I still looked at the trees, unsure if Knox was really listening. That was a lie. I knew he was. I could practically taste his undivided attention. "My grandmother knew nothing of what was going on in New York, with the daughter who sent her two children to have summers with her, no explanation of why she didn't come too. My grandmother worried over this, asking us subtle questions about our home life, about Mom. We expertly lied, still holding on to a loyalty to our mother, even though the truth might've saved us from a lot. Sadly, we didn't realize it then."

I'd spent many nights wondering what life might've looked like if we had told our grandmother the truth. She would've acted, swiftly and immediately. And though I knew that the laws were infinitely complicated around abuse, custody and removal of children, I knew in my gut that my grandmother would've been victorious in saving us from the situation.

Maybe even our mother too. But that was more of a hopeful feeling, that given the real opportunity to escape, to be with her girls, that she would've taken it.

The truth was, I knew she wouldn't have. She was twisted up in my father. Embroiled in a toxic kind of love that sickly trumped the love she had for her daughters.

I didn't know what went wrong with her, how she could've been so different from my grandmother. My mother was the truest example of how loving the wrong man could not only kill you but warp you into an unimaginable version of yourself.

I was there in front of Knox telling my story, and even that didn't tamp down whatever feelings I had for him.

"As we got older, my father decided that the summers spent in Appalachia weren't good for us girls." I sucked in a deep breath. "He realized that we were getting 'too smart for our own good'—his words—since there is no such thing as a young girl being too educated." I sneered with anger, fresh and visceral after all these years, recalling the things my father had said that made it clear he hated women, his children and wife included, yet my mother stayed.

"My guess was he sensed that we were eventually going to tell our grandmother the truth." I clicked my tongue. "She fought against his ruling. She even came out to New York once."

I leaned over to grasp some leaves from a bush, needing to rub the pieces in my hands to ground me as I remembered the last time I saw my beloved grandmother.

The memory was foggy, but I remembered raised voices in our small apartment, my grandmother far too big for the space. Not because she was large in stature but because she existed in such a large place in my mind.

"She likely would've fought harder, until she got to the bottom of it, but she died later that summer." My nails bit into my palms as I spoke, willing my voice not to break.

To that day, the pain I felt over losing my grandmother was still visceral and agonizing, nothing like the way I felt over the loss of my mother.

"A fall." I shook my head. "She just tripped, broke her hip and then died because the night was cold, and Appalachia is unforgiving and brutal to even those who reside there. Even those who love it fiercely."

I looked out upon the silhouettes of the trees, standing like ancient sentinels observing us. Though there were a lot of legends I didn't believe about this place, I believed it to have a kind of sentience to it and that it decided on a whim whether it was benevolent or malevolent.

"It broke my mother, I think," I whispered. "Or maybe that's me being overly generous. Thinking she was still whole at that point. Because if there was even an inch of me still put together, I'd use it to give myself strength to take me and my children out of that situation."

I shook my head, punishing myself for the ugly thought. The resentment I carried like cancer in my insides for my mother. Blaming her for my father's sins.

"It wasn't her fault—" I tried to reason.

"It was," Knox interrupted coldly.

I glanced up at him. "My father, he—"

"Was a piece of shit," Knox finished. "And so was your mother. For staying."

"It's not that black and white," I argued. "It's more complicated. She loved him."

"More than she loved her children?" he replied, his words coated in acid.

It seeped through skin and flesh and bone, right to the core of me.

"Yes," I rubbed my eyes. "Yes, I think she loved him more than she loved us and hated herself even more than that."

Having grace for my mother was hard, as I had longed for her to protect us, to have changed our lives. For her to be something different. Even if it was to just be strong enough to let our grandmother have us.

But it was never that simple.

"You, putting your hands on Daisy," I continued, determined to bring this back full circle, to show him the gravity of what he'd done to me when his hands landed around my sister's neck. Raging at him and calling him names was tempting, but I was attempting a softer route with the hardest, cruelest man I'd ever encountered. As if that would soften him to me.

"Not the same," he ground out.

I tilted my head to eye him. "Isn't it? Isn't it that black and white? You had your justifications for what you did, just like I'm sure my father did. How can I be sure you won't hurt her? Hurt me?"

It was the most vulnerable thing I'd said.

It was a plea.

Please don't hurt us. I'm already too deep to wrench myself out. Please don't turn me into my mother.

"I would put a knife through my heart before laying a hand on you in anger, Piper," he vowed.

I rubbed my neck, the pulsating from his touch. Not with pain. With an electric awareness, a wanting that vaguely sickened me, given the violent gesture.

Knox's eyes went there. "That wasn't anger."

"Then what was it?" I asked, my voice a low rasp.

He didn't answer.

His gaze bore into me, scraped over my skin, ripping pieces of it away until I was nothing but a trembling pile of bones.

Then he walked into the forest, leaving me alone.

Was it smart, following the seething demon into the forest?

He'd stalked off there because he hadn't wanted to be around me. Hadn't wanted to be around the feelings we were drenched in when we were in each other's presence.

Because he wanted to continue to hide his secrets and his true feelings.

No, it wasn't smart, following him.

Maybe if I'd gone into the cabin and created some distance between us, it would've stayed there. The tension between us might have remained tension, coiled so it never released. Like a bomb, long buried, ready to explode but keeping the world tentatively safe under layers of soil and rock.

I had always made smart decisions when it came to men—Daisy had pointed that out earlier. Those smart decisions landed me here anyway. In the place I loved so much. With Knox. I couldn't help but think that was the universe urging me toward him.

Or maybe it was the universe testing me, to see if I was like my mother.

I didn't marinate too much on that thought.

Instead, I followed him into the forest.

If it was a test, I failed.

He wasn't hard to find.

He wasn't trying to hide.

Predators didn't need to hide.

And I knew he heard me approach.

"I was broken. Early on."

His back was to me and stayed to me while he spoke.

I wanted to see his face, desperately, but something told me whatever he was about to say was too painful for him to speak while facing me.

So I stood. Waiting.

"My mother, if you could call her that, wanted a man. She had two sons, but that didn't matter to her."

I could feel the scorn in his voice. The poisonous, unyielding hatred. It almost choked him. An inkling of why he'd had such a visceral opinion of my own mother.

"When she found someone she thought was good for her, she

ignored what he did to us."

My stomach pitted as I heard in his voice agony that no one should have to carry. I had an inkling of what he meant, and it squeezed my heart.

"I like to think she didn't know he was a child molester when she married him," he continued, speaking my greatest fear. "I'll be generous for her, but she was also so fucking desperate that he could've told her that on her wedding night, and she would've stayed. Not that the *how* of it matters. It mattered that it happened."

He turned then, and as much as I'd been longing for his eyes, I wished he would've stayed facing away from me so I didn't see the void in his gaze.

There was no pain, there was no anger, no grief. Nothing but a never-ending black hole of coldness that he'd created to keep him safe from it all.

"I knew there was something off with him from the moment I met him." His voice was a flat monotone, words so heavy I was surprised they didn't drill me chest-deep into the earth. "So I stayed up that night, the first night he was in the house as our stepfather." He laughed. I'd never heard him laugh before. Not that I would ever truly call the sound he made a laugh. I'd never heard a sound so horrible. So chilling. It echoed through the forest.

"He didn't even bother to wait," he continued. "He went for my brother first." He stopped speaking, standing stock-still. I would've thought he turned to stone right there and then had his hand not fisted and his body quaked.

Seeing him shuddering was akin to seeing a skyscraper tremble. You were so used to them standing tall and strong that you forgot they could fall too. And if they did, the wreckage was unimaginable.

"My brother was younger. He preferred them younger. But I managed to avert most of his attention away from him. When I could."

The handful of sentences held decades' worth of meaning. Of pain. Of a kind of evil I couldn't even digest. Logically, I knew terrible things like this happened in the world. Sickening things. But I had never let myself think too much on it. I worked with children. Every day, I saw the brightness in them. The purity. The innocence. What a treasure they were.

And to think a human could sully something like that in such a disgusting way sent my blood curdling. My heart splintered in my chest for Knox.

He was explaining how he averted a pedophile's attention in order to save his brother the trauma.

"How old were you?" I barely resisted the urge to vomit in the dirt beside me.

"I was nine when it started," he said, his voice dead.

I blinked slowly, trying my best not to let my horror and pity seep onto my face. I knew that's not what Knox wanted, that that would only drive him further away.

There was a reason for Knox being the way he was. That I'd known. People did not come out of the womb entirely wrong. Not even my father. The world molded my father to be that way. Sure, there was a rottenness in his core that might've been there since birth. But that could've melted away had he grown in an environment of nurture and love, raised in places where the good parts of him could've bloomed to outweigh the bad.

I'd known Knox was made, not born. And I'd reasoned that something horrible must've happened to him to leech so much happiness and empathy from a man, leaving only a cold, malevolent presence.

But I couldn't have dreamt up this.

"He was the first person I killed." Knox was unapologetic, unashamed. Matter of fact.

"Good," I choked out, never thinking I'd celebrate the idea of someone being murdered. I was against the death penalty; I believed in redemption.

In theory.

But in that moment, when it was personal, I understood the need for retribution. Vengeance. Death.

Knox tilted his head. "Good?"

I nodded. "I hate that he stole even more of your innocence by you taking a life." I was genuinely mourning for the boy who was forced on that path. "But I am glad that he doesn't walk this earth. I'm glad you took him off this planet."

Knox didn't speak for a long time, as if mulling over my words, deciding if he was going to share more.

I was hungry for more, even if the horrid truth of his past stung my insides like a nest of hornets.

"I started by killing those who deserved it," he finally spoke. "You may agree with those early deaths too. They were truly sick. It was black and white. Clean."

When he stepped forward, I quivered. He was Knox, but he was something else inside of his skin too. The killer he'd turned himself into.

"But things never stay in black and white for long," he continued, prowling closer.

I kept shaking at his advance, but I didn't retreat. This was a test, I knew that. He wanted to scare me, he wanted me to run. I wouldn't give him that. I'd show him I was strong enough to handle this. Handle him.

"But then it became clear that I *needed* to kill." The ground crunched as he stopped in front of me, completely in my face. He consumed me, his harsh expression, the danger radiating off him. My body thrummed with fear and need and sadness.

"I need it to breathe, Piper," he murmured. "There's nothing romantic or redemptive about it. I'm not some fucked-up kind of Robin Hood killing predators. You can't make this pretty in your mind. You can't make *me* pretty in your mind. What he took from me is what I am. Ruined. Disfigured."

The weight of his words settled inside of me like lead. He truly believed that he was wrong, damaged. The hatred he felt for himself was palpable.

"You're not ruined or disfigured to me," I whispered, my words broken, tears wanting to escape my eyes.

His brow hardened as I saw his determination to disgust me. To terrify me.

"You still think you want me after this?" he spat. "Want my blood-stained hands on your body? Want me to fuck you with tastes formed by years of abuse?"

I nodded slowly. His words were brutal and ugly, unveiling the attraction we'd been dancing around, but doing it so he tainted it. Made it wrong. And he did that on purpose. Because, I suspected, he'd never had an intimate relationship that felt right in any kind of way. I mourned that for him. I also felt kindred. Although I had been spared the horror of sexual abuse, all of my intimate liaisons were tarnished by fear and feigned attraction to men who wouldn't hurt me.

"I don't fuck like any man you've been with, Piper." His rasped whisper was more powerful than any roar could've been. "I haven't ... enjoyed any sexual touch with a woman. Or a man."

There was a slight difference to the cadence of his last sentence. Almost a tremor in it.

He was still trying to unsettle me. Trying to put me off as if him exploring his sexual identity and agency were something to be ashamed of.

"You haven't found the right person, then." I was breathing heavily.

His eyes flickered over me, purposefully brutal, assessing, unimpressed.

"You think that's you? Because you have a tragic backstory?

You're chipped in places, Piper, but you're not broken. Not shattered. And those chips only make you more stunning. I lay a hand on you and it would all evaporate."

I stepped forward, purposefully pressing our bodies flush together. Knox went statue still.

Forcing my hand not to shake, I reached out to cup his jaw. My palms exploded with electricity when I made contact. The skin was smooth, warm, unlike the cold façade he wore.

"You're not the one who gets to decide how broken I am," I cupped his cheek. "And you're also not going to stand here in front of me, trying to scare me with your trauma, with your sexual history or your biased view of your soul."

"I'm not trying to scare you with my trauma, Piper." Knox took hold of my wrist. Although he didn't yank my hand away, he squeezed my bone. I loved the pressure, the pain on my flesh. I'd thought I didn't want a possessive man, but it turned out I wanted this man to possess all of me.

"I'm trying to scare you with how I dealt with it," he bit out. "Plenty of people who get abused process it in healthy ways, become normal members of society. Or if you're my brother, they become famous by defying death for a living."

I filed away that tidbit about his brother. The tone in which he said it showed scorn on the surface, but I detected other things too. Worry. Reverence. Pride. Love. He was capable of all of the human emotions he thought himself immune to.

"As for my soul." His grip tightened. "You're deluding yourself if you think I have one of those worthy of you."

"I'm aware of the road you've walked down," I replied in a low voice, careful with my words, tasting them before putting them into the air. "Since it brought you to me by way of kidnapping preceding a forced marriage. I'm under no illusions as to who you are and what you've done." I stroked my finger down his neck then rested it lightly against the bullet wound I'd all but forgotten about.

Shit. We had been traipsing through the forest, having this heavy conversation, and he'd been *shot* an hour ago.

I scanned over his face. He was pale, but that was his norm. Somehow, despite sitting in the sun for hours on end watching me garden, that hadn't added so much as a smidge of color to his face. Not a reliable marker for his overall health.

Though it was incredibly difficult, I swallowed my need to speak more, uncover more of him, share more with him.

"We need to shelve this discussion," I said with a heavy breath.

"Shelve it?" His brow barely rose. It was little more than a twitch, really, but I noted it.

I nodded. "You were shot."

"Not in the throat. I can still speak." His hands were at my rib cage suddenly, a ghost over my torso for how lightly they skimmed me, as if he were afraid to touch me. "I can still take you." He grasped my chin roughly, much rougher than his barely-there touch on my torso. "If I want to."

There was a cruel undertone in his voice, in his gaze. He was implying that this was all teetering on *his* decision. That *he* was in control. But I knew that he was trying to convince himself more than anything.

I knew that there was no controlling this. Us. Whatever this was. If I was able to control it, I would've left with Daisy, risks be damned.

"We need to go back," I protested. "You need to sleep. In the bed. Not on the couch."

His eyes skimmed over my face. Slowly over every inch of it. "No way in fuck you're sleeping on the couch."

I swallowed my nerves. "I won't be."

It was time to be rid of this illusion that we were captor and captive.

We were both captives to each other.

Fourteen

Something had changed with Piper.

She'd let go of all pretenses she'd been trying to hold up, crossed the distance between us and made it clear of her feelings. Of her wants.

For me.

Even after I'd told her the truth. Exposed my ugly, rotting insides to revolt her.

But there was no revulsion. I should've expected that. Piper wasn't capable of the cruelty it took to hear someone's greatest sins and secrets and then shatter them while they're most exposed.

That was my job.

If not that then surely me laying a hand on her sister, then laying my hands on her, especially after learning what a piece of shit her father was, should've swayed her. My fingers itched for my knife. I needed to release more blood to sate my need for punishment of that act.

I rarely regretted violence. Killing. The second you began regretting the souls you took was the second you were walking your own way to the grave. Regret was weakness. Too human.

But touching her sister—the five-foot-fucking-nothing ballerina Piper loved most in this world—was a sin I shouldn't have committed. I wasn't in control then. I'd seen red. I'd seen Piper lying lifeless on the floor.

And then I was across the room, choking the life out of her sister. To punish her for endangering what I held most precious.

It was dangerous. Deadly, even, that I didn't have a hold on the beast inside me during those moments. It was another path to the grave. Piper was my greatest weakness. I was only just coming to terms with that.

My thoughts fractured as the door to the bathroom opened. Piper had been in there, cleaning up, getting ready for bed.

With me.

We hadn't spoken on the walk back to the cabin. Hadn't touched. But I still felt her all over my fucking insides. Her gentle tone like one an animal trainer might use to speak with a tiger that had gone feral.

Except I'd never been tame to begin with.

That's what I was then. Tamed by this magnificent creature delicately padding on bare feet through the cabin that was meant to be her doom yet had turned into my salvation.

She was nervous. I could feel it in the air. See it in the way her body moved, the slight stutter in her step, the downward cast of her eyes, her teeth nibbling the soft flesh of her lips.

Those full lips I itched to feel moving over mine, the mouth I was desperate to claim. Yet those needs were clouded by something wrong, a buzz just under my skin, punishing me for having those needs, convincing me that I wouldn't be able to fulfill hers.

The sheets smelled of her when I'd climbed into them. Floral, fruity, sweet with the faint spice of her sweat. A delicious combination, one I held on to as she traversed the short distance across the cabin.

Her eyes roved over me in the bed, and it took every ounce of control I had to stay still, to keep my expression free of any of the bubbling need that singed my skin.

It was a great effort not to explore the exposed skin of her legs in tiny sleep shorts that were basically panties, a tight camisole showing off peaked nipples that I couldn't fucking stare at for a second longer or they'd be in my mouth, my teeth grazing them over the fabric.

No.

The voice was sharp in my mind.

Resist her.

I'd made the concession of sleeping in the bed because of the determined glint in Piper's eyes when she'd declared I'd be sleeping in it, knowing she wouldn't give up that fight. She was concerned for me. Wanted to take care of me. Never in my life had anyone wanted to take care of me. The feeling was overly warm, uncomfortable. My nature urged me to push her away, hurt her before she could get close enough to hurt me. Strike first, damage her as a warning to show her what happened when she thought she could get close to me.

Two of my baser instincts battled against each other as she climbed into the bed. One itched to claim her, bury myself deep inside her. The other sought to break her, hurt her in a way that would ruin whatever lay between us beyond salvaging.

It took all of my effort to lay still as the bed depressed, my body stiffening as her bare arm brushed across the sleeve of the shirt I was wearing.

I was fully dressed, ensuring my bare skin wouldn't touch hers. Sully it.

I could feel the nerves radiating from her as we both lay there, staring at the ceiling, the closest we'd ever been. Though we were physically only inches apart, the depth of the emptiness inside of me formed a yawning distance between us.

She was also coiled with expectation, waiting. For something to happen between us. For me to cross the chasm and show her affection, prove I was capable of it. I imagined bringing her soft, pliant body into my arms, her head laying on my chest, burying my nose into her sweet-smelling hair. I imagined the honor of her feeling safe enough to sleep there, in the arms of a murderer. And she would. Trust me enough to lapse into a state of blissful unconsciousness

She'd give me that gift without hesitation.

The tension lingered between us, her breathing sparse and shallow, as if she was scared too deep of an inhale might spook me. Her hope was what did it, coming off her in waves, hope that I might be the man, underneath it all, to bring her into some sort of safe embrace.

With a sharp and uncomfortable sensation in my chest that had nothing to do with the gunshot wound, I turned my back on her and went to sleep.

PIPER

It went on like that for a week.

It should've been nice. The truce we made, the truth we shared. The acknowledgement of what we were to each other. The redefining of our roles.

It *should've* been a relief.

Except I felt more on edge than I had since the moment I met Knox. Back then, there was fear, yes. Plenty of that. Anger too. At him for being the omen that signified the end of life as I knew it. He was the villain.

But there was a distance. There was a separation between us.

Now we were closer than I suspected a kidnapper and abductee ever had been. We'd shared our insides, our ugliness. He'd exposed parts of himself I knew had never seen the light of day.

My fingers had been in his flesh, sewing him back together. We slept in the same bed. We spent most of our days together. We ate together.

It was the closest I'd ever been with a man. With a person, for that matter, my sister included. Except the distance between us was wider than ever.

Though we slept in the same bed, we didn't touch. Didn't cuddle. Although it had been expressed that Knox wanted to have sex with me, nothing had been acted on. Not even a kiss.

A kiss seemed so pedestrian, so juvenile. Yet my lips burned with an unyielding need for him. To taste him. I didn't act on it, not with the wall he'd hastily put up, not with the fear of rejection, heartbreak. I had to survive lingering on the sidelines, waiting for him to yank us both onto the proverbial playing field.

We were stuck in a kind of purgatory of our own making. It was utter torture. I was hyperaware of my every movement, every word I said, every gesture. Knox watched me like a hawk, his demeanor locked down tight. He'd gone back to speaking in monosyllabic tones and only when forced. No more admissions came from him. I didn't think he had any left.

Me, I had a few, though. Secrets and scars still hidden deep.

My need for Knox was a living, hungry thing, desperate to consummate ... whatever it was between us.

I had never been afraid to make the first move with men I wanted. Granted, those were never men I really wanted; they were men I talked myself into wanting because they were the appropriate choice.

Not a threat.

Knox was most definitely a threat. What if I reached out to touch him, and he crushed my hand? What if I gave myself over to him, and he crushed my heart?

So we danced awkwardly—or I should say, *I* danced awkwardly since there was nothing awkward about Knox. He was ever graceful in that predatory way of his. Never unsure. Never afraid.

But I could see it, the added tension he carried in his shoulders, the lines of his eyes. And though we didn't cuddle in bed, I'd definitely brushed up against the length of him—by accident—and felt the full width and girth of his need.

He was still recovering from the gunshot wound. I had been worried about some kind of infection setting in, since our environment was not sterile, and I was most certainly not a doctor. He let me look at it daily, change the dressing and clean it out. But not with his shirt off. He would unbutton the top of the button-ups he'd now taken to wearing to expose the area to me, but nothing more.

It was as if he was hiding something from me. I didn't know what. He was a muscular demigod—or devil, if we were going for that kind of metaphor. I knew his torso was carved with muscle because I saw the outline of it. Honed and chiseled to be a weapon, I considered him a work of art even clothed. He definitely didn't have anything to be ashamed of.

Then again, what he'd told me of his childhood—the one that was stolen from him—it could have been something related to that. To nakedness, feeling dirty or wrong.

I'd chewed over that for a long time. Sex very well could be a complicated thing for him. He'd never found pleasure in it, hadn't he said that? From his perspective, perhaps there was nowhere for us to go from here. My need for him might not have been the same as his for me, and I wasn't going to try to sate it if it damaged him even a little.

I'd been mulling over this yet again as I sat in the garden, watching the sun set.

Knox had been on a supply run earlier in the day and had forbade me from helping him with the bags. He'd done it rather meanly, if I was honest. Every interaction we had now had a brutal edge that hadn't been there before. He'd been cold but never cruel. Now he cared about me enough to be cruel.

He didn't want to accept help which would communicate that he was weak.

I rolled my eyes.

Men.

Even though he considered himself to be vastly different from the garden variety male, there were a lot of things that weren't too different at all.

I stood, dusting dirt from my jeans, reasoning that he'd had sufficient time to do all the things he needed to do, without the help of a woman who would endanger his masculinity.

Plus, I was hungry, masculinity be damned. My stomach rumbled as I entered the cabin, and the delicious scent of whatever he was cooking invaded my senses. Mushrooms, onions, herbs. His cooking talents continued to impress and enchant me. Not once had he accepted my offer to cook. He hadn't even responded to my offers, actually. He just gave me a withering glare then turned back to the stove.

Maybe it was a control thing. That's what made the most sense given what I'd learned. But I had secretly liked to think of it being him wanting to take care of me in a way he was capable.

And my secret might've proved to be correct when I saw why he'd been so cagey about letting me help with anything from the supply run.

He'd been planning something. For me.

The bed had fresh sheets on it, crisp and dark-colored, inviting. Nothing like the old, threadbare sheets I'd been sharing with him the past week.

My intestines dropped to my feet, looking at that bed. At the singular meaning those sheets could've communicated. That something was going to happen between them.

My womb clenched at the very thought, nerves, fear and desire a fiery cocktail.

He could've just been sick of the sheets from before. He was a man who liked the finer things, if the quality of his clothing was anything to go by. But my intuition told me that wasn't the reason. Not when combined with what he'd done to the rest of the cabin.

My eyes swept over the table, the vase of wildflowers in the middle of it, the food steaming on plates. Two glasses were full of red liquid, an expensive looking wine bottle sitting between them.

"*You* did this?" I asked, my voice breathy.

I felt as if I'd walked into a fever dream, a fantasy that was too impossible to be real. Could this be Knox ... *wooing me*?

"Woodland fairies sure as fuck didn't," he replied gruffly, puncturing through my soft thoughts like a serrated blade.

I chuckled at the hostile tone, directly at odds with the romantic gesture.

One I had never thought in a million years that Knox would be capable of. It might've been a simple, human, romantic gesture, cooking dinner for someone you were dating in the normal world. But I understood it was something pivotal for Knox. It was him wrestling against all his instincts, his coldness, his brutality, to do something nice for me. To show that he could do this. To show both me, and probably more importantly himself, that he was capable of this.

I fought very hard to keep the tears out of my eyes.

My feet carried themselves forward as I surveyed the plates, the glasses, biting my lip.

"I can't drink that." I nodded to the glass. I didn't want to ruin the moment, but I also needed to share the one piece of myself I'd been hiding. Not exactly on purpose, but I'd been holding back. Was it because I still considered it a weakness and didn't want to show that to Knox? Was it because I was embarrassed? Or was it simply because we'd kind of had a lot going on, and there hadn't been the right moment for it?

A mix of the three, most likely.

His expression didn't change, but I could've sworn I saw something resembling 'male panic' in his eyes—my term for a kind of panic that was reserved for the man who inadvertently said his girlfriend looked fat, accidently admitted he thought another woman was attractive or forgot an anniversary.

That was the kind of flash I saw in Knox's usually inexpressive eyes.

I found it incredibly endearing, and a sign that this man actually cared about me.

That even the villain was not immune to something as simple as male panic. Even brutes feared a woman insulted.

"If it's the wrong kind of vintage—"

"It's the perfect vintage, I'm sure," I told him, cutting him off before he could spiral. Though an evil part of me wanted to watch that. Revel in something as human as rambling from him. But putting him out of his misery was kinder. And despite his penchant for cruelty to me, all I wanted to give him was kindness. To show him he couldn't scare me off. "I'm just unable to enjoy it, since I'm sober. In recovery. Ten years."

Knox stared at me. Clearly, I had managed to catch him by surprise. It was vaguely satisfying.

That satisfaction helped with the nerves I felt while exposing this last soft, vulnerable part of myself.

I tucked my hair behind my ears. "Something I should've shared before now, to be fair, since it's something I like to drop on the first date, but we didn't exactly date, did we? Unless you count dragging me out of Central Park against my will our first date."

Knox's expression remained that blank kind of shock, almost as if he didn't know what to say. "You're sober."

I nodded. "Yeah. It's the family curse. My mother, my aunt, my grandmother. Interestingly, the women in our family are the ones who kill themselves or ruin their lives with booze. Then again, it was the women in our family who had to shoulder nasty, violent men who all but caged them in the house to clean, cook and pop out children. Not that I had that excuse for my problem. I had plenty others, though."

I'd been in the program long enough to poke fun at my faults, my addiction. It was the only way you got through. You carried the anvil of addiction long enough, you'd collapse under its weight. You had to find a way to make it light in order to survive. Or at least I did.

Most people tended to become slightly awkward or uncomfortable when I said I was sober, either doing everything they could not to ask questions or asking far too many. Neither overly bothered me; I knew people's discomfort with my problem was a sign of something they were battling themselves.

I waited for Knox's reaction, more curious than anything.

He stared at me for a few long moments before he took the two glasses and the bottle, moving to the sink where he promptly poured them down the drain before rinsing them with water.

I watched the whole thing, vaguely amused.

"That's rather dramatic," I told him when he turned. "I have the problem, not you. You can enjoy a glass, or a bottle of wine in front of me without feeling guilty."

One moment Knox was at the sink, the next he was on me, his long legs crossing the distance between us in a few quick strides.

One of his hands clutched my hip, the other cupped my cheek. "Your problems are my problems, Piper."

I wanted to roll my eyes, but he was just so intense about it. And the intensity with which he spoke after a week of almost indifference socked me in the gut. "Not this one," I whispered. "And it's not a problem anymore. I can exist around alcohol; you can enjoy it."

His grip tightened. "I can't enjoy something that almost destroyed you."

I smiled. "It didn't almost destroy—"

"It did," he said plainly. "I see past your mask, Piper. I know you. And I consider myself an expert in destruction. I see it. And no way in fuck do I care about booze more than you. You don't drink, I don't drink."

My lips were sealed together tightly so he didn't see them quiver. Not once had I required or expected anyone close to me to monitor the way they consumed alcohol. Sure, at first, I had to be careful who I spent time with. At the beginning, I couldn't be around friends who maybe overindulged a little too often. But again, that was my problem, not theirs. Once I got a handle on it— as much as an addict can get a handle on their addiction. They called it 'in recovery' as opposed to 'recovered' for a reason. It was not a static state, it was a constant, evolving battle. Sometimes you didn't even realize you were fighting it, other times you were doing it tooth and nail.

Once I felt secure in my sobriety, I was fine watching people enjoy drinking. My sister did it often, and though I was jealous of her being able to have a mimosa with breakfast and then switch to coffee without issue, I was glad she could indulge.

If Knox had sat across from me sipping what I was sure was an expensive bottle of wine, it wouldn't have changed the way I thought about him. Wouldn't change my feelings for him.

Though I recognized this as a vaguely toxic behavior, it only served to make me more attracted to him.

It was far too intense, far too codependent. Not healthy. But I found that I didn't want healthy, stable. Not with Knox.

"I'm in ... lust with my kidnapper." I sucked my teeth. No way was I going to use the other four-letter word. It was too soon to say, to feel. "My therapist is going to have a field day with this."

"You have a therapist?" Knox tilted his head to regard me, offering his curiosity freely. And I took it greedily like the gift it was.

It was an effort to keep an easy expression on my face, as if we were having some kind of regular conversation and this wasn't changing the trajectory of my life and rearranging my insides. "I'm a thirty-year-old recovering alcoholic with a fucked-up childhood," I told him with a smile. "I'm a self-care girlie too. And I know that actual self-care isn't just bubble baths and face masks; it's speaking to a professional and getting your head right..."

I inclined my head to regard *him*. "You haven't gone to therapy?"

He gave me a blank look, or what I might've seen as a blank look had I not known him. I now knew how to read the smallest of tells. The slight twinkle in his eye, the twitch in his upper lip, the relaxing of his shoulders—all markers of his version of a smile. He was amused.

"Do I *look* like someone who has gone to therapy?" His tone was the same cool baritone as before, but I sensed only I would hear the lightness in the inflection, the teasing.

It felt like I was the only person who understood a secret language no one else in the world knew.

"Would you be very offended," I whispered, barely able to fit the words inside the room, "if we didn't eat the food that you've likely outdone yourself with?"

Knox's eyes flared as he caught on to my meaning, hearing the hungry lilt to my tone.

"I would not be offended in the slightest," he growled.

A beat thrummed between us.

And then there was a burst, a snapping of that taut tension coiled around the both of us.

Who moved first?

It was me.

It was me who surged forward. If I hadn't, would he have?

No, I knew the answer to that. If I hadn't made a move, he would've stayed, simmering with a palpable lust but never acting on it. Partly because of his trauma but also because he didn't want to tarnish me. He wanted to protect me from himself.

It was that knowledge that made him all the more irresistible to me. He thought himself to be beyond redemption, but the darkest of souls would've taken me long ago, regardless of whether or not I was willing, uncaring of how they would ruin me.

Though he was resisting me, that didn't mean he didn't respond the second my lips crashed onto his.

One of his hands tore into my hair, plastering our mouths tighter together. The other went to my ass, pressing our bodies flush, as if he wanted to meld us together.

His erection pressed into my stomach, large, probing.

I lost myself in the kiss, gasping at the coppery taste of blood entering my mouth that followed a sharp burst of pain as his teeth sank into my lip.

"I'm not going to do this without pain, blood," he warned, his voice thick. He held me tight enough to hurt to prove his point. "I don't know how else to be."

"I don't want you to be anyone else." I leaned forward to lick a trickle of my blood that was staining his lip. "I want this to hurt."

My admission shocked even me. I'd never been into any kind of kink. I was convinced that I wanted tender, soft lovemaking.

Vanilla.

But that had never satisfied me. Deep down, I hungered for something darker, more forbidden. But I'd swallowed those needs because of my past, because of my complicated relationship with violent men.

Indecision was clear in Knox's eyes, as if he were thinking that very thought. His hesitation stung my skin as if he'd slapped me.

"I'm not a victim," I snarled at him. "Don't treat me like one."

That was enough to jerk him out of his stupor. He yanked me forward again, only kissing this time, no biting. But that didn't make it any less violent. There was no room to catalogue the kiss as anything but carnal. There was nothing romantic, soft about it. Not that I'd expected that from Knox.

I wanted real. Wanted to feel the utter brutality, the uncontrollable need he had for me.

His hands fisted my hair, wrenching on it to expose my neck before his teeth grazed my carotid artery. I shuddered at my vulnerable position. Exposing my neck to a predator was submission, wasn't it? Trust?

Not that he gave me a choice.

He just took.

And that's what I wanted.

His lips replaced his teeth along my pulse.

And then he was stepping back, only slightly. Just enough to send a groan of frustration through me.

His eyes glowed with feral need, but his face was an emotionless mask.

"Take off your clothes," he said impassively. The words hit me in the throat.

His order was sharp. No warmth or adornment from him.

But I reveled in the command, in knowing that Knox was going to take the helm, and I could let go of coherent thought and just obey.

Which is what I did.

With shaking hands, I tore off my T-shirt.

"Slower." The word cut through the air.

With great pains, I did as he said, slowing my movements as I unbuttoned my jeans then stepped out of them, all under the power of his intense eyes.

He didn't even bat a lash.

Nor did he speak.

It should've been awkward. Slowly undressing in front of a man with nothing but my roaring heart and rapid breaths filling up the silence. No music. No city sounds, no TV on in the background.

But it wasn't. It only served to make the moment more charged. It could've made me feel like some kind of object, bowing to the whims of a man, yet it didn't. I felt powerful, with more agency than I'd ever had in my life.

By the time I was standing in my bra and panties, I was trembling with need. The bra and panties themselves were nothing special, just simple cotton. But Knox's gaze on the fabric made me feel as if I were wearing the finest silks and laces.

With a long exhale, I reached back to unclasp my bra, letting it fall to the floor. Then I hooked my panties with my thumbs, bringing them down and stepping out of them.

I'd barely done that before he was on me, his hand tagging my neck and tugging me forward so my lips crashed against his once more. His hands trailed down my back, clenching my bare ass, pressing my naked body into his clothed one.

Once again, just as I was losing myself in the world-breaking, chaotic passion of the kiss, Knox detached himself.

"Can I just..." He looked violent. Crazed. Half mad with desire. But also something else, something conveyed by the softness of his tone. He looked almost ... vulnerable.

It hit me in a place that wasn't sexual. In my heart, a place I hadn't thought Knox was able to touch.

"Can you what?" I probed. If he was asking for permission, then surely it must be some dirty, sordid thing that he needed my okay for. And I was ready to say yes to anything at that point.

"Look," he ground out. "At you."

He was asking permission to look at me after claiming my mouth? And after kidnapping me? After stealing my heart and soul and ruining me for all other men?

It should've been a complicated response to his simple question, but it wasn't. I found myself coming to grips with the fact that I might've done absolutely anything he asked, without question if spoken in that tone that stroked me in places no hands could reach.

Instead of answering with my words, I untangled myself from

him. It was immensely difficult because I loved being wrapped up in him, having his body so close.

The room was balmy, warm from the roaring fireplace. And my skin was hot with desire. There were tiny beads of perspiration already covering much of my naked body.

Despite this, my nipples peaked as I stepped back onto the rug, naked, for Knox to look at.

It should've brought forward a healthy dose of self-consciousness. It wasn't easy, even with a familiar lover, to stand naked in front of them without moving, without the fervor of sex or even the distraction of life.

Distracted meant men saw tits, ass, pussy—not always in that order. They did not see ridges of cellulite, extra flesh around the midsection, little imperfections that seemed anything but little to women.

Knox wasn't distracted. Not even a little.

His eyes were rapt on my skin. Every blemish, dimple, every imperfection.

He rubbed his hand over his mouth as he catalogued every inch of me. My knees trembled under the weight of his gaze. It was similar to how he'd looked at me when I'd had the towel on. He wasn't worshiping me, not exactly. He wore the face of a man who was looking at something he wanted to plunder, wanted to brand. But there was also something else. He was a man coveting something he didn't feel worthy of yet held a glint of knowing he was going to take it anyway.

After minutes, minutes of him looking over every crevice of my naked body, his eyes found mine.

"You are perfect," he said, his voice nothing but a rasp.

That was a compliment that men tried to throw around because they felt that's what we wanted to hear, but there was always an emptiness to it. Because they saw what they wanted to see in us, what they wanted us to be, considering that to be perfect. But Knox saw all of me, knew all of me and still considered me that way.

It was a dizzying weight, to be something precious to a man like Knox. I felt something lock into me. Something that told me we'd never disengage clean or without pain. That this wasn't just sex. It was about souls too.

Knox let me walk up to him, but in a way, it felt like I was approaching a wild animal. Every one of my movements had to be slow, purposeful, or else he might've turned on me.

I felt it. Fear. I was afraid of Knox. Not as much as I should've been. Yet that was what drew me to him, that fear. It was what excited me. Made me feel alive.

My hands found the hem of his shirt, but just as I was about to peel it up, he caught my wrists in his grip.

My bones protested at how tight he was holding me, and I forced my breathing to stay steady.

Don't betray an ounce of panic, I told myself.

Looking upward, I met his eyes. They seemed to be black pools of darkness, tendrils of it curling around my skin, sinking past layers of flesh and bone to the very core of me.

"It's okay," I whispered, laying one of my hands on top of his, stroking, coaxing.

He flexed his grip, and I gritted my teeth against the pain. He could've broken my wrist if he wanted to in that moment. Doing that would've shattered me. Shattered all that lay between us. Because though I reveled in the pain that he made me feel, the roughness in which he handled me, the danger I danced by being close to him ... the most precious thing about him was the violence he emanated but never truly released upon me. I wanted to be the one thing that was special to him, as delirious as it was. If he hurt me like he did everyone else, he would no longer be anything better than my father.

I was walking on a knife's edge. We were. One wrong move and we'd sever everything between us.

Knox took an audible breath, nostrils flaring, eyes strained. He was fighting against his baser nature. Or one of them, at least. One that was telling him to hurt rather than open to the chance of being hurt.

I waited.

He let go.

My heart swelled at the trust he gave me, the enormity of the gift that trust was.

Taking a deep breath, I pulled up the shirt.

"Arms up," I ordered, my voice only shaking a little. I knew he caught it. He was watching me like a hawk. Every tell my body had that I was afraid and aroused didn't go unnoticed by him.

Despite his predatory gaze, he complied with my request.

I let out a breath as I exposed his torso. Muscled, chiseled, as I'd expected. The skin was porcelain, flawless.

On his torso, at least.

When I exposed his arms, I saw it.

Scars. Ribbons of them. From his wrists all the way up to his shoulder. There must've been *hundreds*.

Though I knew I needed to be mindful, I couldn't restrain the gasp that came out of my mouth upon seeing them. Without even thinking, I reached out to touch the skin to ensure it was real. It couldn't have been. He couldn't have been sleeping next to me, been curled up with my soul while I'd been ignorant to what was obviously a huge part of him.

Knox stiffened as my hand reached forward.

My fingers hovered a hair's breadth away from the ruined skin when I looked up at him once more. His jaw was as rigid as iron; I could see him clenching it. His chest moved up and down heavily.

No one had seen these scars. I knew this inexplicably. Knox didn't let anyone see what was vulnerable, human about him. He was ashamed. That's why he'd been so intent on ensuring I didn't see this, even when he was bleeding from a bullet wound. This was his secret, his shame, the most vulnerable part of him.

And he was showing me.

"What... Who did this?" I asked him in a strangled whisper. Fury simmered low in my gut toward the beast that was capable of inflicting such pain upon someone.

"I did," he replied without dropping his gaze from mine. His tone was cold. Inhuman. I knew it was because he was protecting himself. He was waiting for me to shrink back in disgust or be scared off.

I looked from him to the scars, taking stock. Some of them looked older, others were puckered and raised. And there were a handful, I was horrified to see, that were red and angry, barely healed.

Recent.

He'd done it while here.

I'd been there, sleeping maybe, and he was cutting through his skin to create more scars.

"It's the only way I can cleanse it," he murmured, watching me. "My blood. Otherwise, the filth builds up."

I nodded, even though I didn't understand what he meant by that. I understood it was related to the abuse in his past, the way the trauma had manifested in making him feel unclean. The result of the assault on such a pure, defenseless body. On an innocent, vulnerable mind. My blood boiled at the visible evidence of what he'd been through, corroboration that barely scratched the surface of how far reaching the talons of his abuse had scraped.

My fingers traveled the small distance I'd put between us. Knox flinched as I made contact with the skin, but he didn't push my hand away. I felt the ridges of the scars, the hardness and softness of the healing skin. I went over them, tracing the shapes with the pads of my fingers, thinking of Knox doing this to himself. Over and over again. For years.

I ached to tell him that he didn't need to do this. Didn't need to punish himself for the sin of being a victim since that was not a sin at all. I wanted to take him into my arms and protect him.

But this was not the time.

He had not revealed this in order for me to take care of him. He needed to see that I saw this and still *wanted* him. That was the thing he was holding on to so tightly, thinking that he was too ruined to be wanted, to be desired.

Once I found my way to his shoulders, I slid my hand to his flawless neck and pulled him toward me.

He resisted for a millisecond, but then he understood my request. His mouth was on mine in an instant. I reveled in the warmth of the kiss. It was edged with desperation, a palpable relief from Knox. It was as if he'd expected to never kiss me again after exposing himself. It was the wall I'd been feeling with him this week, since he revealed himself in the woods. He had been bracing for the impact.

I might not have fully understood this man—I got the sense it would take a lifetime to do that—but I was comprehending that this was the first time, maybe ever, that he'd opened himself up for any kind of pain, and he was expecting to be rejected.

It seemed impossible that a man like him could be hurt, even when he showed me the parts of him that were soft. Because even his soft parts were covered in scar tissue.

There was nothing hotter to me, it turned out, than a monster who needed some humanity.

We made quick work of his pants and underwear, though there was nothing quick about the way I regarded his cock. My eyes went wide as I took in the length, the girth, the perfection of it, standing at attention. For me. I'd never been much enchanted by the male member, finding it ... ugly, for lack of a better word. But this was not ugly. I might've even described it as majestic. With great effort, I ripped my gaze from the member between his legs, forcing it up his chiseled torso to his eyes. They were hooded with a hunger that I felt in my core. My hands landed on his defined pecs, warm, skin impossibly soft. I reveled in the ability to touch him.

"I would like," I breathed against his mouth, "very much if you would fuck me."

His eyes flared, and he let out a hiss. He didn't linger in the shock of my request for long, snatching me up roughly. I wrapped my legs around his hips, gasping as my soaking-wet, bare core ground up against his hard shaft.

I got the sense he was going for the bed, but the second I rubbed up against him, he let out a growl and we descended.

My back hit the cold wood floor, juxtaposed with Knox's blistering hot body pressing into every inch of me, his cock brushing right where I needed it but not entering.

"I'm not going to be gentle, Piper." His face was inches from mine. "I have a need to worship your body, taste your cunt..."

One of his fingers brushed past his rigid length, gliding inside my slick core, making my eyes roll to the back of my head from the perfect intrusion.

They were gone much too soon. I was about to protest when he held them up between us, glistening with ... me. Maintaining eye contact, he put those fingers in his mouth, tasting me.

I squirmed at the intensely intimate act that was easily the sexiest thing I'd ever witnessed.

"Yeah, I'll be *feasting* on that cunt." His eyes were clouded with the storm of his carnality. "I'll worship you." His hand circled my neck. "But my form of worship may seem like a form of torture. I don't know how to be gentle."

His words hit like a whip against my hungry skin.

He didn't want to hurt me. He wanted me. It was painted in the air, it dripped off his breath. But he was battling against his baser instincts, believing himself unable to not harm the things he wanted.

I leaned up, grabbing his neck to drag his mouth down to cover mine, to kiss him brutally, brushing my teeth against his lips until the coppery taste of blood filled both of our mouths.

I licked my lips as I pulled back enough so I could see his eyes.

"I'm not asking for gentleness, Knox," I rasped. "I want *you*."

His body twitched with the words I suspected he didn't consider himself deserving to hear, his expression frosting with animalistic need.

He kissed me again, his hunger for me palpable. My back arched as I urged him closer, needing the connection, that final nail in my proverbial coffin.

Even without it, I was done for.

"Protection," he rasped, poised against my entrance, holding back from sheer force of will. I could see it in his eyes, see it in the cords of his neck, the shallow, rapid exhales and the tension around his eyes.

He wanted to thrust into me. He was wild with need, but not completely. Even then, in his most raw and carnal state, Knox was holding on to control. Reason.

"We don't need it." I was nowhere near possessing any kind of reason or control. My body only knew need. And I needed Knox inside me. Right away.

"We need it," he grunted. His cold gaze battled with the hot need of his nature. Even then, he couldn't let go of control. "I want you, more than anything, but I'm not fucking risking it."

We were poised there, in a moment of wild abandon, yet logic was a cold snake, swirling around us.

"I'm clean," I bit out. "If that's what you're worried about."

His eyes glittered. "I'm not worried about *you* fucking tarnishing *me*, Pipe."

My head cleared slightly as I took in his meaning. "Are you..."

"In this one and only sense of the word, I am ... *clean*," he spat the word as if it tasted bad.

Now, I was a worldly woman and knew better than to take ordinary men at their word with such things. I'd never, not once, risked my body nor my health solely on a man's word. But Knox was no ordinary man, and I trusted him with my body. My life.

We'd established that we were both clean, yet he was still adamant about protection.

"If it's pregnancy you're worried about, that can't happen," I told him, my body still wrought with rapture.

Knox was still stock-still. Not even a slight furrow to his brows.

When I arched my back in order to try to coax him inside, he let out a feral hiss but didn't move. His grip was steel, flexing past the point of pleasurable pain to where it just hurt. A warning.

"I'm not taking even a single chance on *that*," he told me in a tone that chilled my very blood.

Faraway, I stored this visceral emotion that communicated how very strongly he felt about procreation. It made a lot of sense, given his past. His present. I mourned that for him.

"This is going to ruin the moment," I sighed.

Knox pressed into my clit with his cock, eliciting a small groan of pleasure from my mouth.

"Nothing will ruin this moment, Piper." His teeth brushed my neck. "Not even if the sun fell from the fucking sky."

My chest ached as his words stole the breath from my lungs.

Well, there were no other options. He wasn't going to give me what I craved unless I gave him a concrete reason as to why we didn't need protection.

"I had cancer," I blurted. "When I was eighteen. Ovarian cancer. I beat it, obviously. But I can never have children."

Those words said out loud should've sucked all the sexiness out of the room. The word 'cancer' and the explanation that I was barren was a surefire way to kill the moment.

Knox had flinched as if I'd struck him when I spoke, but his cock was still rock hard at my entrance, his body was still coiled with lust. His eyes searched mine, wholly clear of the rabid hunger that had been there moments ago. For just a moment, though.

Then, in one brutal thrust, he was inside me.

He was big, bordering on huge, and even though I was soaking and primed, I hadn't had sex in a long while.

It hurt, but that only served to help take the edge off the overwhelming pleasure I felt as he seated himself to the hilt.

My eyes were locked on his as the world exploded in whites and blacks before he came back into focus in stark sharpness.

"You're never escaping me now, Piper." He didn't move, just filled me. "This," he pushed forward ever so slightly. I clasped his back as spears of pleasure cut through me. "This is everything I couldn't have imagined. And you're mine now." He clutched me tighter. "I'm not letting go. Ever. No one is getting in this cunt." He pistoned forward again, harder this time, rougher. I wanted to squeeze my eyes shut, but I couldn't, I couldn't relinquish eye contact with Knox.

"No one is ever touching you again," he vowed. "No one."

I let my breath out in short gasps, desperate for friction, for the release my body was waiting for, my insides coiling as he spoke.

"You need to say the words, Piper."

The possessiveness to his tone, the ownership in the words... Neither made me recoil, didn't make me grasp for a sense of independence that had once seemed so vital to my identity.

"No one is ever touching me again," I agreed. "I'm yours."

His eyes searched my face, as if he were expecting to find a shadow of a lie there.

He wouldn't find anything. I was his. Forever. Even though such a concept was laughable considering the circumstances, that didn't make it any more or less true.

"Good," he nodded, after finding the sincerity on my face.

Then he began moving, thrusting with such force I saw stars, and an orgasm pressed against my very throat.

The sensation was too much, his size, stretching me to my limits, pain accompanying the mind-blowing pleasure.

I exploded.

Into a million and one pieces.

And I'd never collect them again. Never be able to put myself back together the way I had been before that moment.

Whatever happened in the uncertain and scary future that lay outside the cabin didn't matter.

I was gone.

I was Knox's.

Fifteen

Knox

She fell asleep with my cock inside her.

That was the only way I'd allow it.

Once I'd been sheathed in the velvet of her pussy, I understood. This was what it was supposed to feel like. This was why people destroyed their lives over something as simple as sex. I hadn't comprehended it. I got having a life ruined by the sick desires of others, but I'd never experienced it. That need, that craze. I'd reasoned that the abuse had deadened that part of me, shriveled and defiled it in such a way that I'd never grown a healthy enjoyment for sex.

Not that what I was feeling for Piper was anything but healthy. Her pussy was so sacred to me. I wanted to hunt down every person who had ever been inside it so I could ensure no one else on this planet knew her that way.

Only me.

I'd explored every facet of the sexual experience with cold curiosity, waiting for something to awaken inside me.

When nothing so much as twitched, apart from the need for bloodletting, to get out the dirt that piled up by engaging in such acts, I assumed I was dead.

Then Piper found me and brought me back to life.

I stared at her flushed, exhausted, peaceful face, hair splayed on the pillow, trusting enough to fall asleep like that, with me beside her. Inside her.

It defied natural law, her giving herself to me. That I got her.

My mind screeched with pain, with all the ways I could lose her. Lose this.

No way was that happening.

So I began to make arrangements in my head.

To ensure that Piper would never be anyone's but mine.

Piper

I woke up alone.

My body ached from the exertion from the night before, more sex than I'd ever had in a single night. The best sex I'd had in my life. The best sex anyone, anywhere had had in their entire life. I felt changed from it. Unraveled then put back together in a different way, a way that only Knox had the key to.

The reality of that didn't scare me. It wrapped around me like a warm blanket, even though the bed was cold without Knox.

I got out of bed without bothering to cover myself. A trip to the bathroom was probably the smartest thing to do since I *really* didn't want a UTI, but I changed my course when I saw him on the sofa.

It wasn't a surprise to see Knox sitting there, tense, hunched over, his eyes vacant. I'd expected this. Him to be closed off. I understood it. With someone like Knox, life wouldn't be easy. He wouldn't give in to me easily. Wouldn't open up completely. There were too many demons nipping at his door.

Sex, even the most mind-blowing sex in the world, wasn't a cure for everything.

I wasn't mad or hurt to find him there, to feel the coldness and the distance from him. It was intended to scare me away. Not intentionally, I knew that. It was survival instinct for him. I pushed past it without hesitation, running my hands through the inky locks of his hair. How long had I been itching to do that? I wasn't going to let him erect walls between us. Not now that I knew what I'd been missing out on. It was the greatest treasure to have the ability to touch this man, have his arms around me, be coated by him from the inside out. I wasn't letting that go.

He glanced up, his movements stilted as his obsidian eyes caught me. I didn't miss the way they floated up and down my naked body. It was purposeful, not covering myself. It was my way of showing him I was unarmed, vulnerable.

Though I hadn't had a whole bunch of time to think about what he might say, I had garnered a guess it would be something along the lines of, *This was a mistake. I'm an evil miscreant, and I won't maim you with my wretched soul.* Nobility from the man who thought himself to be the villain.

But that wasn't what he said.

"It can come back," he said.

I frowned at him in question, my hand still in his hair.

He turned in the chair, catching my wrist in his grip. It was tight. Too tight. It wasn't a pleasant pressure and would surely leave a bruise. I ground my molars and didn't make a sound because part of me liked it. Knowing that he wasn't in control around me, that I made him slip.

"The cancer," he said, bringing my wrist to his lips, instantly gentle after the brutality of his prior touch. "It can come back."

He didn't exactly structure it like a question, but it seemed like it was since he wasn't a doctor with extensive knowledge of my medical history.

The panic in the air was palpable.

"It could," I said carefully. "There is a small chance it could. Slightly higher than anyone else without it, but the risk isn't high."

I downplayed it like it hadn't been an axe hanging over my head my entire life. Every physical twinge, every bout of the flu, every test I had, I braced for the bad news. Because I knew that it could happen to me. I wasn't insulated by ignorance, thinking things like cancer happened only to other people.

I was aware that fate was a bitch who'd gifted me with horrible parents, addiction and a genome that tried to kill me. But I also tried not to dwell on those things. Which I was only successful in doing after I stopped trying to drink those worries away. Trying to drown them. I quickly learned that worries could swim, even in bottles of Tito's.

"You need a checkup," Knox growled, hoisting my naked body up against him. With his head resting against my abdomen, his hands possessively slid up the backs of my thighs, kneading my backside.

"We need to get you checked out now."

I wanted to laugh at the urgency, the anxiety in his tone, as if cancer were raging in my body right then, and it was a race against time.

"We don't." I ran my hands through his hair once more.

"We fucking do," he gritted out, his head snapping up.

"I've had checkups," I assured him. "Yearly. Since I went into remission. I keep track."

Knox was watching me very carefully, as if cancer might've just ravaged my entire body at that moment. "Yearly isn't enough. We'll get some more. With the best doctor in the country."

I wanted to smile. Don't get me wrong, while talking about my cancer and about the possibility of it coming back, there were many times when I did not want to smile. Often, I only did so to make my sister feel less worried or because if I didn't smile and laugh, I would've broken down in tears.

But with Knox, my need to smile was not a mask, nor was it a replacement for sorrow. My lips twitched out of a general feeling of warmth.

If you'd asked me if Knox could give me any kind of warmth when I'd first met him, my answer would've been that he could only generate heat inside me if he literally set me on fire. Which wasn't out of the question, after he murdered me, to get rid of the body.

He ended up lighting a different kind of fire in me. My body. Last night. And sure, that was life-altering and mind-blowing. But this gentle warmth, like a mug of tea that was the perfect, cozy temperature, simmering inside of me... That was a lot more profound.

"Sure," I told him. "Once we get out of this situation." I waved my hand at the cabin, a sudden feeling of dread overtaking me at the thought of ever leaving it. I pushed that apprehension down, clearing my throat. "We can go see a doctor to get me checked. It doesn't need to be the 'best' doctor in the country, though. Any MD can read the results of the test."

Knox's gaze hadn't wavered, but I'd seen a slight twitch in his cheek when I mentioned getting away from the cabin.

I wondered if he was reassessing his entire plan. He must've been. The previous plan was to keep me here under threat of death for my sister then deliver me to his boss to be married once I was sufficiently broken and terrified.

I waited for him to speak about the elephant in the room, for him to make pragmatic, realistic plans. I ached for that. For him to take care of this. Give me hope that we had a future.

He didn't do that.

"I'm a monster," he said plainly. "I wasn't born this way, though I know some are. Born without feelings, with a penchant for cruelty. People who dissect animals for fun when they're kids then move on to people when they have the ability to." His eyes bore into mine. "I was made into this. By my childhood and the way I chose to deal with it. I moved away from the sunlight where my scars were visible, hiding in the darkness where I could make more. I've killed people, Piper. Plenty of them. Fathers, mothers, daughters, sons."

He moved from where he had been pressed against my torso, letting me go completely to lean back on the sofa as if to create distance from me.

"Almost all of them deserved it, but they weren't all irredeemable." He never broke our gaze. "Some might've found their way back, might've turned away from the lives they'd been living. What I'm trying to explain to you is that there's no justification for who I am, for what I've done. I don't want you to romanticize who I am. Because that would be a mistake. This isn't romantic. I'm not going to change the way I work in the world. The killer that I am. But for you..."

He leaned toward me, as if he wasn't able to help himself, his fingers barely grazing the skin of my stomach, circling my belly button. Shivers reverberated in my bones from the touch. It was delicate, but it felt like a thousand tiny needles were puncturing my skin. "You are the only person on this earth I become human for," he murmured. "I will always be evil according to everyone else, Piper. You can't change that. Not with your smiles, not with your laughter, your gardens, your cooking, your stories." His fingers dipped lower, slipping into my soaking-wet pussy, making me gasp in pleasure. "Not even with your cunt." He dragged his tongue along my bottom lip. "It's important you know that. I'm a human for you and you only."

It took me a second to get my bearings with his glorious intrusion into my tender insides. He rubbed carefully, teasingly, exquisitely.

With great effort, I took hold of his wrist and carefully pulled, making my intention known.

When Knox let out a low rumble in the back of his throat, eyes narrowing on me, I wondered if he wouldn't take his finger out of me. I wouldn't be mad at it, to be fair.

But he gave in to my delicate request, fingers leaving me empty.

"Take off your boxers," I told him, intending my voice to be sexy and authoritative. It ended up being breathy and thin.

Knox raised his brow at my making the demands, but with an uptick of his mouth that was incredibly sexy, he obeyed, lifting his body so he could take off his boxers to reveal his magnificent, hard cock.

I smiled at him and licked my lips.

He let out a low hiss of breath as I knelt down on the rug, using my hands to push his knees apart.

My hands met resistance as he leaned forward to tilt my head upward.

"No, Petal," he shook his head. "You will never be on your knees in front of me."

I smiled against the feral command, not moving or so much as flinching.

"You get to worship me, I get to worship you."

I saw the ghost of desire on his face, but it was mostly overlayed with hardness. "I do not deserve to be worshiped, Petal."

Though the words speared my soul, I kept my sensual, playful expression in place. This was not the time to heal wounds. To convince him otherwise. It was time to show him.

I lifted my finger to place it on his chest, pushing. "I get to be the judge of that, honey."

He flinched at the term of endearment, his body as rigid as stone. I didn't think my chances were entirely good at winning this fight, but I wouldn't back down.

I was shocked and delighted when, after a withering glare, he let me lightly push him back onto the sofa.

I pushed his knees apart to glimpse his impressive length.

"You know, I made myself come on this very couch." I grabbed the base of him in a firm grip, looking up at him. "Thinking of you. Coming in and finding me. Bending me over." I thought the admission would be embarrassing somehow, but it was liberating to share sensual secrets with Knox.

His eyes were clouded with need, his body taut. "I know," he bit out. "I saw you."

My grip slacked in surprise. Didn't see that one coming. Hot embarrassment crawled up my neck.

"It was the most stunning thing I've ever seen," he continued. "I watched you. From the window."

An admission of his own. Though his voice was strong and masculine, I swore I sensed a little shame in it.

I smiled, my embarrassment gone. "Maybe next time I do it you won't be watching from the window," I told him, feeling bold.

His cock twitched in my hand. I was guessing he liked the sound of that.

"You better do something soon, Petal," he ground out. "Because I'm seconds away from burying myself so deep in you, you'll feel me in your throat."

My insides dipped and my mouth pooled with saliva. I quickly leaned forward and took him in my mouth. Fully.

I'd had intended to go slow, teasing him, torturing him. But I no longer had the patience, the willpower for that. I felt rabid, desperate to show him how much I wanted him.

He was too large to take entirely in my mouth, but I took as much as I could, moving up and down his length, my hand following my mouth, tasting his salty precum.

It wasn't long before his hands went to my hips, and I was up. Kneeling at the feet of a man who considered himself evil, tarnished, had been wonderful. Erotic. Especially since he was the most dangerous man I'd ever encountered. Best of all, though I was the one on my knees, he was the one submitting.

"Bend over," he demanded, setting me on unsteady feet.

I clung to the arm of the sofa, gaze blurry from the rapid change in perspective, from the lust clouding my vision. My pussy had a heartbeat.

"Like you imagined." His voice was so hoarse, I barely understood him.

I did as he asked, resting my forearms on the sofa, tilting myself up to him. He didn't make a sound as he approached me from behind.

My knees trembled when he didn't touch me right away, his penetrating gaze falling upon the part of me I was exposing to him. Presenting to him.

A single finger trailed down my spine, and I shuddered with pleasure.

It slid down my lower back to my ass, delving into the sensitive, forbidden area.

My teeth sank into my bottom lip as he teased that entrance.

"I'll be taking every hole you have, Petal."

My insides lurched at how coarse and crude and brilliant those words were. I'd never done ... that before. I'd been with sensitive, missionary men, after all. And I had convinced myself I didn't want to venture anywhere beyond that.

But I ached for Knox to take me there, even if it scared me just a little. Especially because he scared me a lot.

His fingers resumed their journey to where I was weeping for him, spreading my lubrication up and down.

My body was shaking, already on the edge of orgasm, nervous expectation pulsating through me. Was he going to take me there ... now?

His hands bit into my hips as I forced myself to relax, his cock pressing into my entrance. Again, he teased it back-and-forth with a restraint that I hadn't thought he possessed. I could feel his vicious need to claim me painted in the air.

His grip tightened, and I braced myself, ready for whatever intrusion he dictated.

He slammed into my pussy so hard I saw stars and almost instantly came. I would've, if he kept moving. But he remained still, fully seated, grasping my hips, taunting me.

He bent over, his lips at the back of my neck.

"Will you let me take your ass, Petal?" he asked in a menacing whisper.

"Yes," I cried without hesitation.

I felt his smile as he stayed there, completely filling me, holding me on the edge of orgasm.

Then he was moving, slamming in and out, brutally, painfully, perfectly. I came apart, barely able to comprehend that he was still moving, still fucking me into a second orgasm.

His hands tightened at my hips as he let out a low roar and emptied himself into me. My body shuddered with his pleasure, enjoying every stroke he gave me.

We stayed like that for a while, me clutching the sofa for dear life, Knox still inside me, grip not slackening any.

"Was that as good as you imagined?" His deep voice punctured the thick cloud of satisfaction I was covered in.

I turned around to smile at him, sweat making my hair stick to the side of my head. He was the picture of perfection, glistening with perspiration of his own, hair mussed and his electric gaze on me.

"With you, I cannot imagine the amount of goodness you can make me feel," I whispered, as close as I could be to admitting it.

That I loved him.

Because I was too cowardly to say it out loud. Even with everything Knox had given me, something in my soul told me he'd never say those words to me.

And though I couldn't have imagined how the warmth of this new dynamic would make me feel, that realization kept a chill in a place the sun could never touch.

Knox

She went out for a run.

I wanted to follow her. No, first I wanted to chain her to the fucking bed and refuse to *let* her go out running. Not out in the woods where a rogue tree trunk could trip her and make her snap her fucking neck. The exertion of the run could give her a heart attack. She'd had cancer for fuck's sake.

Cancer.

A foreign invader that was invisible, impossible for me to fight against, that could suck away at her life force. With absolutely nothing I could do about it.

She was suddenly so impossibly fragile, the sheer amount of things that could take her from me making my need to have her in my sight, my hands on her at all times, almost overwhelming.

If I didn't chain her to the bed, then I'd follow her on her run.

It was what I'd intended as I watched her move around the room, tying up her hair, lacing her shoes. I was greedy to watch her, to drink up every movement her body made.

Though it was physically fucking painful for me, at the last minute, I'd refrained following her on her run. I was mindful of just how quickly I'd become infatuated with her. Obsessed. She was suddenly the reason for my inhales and exhales.

Not just dangerous anymore.

Deadly.

Giving her the run alone in the woods was a punishment for myself. A test. I could not give in to this obsession.

I'd stayed, my hands finding their way through her bag, if only to touch everything that was hers.

When I found it, I'd sat there, holding it, chain-smoking until she emerged from the trees, cheeks flushed and looking so fucking sinful I almost had to tear across the space between us to take her against a tree until bark embedded in her back.

Later, I promised myself.

She smiled when she saw me. Easy. Lighting up her whole face. An expression that paralyzed me, freed me of every coherent thought.

That smile. So vulnerable. So gorgeous.

And it was for me.

It was fucking *mine.*

I'd somehow found myself with a woman who smiled without fear, without disgust. For me.

Something cracked inside of me with that smile, opening up a well that I was not going to focus on.

"What is this?" I asked, holding up the small drawstring bag.

Her brows knitted together, smile disappearing. "Were you going through my things?" Her tone was saturated with annoyance. I loved it. Her ability to easily get mad at me, show me her anger without fear of retribution. No one in my previous life dared to show me that. Men who killed for a living were scared to act so much as irritated at me.

But her... My woman wearing flowers and hot-pink yoga pants threw her sass easily and without fear.

My *previous* life.

That's what it was. If you could've called the barren wasteland of blood and corpses a life.

I'd left it behind the second I picked up Piper. I'd never be able to go back to that, not now. Not while blood and oxygen flowed through Piper.

"Yes," I admitted to going through her things without shame. She was mine. That meant everything she owned was mine too. Not healthy nor normal. I knew that would annoy her, put her off—just how intense and unyielding my ownership would be. But I didn't care.

She put her hands on her hips. I wanted to slam against her from behind, seat myself inside of her until she screamed. I'd done that hours ago. But I wanted it again, and to take her ass as she'd promised. My cock swelled at the thought of having her in every way I could. It was a greedy, desperate part of me that would never get my fill of her.

"That's an invasion of privacy." Her tone wasn't as sharp, presumably because she'd noted the lasciviousness on my face.

I was sure my tells were small. I'd schooled any and all reactions my entire adult life. It wasn't something I'd thought I could change, but Piper was changing me. Learning me in a way that no human, not even my brother, had been able to do.

She saw that I was imagining fucking her, and she reacted with a flush to her cheeks, a hitch to her breath, and I would bet, a wetness between her legs I itched to coat my lips with.

"I don't want you to have privacy," I replied, not opening the bag. "I want to know all of you. Every inch."

When she plunged her teeth into her pouty bottom lip, I wanted her to break the skin. I wanted to taste the copper of her blood when I claimed her mouth.

"That's a little toxic," she replied finally.

I shrugged in response. What did I give a fuck about toxicity? Me merely breathing, touching her, fucking her was toxic to her.

"And also incredibly romantic," she added.

"This is not a fucking romance, Petal" I scowled.

My tone was brutal, mimicking my reaction to her words, violent and angry.

She didn't even flinch.

She fucking smiled, crossing the distance between us to smoothly take the bag from my grasp. The brushing of her fingers against mine sent shockwaves to my dick, even though I'd touched and licked and tasted every inch of her. She was different now. Had new sweat covering her body, more life. I needed that.

"I beg to differ," she said quietly. "Hold out your hand."

Though I stiffened at the order—no one ordered me around—I replied on instinct.

She tipped the contents of the bag out, then I stared at what lay in my palm.

Cigarette butts, a bullet, a Tarot card depicting The Devil.

I'd already looked at what was inside the bag. I'd inspected each of the butts, understood that she'd collected and kept them from what I'd smoked, the bullet. This was the bullet her sister shot me with. The one she dug from my skin.

And The Devil.

Kept with things that were mine. It boasted what she thought of me.

That I was evil.

And she wasn't wrong.

PIPER

It didn't bother me like it should've when he revealed he'd gone through my things. That he didn't think it was wrong because he considered me his. And that I had no privacy with him.

Things that should have inherently unsettled and angered me about him and warned of the dynamics of a relationship that was already doomed.

Yet like any and all other behavior that should've and would've served as a red flag with anyone else, it only served to wrap me tighter in a feeling of safety.

"The Devil is a misunderstood card," I told him, taking the card and looking at the illustration. My gaze went upward to where Knox was watching me with an iron jaw.

"It signifies feelings of obsession," I whispered. "Also entrapment." My fingers trailed along the edges of the card. "In the entire deck, The Devil is one of the few cards with two people on it." My fingers ran along the figures on the card. "I believe it means those people are energetically linked. For better or for worse. It's up to us. And if you want to get astrological, which I'm sure you're going to turn your nose up at, The Devil is connected to Capricorn. Which I'm betting you are."

Knox's face remained impassive, neither agreeing nor denying. He probably didn't even know his sign.

I'd ask for his birthday at a later date.

"Capricorns are perfectionists. Can be cold. Can give off a ... daddy energy, for lack of a better term."

My cheeks warmed as I said that, not entirely intending on it. But I wasn't wrong, was I? Knox was ultimate daddy energy.

Knox's brow lifted just a hair, and I swore I saw his mouth twitch.

"I may have daddy issues," I blurted. "A lot of them. But I don't mean it in that sense. I mean it in the sexual sense. I'm just going to stop talking now."

I hadn't intended on rambling for so long about a subject that many people rolled their eyes at and dismissed. Someone so rooted in logic and control didn't likely take stock in Tarot.

"It's silly—"

"Nothing about you is silly." Knox circled my hand holding the card. "Nothing you hold dear. Nothing important to you." He looked down at the card then back at me. "It's you, Petal. You can't just see a Devil card. You make it more." He paused, dragging his thumb along the thick veins in my wrist. "You make me more. And that scares the fuck out of me."

It was as if I'd been punched in the stomach, all the air bursting from me. I knew what an admission that was for him.

Knox.

Afraid. Of me.

"You're not going to break my heart, are you?" I asked, fear of my own clawing up my throat with barbed talons.

"I want to say no." Knox regarded me with a calculating gaze.

"But I can't. My nature is to destroy things. Bury things. I'll promise you that if I do break anything in you, I'll be the one to put it back together."

I sucked in a deep, ragged breath.

No promises.

He could hurt me. More completely than any man would or could.

But I'd risk the prospect of being broken, ruined by him, for the complicated joy of being his. Of him being mine.

————

Knox and I were a couple.

The ground shifted from underneath me. The air changed around me. My heart seemed to beat at a different rhythm.

Knox was a force of nature. He had the power to destroy. That much was evident right off the bat. Just glancing at him on the street, you'd get the inkling he had that power.

But he also had the ability to make things grow.

Make *me* grow.

His presence had always been intense, but the weight of it had become something else. Every inch of my skin felt Knox's attention. He watched me in a different way. As if a hole in the ground might open at any moment to swallow me up.

His hands were almost always on me. Possessive to the point of pain. Not just bordering on toxic.

I knew his attention might've stifled and suffocated anyone else, but not me. I liked it.

We were in a bubble. Stretched to its limit. I could feel it. The tautness of every moment, balancing on a sword, wondering what would puncture it. I could feel the tick of the metaphorical clock that was counting down our time there.

A whole other world was thriving below us. One that included

Stone, my sister—who I worried about constantly and who I considered myself having betrayed for being so happy.

Though *happy* was far too simple and pedestrian a word for what I was with Knox. It wasn't exactly true happiness. The dynamics between us were far too gnarled and complicated and threaded with trauma to make our relationship happy.

But those dynamics were the very things that tangled into the core of me, making me understand that no matter what inevitably happened when the world rushed in, I would always be Knox's.

Though it couldn't be that simple below this mountain. Even without the pressing threat of Stone—which was pretty hard to think of a solution to—I was a kindergarten teacher with a normal life. Knox was a killer and a man who I knew would be unable to fundamentally operate in the normal world. What would introducing him to my friends look like? Dinners? Takeout and Netflix? Could he be satisfied with a life free of what fed the darkest sides of him?

And though I ached to heal him so that he didn't need to feed himself pain and suffering—I hadn't missed two new lines of scabbing over cuts that had appeared on his body—I had to admit that I didn't fall in love with the sides of him that were normal. I fell for him because of his depravity.

It was all much too complicated, and I wasn't brave enough to face it. Instead, I chose to drown in Knox. For however long I had him.

"What would you have done?" I'd asked the night before, tangled in bed, staring at the ceiling, my body aching from the attention of his licentiousness, which was near insatiable.

He'd been denying himself pleasure for years, so he had a lot to catch up on. Not that I was complaining.

"If you had been given the opportunity to pursue your passions, have whatever passes for a normal life?" I continued my question. He always waited patiently in the silences that I put between sentences, a quirk of mine that annoyed previous boyfriends to no end. Not Knox. He gave the impression that he'd wait in the valleys of my words for a lifetime.

"If someone hadn't stolen that future from you," I added through my teeth. I still breathed in venom when I thought of how Knox had been abused. Though I was an expert in knowing no amount of vehemence could change the actions of monsters, especially not dead ones.

It was maybe an unfair question, akin to someone asking me who I'd be if I hadn't had a father who'd murdered my mother. But I wanted to know Knox beneath his layers of coldness, his bloodthirstiness. I understood there was more to him, a never-ending depth.

He ran his hand along my hip. It was colored with bruises the same size and shape of his finger pads, evidence of the way he held me, as if he wanted to imprint his touch onto my bones.

I truly hoped I wore his bruises for the rest of my life. That every day I'd wake up with a mottling of black and blue in intimate places, proof of just how hard he was holding on to me.

I, too, was learning to bathe in his silences before he answered my questions. If he did. He didn't always respond to me. Not because he was ignoring me but because he didn't have words. Usually he did very well by communicating with me through actions.

I thought that he might not answer this time. That I was asking him to be too vulnerable, not just with me but with himself.

"A painter." His voice was ice cold, a sign that he was covering up his true feelings.

My heart skipped at that large victory he gave me.

"A painter?" I repeated, using considerable effort to keep my voice smooth, even.

He nodded once. I waited for more explanation beyond that, but in Knox-like fashion, he didn't give me one.

Which was fine because I had all the information I needed.

Later, we were at the bottom of the mountain on a supply run. Together. He hadn't so much as asked me but made it a forgone conclusion that I'd be coming. That he wouldn't let me out of his sight. I felt the same.

The warning of The Devil card lingered in the back of my mind, about an intoxicating, addicting attraction that would be my destruction.

I had experience with that. I'd conquered addiction before—as well as anyone could. But Knox was no substance, and there was no way I could quit him.

I pushed those thoughts from my mind and made a plan instead.

———

"I need you to put some trust in me," I said when Knox stopped the car.

"I trust you with my life," he replied instantly. He was still gripping the steering wheel. "But not with yours. That's too precious."

My throat seized with his words, both with the value he put on my life and the intensity in which he spoke. It was almost stifling, the new obsession he had with me. Or maybe it was an obsession that had been there all along, a beast only recently let out of its cage.

And I didn't hate it. No. I was quickly understanding that I didn't know what I'd do without it. I was swimming in an obsession of my own.

"I'll be right in there." I nodded to the building. I'd directed him to the nearest big-box store in the small town that was a thirty-minute drive from the base of the mountain. Which wasn't actually that far, considering this was America and we lived on big-box stores, franchises and fast food. Among other things, but those were the things you could rely on, even in the middle of nowhere.

"Alone." I could practically hear his teeth gnashing together. "Not gonna happen." His word was threaded with authority. His word was law.

"If you'll remember, I walked around New York City alone for years before you stumbled upon me," I teased.

"Luck. Dumb luck," he gritted out. "You may have it. I do not."

I smiled, unbuckling my seat belt then leaning over to grasp his face to lay a close-mouthed kiss on his lips.

This was where I lost control. Knox wasn't one for chaste kisses. His mouth plundered mine, a brutal invasion of pleasure to the point that he'd hauled me across the car so I was straddling him, grinding against him like an animal in heat before I knew what was happening.

"You're not going anywhere without me, Petal."

Pulling back and grinning, I rubbed against where he was hard for me.

"Hold that thought," I told him. Then in a rare act of stealth, somehow, I managed to open the car door and jump out of it without Knox stopping me.

I closed it behind me, finger waving to a furious Knox, knowing I had at least a small head start since he couldn't go waltzing into the store sporting a giant, visible boner.

Time to execute my plan.

———

"You are in so much fucking trouble."

I was yanked away from my perusal of acrylic paints and into a hard, furious body.

I smiled, though his tone was meant to be scary and threatening.

"Worth it," I snickered. "And I think I'll like your form of punishment." My body was already melting into him, singing for him.

Knox stilled for just a moment, his grip tightening. "I'll tie you to the fucking bed in the cabin and won't let you come for hours," he whispered in my ear.

My entire body tingled. "Like I said, not exactly punishment."

Knox let out a low sound at the back of his throat. "You will ruin me."

"I'm counting on you ruining me."

Before he could say anything, he looked into my cart and froze. "What is this?"

"Well, you ruined the surprise, which isn't surprising." Fluorescent lighting was no one's friend, but he managed to look like a dark god in the aisle of Walmart, eliciting stares from the people who passed by.

I ignored them without much effort, since he was my solar system, a whole universe in his gaze. "I want you to paint."

I'd managed to find a canvas and an easel. I'd been surprised and delighted they had them in stock along with a scant paint selection that I was sure would do for a start.

"I'm not doing that," Knox's voice was glacial. He was wearing his mask, all affection gone from his eyes, his features turning sharp.

I'd expected that. Him to close down.

"Yes, you are," I returned, pulling myself from his hold so I could face him with my hands on his hips. It felt daring and gratifying to be able to touch him like this in public. To show the world he was mine. Maybe I was a little possessive too.

"It can be my birthday present," I whispered.

Knox blinked once. "It's your birthday?" There it was again, the male panic he'd had the first night we had sex, with the wine.

I nodded curtly, feeling a teensy bit bad for the lie, but it was for his own good. I was using his one weakness ... me. Knox was a lot of things, and he considered himself inhuman, but he cared about me. A lot. He tortured himself over it.

"I'll buy you a fucking diamond," he snapped. "Fancy bag."

I shook my head. "I don't want a diamond or a fancy bag." Though I couldn't help the image of a diamond on my left hand, given to me by Knox.

Such a fantasy could never come to fruition, and thinking of any kind of future, let alone one so normal, was fatal at that moment.

I focused on Knox, the present, showing him I meant business with what I hoped was a dedicated stare.

He didn't look like he was going to budge. I had to pull out the big guns.

I jutted out my bottom lip and made my eyes go wide. "Please?" I asked in a small feminine voice.

Again, more than a little manipulative, but it was for the greater good.

Knox glared at me, gaze unyielding and frigid.

I worried that even the plea hadn't melted him.

Then he lunged forward. "For fuck's sake." He snatched a handful of the paints I'd been deciding between and a fistful of brushes before hurling them in the cart.

"We're going," he ordered, taking hold of me and dragging me along with the cart.

I smiled all the way to the checkout, letting Knox shove all the items on the belt with his surly energy.

I hadn't even noticed he'd stopped or that his attention wasn't on me until he spoke.

"You look at her for a second longer, I'll rip out your eyes and feed them to you," Knox quietly told the man behind me.

I couldn't be sure, but it did seem like the man had been looking in the vicinity of my ass that Knox now had his palm on possessively.

I swallowed my smile as the man paled and looked ready to pee himself.

"Let's fucking go." He snatched up the bags, flattening his hand on my back as we walked out.

"I like shopping with you," I said cheerfully as he glared at two men who dared walk past me.

His eyes darted to me. "Jesus Christ," he muttered.

I wasn't sure what that meant. Maybe he liked it too.

Sixteen

Piper

"It's not your birthday is it?"

I smiled into the canvas I'd propped up on the easel I'd erected after pushing aside the dining table so he could paint in the middle of the room.

Knox hadn't offered to help; he'd just sat on the sofa, chain-smoking and watching me. The windows and doors were open to let in the warm breeze, the only way he'd even entertain smoking inside. I'd urged him to do it, which was against everything I stood for since I'd previously thought it was a bad, deadly habit that shouldn't be engaged in and certainly shouldn't be inflicted upon others.

But now the bitter and acrid smell was intoxicating to me. Comforting. The simple act of him sitting on the sofa, watching me, smoking was calming.

He'd put out the cigarette, his hands on my hips, featherlight. He smelled faintly of tobacco.

"No," I told the blank canvas.

"You manipulated me into getting what you wanted." His lips brushed my neck.

I shivered as they traveled to the base of my ear before he lightly bit down on my earlobe.

"Yes."

His hands went under my shirt, feathering up my stomach and then my rib cage.

"I'm proud," he murmured.

I smiled in surprise. "You're not mad?"

He continued brushing against the ridges of my collarbones, the base of my breasts, but not moving upward to where my peaked nipples were crying out for attention.

"I'm not mad," he replied, a rasp in his voice. "Manipulation and cunning are what you need if you're going to survive me, Petal."

Though his velvet words were meant to be some kind of ominous threat, I didn't take them for that. Knox was so sure that my character would have to degrade if I stayed in any kind of life with him, but I knew the opposite was true.

This was not the time for debate, though.

"What do you want to paint?" I asked, staring at the blank canvas, anxious anticipation rising within me.

Knox's form was tight, coiled. I could feel the discomfort radiating from him. He was in uncharted waters, feeding parts of himself that he'd long starved.

My soul cried for the ways he was damaged. And I vowed that I'd be there to help repair whatever I could and treasure whatever I couldn't.

He put gentle pressure on my torso so I turned to face him, his hands still grazing my ribs. "The most beautiful thing I've ever seen." His eyes ravished me. "You," he added after a heartbeat.

My breath fled from my lungs. He'd called me beautiful, perfect before. But the power in the words, the reverence in them floored me.

I nodded, trying to play it cool. "Okay."

"Naked." He trailed his finger along the hem of my tee, pulling at it to expose my collarbone. My breath hitched at the simple touch.

"Naturally," I said, breathing heavily. "I'll ... go get ready." I gestured to the bathroom, unaware as to why I was suddenly acting so chaste when this man had seen all of me.

So I did what any sane—debatable—woman would do. I went to the bathroom to get naked for her captor to paint her.

***

"Ready?" I asked him, grinning. Once I'd set up the easel, he'd taken over arranging everything else he needed.

I'd watched him with rapt attention, enchanted by him moving in this way. His deft fingers arranging paintbrushes, paints, precisely lining them up beside him. If I got a ruler out, I'd bet they were the exact same distance away from one another, down to the millimeter.

He looked up from his paints.

I saw it. The flicker of uncertainty. Of ... fear? Unease? He was out of his comfort zone. And that satisfied me. That he was willing to go there with me.

He nodded once, curtly, instead of speaking. Once again retreating to that cold part of himself. But his mask didn't hurt me. It didn't fool me.

I dropped the robe I'd been covering myself with.

Knox let out a sharp hiss although he'd seen me naked many times in the short amount of time we'd been ... whatever we were. He'd made it his business to learn every inch of my skin. To own it.

But he still reacted with visceral hunger that I felt in my synapses whenever he looked at me. I wondered how long that would last for. Surely, the shine would come off the diamond, so to speak. Then I thought about my need for him. It surely did not seem to have a bottom. I couldn't even envision myself not reacting with feral desire for Knox.

"Where do you want me?"

His eyes flared with lust as he fingered a brush.

My core hummed, and my nerves tingled with salacity.

His very gaze told me where he wanted me. Riding his cock. Which was very much where I wanted to be too. I'd never felt more complete than when Knox was inside of me. Never felt more healed. And I was never sated either. Despite the amount of times we'd had sex, my insides aching from exertion.

I denied the hungry goddess inside of me, urging for more of him.

Again, Knox didn't speak, he merely canted his head toward the bed, still rumpled and unmade from us. The scent of our coupling still lingered in the air.

I breathed it in as I sat on the bed.

"How should I sit?" I asked, unashamed of my nakedness. I'd always been confident, but the way in which Knox had shown reverence for every inch of my skin made it impossible to feel shy about any of it.

"Show her to me," he commanded, voice as rough as a handful of rocks, grazing my bare skin in the most delightful way.

I knew what he was talking about. It was impossible not to. His possessive gaze was zeroed in on the space between my legs. The core that throbbed for him.

"Make yourself comfortable too," he added. "Read."

I smiled against the command that I might've bristled at a week ago. A lifetime ago. Now his commands made me feel warm, secure. Safe.

I reached over to where I'd placed the book on the wooden nightstand, never able to get more than a few paragraphs in.

"You think I'm going to be able to concentrate on this?" I waved the paperback at him as I settled, arranging the pillows behind me to sit against the headboard, exposing my naked core to him.

"If I'm going to concentrate on this," he nodded to the easel,

"I'm going to need to have you not look at me like you're going to impale yourself on my cock."

His voice was significantly less restrained than it had been moments ago.

My body quivered at his words as I struggled to hold my need back. I opened the book with shaking hands, smiling at him above the pages.

"I can't make any promises," I said seductively. "But I'll try my best."

Veins in his neck protruded as he held my gaze, not returning my smile. I'd never seen him smile, not once, just small twitches to his mouth.

It didn't bother me, him not returning my smile. I didn't need such benign things from Knox. I just needed … him.

A lifetime simmered in the moment we stared at each other before he broke the gaze and dipped his brush into the paint.

"Don't expect a masterpiece," he grunted as I tried to focus on the words in front of me. This wasn't a killer. A monster. Just a self-conscious man.

I glanced up at him, smiling. "I've already got one." Corny, but I wasn't lying.

He didn't respond.

He just started painting.

———

He painted for hours.

No breaks.

Not that that surprised me. Knox was not a man to do anything by halves. My limbs had started to cramp from sitting in the same position, but I didn't dare complain. I would take a little pain to watch Knox like this. Forever. I'd let my bones calcify, my body waste to ruin if that's what he needed. And I knew that he'd never let me wither. That even in his trance, he'd be aware of my needs. He'd asked me intermittently if I needed water, food, bathroom breaks. The smallest shake of my head was all I'd given him, unwilling to puncture his groove.

His brows were pinched in concentration, his hands moving in sure, careful strokes.

I'd never seen his face move that way. Be so expressive. Maybe when he was inside me, but that was it. I watched at first, him being tense, like an animal out of their habitat, unsure of the air, the environment, the threats.

But then I saw it, the muse, the art... whatever it was took over him, and he changed. He was still Knox, but he seemed ... lighter somehow. And heavier too. All at the same time, embodying all facets of himself in a single moment.

Over the hours, I read the same page over and over again. Most of the time, I just watched him.

Until he stopped painting to stare at me.

"You keep looking at me like that, Petal, there will be no more painting, and you'll be on your back, screaming my name, milking my cock."

My body jolted at the words, puncturing the silence I hadn't realized had been so heavy. Need flooded my sore limbs, and I fought not to react. Although I really wanted him to do those things, I wanted him to paint more.

I painstakingly ripped my eyes off the masterpiece that was the killer painting me and stared at the words on a page until he was done.

He didn't tell me he was done; he just stepped away from the canvas, rubbing his jaw and staring at his work with a critical eye.

After waiting to make sure he wasn't just taking a break, I stretched, my aching muscles thankful for the movement.

Knox's eyes snapped up to where I moved, running along the bare skin. His gaze was no longer critical. It was hungry.

"Uh-uh," I waggled my finger at him, snatching my robe and ignoring the groan of my hips as I jumped quickly off the bed before Knox could prowl toward me and make me incapable of coherent thought.

I tied the robe quickly and walked to the canvas, tentatively, as if I were walking toward a bomb.

"Am I allowed to...?" I motioned to the painting.

Knox's posture was ramrod straight. He barely moved his head in a nod that I took as permission.

Gingerly, I stepped around the easel so I could look, suddenly scared that he painted like shit and I'd have to pretend it was good. And I wasn't good at pretending. Knox would see through me in a minute and feign not being wounded. But he would have to be since I'd coaxed him to do something creative and good, and if he got a bad reaction to it, he'd slither back into his dark shell, never to come back out.

I hadn't really put much thought into the carnage I'd wreak if my little plan backfired. Not smart of me, considering what was at stake.

But I needn't have worried.

I blinked when I stared at the canvas, my jaw slackening. I didn't say anything. I couldn't.

The painting was unlike anything I'd ever seen before. I didn't know why I was expecting a simple portrait. Knox was anything but simple.

It was me. Naked and reading on the bed. Painted in exquisite and painstaking detail. I could feel the reverence, the worship he had for my body in it. There was a radiance to me that I couldn't describe, soft pinks and whites merging together to elevate my form. I was perched on a bed, but the walls of the cabin weren't behind me.

It was The Devil card from my Tarot deck, towering behind me, painted in harsh strokes of black and red, contrasting the gentle pastels he'd painted me in. Hovering above me. Casting me in shadow. Swallowing me whole. The Devil was also painted in exquisite detail, almost exactly like the card in my little bag of mementos. How he'd painted it from memory was beyond. It was unbelievable.

I looked from Knox to the painting, tears crowding my eyes. It was that mind-bendingly perfect. That visceral.

"You were born to do this," I whispered, once again captivated by the painting. I was unable to look away from it for too long. It encased beauty and darkness and the harshness of life in a way that I couldn't quite pinpoint.

I knew what the not-so-subtle symbolism was saying. That he was The Devil. The dark cloud casting a shadow over my life and spirit. It saddened me greatly that he saw himself like that, but I understood it. He was saying it in every way he could, screaming it at me through this exquisite piece of art.

What he didn't understand was that the coolness of his shadow was more comforting and warmer than the brightness of any sunshine in a world without him.

"No," he said harshly, yanking at the tie of my robe so it opened. "I was born to do *this*."

He lifted me onto the table that had been cluttered with paints and paintbrushes, both the former and the latter tumbling to the floor as Knox placed me there. He immediately propped my legs up, spreading them and barely giving me a moment to prepare before he dove in. His mouth landed in the perfect spot, and I arched my back, pleasure shooting to my very fingertips. Knox was a wild animal, devouring me without restraint, without respite.

My orgasm washed over me in a wave of pleasure that shrouded me, taking me out of the room for a moment. And a moment was all he needed to remove his mouth, take his cock out of his pants and thrust into me with the same ferocity he'd eaten me with.

My toes curled at the pleasure of his glorious assault. He grasped my hips, towering over me like The Devil in his painting. His fingers were flecked with black and red, staining my bruised hips with paint. I wished the paint would sear into my skin forever.

"I was born to do *this,* Piper," he grunted, not halting his rhythm even for a moment. "For you." He slammed his hips harder to punctuate the point, sending me exploding around him all over again.

The entire time, I stared at the painting, transfixed by it.

I couldn't help but believe I was born for this too. Born for him.

SEVENTEEN

PIPER

My toes curled into the damp grass, head tilted upward at the gentle breeze.

I hadn't been able to sleep. There was no way I could sleep. Not with the energy thrumming through me. Even though Knox had thoroughly tired me out, my limbs heavy and my body sated.

He was sleeping, his arms tight around me like they always were. He didn't exactly cuddle me; he encased me in the vice of his arms as if someone might try to take me in the night.

As someone previously accustomed to their own space, with strict no sleepover rules, initially, I wasn't sure I'd be able to sleep like that. Turned out I could. I slept deeper than I had in my adult life.

But not on this night.

Not with the looming pressure of the outside world, oppressive like a weight in the room, pushing at the walls, the ceiling. Not with the exquisite painting sitting in the room like a living thing, staring at me.

My body was still stained with the paint smeared from Knox's hands, and the paints cluttered on the dining room table. Knox didn't seem bothered when I refused to let either of us shower. He was trapped in a hungry trance for me. As if he needed to fuck himself into oblivion in order to distance himself from whatever had opened up inside him as he painted.

I hadn't complained.

The door to the cabin opened and closed. I'd anticipated it, though he took longer than I'd thought. I'd expected him to wake the second I crept out of bed, his arms locking around me. But he'd been in a sleep so deep, I hadn't roused him when I extracted myself from his brutal grip.

The deepness of his slumber spoke to just how exhausted he must've been. How special it was for him to give away completely to slumber, be that vulnerable with me. It was something beyond extraordinary when a man who defined himself by his strength let himself be 'weak' in front of you.

I'd wanted him to sleep. But my absence must've roused him.

Arms went around my waist as he pulled me to press against his torso, mouth nuzzling into the curve of my neck. His teeth brushed the skin, sending a delicious shiver down my spine.

"I don't like waking up to you being gone."

"I didn't go far," I told him, my body prickling in awareness of the threat in my midst, my skin tight with excitement.

His hold on me tightened. "Anything outside of the bed is far."

I rolled my eyes. "It's a full moon," I pointed out, though I didn't need to since the moon was shining in our faces, refusing to be ignored.

"I like to bathe in the moonlight," I whispered. "Though it's a little more difficult with the city lights battling against it. And I doubt I'll be here for another one. So I wanted to ... make the most of it."

I trailed off as I spoke the words, cloaked in anxiety, stifled by it. It was highly unlikely we'd be there much longer, I didn't think

Stone would allow it. The moon pressed against me, a firm reminder of action required. Change required. The power of it all shifting me.

Knox didn't speak for a long time. I yearned for words of reassurance. For promises. Plans. Anything to give me hope for a way out.

He didn't give me any of those.

"I've always wanted to fuck you in the garden under the moonlight," he said against my neck.

My skin erupted in exquisite chills, and my body buzzed with need at the words.

"Why are we still standing here, then?"

The words were barely out of my mouth before Knox lifted me, spinning me. My legs wrapped around him as he carried me with considerable strength to the garden.

Our mouths fused together, the kiss carnal, animalistic. He didn't waste time, quickly lowering me onto the dirt, prying the blanket away from my naked body so my skin pressed into the soil, the earth, the plants. Soil I'd turned over, life I'd created crushed beneath me, surrounding me, us.

Knox knelt above me, cut against the moonlight in a brutal glow, like some kind of dark god.

His eyes roamed over me hungrily, his erect cock twitching with need.

My own body overcome with desire, I opened my legs to him, willingly inviting his gaze to where I knew I'd be glistening for him.

It felt lewd to be naked out there like that, lying in the dirt. Forbidden yet natural all at once.

Knox looked at me a moment longer before his body covered mine, hooking one of my legs around his hip before he entered me inside.

I clawed at his back and cried out as his brutal strokes didn't slow, as the ground, rough and soft and gritty, pressed into my back.

I thought that he'd already marked me, claimed me as his. But that was it. That act in the dirt, underneath the moon, that was Knox claiming me down to my soul.

In view of the Appalachian wilderness, under the glow of an ageless moon, that was it. The world witnessed to us, no going back. Only forward. Only through.

Whatever darkness might come.

———

Later, once we were sticky, sated and covered in dirt, Knox carried me inside and right to the shower where the hot water cascaded over us. There he took me again, coaxing more orgasms out of my spent body to the point that every ounce of pleasure and energy was drained out of me.

My legs couldn't hold me. Not that they needed to. Knox carried me from the shower back to the bed where he dried me then proceeded to brush my hair. Soft, careful, rhythmic strokes. I drifted off just like that, enjoying such an unexpected showing of caretaking, of love.

It was the best night of my life. I felt loved, worshipped, owned and devoured. Knox took every part of me, and I would've given him more if he'd asked.

It felt pivotal. It felt permanent, something between us. Not that it hadn't been from the start. But there was no denying it after that. My world could not have kept spinning without Knox. I couldn't have breathed without him.

Again, toxic. Completely untenable. Something I should've guarded myself from. But I didn't want to. I wanted to be loved the way he loved me. Too much. Enough that he would've burned the world down for me.

After last night, I was sure that was the way he loved me.

Until I woke up in the cabin.

Alone.

The SUV was gone.

Knox was gone.

KNOX

It was a long way to Maine. Around sixteen hours of driving. Each way. Too long to leave Piper for. But I had no other choice. Not only did I have to get out of that cabin, but I had to talk to my brother. I reasoned that the drive would also serve to give me distance, help clear my head of whatever fucking enchantment had been put over me.

Away from her smell, her smile, her soft body and the little mews of pleasure she made as my lips explored her body. Yes, that would turn me right. Or turn me wrong. Back into the cold, unfeeling, familiar creature I had been quite comfortable being.

That was the only way to ensure my survival. Both of our survival.

That's what I told myself the entire drive to Jupiter, Maine, where my brother lived.

I'd visited three times. Once to deposit the battered body of my brother's piece of shit agent for his punishment, another time to meet Mabel, my niece, and the final time to plant a bullet in the brain of the piece of shit agent who almost killed my six-month-old niece and sister-in-law.

Neither Avery, my sister-in-law, nor my niece seemed scared of me, even when I murdered a man in front of them. Avery was nothing but thankful, welcoming. Mabel, well... Mabel was perfect. The embodiment of it. A small person I would do literally anything to protect. That included keeping my distance from her. Which she didn't seem to understand, since her chubby fingers reached for me whenever they could.

A long time had passed since my last visit. Mabel would look completely different. I ached to see her, watch the changes, see how she'd grown. But I knew the best thing I could do for that child was to be nothing but a shadow whenever possible.

I watched them from a distance for hours. They had their lights on, no curtains. I shook my head at that. My brother was famous, his relationship with Avery Hart had made headlines, was a fucking sensation in the past. Paparazzi had once stalked along this beach in order to get one photo of Kane, Avery and most importantly, Mabel.

My fists clenched at the thought. I couldn't protect them from that. I couldn't kill every asshole with a camera. Couldn't dispose of a body without it never tracing back to me like I had with the piece of shit who'd tried to steal Mabel.

But I hadn't needed to. Their town, Jupiter, had closed ranks. They'd accepted Kane and Avery as their own and protected them from the media. There were still stories, ongoing interest, but no one dared to breach the limits of their beach.

Kane had a family there, friends. Good ones. I'd done the background checks on them myself to ensure they weren't threats.

Rowan Derrick and Kip Godman were threats if they chose to be. Former SEAs. They were honorably discharged, despite some of the Black Ops shit they'd been a part of. They weren't squeaky-clean heroes by any means, which was why I liked them. Because anyone who looked squeaky-clean, like a hero, was likely the worst villain underneath it all.

I shouldn't have even been there, on that beach, watching my brother kiss his wife as she cooked dinner, holding their daughter. Shouldn't have been intruding on the life he deserved, polluting it with my toxic presence, poisonous problems. It had been my job since before I could remember to protect him from everything, including myself. I'd never resented it, not once.

It seemed like he might not have needed me to protect him any longer, and the loss of that role felt unsettling, even if it was a good thing.

Though it wasn't actually the loss of that role that unsettled me. It was the fact that I had come to him for help. Fuck, did I hate myself for it. I'd spent the entire evening on the beach for a reason, full of shame, unable to move toward the house. But I couldn't leave either, not without some sort of guide for how to survive this.

How *anyone* survived this.

I couldn't believe that people who declared themselves 'in love' felt the way I was feeling. How they said things like that then went about their lives as normal, as if they weren't crippled by the sheer weight of the emotion inside them. As if they weren't half mad with their need for her and the need to have eyes on her, hands on her at all times to ensure nothing happened to her.

What I was doing went against every single cell in my body. To be so far from her. Leaving her so vulnerable. But surely, there was no way walking around like I was could've been sustainable.

The reason I came there—beyond the fact that I had no one else to go to—was I'd seen it in my brother's eyes when I'd delivered Brax to him—the fuck who had almost destroyed them, almost robbed him of his pregnant woman and then tried to kidnap his daughter.

But on that day, I'd seen it in my brother's eyes. A darkness that hadn't been there before. A resolution that he'd slay any and all dragons for Avery. I saw the way he looked at her, even before their daughter was born. It was a look that said his heart beat for her. His previously aimless, wild existence had become nothing to him. There was something so fierce in my brother's eyes, I couldn't look at them. Something that stretched the chasm between us even further. He presented to me what I'd never be capable of, and I was glad for it because there was nothing in the dedication in my brother's eyes that was *appealing* to me.

To be so chained by a feeling, by another person, breakable and mortal and temporary, was beyond comprehension to me.

Until Piper.

And there I was, sitting in the sand, unravelling as nighttime cloaked the world.

There was no way I could talk to Kane at that point. That would require waiting until the sun rose. More time away from Piper. I was already at my limit, my skin prickling with unease caused by the distance between us.

Luck, for once, was on my side as I watched the door to the house open and my brother walked through it, coming to sit on the back porch.

It took a second for me to work up the nerve to make my presence known. This would forever change the dynamic between us. I'd kept as far away from Kane as I could throughout my life. So I didn't tarnish him with my presence. Didn't let him into my world. Nothing existed there but death.

But now there was life.

Now there was Piper, bursting from the seams, driving me fucking crazy.

Making me *paint*.

The thing I'd done early on, after my first kill, thinking I was done killing once my abuser was worm food. Thinking *I* could be done. Thinking I could do something more than kill. Be more than a killer.

And it had been proven quickly that I couldn't. That I wasn't normal. I was wrong. Killing was my only option.

I'd pushed away any worldly needs or wants and focused on nothing more than that.

There was no way back to my old life, only forward, so I pushed my way through the sand, up to where my brother sat.

The evidence that the demons of his past hadn't left him showed as he heard my approach. The previously content, relaxed look on his face disappeared, replaced by a cold fury, a readiness to defend and kill that was stony and unfamiliar on my brother's face as he stood, squinting into the shadows that still cloaked me.

He had softened with his wife and daughter, but toward anyone who would cause them harm, he'd become as hard and as brutal as me.

His sense of threat was honed, every limb in his body taut and ready to attack as he recognized a predator was near.

"Easy," I told him as the soft light from the kitchen illuminated my form enough for him to recognize me.

The tension didn't leave my brother's face completely, his brows furrowing in irritation.

"You gotta stop doin' that shit," he growled, hands still fisted.

It wasn't kind, me creeping out of the darkness, given the experiences he'd had with people threatening his family, but I wasn't kind, was I?

"What am I gonna do?" I asked him, keeping my gait slow as I approached him. "Ring the doorbell at two in the morning?"

Irritation quickly left my brother's face. Ugly emotions melted off him as easily as they always had. He shook his head, sitting in the wicker chair he'd burst up from.

I sat in the one beside him, glancing back into the house where I could see little but the large kitchen, a fridge tacked with photos, memories.

"Baby and Avery sleeping?" It might've been considered a stupid question at two in the morning, but I knew my brother and his wife still struggled with sleep.

He nodded, rubbing his jaw, looking tired.

"She doing better?" He knew who I was talking about. Avery had witnessed a man killed in front of her, after believing he was going to kill her and kidnap her baby. Not things easily recovered from.

Kane's face instantly softened with reverence. "She's doin' fuckin' great." Pride and love burst from his tone.

That pleased me. I cared for Avery. As much as I had the ability to. I'd be forever in her debt for what she gave my brother, a life, a purpose, a child. A way out from our wretched fucking past.

."Good." I looked out toward where the ocean was enveloped by the night, listening to the gentle rumble of the waves, wondering if I'd ever have what my brother had. A home. With Piper.

So simple. Yet so out of reach. Even sitting there, my skin crawled with the need to escape, to slink back into the shadows where I was more comfortable. Where I belonged. Alone.

"How do you do it?" I choked the words out as if they were covered in blood and shards of bone. Which they were. I'd wrenched them out of my chest cavity.

Out of the corner of my eye, I saw my brother's head turn toward me. I kept looking out at the blackness.

"Do what?" he asked, what I assumed was a forced casualness in his tone. He knew me, which meant he clocked the difference in my words, the cadence in which I spoke them.

My hands itched for a knife to tear through my skin. I let words do it instead. "Love someone." The words themselves attacked me with pointed barbs, hurting me in the way I deserved for daring to love someone as perfect as Piper, sentencing her to a lifetime with me.

I could fucking taste my brother's shock. He'd known the road I walked. None of the specifics, but he was smart enough to understand what I did. He was smart enough to recognize the cold creature I was. Endlessly, he'd tried to reach out, foster more of a relationship with me, yet I'd rebuked him every time.

Beyond the shock, I could feel the fucker's elation. This was what he'd wanted for me, especially since he got married and had Mabel. Wanted to believe it was possible for me too.

He clapped me on the shoulder, and I was surprised I didn't

shatter into irreparable pieces. "It's not something you do, brother." There was warmth, and yes, fucking joy in his tone. "It's something you ... surrender to." He paused, and even though I wasn't looking at him, I was certain the prick was smiling. As if this were something to smile about. "Know you're not exactly practiced in surrender.'

A bark of laughter escaped me. Nothing like his. Mine was cold and ugly and resentful. "No, I'm not," I agreed, mulling over what he said.

Surrender.

Surrender to Piper. The life she promised. The redemption. At the cost of her soul.

"But I can't," I added. "I won't ruin her life."

It was clear then, crystal fucking clear. The clarity I needed.

I stood, running my hands through my hair, wanting to snatch it out at the root. Wanting to peel my feelings for Piper from my insides. But I couldn't, they were already connected to all of my organs. Everything that kept my heart beating.

"This was a mistake," I said, not looking at Kane, knowing that I'd given him something dangerous.

Hope.

"All of it."

Without waiting for him to respond, without giving him another moment to believe that I was anything more than a subhuman, I walked back onto the beach.

I'd go back to Piper. I'd get rid of Stone. And then I'd leave her life forever. Give her a chance at a happiness that she'd never get with me.

Eighteen

Knox

During the long drive back to the cabin, I'd been filled with a feeling of wrongness. A churning in my gut for every mistake I'd made since I'd brought her here. The biggest one was touching her, giving in to my needs. Yet my steadfast resolve melted with every mile I grew closer to her, hungry, ravenous for the salvation she provided. The knife through my flesh no longer did anything. No release, no purification. Nothing.

She was it.

Could I let her go?

No.

I knew that instinctively. I would have to make her let me go. Make her hate me. The idea sent acid through my chest.

My dread crawled higher up my throat, strangling me with unease, and I knew something was wrong the second I turned off the highway onto the overgrown road that led to the cabin. The overhang of trees that had partly obscured the road had been disturbed. It had rained, and there were fresh tire tracks in the drying mud.

My foot flattened on the gas of the SUV, tearing down the road, my guts in my throat. Something told me I was too late, yet I did something I never did... I hoped. Fucking hoped that somehow, Piper was still there, breathing, battling. Hoped that I could get there to kill every single intruder to our cabin, whoever dared come near my woman.

There were no cars when I pulled up to the cabin, but the front door was wide open, so I knew. I fucking knew.

They'd come. Found us somehow.

And they'd taken Piper from me.

I'd done this. By leaving in the first place. By wishing that she would be rid of me. And now she was. Rid of one horror yet thrust into another that would strip her of everything, if it hadn't already.

My palms slammed down on the steering wheel.

"Fuck!" I roared, unable to keep the cool that had been my trademark for however long. Since I made my first kill, ruined my already tattered soul.

Except it wasn't ruined, my soul. It seemed there was a shred of it left, enough for Piper to hold on to, to fucking own.

My boots sunk into the mud as I got out of the car, not even bothering to draw my gun. There was no one there. Senses honed over years told me that.

Inside, I took in the cabin, the curtains blowing in the crisp wind, the unmade bed that still fucking smelled of her. The flowers in the vase were drying at the petals, about to die, still hanging on.

Her presence was undeniable, her absence fucking visceral.

The painting was gone too. That didn't matter. I had it etched in my brain. Seared into my insides.

I'd find her. I had to find her. Alive. Stone took her, it had to have been him. The loss of the painting meant he'd gained the knowledge that Piper was something more to me. That she was everything. I knew the man well enough to know that he was going to try to prove that only he could own her. He'd use Piper as an example of how no one crossed him.

My fists clenched at my sides, thinking of him laying a finger on her.

If he did, I'd put her back together. And if she was too broken to fix, I'd love every single piece of her till the moment I died. Then I'd tear Stone apart with my bare hands.

My plans for revenge were cut short by a cool barrel against my temple. I hadn't even noted that someone had entered the cabin. Clumsy, too fucking clumsy of me. Not that I was afraid of death, but if whomever this was pulled the trigger, Piper would be fucking doomed.

And that was unacceptable.

"You better be ready to die," I said to the person holding the gun to my temple. "Because I sure as fuck am not."

Nothing, not even a bullet, would stop me from getting to my woman.

PIPER

They'd come in the night.

I hadn't been sleeping. I hadn't slept well since Knox left. Couldn't sleep in the bed that smelled of us. Of him.

I'd been waiting for him to come back. He hadn't left me. Of that I was sure, once the sting of abandonment had worn off. What was between us was real. Was solid.

There was no acting there, there was no escaping or running from it.

Knox had left because he had to. For whatever reason, I didn't know.

What I did know was that he was coming back. I had to trust in him. I'd forced myself to go about my days, not wallowing, not crying. Tending to the garden, cooking, reading, cleaning.

I hadn't thought he'd be gone for long. We had enough food

and supplies for about another week. He would likely not push it that far. Three days, maybe four was what I'd guessed.

Despite my certainty—in the daylight, at least—that he was coming back, night brought with it doubts. Doubts about his nobility, thinking that if he left me, I'd be better off. But those thoughts quickly evaporated. Knox wasn't noble. That's what I loved about him, his villainous soul. And even if he had decided to be noble, he wouldn't have left me alone in a remote cabin with limited supplies and no vehicle.

So that was out.

The more likely reason was that he was off on some sinister, dangerous task. My fear came out of the worry that whatever task he was completing had gone wrong somehow, that he'd been hurt.

The thought of it had my heart hammering, my breath shallowing. Knox was like a marble man, unbreakable in my eyes, his skin too thick, impenetrable, to wound.

But he bled. I'd seen it.

I had not forgotten that we were in the midst of a bit of a pickle with the Italian mafia. If we *were* going to be together, it was infinitely dangerous for us. I didn't think Stone would casually step aside and just let Knox have me.

No hard feelings. I tasked you with breaking the woman I wanted to forcibly marry, and she fell for you instead. It's not a blow to my masculinity at all.

Yeah, right.

People would need to die for us to be together.

Stone likely needed to die for us to be together.

That didn't bother me. I thought it might have, but the people who had to die were the same people who were part of the plot to force me to marry a man decades older than me who just so happened to be the head of a major crime organization and likely was responsible for the deaths of hundreds of people.

I'd lose no sleep over that.

It was Knox.

He was powerful. But he was one man against … however many were in the mob. Fifty? A hundred? More?

He already told me he didn't have friends, allies. He'd have to take them on alone.

So that's what kept me up at night, him going to battle for me, for us, alone.

And when I heard the crunch of tires against gravel, I lost all sense. I leapt out of bed, not even bothering to put on shoes or pants then sprinted out the door in nothing but his tee and my panties.

I immediately knew it wasn't Knox.

But it was too late.

———

They'd left me in a cheap motel room bathroom, handcuffed to the sink, I'd started on the bed, before they left me. My wrists were bleeding. So was my lip. My eye was swollen, and it throbbed like a motherfucker.

I'd fought them. Which maybe wasn't smart, but I'd reasoned that I was fighting for my life. Knox was either dead—unthinkable —or hurt enough to leave them to hurt me. And he'd have to be heartbeats away from death to stop protecting me.

Either way, I wasn't going to go quietly.

The men I'd fought against were much stronger than me and had no qualms about beating an unarmed woman.

I was still wearing a tee and panties. Luckily, the panties had remained intact, even though one of the men—Groves, was his name—had tried to wrench them off as I'd writhed on the cheap sheets of the bed, terrified that I was about to be raped.

But the second one, the one who was quieter, older and likely in charge, had stopped him.

"Stone wants her untouched," he growled, ripping the man off me.

The younger, vile one was breathing heavily, eyes on me, on my exposed panties. "What does it matter?"

The man had let him go. "It's your hands. Then your life." He shrugged.

For a terrible moment, when I thought that man was willing to risk an empty threat and go for me again, my blood sang with real fear.

I exhaled with relief when his eyes darted away, and he muttered a string of curses. "What's the point of this shit gig if I don't get pussy?"

The older man glanced at me, sighing, as if to say, *Can you believe this guy?*

I scowled at him, refusing to engage in any kind of false comradery with my captors. I was under no illusions that this experience would be anything like what I had with Knox. This was different. This was real. The throbbing in my eye, the stinging in my wrists and the bone-deep fear coursing through me told me that.

Before Knox took me, if I was tied to a bed in a tee and underwear with at least one man who had made it clear he wasn't opposed to rape, neither of them shying away from violence against women, I'd likely be a simpering mess. I would've been begging for my life.

But I'd changed in the cabin with Knox. I knew I'd softened him in a way that couldn't be described, and he'd hardened me.

The strength he helped me discover inside myself meant I was able to scowl at both men, refusing to give up my power.

They stopped speaking to me after that, my would-be rapist sulking and scrolling on his phone, the other just sitting there, staring off.

My mind raced with escape attempts, with worry for Knox, wondering about my sister, if this meant that they had found out where we were because of her.

I knew she wouldn't give up our location easily. The vision of how they might've extricated the information from her turned my stomach.

With my mind torturing me relentlessly, I struggled to keep my expression even, to hold the tears at bay. Creating grief in the unknown was a surefire way to insanity. I had to maintain my head. I gathered all of those panicked, painful worries and images, then I shoved them into a closet, bracing the door shut.

It rattled, but it didn't open.

Stone had arrived at the motel after a few hours, wearing a three-piece suit and a sedate expression. As if he were walking into a boardroom and we were having a civilized meeting rather than a cheap motel where he had me cuffed to the bed.

"Piper." His oily gaze traveled up my exposed legs. "Not the circumstances I wanted us to see each other again in."

I pursed my lips, refusing to greet him.

"I'm disappointed," he sighed, unbuttoning his jacket before sitting on the edge of the bed. "I thought Knox was loyal. But it seems he is just another snake who can't control himself." His eyes ran over me again, and I shivered in disgust. "Not that I blame him. I can understand why he thinks you're worth dying for."

My vision went blurry and a low roar erupted in my ears. I struggled to catch a full breath, as if all the oxygen was stolen from the room. "He's dead?" I whispered, forgetting my vow to myself that I wouldn't speak. The two words were rasped out, coated in pain, agony so visceral I could barely swallow a scream.

Stone smiled with satisfaction. The pain, the despair in my breath made him happy. "People who betray me, Piper, do not walk this earth for long." He gripped my neck, hard. I might've focused on that pain if my heart hadn't been splintering in agony right then. "You'd do well to remember that."

I wouldn't cry. Not in front of him. Knox wouldn't want that. I wouldn't give him that. "Fuck you," I spat.

Another smile. "I will be fucking you, Piper," he returned placidly. "The night you become my wife. And I'll ensure that I do it so thoroughly that I remove any trace or memory of Knox that remains."

His cologne was sickly-strong, an assault on my senses, making my head pound. Or maybe that was his grip on my neck. Or maybe it was the world falling apart on top of me.

"Where is my sister?" I demanded. I needed to understand how much pain I was going to be in.

"Safe," he smiled pleasantly. "She's dancing in a production tonight. I hear she'll be wonderful. Such a talented dancer. So much ahead of her. But that future is so fragile. So reliant on her small body staying healthy. Whole."

My mouth went dry. Not from the fear of his threat—I'd been living underneath that pressure for months. But from relief that she was okay. Unharmed. Stone might've been the biggest piece of shit to walk the earth, but I didn't think he was a liar. Killing Daisy was losing the leash he'd fastened on me. He was smart enough to understand that.

Still, the question remained of just how he'd found me. Not that the *how* of it really mattered at that point. He had found me.

I was screwed. I understood that. I was cuffed inside a motel room with men with guns, the mob, guarding me. I didn't have a weapon, no protector, no man who loved me more than anything coming to rescue me.

Knox was dead.

Dead.

I couldn't breathe around the agony of that.

Cold certainty circled around my neck like a noose. There was no escaping this. My fate was sealed. Because Daisy was their bargaining chip. And I'd give up for her. My fight was over.

Don't you dare, Knox's voice growled in my ear. *Don't submit.*

I steeled myself and stared into Stone's brown eyes. "You can try," I hissed. "You and your pathetic excuse for a cock can try. But Knox has ruined me completely and utterly for all men. No matter what you do to me, I'll always be his."

Fury, white-hot, flashed in Stone's eyes, and I thought he might hit me. I wanted him to. I wanted to show him that I could fracture the control he valued so dearly. But he tamped it down, sucking in a deep inhale and squeezing my neck harder.

"We will see, fiancée," he murmured, pulling me so our lips almost brushed. "I know I seem civil now, but I have thought of all the ways I will bring you to heel. I will break you, Piper. And you'll be nothing but my obedient wife. If you're not, I'll throw you to my men and let them fuck all of your holes until you're bleeding from the inside out and begging for death."

His threat was a velvet promise.

Dread wrapped around my heart, squeezing. I knew that threat wasn't empty. He'd do it. And though parts of me wanted to die right then, I didn't want *that*.

One monster or many? Was that my fate?

I struggled to keep my breathing even. There was only one monster I wanted, and he was gone.

Stone stared into my eyes a moment longer before letting me go and standing, putting his jacket back on and smiling at me as if he hadn't just threatened to have me gang raped.

"I'll give you time to consider." He glanced at the expensive watch on his wrist. "Twelve hours should be sufficient. Enough time for my staff to pull together a wedding. Daisy has already been informed that she'll be your maid of honor. We'd hate to disappoint her, wouldn't we? Then she'd feel as if we no longer have any use for her, and that would be terrible indeed."

On that warning, he left.

He stared at the man who had been standing silently in the corner of the room. "No more marks on her face," he barked. "I want my wife presentable. We can cover this with makeup." He waved to my black eye as if he knew what could and couldn't be hidden by cosmetics. As if he had experience in that. I shuddered at just how many brides he might've considered before me.

"But I want her looking presentable. Arms too. They'll be exposed. If she fights, make sure you don't leave any marks." His eyes went to my exposed thighs. "And no one touches her sexually, unless I decide that this wedding will no longer be prudent."

My eyes clouded with tears I refused to let fall. I was nothing but a piece of meat, property, to a man assuming my body was a collection of trophies, his to control.

"I'll be seeing you," Stone promised, looking at me again. "It would be in your benefit to wear white and be smiling at me as you walk down the aisle. You'll like your life. I'll make sure of it. I'll plant babies in you, and you'll be the dutiful wife and mother I know you can be."

And then he left.

Left me with the horrifying knowledge that Knox was dead, and I was destined to marry a true tyrant.

Plant *babies* in me.

I felt triumphant knowing that at least that threat would never find its way to actuality. I felt grateful for the cancer that had made it so my womb would never be home to babies that bastard could use to control me. But that didn't mean I wasn't going to be tortured in all the ways a woman could—and those were many.

I'd lain, staring at the ceiling, mute for hours. It had bored my captors, who had probably been expecting, hoping, for more of a fight. They were bloodthirsty to cause me more pain. Their boss had okayed it, after all.

But I didn't give them a reason. They couldn't cause me any more pain anyway. Nothing would rival the excruciating anguish tearing at my insides

"I'm hungry, and this bitch isn't going anywhere, so let's eat," Groves said.

The older one eyed me with a more practiced eye, as if he thought my behavior was all an act to lull them into doing something just like that.

I didn't care what they thought. I was drowning in my fate. In the knowledge that Knox was gone. The ceiling tiles numbered 148, with three of them peeling, thirteen of them covered with a yellowish water stain. I'd counted and roamed my eyes over every one, cataloguing precisely so I didn't have to think of *it*.

Knox is dead.

Knox is dead.

Knox is dead.

I knew I couldn't give up, that this weakness was essentially spitting in the face of his memory, but I couldn't find any fight in me when I was untied from the bed and carried roughly into the bathroom before they dumped me on a cold tiled floor and refastened my cuffs to the bottom of a filthy sink.

I barely even whimpered when one of them kicked me, hard, in the ribs. There was a loud crack then a feeling of warmth in my abdomen, but I barely noted it.

"Don't scream," Groves hissed, yanking my hair so my face was exposed to him. His eyebrows needed plucking, and he had pockmarks from acne dotting his skin.

Scream? I was already screaming, wasn't I? Maybe it was just on the inside.

"You scream, anyone hears you and calls the cops, it's goodbye little sister." He grinned, showing gleaming white veneers, fingers bending in a daunting wave. "Not before we chop off her limbs. Or maybe we do that and keep her alive? That would be a fate worse than death for a dancer like her, wouldn't it?"

The mention of Daisy jerked me out of my stupor. My mind cleared as I focused on his dull-gray eyes.

"You hurt my sister, and I'll pull your fingernails out and feed them to you," I promised him, my voice cold, unfamiliar.

He laughed, pulling my hair harder so pain exploded in my scalp. "Big talk from someone about to be chained to Stone forever. Which, for you, may not be long." He leaned in and laid a long kiss on my lips, shoving his tongue in my mouth.

I bit it.

"Bitch!" he yelled, rearing back as if to hit me in the face before remembering Stone's instruction.

Another kick to my ribs. More warmth flooding my body.

I hoped that he had punctured something vital. Then I'd die, and Daisy would be safe. But would she?

There was no way to be certain of that. All it would've ensured was that my bright flower of a sister would be utterly alone in a wasteland full of violent criminals. Not an option.

Dying and leaving my sister alone in that world wasn't an option. Even when grieving, toxic parts of me wanted to escape into whatever afterlife Knox was in.

I had to stay alive, I told myself as darkness clouded my vision.

Stay alive, I told myself.

As if I had any kind of control over that.

Nineteen

"You're sure this is where she is?" I asked Joey as we pulled up to some piece of shit motel over the state line in the middle of nowhere.

The sun was just about completely set, the dull glow of twilight doing nothing to improve the appearance of this ramshackle place. Only two cars were parked in the lot—an ancient Ford pickup and some cheap Toyota packed to the gills with crap. No black SUVs to be seen, no sign of Stone's men.

Joey nodded beside me. "I was supposed to meet them here after I waited to see if you turned up," he explained. "Then we'd take Piper back. For the wedding. Or..." he trailed off, swallowing, understanding the energy in the car right now and how fucking loose of a hold I had on the beast inside me.

"Or we'd be burying her body once we were ... done with her," he continued, fear in his eyes. Though there was also a touch of bravery for his honesty. "If Stone didn't like the state she was in, if she refused him."

Joey was right to be afraid. He was just the messenger, and he was helping me, but that didn't make much difference to the urge inside of me to smash his head against the dash until his skull cracked and his brain was leaking out of his ears.

I'd never had so much blind, violent rage inside me before. I didn't lust for blood, gore. Didn't find the need to drag out a death for some kind of thrill. The snuffing out of life, quick, clean, painless—that satisfied me plenty.

But right then, with Piper gone, her fate undetermined, her mental and physical state unknown, there would be no satisfaction until every person who'd had a hand in this was drenched in their own blood. I would tear them apart limb from limb with my bare fucking hands if they took her from me. If they broke her. They were dead, for merely laying hands on her, but the nature of their deaths was to be determined.

Joey was still watching me. I knew he was on guard, waiting for me to strike. He wasn't exactly a genius, but at least he was smart enough to understand that he had been seconds away from death since he'd made his presence known.

I held it together only because he had helped me.

He'd informed me—after taking the gun from my head but still unarming me because he'd rightly deduced I'd kill him on sight— that he was ordered to kill me if he found me.

It was clear that they'd thought that I was long gone, leaving Joey with the shitty job because he was likely suspected of being a weak link. I didn't doubt Stone had seen his real feelings for Daisy and was biding his time to end him. Fuck, he might've been counting on me coming back and killing Joey on sight, doing his dirty work for him, ensuring that the blind loyalty his henchmen had for him in the name of 'family' remained intact.

Joey had quickly said that he was going against Stone, that he didn't give a fuck about his orders. He was *in love* with Daisy. A twist I hadn't seen coming. I'd been sure she was nothing but a quick fuck to him, and he had been a loyal solider of Stone's since he was a kid. That's how Stone made his soldiers, after all. He preyed upon the young men malleable enough to be romanced by the life he promised them. The wealth, the brotherhood, the riches. He got his hooks in them then stole another piece of their humanity with each act of violence he ordered them to commit. He coaxed out a cruelty that was latent in most men.

Joey was softer than the rest, not that I'd paid much attention to him beyond subtly learning him like I had everyone, lest I need to take them down.

Just because he was softer, didn't mean he was weak. He'd killed on command, he'd never once disobeyed Stone's orders, viewing him as the father he didn't have.

But apparently, having your mentor threaten to have your girlfriend killed so he could forcibly marry her sister took the shine off the relationship.

He explained how they'd found me—not from Daisy's trip there. Thankfully, even Joey didn't know about that.

Stone was smarter than I'd imagined. He'd been tracking me since the moment I left the city. Or tried to. I'd dropped off the face of the earth because I was good at what I did. They never would've found me if not for that day. What might've been classed as the best day of my miserable existence. When Piper had been unafraid to expect something more of me, deceiving me by running into that store, knowing my cock was hard, and I couldn't immediately chase her. I'd been off-kilter. Aware of too many male eyes on my woman. Hungry eyes as if they had the right to look at her.

I'd been so clouded by fury I'd used the wrong credit card. Such a pedestrian mistake that could be the difference between Piper's life and death. *My* life and death. The card was one issued to one of my aliases, so it should've been safe, but it was easier for Stone to track. The one I'd been using for supplies would never have shown up on his radar. Simply grabbing the wrong card was my crime. Evidence of just how dangerous this weakness was. How the simplest error had turned our world to fucking ruins.

Joey explained all of this, and how they'd taken Daisy from him two days prior, after they found me and watched us.

Watched us.

He'd flinched when he said that, eyes averted so I understood just what they'd watched. I'd dig their fucking intestines out, whoever had laid their eyes on my fucking woman.

Joey didn't give the information to me up front, smart enough to know I'd kill him the second the words left his lips. I could get the location out of him with a few swipes of a knife, but I didn't have the time for that. Every minute counted when Stone's men had Piper. Every second once Joey informed me Groves was one of the men tasked with taking her. That sick fuck.

I'd stoked the fire within her, the spark of survival, of fight. She wasn't one to go down quietly. Fuck, she might've been brave—and stupid—enough to refuse Stone only to get raped...

"Our life is like living in Alaska," Joey interrupted the thought that had me gripping the steering wheel so hard, I was surprised I didn't pry it off.

I had no fucking clue how our life was anything like living in Alaska, but no way was I going to inquire into his reasoning. Hopefully, he'd shut the fuck up so I could think. Every instinct I had was screaming to run into the motel in case Piper was in there, but I needed to scout the area a little longer, to ensure it wasn't a trap.

"You know, living in perpetual darkness."

I wanted to shake my head. I didn't bother to do that or tell him that was only in specific regions of Alaska, and the darkness wasn't perpetual, it was seasonal. But there was no point.

He was a fucking idiot.

"That's what it is," he murmured. "Not even shadows. True darkness. And I was so accustomed to it that I didn't realize how dark it was until I saw Daisy." He paused, a slack-jawed, dumb look on his face. "Until I saw sunshine."

I didn't respond to him, which I doubt he expected in the first place. I didn't speak superfluously or discuss overly romantic shit.

Though his stupid fucking words struck me somewhere vital. That's what it was. The feeling over my skin that I'd been unable to pinpoint. It was sunshine. After living in darkness for so long.

"We need to go in," I said, taking out my gun then checking the clip and screwing on the silencer.

I didn't need to feel right now. We were going into a situation where I needed to be emotionless, cold. I needed to rip apart anyone and everyone keeping me from my woman. I needed to wear the blood of anyone who had touched her.

———

It was unbelievably easy to find out where Piper was. The proprietor of the motel had informed us that one room had been rented by "your buddies" after taking one look at our suits and making a correct assumption.

Joey was adept at picking locks—granted, the motel lock could've been picked by a toddler—and I let him, although the fire in me itched to kick the door down.

I didn't make unnecessary scenes like that. Didn't let emotion leech through in situations such as this. That was sloppy. That was how mistakes were made.

The door inched open, and my heartbeat slowed. My mind cleared then I entered, ready, desperate to find my woman, unharmed.

But the room was empty.

Well, not entirely.

The bed was mussed. The piece of shit headboard was scratched with marks made by what I assumed were handcuffs.

And the room smelled of her. And of blood. Peaches and old pennies.

A sickening combination.

My throat shrunk to half its size as I tightened my grip on my piece.

Joey didn't speak, just nodded his head to the closed bathroom door I'd already spotted but had been unable to make my way toward. Frozen. I'd never been frozen with fear in my life. Not even while facing the man who put me on this path to begin with. Who abused my brother and I, had ruined countless other childhoods with his perversion.

Not then, not ever.

Until that moment.

Until I smelled Piper and blood and stared at that closed bathroom door. It was Schrödinger's cat—a thought experiment that illustrated how a being could be in two states at once, both alive and dead. Fate was linked to a random event that may or may not occur.

Behind that door could be Piper's brutalized, bloody corpse. Or she could be alive, waiting for me. With fire still burning in her eyes.

If I didn't open the door, I could continue entertaining the thought that Piper was alive.

If I did open the door, she might be lying dead on the cheap, cracked tile.

Standing there, I observed my greatest nightmare and singular salvation simultaneously.

I knew Joey's eyes were on me. He was waiting for me to take the lead, and my pause was a sign of weakness. One I couldn't afford right then.

It was the hardest thing I'd ever done, taking a step toward that door then turning the knob to potentially reveal Piper's lifeless body.

The coppery smell of blood intensified as I turned the knob and switched on the light to the small room.

My own blood roared through my body as I took in her form, huddled on the floor, motionless, bloodied, beaten.

I paused for a second, just a second to envision the ways in which I would torture those who dared touch what was mine.

All I took was a second, though. Because I saw the gentle, slow rise and fall of her chest, and my heart continued to beat, my world continued to spin, and I had a reason to exist beyond vengeance.

My feet took me to her, and I gathered my world in my arms as tenderly as a savage like me was capable of.

But I was glad. In that moment I was glad for every bit of brutality I'd gained in my life, the skills I'd amassed which would ensure I'd avenge her to the highest possible degree.

Piper

"Petal."

The voice was gentle.

Impossibly so.

I must've been dead, then. Because though I recognized that voice, there was no way the owner of it would be gentle. It wasn't in his nature.

"Petal."

There it was again. More of an edge to it that time. I felt a sensation on my body. Light at first then firmer.

My body throbbed as I heard a metallic click followed by instant relief from aching wrists as they were freed from the handcuffs.

Then there was a warm, hard chest. The smell of spice, earth and *him*.

Knox.

Panic forced me up to the surface from wherever I'd been drowning.

My eyelids were impossibly heavy, so it took every ounce of strength I had to open them.

It was Knox. I was in his arms, the watery-yellow light from the lamp in the bedroom of the motel room illuminating him. He was a shadow against that light, harsh edges etched in fury as his eyes traveled over my face.

I searched his cheekbones, his smooth jaw... No bruises. No blood. Only slightly bloodshot eyes, his inky hair more mussed than usual. He was wearing a suit, open at the throat, showing off the taut protruding veins in his neck.

"You're alive," I croaked.

His eyes flared at hearing my voice. "And so are you. You're going to stay that way," he ordered. "And every man who did this..." he stroked his finger down my tender face with an impossibly delicate touch. "They're going to die in the most painful way possible."

My body chilled at his words, hearing the killer lurking beneath them.

"Turn your fucking back," he snapped at someone. I was confused as to who he could possibly be speaking to; I was still in a daze from the experience, from preparing to die, wanting to die, thinking Knox was gone yet seeing him there now.

I let him gradually move me to where he reached into a bag on the rumpled bed that assaulted me with memory, shocking me into an immovable state. That was the bed I was almost raped in. That was the bed where Stone had threatened me, where he had informed me triumphantly that Knox was dead.

My limbs turned to stone then began to tremor as if an earthquake were shaking my very foundation.

"Petal."

His voice was no longer gentle. It was a cold and sharp blade cutting through my haze, the heavy memory of—minutes? Hours? —ago that caused my heart to thunder like a racehorse through the delicate cavern of my chest.

I blinked him into harsh focus. His face was etched in harsh lines, his eyes electric, nostrils flaring, a crease in the center of his brow. A picture of cold fury.

He didn't say anything, just let me hold on to his form, his face, his scent like a port in a storm. All I could pull in were shallow breaths.

"Hands on my shoulders," he ordered, his voice a strange mix of tender and brutal that I'd never heard from him.

Confused for a second, I realized what he meant when he knelt at my feet, a bunched-up pair of sweats in his hands—my sweats, I noticed dazedly. I did as he asked, balanced unsteadily on one foot then the other as he threaded my feet into holes like I was a child before pulling the pants up my bare legs.

He did it slowly, his eyes honed in on my inner thighs, where there were small but unmissable fingerprints from Groves trying to hold my legs open.

His hands had stuttered, just for a second, but I'd felt the world tilt as the energy of his body completely changed.

He was robotic as he settled the sweats onto my hips.

Knox thought I'd been raped. He'd found me chained to a sink, beaten and in my underwear, with fingerprints on my thighs. It made sense.

"Knox," I began, wanting to reassure him that that didn't happen, since he looked like he was a man unhinged. Beyond anything I'd ever seen.

"Go to the next room," he ordered the person I totally forgot was in the room, the one who hadn't uttered a single word during our exchange nor made a single sound. "They'll be coming back, so I want you to alert me if it's before I can tend to Piper."

Though it seemed impossible for me to be able to tear my gaze away from Knox, I had to see who he had trusted enough to bring with him.

I frowned as I took in Joey's face, pale and serious.

That tore me completely out of my haze.

"Daisy!" I yelled, or I tried to project my voice as loud as possible, cold dread clutching at my windpipe. My voice was scratchy and hoarse.

I watched his jaw harden and fury paint his face. "She's alive," he told me quickly. "But they have her."

"Then you go get her," I ordered through gritted teeth.

"Petal," Knox murmured.

My gaze darted to him, my heart skipping a beat again, seeing that he was alive and there. My joy held fast, but it didn't win in the battle over my concern for my sister. Who was currently completely unprotected. "Don't *Petal* me," I snapped. "You're here to presumably kill his men—"

"Not presumably," he interrupted, his words harsh as a lashing.

I recoiled at how ... unstable Knox was. Upon first glance, he had seemed placid, in control. But I could feel the fury radiating off him. See the way he held his limbs, the tic in his jaw, hear the feral edge to his tone, no longer smooth like a honed blade but serrated and sharp enough to do damage, to shred.

"Okay, you're here to kill them in a horrible, painful way," I relented, not showing my unease at his raw emotions. "But that means that Stone will eventually get word of that and Daisy..." I sucked in a sharp breath, wincing as the simple motion sent spears of pain through my injured ribs.

Seeing my discomfort, Knox's hands flexed as he lifted them toward my ribs, curling and unfurling them into fists as he set them there for a second before ever so soothingly pulling up my shirt to expose the mottling of redness.

He didn't make a sound. He didn't need to. His wrath was a physical thing, trailing around my injuries, featherlight across my skin.

I yanked my shirt down. We didn't have time for this. I didn't look at Knox. "You need to go get her," I repeated to Joey. "Since I'm guessing your presence means you do actually love her and are against Stone using her life as a bargaining chip."

"Nothing is going to happen to Daisy," he vowed, suddenly seeming older and more badass than he had during our previous meetings. Him being a badass in front of Knox was akin to a puppy growling in front of a roaring bear, but I got the energy.

He loved her.

That was good.

"I'll believe it when I see it," I ground out, pain making my voice catch. I'd used up a lot of my strength doing so much yelling. "You're going to get her."

Knox's arms tightened around me, despite seeing the pain likely on my face, feeling it in the tension of my body. I knew he needed to feel me, grip on to me like I was *his* port in the storm.

"Enough, Piper," he barked, his control fraying. "We'll take care of Daisy later."

I gave him a cold look. "No, you'll send Joey to do *it now.*"

Knox searched my face. He was the man who knew me better than anyone else, who understood me. And I understood him. He wanted Joey there to presumably look after me while he tortured and killed the men.

He wanted to shield me from whatever he was going to unleash on them for marking me. And he was determined to get his way. He was used to that. No one challenged him. Especially not when rage was simmering in his bloodstream, seeping from him. Not now when he was a paladin with a singular goal: vengeance.

No one, that was, except me.

I watched him battle, his jaw twitching from the force he was exerting to keep himself locked down. I hadn't looked in the mirror, but I guessed I looked bad.

"Outside," he roared the command so brutally, it made me jump. Granted, one was bound to be a little jumpy after being kidnapped—for real this time, not whatever Knox had done to me —almost raped, beaten and handcuffed to a sink.

I didn't look to see if Joey obeyed his command, I couldn't take my eyes from Knox. I'd truly believed he was dead earlier, so I was afraid he was some kind of mirage. The attachment I felt to this man was nothing short of unhealthy. I didn't want to breathe air where he didn't exist. I didn't want him out of my sight.

I guessed the feeling was mutual.

I heard the door shut, relief racing through me to know Joey had left.

"No one is allowed to mark you but me." Knox's voice was low, desperate as he ghosted his hands over every throbbing mark on my face, picking up my hands as if they were made of tissue paper before tracing the red, raw, angry marks from the handcuffs.

"The fact that I left you unprotected so they could do this…" He looked down at my wrists, rage strangling his words.

"This is not your fault," I told him gently.

His eyes once again roved over the throbbing marks on my face, as if he was concreting them in his memory, for him to revisit when he wanted to engage in emotional self-flagellation.

"Yes, it is," he scowled. "I left you thinking you were safe without me, but…" He trailed off again, as if he kept losing his train of thought. Very unlike Knox, who calculated and measured every one of his words before he even spoke them.

"I must make them suffer."

The words were pulled from the very reaches of his insides, sending a cold prickle up my spine.

There had always been the background knowledge that Knox had killed. Not even background knowledge, he'd come right out and said it. Multiple times. I'd never been in the presence of a killer, unless you counted my father, and he hadn't killed yet. Although he essentially had. He had killed my mother long before her heart stopped beating.

I abhorred violence and violent men because of my childhood and also because violent men were despicable.

Yet I'd fallen in love with Knox knowing that, not even squirming at him openly telling me he killed.

And I was there in front of him, listening to him muse about the ways he might torture those who'd hurt me. *Torture*. Something I also abhorred, as did most sane people.

Yet my stomach did not turn, my soul did not flinch in front of the cold certainty of what Knox was going to do.

"Making people suffer does not change anything," I motioned to my hands, to my face, to my body.

To my immense surprise, Knox flinched as I gestured to my bruised torso.

Flinched.

As if looking upon my body *hurt* him.

When he opened his mouth, I gingerly pressed my fingers to his lips. They were so soft despite all the harsh declarations coming out of them.

"I know that it's not as easy as that for you." My gaze never left his. The fury and hunger for violence swirled within his irises, a living thing, separate from the facets of Knox I'd come to know. The Knox who put wildflowers in a vase, who painted me in pastels, who cooked me flavorful feasts, who gave me seeds to grow a garden.

Who seeded something inside of me that grew and bloomed where he'd thought he could only make things wither and die.

"I know that's an impossible thing to ask you, to not kill those men—" I continued.

"I will do anything you ask," Knox interrupted me. "But not that. You will not get in the way of my revenge, Petal."

I licked my chapped lips, throat suddenly dry as I realized I hadn't had a sip of water in ... how long?

Knox noted this and immediately stopped his menacing, threatening dance to direct me to the small fridge in the room—surprising that it had one—where he found a bottle of water he uncapped then passed to me. He did this while keeping one hand on me at all times, as if he were afraid I was going to fall off the face of the earth if he let me go.

I greedily sipped the water, all the while feeling more and more in love with the caretaking side of Knox coexisting right alongside the cold-blooded murderer.

Once I was done, I looked up at Knox, who was cataloging my bruises. He capped the water bottle then lifted up my shirt once more to regard the swelling on my stomach.

His fingers brushed the skin in a barely-there touch.

"We need to watch for internal bleeding," he said, his voice chilly. "Might've cracked some ribs, though there's nothing to be done about that except time. And blood." He glanced up. "No more of yours will be spilled. But don't ask me to take *this* without punishment."

It was as close to a beg as I'd ever get from him.

I stroked his cheek. "Don't ask me to put your vengeance before my sister's safety," I pleaded.

I saw the change in his eyes. Not before the battle, though. This was someone who had previously defined himself by not caring for others, not having a weakness. I was asking for him to show what he perceived as weakness.

It made sense that it would be a battle. I worried he simply wouldn't be capable of it. Not in the face of the brutality I'd endured. I knew that woke something primal in him.

After a long pause, he nodded. "I'll send Joey to get her right away."

My body sagged.

I leaned up to kiss him on the lips. Gently.

And he kissed me back. Gently.

"But that doesn't mean I'm not going to kill them with my bare hands."

Although I thought such a gesture was impossible minutes ago, I smiled against his lips. "I wouldn't expect anything less."

———

It was somewhat of a dilemma as to what to do with me once Joey left. Knox didn't want me anywhere near what he was about to do. But he also didn't want to let me go.

His hands were on me every moment, moments we knew were scant. I wasn't sure how long ago my captors had left for dinner, but they were likely due back any moment. We had rented the room next door, situated in there waiting. Knox's eyes remained firmly on the window that opened to the parking lot, watching for headlights to illuminate the dark room.

He was coiled, tense, had retreated back behind the façade of the killer he wore so well. But he hadn't retreated completely. He cast concerned glances my way every few seconds.

"Where did you go?" I asked, a question that had been bubbling around in my mind for a while now.

He didn't look at me, clutching the ragged curtain. "I went to Maine."

I frowned, thinking about the distance he covered and how it explained why he was gone for so long.

"My brother lives there," he continued.

His brother. The one other person he said he cared about.

"I went to him for ... help."

His voice was strained, fractured. Mingled with coldness and vulnerability

"Help?" I repeated. I couldn't fathom Knox asking for help. What a huge battle that must've been for him. He would've had to abandon all of his pride, the story he told of himself being unbreakable, in order to ask for help.

"I don't know how to walk this path, Piper," he said looking back to the window. "I don't have the parts for it. I—"

He was cut off by the lights that passed then pulled into the parking lot.

My body strained with tension, both of us silent as doors closed.

Muffled male voices and laughter sounded as the door next to us unlocked, opened and closed.

"Stay here," he demanded, not waiting for me to speak, not looking at me. He just left.

———

It was quiet. However he did it. I barely heard anything beyond a small muffling of a shout and a thump.

That was it.

I was wringing my hands, sitting statue-straight on the bed, unable to move, though I longed for a shower to wash off the filth and blood. I used the restroom because the cramp against my stomach felt more to do with nature than man at that point. And on top of the shit sandwich of a situation, I'd gotten my period. Another fun little tidbit about being barren... You got to keep all the horrible things that show you're fertile except you're actually not.

I'd gotten a tampon from the bag on the bed, a bag of clothes and toiletries Knox had had the presence of mind to grab from the cabin. He'd not only understood that we wouldn't be going back there but he'd had hope that he'd find me, and I'd be alive to use the contents of the bag.

I wasn't sure how long it was supposed to take. Knox had wanted to punish—read, torture—those men for hurting me. How long did that take? Probably longer than an hour.

It had only been a handful of minutes.

That felt like eons.

I worried for Knox, though I didn't doubt his ability to go up against two men in the state he was in, fuming with a kind of rage that I hadn't known existed outside the animal kingdom. But I was still aching from thinking he was dead. I didn't love the idea of him risking his life so readily after so recently coming back to me.

Then again, I reasoned this was only the beginning of Knox risking his life for me. Two men were the appetizer when you considered the behemoth we had in front of us.

I jumped at the sound of a door opening and closing, scuttling back on the bed, ready to fight my way out of this as the predator in black stalked in my direction. It took me a couple of seconds to realize it was Knox, not one of Stone's henchmen.

My eyes cast over him, looking for any injuries, any obvious harm. There was none. His hands were white, pristine, not even a speck of blood that I could see.

"It's done?" I asked, surprised.

Knox dipped his chin in confirmation.

He then prowled toward me. Though I knew the threat was gone, my heartbeat didn't steady as I reflexively backed against the wall.

Knox caged me in.

His hands landed on either side of my head, and his body pressed against mine, his face hovering inches away, eyes landing on my bruise for a long moment before making true eye contact.

I winced at the abyss I saw in his gaze. The emptiness quickly retreating but first showing me a glimpse of who he turned into when he was killing.

Killing.

There I was, with a man who was the embodiment of violence, who had presumably just killed two men. Two very bad men to be sure, but he had snuffed out their lives.

Did that change how I felt about him? Did it kill any love inside me?

No.

The answer came within a second of the thought popping up in my mind.

No.

Nothing would ever stop me from loving this damaged, dangerous, deadly man.

"I need..." His tongue ran along his front teeth.

"What?" I asked immediately. "What do you need?"

He shook his head as if he were trying to banish thoughts, images. "This is when I would ... clean my blood."

This was when he'd score his skin with a knife. Purge himself. Hurt himself. As punishment for what he'd done? For who he was to his core?

I didn't want to shame him for his coping mechanisms, but I greatly wanted to end the act of Knox hurting himself. Adding to an already overabundant collection of scars.

I licked my lips. "Can I offer you another option?"

My pulse thrummed, and warmth crept into my limbs. Need. It seemed impossible for me to have this feeling given the events of the past—however long it had been—but I did. I had a desperate feeling to feel alive. To be full.

Knox's eyes widened a smidge, the tension in his jaw intensifying at my words.

"Piper," he warned. "Do not offer something that you are not ready for in order to try to protect me."

I reached up to cup his jaw. His body was a statue under my hand from the force he was using to keep himself still.

My other hand, rather crudely, went to cup him where he was already rock hard.

Flutters stirred between my legs.

"I offer you everything," I whispered. "In fact, I demand that you take it. I demand that you take me so you can erase every touch from those who weren't you."

He jerked at my words, but he didn't take a second to ask if I was sure. His mouth plastered to mine, and I hungrily sank into the kiss. Into him.

"They didn't rape me," I said, disengaging from the kiss with great effort.

Knox searched my face for a lie then nodded quickly. He didn't visibly relax, but I swore I saw a wrinkle leave the corner of his eye.

"And, uh, one more thing," I added before he could kiss me again. "It may make you rethink what we're about to do."

He clasped the back of my neck. "Nothing could make me rethink what we're about to do, if it's within your consent."

My body seared with need for him. While in the midst of his animal state, still establishing consent. So hot.

"I'm, I've, uh, got my period." I was irrationally embarrassed about a normal bodily function.

Knox froze then blinked once. "Does it make it uncomfortable for you?" he asked practically.

I shook my head. "Not at all. It's just ... messy."

Knox showed his teeth in an expression that certainly could not have been described as a smile. "You think I'm scared of a little mess? A little blood?"

His hands slowly, gently went to the waistband of my sweats, keeping his eyes glued to mine, searching for any kind of negative reaction.

I knew this because for the first time, his touch was hesitant, waiting. I could see that he was holding himself back.

And though I was overcome with yearning for him, I was thankful for the slower pace. My body was ready for Knox, but my mind was not quite there. I was still rattled, my edges frayed, my fight-or-flight response still in place, still recovering. Then there was the physical pain I was feeling. Tamped down somewhat by painkillers Knox had given me before he'd left to ... take care of the men.

Sex wasn't the most sensible thing to do right then. There was a laundry list of other, safer, more practical things to do.

But my soul needed that connection, to feel alive. Encased in Knox.

So though I was tense, I let Knox's hands venture into my

sweats.

———

"What happens now?" I asked.

We had showered, after we were done. He'd carefully washed my body then catalogued every one of my wounds with a precise eye. Nothing needed any extra care beyond time. He'd cleaned my raw wrists with antiseptic then carefully rubbed cream on them, his fingers shaking as he did so. With rage.

I was wearing my own clothes that still smelled of the simple soap I'd washed them with in the cabin. I swore, I scented the moonlight, the pine trees, the wildflowers. I longed for the place I knew was lost to us. If not forever, for a long time.

Because there was a fight ahead of us.

Knox didn't answer, just continued brushing my hair, strokes precise, tender.

"What happens to Stone now?" I asked him, unable to stew in the uncertainty anymore. "He isn't going to just give up."

"No," Knox agreed. "As long as he lives, he will hunt you."

Unease burrowed under my skin at his words. The cold certainty in them.

"So what now?" I probed again. I trusted Knox. With my life. But I couldn't sit with the proverbial wool pulled over my eyes and just wait for him to take care of things while I sat there wondering about what the future would bring.

"He will die," Knox said as if it was obvious.

I stared at him. The man who loved me with a darkness that engulfed me wholly. That wrapped around me like a second skin. The man who would and had killed anyone who hurt me. Who walked this earth now with the sole purpose of protecting me.

So yes, *of course,* he was going to kill the head of an international crime organization to keep me safe.

TWENTY

KNOX

I didn't have friends. It wasn't smart in my business. Beyond that, I just wasn't capable of forming those kinds of connections. I had begrudging acquaintances who were terrified I'd kill them if they didn't act accordingly and then targets whom I quickly killed.

No one I trusted with my life, let alone Piper's.

Except for my brother.

My *married* brother with a baby daughter.

No fucking way would I involve him in this, put them in danger. Driving to Maine had been a stupid fucking mistake, so I had surveillance installed all over his house to make certain I wasn't inadvertently tracked there.

I'd gone to great pains to ensure that Stone didn't know of my connection to Kane, but I knew if he looked hard enough, he'd find it. There was no way I'd point a needle in that direction.

I only had one choice.

And it wasn't a comfortable one. But Piper needed to be somewhere safe while I ended this. There was only one place, two people

I considered capable of keeping her safe. If I wasn't killed on sight, that was.

"This is a nice house." Piper craned her neck to get a better view of the architecture. I had my eyes on the very discreet security cameras I knew had followed our every move since we'd approached the gates.

My entire body was on alert, tense. All of my instincts were shrieking at me. I was ready for an attack at any moment, and it was taking all of my effort to park the car.

Piper was unaware we had just pulled up to the house of the most dangerous and notorious hitman in the country. Doubtful anyone would've expected a hitman to live in an affluent suburb in fucking Connecticut.

Piper was talking about the wisteria and the charm of the house.

Only she would call a hitman's house *charming*.

Despite my unease, I was almost overcome by my love for her. This person who had been kidnapped, beaten and threatened with rape, yet only twenty-four hours later could smile when talking about fucking *flowers*.

Her hand rose to the door handle as I pulled the car to a stop. I caught her before she could exit.

She immediately looked at me, her cheeks flushed from my touch. Despite the overall situation, my cock swelled. A simple touch from her did that to me. The way Piper's eyes lit up, her body leaned toward me, opened for me. My gaze stuttered on the angry swollen bruise on her eye, the split lip, recalling the purple-black spots I knew lay underneath her white, cotton blouse.

Fire crawled up my throat as I reminded myself why I was risking this. To get my revenge.

"The people who own this house are not friends." It took immense effort to keep my voice flat. I wasn't going to scare her by telling her who they really were, but I needed her to be mindful. "People in my business don't have friends." I glanced up to see the door already opening. Hopefully, he wouldn't shoot first and ask questions later. "But you will be safe with them."

This was an unannounced visit. Surprising people like this wasn't wise, but I was desperate. And I was more than happy to risk my life for Piper's safety. Though this man had few morals and killed without hesitation, I knew he wouldn't kill Piper without reason. Though he had plenty of reasons to kill me.

She licked her lips, and I followed the entire journey of her perfect, pink tongue. "I am safe with *you*." Her statement was firm, argumentative. She thought we were coming here for help; she didn't know I planned on leaving her behind.

I caught hold of her hand, bringing it to my mouth, relaxing somewhat with her skin at my lips.

"Yes, you are." The lie singed my tongue. "Stay in the car," I ordered, then I got out, Lukyan's eyes watchful as I rounded it, going to Piper in the passenger seat, who smiled and waved at him.

I caught the slight twitch to his eyebrow, surprised that she was smiling and waving at him. That she seemed happy, normal, utterly stunning... And she was with me.

His posture was tense as I approached, and I knew he was armed, ready to fire if he so much as didn't like the way my lips moved.

My expression was, as always, carefully blank.

"Lukyan," I greeted.

His eyes were chips of ice, his dark brows raised. "You must be entirely fucked if you're coming here, uninvited and unannounced. With a civilian." His eyes slid to the passenger seat again.

I hated his eyes being on her. It went against everything inside of me to have a man like Lukyan—a man like me—touching her with his gaze.

"I came to ask a favor," I replied, voice tight. I was unaccustomed to asking for help, and it was physically painful. Admitting weakness in front of a threat such as this went against all of my instincts. But for Piper, I would've done anything. For Piper, I would've begged at his fucking feet.

His left eyebrow shot up. Then his gaze returned to the car, where I heard the telltale sound of a door slam.

"Hi," Piper greeted cheerfully, her hand slipping into mine with ease while the other stretched out to Lukyan to shake his hand.

Of course. Of fucking course, she didn't listen to me. She was far too stubborn for that. Not afraid of me. And I'd liked that. Fucking loved it. Only then, I wished she was at least a little bit goddamn afraid of me.

"I told you to stay in the car." My grip on her hand tightened to the point of pain, but she barely winced.

She gave me a megawatt smile. "I don't do what I'm told." Her hand was still outstretched. "I *love* your house," she spoke to Lukyan then. "You have to tell me about how you maintain such a lovely garden."

Lukyan looked at Piper, examining her black eye, the marks on her wrists where the handcuffs had rubbed them raw. The blemishes on perfect skin that still haunted me even though the ones who'd put them there were rotting in a cheap motel room.

Because the man who ordered her suffering was still breathing air.

Lukyan took it all in, Piper, her state, my presence. I saw him putting the pieces together.

I watched him on the precipice. Of killing me despite the audience, despite Piper's warm smile. That's what his true nature hungered for. And he was a man who rarely deprived himself of that.

My body was nothing but a taut fucking wire in those handful of moments, Piper's hand in mine while my fingers twitched for the gun in the holster at my shoulder.

It would be the smallest tell, enough for Lukyan to decide to kill me, scant seconds for me to decide to kill him first. In front of his home. And then we would've been shit out of luck.

I squeezed Piper's hand even tighter as I waited for Lukyan to make a decision.

When he put his hand out to shake hers, I had to tamp down the beast inside of me roaring at his touch on hers. I ached to rip his fucking arm off.

"You'll have to speak to my wife about that," he replied smoothly. "She's the green thumb. I just kill everything." His eyes gravitated to me for a split second, and for an insane moment, I wanted to laugh. "I'm Lukyan." Surprisingly, he offered her his real name.

The moment he let go of her hand, my lungs began working properly again. "Won't you come in? Elizabeth is inside, and I'm sure she'll be delighted to talk to you about the wisteria while Knox and I discuss ... other matters."

His threat was clear, even if I was the only one who could deduce it. We were not out of the woods. Or at least I wasn't.

Entering the house wasn't a surefire guarantee that I would exit it alive. But it was a risk I'd take for Piper.

I'd die for her in a heartbeat.

Though I was hoping it wouldn't come to that.

I had an ache for something unfamiliar.

A life.

With Piper.

It was fucking ironic that I was walking into the home of the deadliest man in the country—myself excluded—in order to attempt to make that happen.

PIPER

I hadn't known where Knox was taking us. We'd spoken little since his declaration last night. We'd left the motel—sensible, considering we'd lingered too long next door to two dead bodies Knox was responsible for—driving for an hour or two before Knox checked us into a moderately nicer hotel off the highway.

He'd taken me urgently once more until my exhausted body had lapsed into a deep and dreamless sleep.

It surprised me that I didn't have nightmares about what happened. Maybe my brain knew that the nightmares were not over. Save all the falling apart for when we were safe. If that was ever going to happen.

I sensed it. The tension in the air, a knowing deep in my marrow. Knox had come to 'save' me, but the battle was far from won, the story far from over. I was a sucker for a happily ever after. In fact, I refused to consume any art that didn't promise that. But I had a terrifying premonition that this story, our story, wouldn't have one.

I tried to keep that panic at bay, choked down food that Knox had ordered for me at a diner, had let us sit in complete silence, eating.

He had watched me intently, waiting. He knew it was unusual for me to go so far inward. I could sense his concern, almost as palpable as his ownership, the ferocity simmering underneath his skin.

It had taken the drive to Connecticut for me to find my trademark optimism. We'd stopped at a gas station for me to pee, and I'd bought two matching keychains.

When I handed him one, he stared at them as if I were presenting him with a severed body part instead of a kitschy keychain.

"They're souvenirs," I explained. "Every good road trip needs one."

The slight narrowing of his eyes communicated that he was worried I might've gone completely insane. Which was fair enough since I didn't think any of our trips should've been immortalized with tacky keychains since the first one was a kidnapping, and this one was a journey toward some sort of battle to the death.

Nevertheless, I ignored him, taking the keys from the ignition so I could thread the keychain into them.

I put mine around the handle of my bag.

I needed something tangible, something unthreatening and real to ground me. To provide evidence that this trip existed, that Knox and I existed, even if it was a gaudy keychain.

I mourned the loss of the painting that they had taken along with me, never to be seen again.

It was so precious, so pure. A piece of Knox's untainted soul immortalized in art, now soiled by the grubby hands of Stone's men, lying wherever they'd deigned to discard it. Like it was trash. Not the single most priceless item on this earth.

Luckily, I was distracted by the charming house we pulled up at, the incredibly handsome man who had emerged from it, and the intense energy radiating from Knox.

I understood that the man, Lukyan, was dangerous. You could see it. Feel it. He was older than Knox, silver threading through his close-cropped, midnight hair. A small gathering of dark stubble covered his square jaw. He was dressed impeccably in a suit that was quite obviously tailored to his large, imposing frame. This imposing energy was quickly counteracted by his wife joining him outside.

She was small in stature, delicate, striking with soft features. Her hair tumbled down her shoulders, and she was wearing an exquisite sundress covered in lemons—quite obviously designer. Her heels were as well.

I suddenly felt shabby in my jeans and hot-pink sweater with the glaring shiner that I'd poorly covered with makeup.

She didn't look at me as if I was beneath her, though. Instead, she'd taken a glimpse at my eye, smiled warmly then invited me in for tea.

"I'm Elizabeth," she said as we entered a grand foyer with fresh flowers and a whole wall of ... birds. Birds in frames.

Dead birds. With colorful, exquisite feathers and interesting shapes. An odd décor choice for an otherwise traditionally decorated home. The sight and the presentation of such glorious creatures trapped in a frame in their death, never decaying, was eerie, sending an unpleasant chill down my spine.

I was instantly curious to hear the story behind those birds, to hear the story behind Lukyan and Elizabeth. I knew it must've been interesting. Though Knox and I were embroiled in our own story at the moment.

I'd never seen Knox tenser than he was while in this house. Which was saying something. He was not pleased to be here, that much was clear. I wondered why he'd brought us here. I kicked myself for not asking more questions and for once again being on the back foot, scrambling to make assumptions on a scant amount of details.

This man, Lukyan, was obviously an acquaintance of Knox's. Presumably another member of the underworld yet pledging no allegiance to Stone since he didn't kill Knox on sight. They weren't friends. Cordial enemies was the vibe I got. My molars ground together in irritation at Knox not preparing me better.

I hid that well, though, since sulking would do no good.

Plus, it felt nice to be in what passed for a normal situation for once. Engaging in pleasant, friendly conversation and being offered tea. Even if it was a thin veneer of normalcy covering whatever was happening here. It was a sojourn from what awaited us, so I needed to enjoy every second of it.

"Knox," Lukyan's voice punctured the conversation Elizabeth and I were having, and if possible, Knox grew even more tense at my side.

"Let's let the ladies have their tea while we have a cigar," Lukyan suggested without warmth. "For old times' sake."

Though I didn't know the dynamics between the two of them, I could discern that it would not be a friendly cigar. There was an underlying animosity between the two men that went beyond the fact that they were both apex predators. History, not good history, lingered between them.

Yet here we were.

Knox's hand, which had been resting at the small of my back, moved to grasp my hip. Tightly.

He paused for a second, the tension in the room reaching a crescendo, my heartbeat roaring in warning that something was on the edge of happening.

Would they get out guns and just start shooting? Surely not. Yet I noted the way Knox's body angled slightly in front of mine, as if he was waiting for that exact thing.

But then Knox let me go.

"Yes, let's." He nodded.

Then he dropped his hand and walked away, not looking at me.

Knox

Lukyan closed the door, but not before I heard Piper's laughter carry through the house. Only she would be laughing with a stranger married to one of the most dangerous men in the world. A woman who I knew had become dangerous in her own right. I might not have had friends to drink and share idle gossip with, but word of Elizabeth and Lukyan had reached even my ears. The piranha brought down by his prey.

"Drink?" Lukyan offered once we entered the office, decorated in dark browns, a wall of books behind the large mahogany desk.

I hesitated. I didn't want Piper to taste it on me afterward, but fuck, I needed something to take the edge off.

"I'm not going to poison you," Lukyan said over his shoulder, misinterpreting my silence. "If I planned on killing you, you'd already be dead."

"Consider yourself that talented, do you?" I asked, not moving, not blinking.

"You're on my property," he reminded me. "Where my wife sleeps."

That said everything. His wife was his greatest treasure. And when it came to her, he was indomitable.

I understood that.

I took the drink he offered, sitting at the other side of his desk in the chair he nodded at. I was being deferential through gritted teeth. Lukyan saw that, and I knew it surprised and delighted him.

We weren't exactly adversaries, but we both waded in the underworld with reputations for our vacant souls, our kill counts. We had always operated under the assumption that one day we might be ordered to take out the other.

It had been a foregone conclusion. Until Lukyan went rogue and decimated everyone who had previously employed him, unraveling the entire Russian mob.

For his wife.

Which was why I was here. He'd managed to do the unthinkable with no allies.

He didn't speak when he sat. He waited, watching me, the low murmur from his wife and the slightly higher pitch from Piper the only sounds in the room.

"A woman has made the ogre human, I see." When he finally spoke, amusement danced in his tone.

"Not quite," I answered, sipping my drink. I reveled in the rich fire traveling down my throat.

His fingers thrummed on his tumbler. "Enough to have you sitting here. Asking for help, I assume."

"No." The insinuation that I needed *help* keeping my woman safe damaged an ego I wasn't sure I possessed until that moment.

Weakness.

That's what I was showing.

Something deadly in my life.

Yet I didn't hesitate when it would keep Piper safe. I had no ego when it came to her.

"I don't need help with my task," I stated evenly. "But I cannot take Piper with me."

The thought of being without Piper after everything that had happened to her sent my blood boiling, but I had no other choice. I would not risk another mark on her skin, any more harm coming to her. She needed to be as far away from this, from me, as possible.

Lukyan was not a man prone to surprise, but I knew I'd shocked him with my unspoken request.

Though he'd only met her a few minutes ago, I knew that Lukyan was smart enough to deduce that Piper was *my* greatest treasure.

"You trust me to keep her here? Unharmed?" Intrigued, his eyes narrowed on me as if I were a fucking insect under a microscope.

My fingers curled into fists as I nodded once, violently.

"You are going to punish those who marked her, I assume?" he asked instead of offering any inkling of whether he would keep her here or not. He was going to torture me with that. It was his way. He could not provide kindness without cruelty. Though it infuriated me, I understood it. If he had come to me with the same situation, I never would've let him through the door.

Before Piper, at least. She wouldn't have allowed me to keep someone on the doorstep with a bruised woman, even if that someone was the most dangerous hitman in the country.

"I'm going to take down Stone and everyone who is loyal to him." It was folly, telling him my plan. Lukyan held no loyalties, but I knew he collected favors. It would be a big one he'd collect indeed if he were to inform Stone of my plan and whereabouts.

"No small feat." He sipped his drink.

I didn't respond to that.

"And you expect to come out of it alive?" Again, the mirth in his tone was clear.

"I expect to accomplish my task," I told him, gripping the tumbler so tight I feared I'd shatter it.

I'd accomplish my task. Whether or not I lived afterward remained to be seen. But I knew that there was no way I'd take my last breath until the threat against Piper was bleeding out at my feet.

Lukyan nodded as if he understood the sentiment behind my meager words. "What would you like me to do with her, if you don't come back?"

I was surprised. He was agreeing to keep her here. It was my last-ditch attempt, and I'd expected it to be much more difficult, thornier than this.

"I will make arrangements for her and her sister." I didn't let my relief show. "To go back to their old life."

"You think she'll just go back to her life before this?" He studied me, leaning back in his chair.

"She'll have to." Poison ran through my body instead of blood. I leaned forward, elbows on my knees. "You'll take her?"

I didn't beg. Wouldn't beg. But that was pretty fucking close.

Lukyan let me stew in the unpleasant feeling, likely entertained by my discomfort. "Yes, I'll take her," he eventually replied.

I didn't show my relief, just sipped my drink.

Piper would live, I told myself.

That's all that mattered.

PIPER

Knox didn't come out of the cigar meeting looking at all relaxed. In fact, he walked toward me like a man walking toward an executioner.

The sight of him sent ice through my limbs. I understood that things were happening. Big things. He was planning on taking down the head of an international crime organization in order to keep me safe. I had already tried to argue against this, but he wouldn't be swayed. And logic dictated that this was the only way that we'd ever actually be able to be together. It was the only way I could go back to my life. If that was even an option after everything I'd been through.

It didn't mean I had to like it. It didn't mean that I didn't have a cold pit at the bottom of my belly that made my skin itch.

The home was expensively appointed with rich colors—purples, deep burgundies—with oil paintings, candles, dim lighting. I felt like I was in an English castle.

We were drinking tea from intricate teacups, eating fucking Madelines.

The woman in front of me was interesting. She was slight, pale, fragile. But fragile like a stick of dynamite might've been. Vulnerable yet dangerous. I already knew the man, Lukyan, was. He walked and talked menace. It might've set my teeth on edge had I not already cut them on Knox. Regardless, it didn't prevent me from feeling a prickle of fear in his presence, despite his polite greeting.

He was a man in the 'business.' The business of killing, I guessed. I couldn't be sure. Some kind of criminal. One who'd amassed considerable wealth.

They emerged from the hall not smelling of cigars but of whiskey. That surprised me but didn't anger me. I even liked the smell of whiskey on Knox's breath when he laid his lips on my neck.

He'd pulled me away from the kitchen where Elizabeth and I had been preparing dinner. It felt foreign to be doing something so … normal in the midst of such chaos. But it was nice. I needed something to busy my hands. Elizabeth spoke little, of benign topics, studiously avoiding our abrupt arrival, acting as if we didn't just turn up on her doorstep. She didn't ask about the bruises either.

"I'm going to ensure that Daisy gets word to you as soon as it's safe," Knox said once he'd dragged me off, his voice low.

I blinked at what he was saying. Definitely not what I expected, even though my worry for Daisy had been pacing at the back of my mind at all times, like a caged tiger.

"Once it's appropriate, you'll meet up with her and Joey," he continued, voice strange and tight. Distant.

A lump of dread formed in my throat even though he was telling me things that should've made me happy.

"You're leaving me. Here," I deduced though it didn't take a rocket scientist to understand.

"Yes." He tucked my hair behind my ear. He had his mask in place, as it had been the entire visit. He was edgy, stilted, on guard.

The intensity of it was comforting yet also pinching too tight, bordering on painful. But that was how I liked it. I liked it immensely, seeing that outside of the cabin, he still had that feeling for me. It wasn't born of the surroundings, the situation in the cabin, the dark magic of the woods.

But my soul grieved through the pulsating energy of loss as he was saying goodbye.

"You're going to be safe here," he continued, never taking his eyes from mine.

My own eyes shifted behind him, to where Elizabeth was moving around in the kitchen, engrossed in her task. To where Lukyan was making no effort in hiding that he was watching us with a stare that could not be described as *friendly*.

Prior to this entire situation, that stare would've almost made me pee my pants, avert my eyes and run away. But now, I met the gaze levelly, without fear, communicating that I had tamed my own predator and wasn't scared of other housebroken ones. His wife was baking *cookies* for fuck's sake.

After a beat, Lukyan seemed to sense I wouldn't scare like the general public did. The side of his mouth lifted, he nodded subtly to me, then he turned to his wife, pulling her into an embrace.

My attention went back to Knox, who had been watching me the entire time.

"There's only one place I'm safe," I told him. "And that's with you."

His gaze didn't waver, didn't so much as twitch, but his grip on my neck tightened.

"That's the one place you'll never be safe, Piper," he rasped, all intense and foreboding.

I huffed in his face, rolling my eyes. "We're going to agree to disagree on that. I've made my choice. It's you." I was determined to show him how serious I was.

He was still entrenched in the worry that he was going to taint me, ruin me. Not enough to let me go, thank God. He wasn't that honorable.

I saw his jaw flex at my response. "In order for you to be safe, I need to take care of this."

He didn't elaborate as to what 'this' was. He didn't need to.

"Stone... You're going to kill him." Why I repeated something I already knew, I wasn't sure. I ached for him to explain to me what that entailed. Why I was being left here. How he could do it all alone.

"I'm going to take care of it," he replied. I didn't know if he wasn't saying it outright because of Lukyan's proximity or if he was trying to spare me from something.

"You can't go alone," I told him, worry suddenly clutching my neck harder than he ever could.

In my head, Knox was impenetrable. There was no way anything or anyone could hurt him.

But that was in my head. He was human, he'd shown me that much. He bled. Now that scared me. Knowing that he could be taken from me.

That simply wasn't an option. I couldn't be without him.

"You worried about me?" he asked, a very slight teasing in his tone. No one would've caught it but me.

"Obviously, I'm worried about you," I snapped, mindful of Elizabeth and Lukyan within earshot. "I love you."

Knox jerked as if I'd hit him.

I hadn't previously said that out loud, I realized. I'd figured Knox was attuned to me, to every one of my small tells. I'd said it in not so many words a thousand times.

But maybe he truly didn't believe it. Truly didn't believe himself worthy of love.

Regardless of the audience, I moved my hands up to cup his face, clutching it as hard as I could, wishing I could fuse myself to him. Wishing I could will my need for him to live into his skin.

"I love you," I repeated, going up on my tiptoes to brush my mouth against his. "And I am telling you that you will hurt me more than you could ever imagine, you would *ruin* me, by dying. Or getting maimed. But I'll deal with a maiming if your heart is beating." I moved one of my hands to his chest, letting the thump lull me into some sense of peace.

I'd expected Knox to stiffen at this display of affection, especially in front of this man who I knew he considered an enemy.

But he didn't. He completely melted into my touch.

He didn't return the words.

He hugged me instead. A hug from Knox, in front of witnesses, no less, felt like the most precious gift in the world.

For only a handful of seconds. Then he let me go.

He turned to give Lukyan what looked to be both a threatening and thankful nod, then he walked out the door.

Without looking back.

Again, his walk had the gait of someone walking to the noose.

TWENTY-ONE

PIPER

"How long does this stuff usually take?" I asked, interrupting a question that Elizabeth was in the middle of asking me.

It was incredibly rude, especially since they were gracious, if not slightly intimidating hosts.

Elizabeth was small, unassuming, even delicate at least upon first glance. But since I'd become somewhat of an amateur expert at spotting dangerous people, I had come to understand that she was one of them. The way she carried herself, the way she moved... She was powerful in a subtle way. Her husband was deadly in a much more obvious way, but I didn't doubt she was just as fearsome if she needed to be.

I'd contemplated them as a couple. I couldn't ask outright if they were some sort of super villain power couple, but I assumed it was likely. Would that be me and Knox if this all worked out? Living in the affluent suburbs, masquerading as normal people? Me baking cookies while Knox buried bodies in the backyard?

I didn't have it in me to transform into the kind of partner Elizabeth most obviously was to Lukyan. Sure, I'd survived Knox, but most of that was on the luck of him falling in love with me.

I wasn't a victim, but I sure as shit wasn't a villain either. I was a *kindergarten teacher,* for goodness' sakes. But the fact remained that I simply wasn't okay with sitting here, playing the polite houseguest to two morally gray people who made great food.

Hence me interrupting Elizabeth with my question that was almost a shout across their dining table.

Luckily, Elizabeth wasn't insulted by my lack of manners; she just smiled knowingly and looked to her husband.

He did not smile. He didn't seem capable of such a gesture.

He sat as close to his wife as humanly possible, something I'd noted in my short time as their guest. The way he watched her, moved around her... It was familiar. It reminded me of the energy Knox had around me.

It wasn't love.

It wasn't that simple, that easy to define. Love was fallible. One could fall out of love. Love did not conquer all, lest what all popular culture said. But what these men felt, it could. It could conquer countries, take down regimes, raze the world.

Lukyan looked at his wife when he spoke.

"It takes as long as it takes."

I drummed my fingernails on the table. My stomach turned at the food in front of me, even though it had smelled delicious moments ago. "Ballpark?" I pressed.

He considered me with rapt attention, holding a wine glass full of what I was sure was delicious and expensive wine. Not for the first time, I resented my biology and the fact that I wasn't able to use substances in moderation to take the edge off.

Not that I thought a glass of expensive red would make me any less keyed up.

"I don't think there is a ballpark amount of time for dismantling a hundred-year-old criminal enterprise," he replied dryly.

He found me amusing, that much was clear. Which only served to piss me off further.

I knew that getting annoyed with him was dangerous, if not just impolite. I was his guest, after all. And not just the garden variety guest. I was technically on the run from a very powerful and dangerous man. It was a liability, having me under his roof. He was doing me a favor, a big one, by letting me stay. Yet I couldn't swallow my tongue. "Well I'm not going to just sit here and wait."

"That's exactly what you're going to do," he answered, sipping casually.

I didn't miss the order in his tone.

Sure, I might've in my previous life, sat back and obeyed him, sitting on the sidelines, away from the peril, letting a man save me.

But not now.

This was *my* life. This was *my* future. And I wasn't about to just sit here and let a man take care of it for me. Even if that man was Knox.

I didn't lower my gaze. "What do you think his chance of success is?" I asked Lukyan. "Don't sugarcoat it."

He laughed. The sound was chilling. There was no warmth in it. No humanity. I was baffled that a man with such an obvious devotion to his wife was so cold in every other way. But that was the pot calling the kettle black, I guessed. "I'm not in the business of sugarcoating anything, Piper." He looked once to his wife, as if he was taking cues from her. Interesting. She nodded almost imperceptibly before he looked back at me.

"Even knowing Knox and how ... proficient he is at what he does, I would say without you in the mix, his chances would be zero."

I swallowed sand at his answer, one I'd already suspected.

"And *with* me in the mix?" I probed.

I struggled to meet his arctic gaze. "Slightly higher than zero.

But not by much."

My heart fell to my toes. "And why do I change the situation?"

His eyes once again went to his wife, for longer this time, and when he spoke, he was still looking at her. "Because organizations like that, ones headed by men used to getting what they want, used to controlling, dominating people, see women as weak. They underestimate them. And that will be their downfall."

He finally looked back at me with his steely gaze.

"That's not to give you hope. Unfortunately, women still don't win wars. They don't prevail. Because men will always fear them. And weak men will always destroy what they fear. The world is run by weak men, Piper."

I stared at him, surprised by the feminist tilt to the most words I'd heard him speak since I met him.

He didn't offer me any hope. I didn't think Lukyan was the kind of man to do that.

But he offered a chance.

A chance, a small chance, at life. The odds leaned toward death, but I was ever the optimist.

I pushed my chair back.

"I know you made all sorts of promises to Knox, but would you consider breaking them?"

Lukyan smiled, if you could call it that, the expression was sharp and thorny and intimidating.

"I think I can do that."

———

There wasn't a timeline on what Knox was doing, therefore, we needed to make a large plan in a small amount of time. I was apt to follow Lukyan's lead when it came to the nuts and bolts of taking down an international criminal organization.

In the end, the plan was simple.

And it was not thought up by Lukyan, who I was kind of suspecting to be some evil genius in his own right.

The plan was thought up by Elizabeth, her husband immediately deferring to her. The dynamic between the two could be studied. And if I wasn't wrapped up in the terror of the only man I'd ever loved potentially dying and petrified at what I would have to do to save us both, I would've been *a lot* more curious.

As it was, my mind was focused on the almost impossible task at hand.

We were in Elizabeth's closet. The space was as large as my bedroom in my apartment, opulent and decorated in creams and whites with plush carpets and rows of exquisite clothing organized on hangers. It looked like I was in a designer store.

The wealth they both obviously had was vast. Crime paid. And despite my reaction to Lukyan, I couldn't convince myself that they were bad people.

I was trying on clothes. Not something I would have expected to do when preparing to go to battle. When men went to battle, they wore armor, or bulletproof vests in this generation. When women went to battle, they wore couture and cashmere. Soft. Pliable. No protection from bullets, knives or fists.

After laying out the plan, we had spoken little. Lukyan had retreated to his office to *make arrangements,* and Elizabeth and I had gone to assemble my wardrobe.

Once that was done, she sat me down in front of a large vanity to do my makeup.

"Lukyan and I were up against some pretty terrible odds," Elizabeth said, her voice soft and sweet as she applied bronzer to my cheeks. "We began our relationship in a manner that was not dissimilar to yours."

I snorted, looking at her in the mirror. "Doubtful. Was he hired to kidnap you as well?" She didn't deserve the snark in my tone, and

I wasn't usually a person to direct it at someone who had been nothing but kind to me but, I was feeling prickly.

And I needed to be prickly in order to pull off my plan.

"He wasn't hired to kidnap me, no." She smiled at me, brushing blush onto my cheeks. "He was hired to kill me."

I gaped at her slack-jawed, shocked by the offhand way in which she said it. No, it wasn't offhand. It was *tender.* As if the memory was somewhat warm. Like recounting how you met your husband at a wedding or by accidentally getting in the wrong taxi.

Not a meet-cute that would do well in mixed company.

I let out a half-hysterical laugh.

"It's ironic," she nodded. "That we'd meet these men in such ways. But that's the only way you come across them, if they think you're their prey."

I agreed, my stomach swirling with unease.

"And the odds you were up against?" I questioned.

She was quiet for a moment, her nostrils flaring, brackets forming around her mouth. "We had a criminal organization of our own to take down. And we did."

I rolled my lips together. "I doubt it was that simple."

She smiled again. "It definitely wasn't. But we don't have time for the details right now, and you don't need them. You just need to know it's possible. And I think you can do this." She squeezed my hand reassuringly.

"Why do you think that?" I asked, staring at the foreign person she was turning me into in the mirror. But underneath it all, I was still me. A kindergarten teacher who liked Tarot and fantasy books. "You don't even know me."

Her brows pinched as she focused on her eyelash curler for a beat, presumably thinking. "I know what kind of person it takes to love a man who thinks he's monstrous," she countered. "And I know how feral, dark and deadly that love is. You'll go outside of your character, your morals, your ethics ... just to keep hold of it."

She finished my makeup then stepped back, raking her fingers through the hair she'd already curled and sprayed.

"You'll do anything to keep hold of him," she continued. "Even if it costs you your humanity."

Her words were not reassuring. Not in the traditional sense, at least. But I held on to them for dear life.

Because I would do anything to keep hold of Knox, of us.

If my humanity was the cost, I'd pay it. Consequences be damned.

———

Elizabeth had left me in the bathroom of the guest bedroom to take care of my basic needs in preparation for our trip. The plan was for us to get on a plane first—a private jet—then they'd be driving me to where I needed to go.

After that, I was on my own.

I stared at myself in the mirror. My hair was shiny and tamed into loose curls trailing down my back. The bruise on my eye was almost invisible. Elizabeth had glued fake lashes onto my eyes, making them feel heavy and uncomfortable, but they made my eyes pop and made me look more feminine. Feline, almost. The blush high on my cheekbones was a baby pink, making me look like I was flushed from sunshine.

The gloss on my lips was that same baby pink, and I wore all white. White sheath dress, clinging to my body and curves, finishing just below my knees. A light cashmere cardigan was on top of it, and sky-high, pink heels were already making my feet hurt. How I was going to run in these was anyone's guess. But that was the point, wasn't it? I was going into the wolf's den dressed as a lamb.

I was as prepared as I was ever going to be. Dressed to the nines in foreign, expensive clothing that melded to my body and made me look like a completely different person. Made me look how I supposed a mafia wife might look.

Which was the point. I was playing a part. I couldn't look like me. Couldn't *feel* like me.

On unsteady feet, I left the bathroom, barely seeing anything while making my way through the decadently decorated home, my heart in my throat.

"You ready?" Lukyan's rough voice filtered through the foyer of the house.

I thought he was talking to me, which was weird since his voice, though rough, was full of an intimate tenderness that was not for me.

And it wasn't.

When I looked in his direction, all of his attention was focused on his wife. She was standing in front of the door, a tight look on her face. Her eyes were faraway, and her hands were fisted at her sides.

She no longer radiated a subtly strong demeanor. Suddenly, she looked smaller, much more vulnerable than I ever thought she could be, staring at the front door.

The way he spoke to her, looked at her, betrayed a gentleness that mixed with his rough exterior.

You could feel it. The way his existence was tied to hers, how he was wrapped up in her, dedicated to her in a way that wasn't healthy but in a way I coveted.

Elizabeth took a deep breath and looked to her husband, her expression relaxing as a small smile lit up her lovely face.

"I'm ready," she nodded.

He stroked her neck. "This is not required of you, you've done enough, *izyubov moya.*"

The endearment struck me with its tenderness and the smooth way in which Lukyan spoke it, betraying a heritage that I guessed was Eastern European.

Elizabeth looked back up at him, her expression sharp. "It is something I would hope someone would do for me if it was you," she returned in a low voice.

He stared at her for a long while before leaning in to kiss her lightly on the lips in a gesture of tenderness that felt illegal for me to see. I crept backward then made purposefully loud steps on the marble floor to announce my arrival.

By then, they had their masks in place. But they were still close to each other, as if it were impossible to stand farther apart, connected by an invisible string. One made of titanium.

A team.

"Ready?" Elizabeth asked, directing her question at me. None of the vulnerability, fear I thought I'd glimpsed, remained.

I nodded.

"Ready," I lied.

———

I'd never been on a private jet before. The level of wealth was beyond my comprehension. The actual flight was beyond my comprehension. I listened intently to Lukyan offering me advice on how to play my hand, what to do, what not to do. I'd nodded and replied at the appropriate times, but I could not, for the life of me, remember the majority of what he said.

And it was my very life that depended on survival tips from a hitman.

The absolute absurdity that was my life would've been funny if, well, if it were happening on a movie screen instead.

I had watched New York City underneath us, trying to prepare myself for it to be my battleground. My entire future, or lack thereof, would be decided there in just a few hours.

My fingers had clutched the arm of the seat as we landed, then I'd gotten into the black SUV waiting for us on the tarmac without speaking. Elizabeth and Lukyan stayed close together, the latter almost never taking his eyes off his wife.

I couldn't watch them for too long. They were the image of what I might have if I was lucky enough to be successful. They were also the image of what I might've already lost.

It was only when we were almost at our destination that I spoke.

"This could go bad," I said, wringing my hands.

"It likely will," Lukyan agreed.

Not comforting.

"You can still pull out," he remarked. The offer was given in a tone free of judgment, yet I still felt the label of *coward* hovering in the air, waiting to be plastered on my forehead if I took him up on it.

We could turn around, go back to the expensive house with the no doubt comfortable bed I could safely toss and turn in all night while Knox did ... whatever he did.

"No." I straightened my shoulders. "No, I can do this," I repeated. Who was I talking to? Lukyan? Myself?

Lukyan nodded then didn't say anything else. Nor did Elizabeth, though I locked eyes with her, and she gave a smile that wasn't just warm. It was dark, cold, knowing. A flash of feminine power that communicated that she had faith in me to do women's work.

Not the work of cooking, cleaning, bearing children, but bringing down the men who sought to control us.

I had tried to live up to that, hadn't I? I talked the talk, walked in women's marches?

Now it was time to walk the walk. In shoes I could barely march in, that speared my feet with searing pain with every step I took, the pain reminding me how a man could never walk in these shoes.

The pain. I held on to that.

I smiled back at Elizabeth, feeling nauseous as my lips stretched.

Yes, it was time to do women's work.

Lukyan's 'intel' had told him that Stone was at Rosso.

Ironic, for us to end it all where it began. He could not gather any intel as to Knox's whereabouts. I didn't know if that was a blessing or a curse. Surely, if he had come in guns blazing, going all *Scarface*, Lukyan would've heard about that.

Then again, that wasn't Knox's style. He was more subtle. He'd watch, make plans first. That's what I was counting on, at least. Him being measured and patient, paving the way for me to be impulsive and reckless.

"You're on your own from here," Lukyan said. "We won't be waiting in the wings to save the day. It's not my job."

It was uniquely terrifying to know I was on my own and that Lukyan wasn't fashioning himself into some kind of hero. It was me. Only me.

"Thank you," I nodded. "For taking me this far." I looked at Elizabeth. "For everything."

She smiled and reached over to squeeze my hand. "You can do this." Her words expressed a faith she shouldn't have had, barely knowing me. "Do whatever it takes to hold on to what is yours." Her gaze touched Lukyan before traveling back to me. "It's worth it. And humanity is overrated."

That was it. That was my invitation to leave and go forth with no one at my back. I stayed frozen for just a second before I opened the door and hopped out onto the New York street.

The car quickly left the curb, the noises of the city creating a muted roar in my ears, before going completely quiet, as if I were in the center of a tornado. My brain went still too.

Taking a deep breath, I stepped out of the calm and into the storm—wearing wildly-impractical shoes.

. . .

Twenty-Two

I had planned for every eventuality.

As well as one could in a situation like this—with as many moving parts as there were. There were a lot of elements outside of my control. But I felt confident I could handle it.

I'd spent the majority of my life preparing for a moment like this. Every second I was in Stone's employ, I'd been watching. Learning. Prodding weak spots, understanding the structure of the hierarchy. Cutting the head off the snake would ensure there was chaos for a time, but the serpent would grow a new head eventually. My goal was to create the most chaos possible. And the person who became the new don would have a lot to deal with before they even thought to try to pursue me. That's if they were stupid. If they were smart, they'd know to thank me or leave me alone lest Stone's fate befall them.

Though I was realistic, I understood that even I might not have the skills or stamina to be successful in my mission. But I had the cold determination of knowing that I *had* to be successful in my mission in order to keep my woman safe.

I'd happily bleed out if I knew that my death meant keeping her safe.

I'd already put plans in place if I wasn't successful. A bank account with more than enough money for a lifetime, new identities for her and Daisy, a way out of the country if she wanted or somewhere to disappear to if needed. All of my holdings would move to her name, except a considerable sum to be put in a trust for Mabel.

I didn't think that it would go that far since I was confident I would at the very least kill Stone. There was no way I'd submit to death if the man who had caused my woman pain and suffering was still bleeding.

I'd considered a lot of different options for how I'd go about my task. Maybe the smartest one was to stick to the shadows, wait until he was alone in bed then just put a bullet in his brain. Clean. Safer. No witnesses.

But that wasn't what the hungry sadist inside of me wanted. In my fury, I'd let myself become a victim of my own ego. Not only did I want to kill him, I wanted to do it where he felt safe. When he felt like he'd won.

And I knew that he was stupid enough to not order me to be killed on sight. As if his soldiers possessed the skill to kill me in the first place.

He likely expected some surprise attack, knowing that I wasn't dead. He'd upped his personal guards. He was scared. Oh, how I relished that.

What he expected was the attack in the night. Because that's what *he* would've done. He'd wait until his prey was at their weakest.

I wanted them at their strongest, to show them just how helpless they were.

So I walked in the front door.

I let them divest me of my weapons—I didn't need them—

reveling in the unease of the heavily armed men watching me sideways as if they expected me to set off a bomb at any moment.

They were inconsequential to me. Little more than flies buzzing around my face. Swatting them wasn't worth the energy I'd expend.

Stone didn't stand as I entered the room, merely looked up with what could only be described as a shit-eating grin on his face. It took me seconds to understand why, eventually seeing what he had mounted behind him, for every single person to see when they walked into the room.

It took every ounce of control I possessed to keep my expression blank, to not jump across his desk and rip his throat out with my bare hands.

That's what he anticipated, after all.

"Knox," he greeted as if he were expecting me. I could see past his veneer of civility to the fury that lay underneath. It was in the stiffness of his shoulders, the tautness of his body, hand underneath his desk, no doubt touching the gun he kept there. He was scared and angry.

"You are full of surprises," he said smoothly. "I knew you had talents, but artistry wasn't one of them. With a paintbrush, at least. We all know your talents with a knife." He turned his head to stare at the painting, to leer at the ridges and valleys of Piper's form.

I stood stock-still, noting the men behind me had their fingers on the triggers of the guns they were holding. I supposed they were ordered to shoot at any sign of movement.

Not that I cared.

After a long silence, Stone turned back to me. His expression was still pleasant, lips turned up, features relaxed but I didn't miss the glint of fury in his eyes.

"And here I was, thinking that you had no sexual appetite to speak of," he continued, his voice straining with fury as he lost hold over his faux civility. "And all it took was the right woman to wake you up. *My woman.*"

Anger gushed through my veins, but I didn't move. "She's mine," I said, keeping my voice cold and even. "Not that I seek to own her. She belongs to herself first. Women are not possessions. Men like you unfortunately don't learn that often enough. It'll be my pleasure to watch you learn the hard way."

Stone froze for a moment in fury before he threw his head back and laughed. I knew the gesture was forced, for his audience. His bodyguards. Because he was too cowardly to face me alone.

"Look at you, the heartless eunuch now an expert on pussy just because he's been bewitched by a cunt." He said the words in his trademark polite tone.

My insides roiled, thirsted for vengeance, to punish him for the way he spoke about Piper.

But that's what he wanted. He saw me as a feral dog, and he expected that he could just dangle some poisoned meat in front of me and that's all it would take.

"Should we end the theatrics?" I asked, sounding bored. "We both know this only ends one way."

Stone looked at me with barely restrained fury before he sighed. "Yes, we know it does." He stood, making a great show of taking a knife from the sheath at his waist. It shone in the light, polished and clean.

When he rounded the desk, the men beside me came in tighter. A cage. That's what he thought he had me in, thinking it would be as simple as slitting my throat.

I wanted to smile, but that would've given me away. So I waited.

"Such a shame." Stone took his time, making his way over to me, the showman he was. "I really considered you as my own son."

"Makes sense, since my father was a piece of shit."

His brow twitched. "I didn't think I'd enjoy this." He examined the knife. "But remembering how you tasted my fiancée's pussy before I had the pleasure reminds me I will." His eyes locked with mine. "And you'll die knowing that she's going to be mine for the rest of my life." He clicked his tongue. "Or hers, which likely promises to be shorter."

There it was. Just a few seconds away from my moment. My body prepared, coiled, the beast inside me licking its lips.

But Stone didn't take the step forward I needed. He stopped at the knock at the door, his irritated gaze turning that way.

"I was not to be disturbed!" he shouted. But once he saw who was at the door, his expression cleared.

Then he smiled. Truly smiled.

And it was the smile that sent dread through me.

I didn't need to turn to know what had turned him so victorious.

I knew. I fucking knew.

"Piper," he drawled, stepping back. "I'm so glad to have you here."

And just like that, all of my plans, all of my control, went out the window.

PIPER

My heart was throbbing in my feet as I walked into the room. And not just on account of the uncomfortable shoes. I felt the eyes of every man in the room on me as I slowly and with faux confidence walked into the opulent office behind the kitchens of Rosso, the building much larger than it first appeared.

Stone's inky gaze coated me in filth, but that's not what almost brought me to my knees.

It was Knox, standing there, flanked by two armed men, standing stock-still, almost shaking with rage, not meeting my eyes until I was almost right in front of him. I might've flinched had I not retreated into such a deep part of myself. He was furious. I could feel the rage emanating from him, lashing against his skin like knives. I knew that he'd been confident in whatever he'd been about to do, willing to die in the process and without regret. And I knew I'd gone and ruined all of his plans. Which was the point.

With a deep breath, I looked toward Stone, but not before I caught sight of what was behind him.

My breath caught, and my mask slipped when I saw what was on the wall.

Stone, who hadn't missed what caught my eye, smirked. "Ah, yes. I was just discussing with Knox my appreciation for his talents. Though I haven't yet had the pleasure to see you in your entirety, Piper, this paints a picture that you will not disappoint."

The way he spoke, the ownership he obviously felt over my body, made my skin crawl. Not as much as that painting, that sacred object being on display there, used as a torture device, a trophy for Stone. Sullying it in a way that should've been against the laws of nature.

"I'm glad you like it." Somehow, I kept my composure. "You can consider it a wedding gift."

Stone paused, his smile clearing from his face as confusion took its place. I reveled in unsettling him. A marker that I was going in the right direction, that I just needed to hold steady.

"I'll marry you," I told Stone, refusing to look at Knox even though his stare was flaying layers of my skin and flesh, down to my soul that was his and his alone. "On the one proviso you let him go." I tilted my head to Knox, keeping my stare on Stone.

Stone's confusion turned to contempt, his lips pulling back in a sneer. "And what convinced you to think I'm deluded enough to believe that you've had such a quick change of heart when you were so ... insistent about where your heart, and your cunt, lay at the motel?"

His tone was pleasant, which made the crude words all the more biting. Stone's true nature was leeching out of his $10,000 suit like snakes slithering through crevices. The anger he felt was fraying his control.

It gave me hope. That he was so furious, betrayed by thinking he could own a woman without consequences, that she'd bow down to him. That anger was my way in. And the delusion that despite all the evidence presented, he still had the arrogance to think I wanted him.

"My heart hasn't changed," I told him honestly. "I'm still repulsed by the way you've gone about this whole thing." I waved my hand. "I wasn't lying in the beginning. I wasn't interested in you. Not in the slightest." I paused to lick my lips, moving just a little closer to him, though even the small distance disgusted me. "But now that I've had a taste of what it's like to walk on the dark side, so to speak, I'd be lying if I said it didn't tempt me. The life you offer."

I leaned forward, ignoring all of the tension in the room as I straightened Stone's already perfect tie, my fingers steady as they stroked the expensive fabric.

In my periphery, Knox shifted on his feet where he stood, unable to remain still with the outrage he obviously felt as I touched Stone. I ignored him, gazing at Stone through my heavy lashes. The man was tense, not wholly convinced, but I didn't miss the hunger, the triumph in his eyes. He really was fucking stupid enough to think a woman could still want him after kidnappings, beatings, attempted rapes, just because he had money and power.

After silently counting to three, I let go. "And then there's the case of my sister's life being in danger." I took time to inspect my nails, which had been polished just a few hours before. The dirt underneath them from the garden in the mountains of Appalachia was long gone. I missed it like a body part.

I looked back up at Stone who was regarding me with distrust. "It'll push a girl over the edge. I don't want it to run my whole life. I want a secure life. You can give that to me, can't you? You have the power to give that to me, don't you?"

Though he surely hadn't become the head of a crime organization by believing everything he heard, I knew that I was breaking Stone down. Men were so simple. Stroke their ego, tell them they're powerful, and they'd be putty in your hands.

"Yes, Piper," he replied, the knife still in his hand. "I have the power to give you *everything* beyond your wildest dreams."

I nodded, batting my lashes. "I expect you've done your research on my past." I'd been thinking a lot about what Knox didn't know about me. He'd explained that his 'job' had been rather last minute, that he'd been overly confident in his ability and hadn't done the usual research into my background.

It only made sense that Stone would've, especially with the resources and time at his disposal. He wanted to control me. And he was smart enough to study me in order to do that.

Stone bobbed his head in response.

"Which may serve as more evidence as to why security is so important to me. Recent events made that all the more clear. And the violence your men didn't hesitate to inflict upon me." I raised my hand to my eye. "Along with their casual references to gang rape and attempted rape."

I could feel white-hot ire radiating from where Knox stood, inches from me. The need to reach out to touch him was so overwhelming it hurt.

But I kept my attention on Stone. "I'll have to request that there be no more violence against me and my sister, nor threats of sexual abuse." I said this all blandly, as if the existence of such things didn't fill my belly with immeasurable feminine fury.

Stone watched me carefully. "As my wife, no one would lay a hand on you. But me, of course."

His gaze went to Knox, taunting.

I didn't follow it. My nails cut into my palms from the force it was taking to remain calm. "Of course," I purred in a way that I hoped was convincing.

The air between Stone and I was electric as he dissected my gaze, looking for falsehoods. I hoped my acting skills were good enough.

"Back to my earlier request," I broke the silence, my voice sharper this time. "That Knox leaves. Unharmed. And with no one following him or killing him once I'm out of sight."

Stone's brow lifted, clearly amused but not convinced. "You think that I'd let him continue to breathe after betraying me?" His tone was eerily civil.

"You'll have to ensure you do a good job of killing me," Knox spoke for the first time since I'd walked in, voice coated in furor. I gave myself permission to sneak a glance at him, finding his stare on Stone to be unyielding, free of any kind of defeat. "Because if there is an ounce of breath left in my body, I'll be coming back. For you. For her."

I flinched at the sheer reverence in his words. His vow was full to the brim with the enormity of his feelings for me, his devotion to me, that it kneecapped me. I struggled to stay standing, to keep the sob in my chest from escaping.

"He did his job, even if it wasn't the way you intended," I told Stone, taking every ounce of strength that Knox had shown me I possessed in order to keep up the façade. "He broke me. He brought me here. To you. Willing. To marry you."

When Stone looked from Knox to me, I didn't wither under his glare, despite how uncomfortable it made me. Despite how much agony I was in.

I felt it. Knox's life hanging in the balance. The need Stone had to punish him. To show me that no one was coming to save me.

"He has said himself that he'll come for you if I leave him breathing," Stone pointed out. Though I could hear acquiesce in his tone. It might've been working. I thought I could maybe save Knox. If I was willing to abandon my humanity.

I drew in a deep breath.

This was it. This was the part that required every ounce, every shred of my strength, scraped from my insides, from my organs. It tore at my soul as I finally looked at Knox.

I might've jolted at his expression, it was so utterly determined. His eyes were blazing, nostrils flaring, mouth parted.

Utterly devoted.

To me.

But I couldn't flinch. Couldn't break. I was there to save us, after all, even if it ensured there would never be an 'us' again. Even if I broke him in a way he didn't deserve.

"He will only come for me if he thinks I want him," I told Stone, my voice detached, foreign. I took a measured breath, forcing myself to look Knox up and down with distaste I couldn't feel. Not ever. Not in a million years.

Outwardly, I looked as if I found him lacking—at least that's what I hoped I looked like. Inwardly, I was committing every piece of his beauty to memory. Preserving him as perfection inside me, where I could treasure him long after the dust settled from the ruins.

"I don't," I declared when I found his eyes. "Want you. I don't want you."

Again, my voice was impressively strong. Mean. Cold.

"You are … *wrong*," I continued, my heart shredding into countless pieces, pain spearing every inch of my soul as I forced revulsion I didn't feel into my tone. "You are … ruined. It's not your fault, I know." Sickly sweet, poisonous pity seeped from my words.

Pitying him. In front of an audience, no less. It was the worst thing I could've done to him. The most hurtful thing. To imply that his damage and his trauma made him weak. Like it didn't make him the strongest, most complicated, multifaceted, extraordinary man I'd ever had the honor of knowing. Loving.

"I thank you." I clasped my hands in front of me so he wouldn't see them trembling. "For showing me what I really need. What I really desire." I looked to Stone. "A powerful man who is able to operate in society, not chained by the shadows like you are. You'll *never* be able to give me the life I want."

There it was. Poison, sickening and vile, but hopefully convincing enough.

I turned away from Knox. I couldn't bear to look at him. Instead, I took my cues from Stone, whose smile had grown wider and wider as I spoke. He believed me, I guessed.

"Ah, isn't this *nice.*" He clapped his hands together before grabbing me roughly and pulling me against his body.

I squeezed my eyes shut for a second to survive the unwelcome touch, steeling myself from fighting against him or kneeing him in the balls.

He was still holding the knife. Which meant my life wasn't safe. He wasn't wholly convinced. And he enjoyed torturing Knox.

His hand stroked my hip, creeping upward, across my bruised ribs to the underside of my breast, not quite fondling me, but it was an assault. I winced at the pain from it, yet Stone only held me tighter. Tears stung my eyes, and I tasted copper as I bit into my lip to stop from crying out.

Though I knew it was a mistake, I looked at Knox again.

His face was blank.

Completely blank. Not even like it had been when he first took me, devoid of human emotion. This was something else. I couldn't explain it. It was as if he'd left, the shape of his face changed, and I swore, something inhuman and feral lurked beneath his eyes. His wrath was that deep.

"You'll forgive me, my darling, if I don't believe you at face value," Stone's voice was deep, warm. "It is partly on account of you *whoring* yourself out to the first of my men you encountered." I had to swallow a whimper of pain when he held me rougher. The grip promised more violence. "I'll be taking measures to ensure your ... loyalty to me." I forced my limbs to remain where they were when he leaned down to lay his lips on my neck. "I could make you bend over for me, right here, in front of Knox to show him what you're giving to me," he whispered, but not quietly enough for Knox and his men not to hear.

My stomach lurched at the threat. Not quite a threat either. He was actually considering it. Weighing his options. If he did order me to do that, it meant I was dead. I understood that if he truly wanted me to be his wife, he wouldn't expose me that way. He held a fucked-up version of honor. He wouldn't let his men see me like that.

I didn't have a plan if he did do that. Other than fighting like hell and hope I won. Hope Knox won.

Stone kept me there, in the purgatory of his indecision for a full minute. I counted the seconds. It was all I could do to keep sane. It took him fifty-seven seconds to act.

Keeping a firm grip on my ribs, he pulled back, his fingers again brushing below my breast. The sound that came out of his throat sounded like a laugh, but it scraped down the sides of my soul.

"I had planned on disposing of you." Stone tucked a loose curl behind my ear. "Not before tasting what has bewitched the most ruthless of my men." His eyes flit to Knox for a split second before returning to me. "But you have changed my mind. I'll have you. Knox, you did me the great favor of disposing those of my men who had knowledge of you fucking her." A pause, Stone's gaze never leaving mine. "Well, *almost* all of them..."

In one swift movement, Stone had removed something from his jacket, two loud pops sending the men at Knox's side tumbling to the ground with heavy, wet thumps.

There was a ringing in my ears.

I gaped down. To where Stone had shot his own men. In cold blood.

Blood trickled from their heads. Warmth dripping down my cheek told me it coated my skin.

Knox was immobile in front of me. I struggled to do the same, but my knees trembled, and I was glad that I didn't have much to eat today or it might've been all over Elizabeth's designer shoes.

Suddenly, the room was smaller, shrinking so it squeezed against my ribs harder than Stone's hand. It was incredibly intimate—and not in a good way—to have the only living men in the room be Stone and Knox.

My savior and my captor.

Stone was still holding me. Armed. His dangerous energy strangled me.

"Now, I'm sure you're still filled with all sorts of intentions," Stone addressed Knox. "Revenge being the most pressing of them. Even if my fiancée has made it clear that she finds you ... lacking." He sighed. "I know it's hard to let go. Bear in mind, if I so much as catch a glimpse of you..."

My breath caught as I felt a cold barrel on my temple.

"I won't hesitate to put a bullet in my pretty wife's skull," Stone explained pleasantly.

He kept the barrel there as my eyes locked with Knox's, drowning in the waters I'd so willingly jumped into, thinking I could swim.

The gun stayed at my head, my heart hammering in terror. Not for me dying, but for Stone pulling the trigger and having Knox watch me die. He'd never come back from that. Never stop punishing himself.

"Have I made myself clear, Knox?"

Knox looked as if he might grind his teeth to dust, not taking his eyes off me. He was furious. He was also making promises. About coming for me. Saving me. Not out loud. He said it all with his eyes. Even if we both understood that couldn't happen. Not anymore.

He nodded once, brutally.

"I'll give you ten seconds to get out of this room," Stone's voice was feather soft, gun still at my temple.

Knox used only five of them before he took measured, unhurried steps to the door. When it closed behind him, I got the distinct feeling that I was never going to see him again.

My plan hadn't been overly complex. Get close enough to Stone to kill him. Simple was good, it couldn't go wrong. How hard was it to get close to the man who wanted to rape and kill me at best and marry me at worst? Like Lukyan said, Stone was conditioned to underestimate me, and that would be when I'd strike.

I hadn't accounted for Knox. On Stone killing two of his men in cold blood and then hurriedly having me taken from the room and put into a car, en route to his home.

Which was where I'd ended up. An hour outside New York, on a sprawling estate, grand with vast gardens. It was picturesque, like it had been plucked out of an English countryside. Made of stone with large, stained glass windows and exquisite marble statues in the entryway.

How such an evil man could live somewhere so seemingly pristine and magical was beyond me. The pretty walls contained revolting memories, blood that had been wiped clean. Of that I was sure.

Stone had handed me off to men in suits who obviously didn't know of my past with Knox and weren't aware that their mighty leader would kill them in a heartbeat if they so much as overheard the wrong information. I wanted to tell them that, but I doubted they'd listen to the word of a captive.

I wasn't under any false illusions that Stone was actually going to marry me. How could he? He was a man of a certain code, and him knowing I'd been with Knox was him thinking that his property—me—was tarnished in some way. An absolutely absurd way of thinking but there I was, feeling like I was back in the 1800s where women were property to powerful men.

I was sure he was going to play with me, torture me maybe, rape me, but not marry me. I had a deep knowing he considered me nothing but a toy to be ruined then discarded.

No one told me anything as I was walked through the hallways of the home, without a speck of dust to be seen, decorated in rich reds and reminding me of an old Italian villa with the furnishings to match. Everything was tasteful, elegant.

The ogre had good taste. Or enough money to pay someone who did.

The men in suits didn't speak to me, and I didn't attempt to make conversation. There was no point; I wouldn't make friends here. I was alone.

The thought was distinctly terrifying but also ... empowering. I wasn't weak or simpering, and I was unwilling to give up and wait to be saved. Knox had showed me the power I had inside me, the strength, coiled and waiting for me to let it out. My mother was a victim to a man who took everything from her, and I'd learn from her fate.

I'd make my grandmother proud.

I'd make Knox proud.

Most importantly, I'd make *myself* proud.

The room I'd been shown to was lovely. An enormous bedroom with a wooden, four-poster bed, a fireplace, a balcony that jutted out with a view of the pool and courtyard below. The smell of roses swept into the room through the open doors. A seemingly tempting escape—it wasn't that high, and there didn't appear to be any armed guards patrolling the perimeter, but I wasn't technically a captive, was I? I'd gone there of my own volition and had said I'd wanted this.

Stone was smart enough to see through my lie, or at least

suspect it. The balcony was some kind of test, I was sure. Or maybe a taunt.

I went to the ornate marble bathroom to splash water on my face until I remembered it was covered in a thick layer of makeup. I blinked through the heavy false lashes, wanting to rip them off.

But I didn't. Couldn't. I had to be this poised, false woman in white, standing in a marble bathroom with no allies for miles.

I jumped as the sound of ringing echoed from the bedroom. Following the sound, I was surprised to see a phone on the night-stand beside the bed. Who still had landlines? Mafia dons needed to communicate with their captive fiancées somehow, I guessed.

Figuring it was for me, I answered it.

"Piper, I trust your accommodations are to your satisfaction." Stone's tone was warm, as if he hadn't just murdered two men in front of me hours before.

I clutched the phone tighter. "My ... accommodations?" I repeated. "You're not expecting me to sleep with you?"

I'd known upon first glance that I wasn't in Stone's bedroom. There were no personal effects, nothing male about it, and the large closet was empty. No shrines to the horned god or stone slabs with chains for sacrificing virgins. Not that he'd leave evidence of the true sadist he was.

"So eager?" he teased in a charming deep tone. "No, I'm afraid I'm old fashioned in that regard." There was a loaded pause. I picked at my cuticles so I didn't rush to fill it. "I know you don't stand on ceremony in regard to who you fuck."

I flinched at the words delivered in that same polite tone but I didn't miss the bite, even through the phone.

"I'd rather let some time go by before we venture into that portion of our relationship," he continued placidly. "We have forever, after all."

Forever. Or as long as he deigned to keep me alive, was what was left unsaid.

I didn't speak. What was there to say?

"I'll be home for dinner by six thirty," he continued. "I'll expect you at the table not a moment past." Order saturated his tone. And the promise of retribution should I not heed it. An omen of what life would be like under the thumb of this man. I reveled in the fate I was saving the next woman from.

"I'll be there," I promised, glancing at the clock that had barely struck twelve. My stomach panged with hunger and thirst. I ignored it.

"Good. I'm so sure you'll like it here, Piper," he added before he hung up.

My hand was shaking as I put the phone down. I was most definitely out of my depth here.

Six hours. I had six hours to learn not only how to swim in these shark-infested waters but to become a shark myself.

Knox

Powerless.

I had promised myself I would never be powerless again. Never in a position where my life was controlled by outside forces. People.

I'd always been the most dangerous person in the room. The most feared. My fate my own. My demons my friends. I'd never been more in control than I had been in Stone's office, poised to kill him.

Yet since the moment I'd laid eyes on Piper, I'd become untethered from all of it. I'd been operating by lying to myself that I was still able to grasp on to the reins.

It had all come crashing down when Piper entered Stone's office, clad in white, looking like a dream and embodying my worst fucking nightmare.

Powerless. I'd been powerless while watching her offer herself up to save me. Spouting lies, thinking that she was convincing enough in her coldness to make me think she didn't care. When her whole fucking soul burned for me. When I knew every inch of it and could tell by the flutter of her eyelids and the tremble of her bottom lip how much her words pained her.

Watching the pain she felt while she thought she was hurting me was the most agonizing thing I'd experienced in my existence. Followed closely to Stone's hands on her, her wincing in pain, the fucking barrel of a gun to her head. One twitch of his finger and every part of her would've been extinguished.

I paced my penthouse, vowing to kill Lukyan. He'd given me his word that he'd take care of her, yet she'd somehow been able to make it to Rosso. And no fucking way did she accomplish that alone. I didn't doubt Piper was capable, but no one outsmarted or escaped Lukyan. He'd helped her. Led her to her death like a lamb to the slaughter. Dressed her in fucking clothes she couldn't even fight in, that constricted her, packaged her up like a goddamn treat.

Powerless. He'd made her appear powerless.

Which I knew was the point in their little, fucked-up plan, but it was by no means infallible. In fact, it had a less than 1 percent chance of fucking working.

Yes, I'd make him pay. But now was not the time.

Think... I had to fucking *think*.

Piper was in Stone's hands.

His hands were likely all over her, his lips on her skin.

I sent a vase smashing against the wall as if destroying something so meaningless would take the edge off the fury practically blinding me.

I eyed the shards and craved the feel of them cutting into my skin, the relief of some pain, subduing the buildup of poison barreling through me.

But that wouldn't help. Not then.

Piper was no longer at the restaurant. I knew Stone well enough to know that he'd taken her to his residence outside of New York.

Because he was smart. Because he expected me to come for her, and he had every inch of that property surveilled. He would've scented me from five miles away if I hastily tried to approach it.

And he'd kill Piper. Of that I was certain. He wouldn't wait for me to come to make a big production out of it. He'd do it, then he'd wait for me to come upon her lifeless body, watching in satisfaction as I crumbled before his eyes.

There was no way for me to get to her. Not immediately anyway.

That meant she was alone. Alone with him and his whims and cruelty.

The simple thought had panic, sheer, unbridled panic hurtling through my heart.

She'd been alone with me and survived it, I reminded myself.

I must've had something foreign in my blood to believe she'd survive him.

Yet I had to have *faith*. Not in some obscure deity created by man in order to control women. I had faith in *Piper*.

But nonetheless, I was completely fucking powerless.

I wanted to reduce the world to ashes to protect her, to save her, but all I could do at that point was trust she had the flame inside of her to do it herself.

PIPER

I didn't change for dinner. There was nothing for me to change into. Was that another sign of Stone's temporary plans for me? No clothes or personal effects because I wouldn't be alive to need to brush my teeth or change my panties?

That only served to motivate me in my mission even more. Kill one of the most dangerous men I'd ever encountered when I didn't even believe in killing or eating animals. Though I was a vegetarian, appalled at even the thought of helpless animal blood, the blood of men, on the other hand... I could admit I was a little thirsty for it.

I'd spent hours in that room, thinking, stewing. Gazing upon the beautiful vista yet seeing nothing but the woods of Appalachia. I'd spent my hours there, combing over every memory I made with Knox, using it to fortify myself, to build me up.

When the hand on the clock read five minutes to six, I went to my door. I'd been expecting someone to come to escort me, but no one came, and nobody was waiting outside when I opened the unlocked door. I peered down the long hallway. Sense of direction wasn't my strong suit when it came to mansions. I knew my way around Manhattan and the woods of Appalachia, but not here.

My stomach turned at the memory of a cabin thousands of miles away, half a world away, forgotten by anyone but me and Knox.

With great effort, I pushed him out of my mind, turning left from the bedroom then walking in the general direction I'd come from. Because I wasn't practiced at being an assassin—if that's what I was—I hadn't taken in the layout of this huge house beyond appreciating the Mediterranean furnishings. Rookie mistake.

After a few wrong turns, I found myself in an opulent dining room complete with oil paintings and an outrageously-long table that could've comfortably sat twelve people.

The room was bathed in soft candlelight, and the figure sitting at the end of the table was an imposing shadow, coming into focus once I'd traversed the length of the table, doing my best not to limp. I made a mental note to give Elizabeth a tongue-lashing for her choice in footwear for my task.

That was if I survived it.

"Piper, you found the dining room." Stone's smile was warm as he stood to pull out my chair. He glanced at his watch. "Two minutes late, but we'll address that later." Cold promise threaded into his tone, and I restrained a shudder.

I wondered if it was a game. All of it. Leaving me in the room without guards, letting me roam about freely. If this was something he did on the regular, a hobby for the man who didn't like golf— terrorizing women. It made sense. It was a pastime enjoyed by powerful men for centuries.

Despite my hatred for the man, I kept my expression docile, let him pull out the chair, didn't squirm when he brushed hair from the nape of my neck and inhaled.

There was a wine glass in front of me, full of amber liquid, and a tall water glass beside it.

"I have come to understand my mistake when I served you wine during our last dinner," Stone said, taking his own seat. "Rest assured, this is nonalcoholic wine." He scrunched up his nose. "It does go against my very nature that such a thing exists, but we make sacrifices, don't we?"

I again did my best not to scowl at him and hurl the nonalcoholic wine in his face.

"Forgive me if I don't take you at your word." I picked up the water glass when I realized I hadn't had a sip of water in hours.

Because of that, I drank greedily and had already taken a large gulp before the burn hit my throat, and I realized it was not water.

I choked the vodka back into the glass, the liquid spilling all over the napkin in front of me and my hands.

Stone had been watching me carefully, hands clasped in front of him. "I suspected you wouldn't take me at my word." He shook his head. "Rest assured, Piper, there will be consequences if you don't trust me in the future."

I coughed, desperate to get the taste from my mouth, yet unable to find anything at the table for me to wash away the vile taste. Except the wine that Stone assured me wasn't alcoholic.

My body revolted, reviling the warmth from the small amount of vodka that made it into my system.

I looked at Stone, horrified at the realization of what he had done to me. Just the beginning of the tortures a life with him promised. A bitter taste of my future.

"It's good for me to gauge how much control you have over your addiction," he said genially, reaching over to mop the rest of my mess with his own napkin.

"It would serve me well to have a wife who fell apart if she happened to be exposed to a bit of wine every now and then," he continued, belittling my addiction with a handful of words. "I'm sure you'll taste it on me often enough." I barely suppressed a shudder at the glint in his eye when he said that.

I was still gaping at him, offended and electrified with fury at this man.

Unbidden, I thought of how instantly Knox swore off alcohol the second he understood my addiction. He didn't want to cause me even a second of discomfort, didn't want to consume something that almost destroyed me. Yet Stone delighted in the taste of it on his lips, on forcing it onto mine.

My heart pulsed with pain.

Stone lifted his hand, clicking his fingers. I jumped when the doors opened, and a well-dressed man appeared, holding two steaming plates.

"Giovanni, would you mind getting my betrothed some water and fresh napkins?" he kindly asked as the man—Giovanni, I guessed—nodded once, taking the vodka glass and the sodden napkins away, not even glancing at me as he placed a bowl in front of me.

I stared at the bowl of soup, crusty bread beside it, and my stomach growled painfully.

My body hungered for his punishment more. This horrible, cruel, entitled man. Seconds passed without either of us speaking, me marinating in outrage that reeked of vodka.

Giovanni returned with what I presumed was water and more napkins.

"Thank you, Giovanni," Stone said cordially, then the man left.

"It's not poisoned, I assure you," Stone informed me when I didn't do anything but stare at the soup in front of me.

He picked up his spoon and started eating, as if to prove it to me.

Still, I stayed frozen. No fucking way would I sit there and enjoy a meal with him.

"Eat!" he yelled, the unexpected violence in his tone making me jump.

I quickly picked up my spoon with a clatter to obey his command. With Knox, I'd so readily battled him against all of his orders, despite the sheer danger that emanated from him. Yet with Stone, I had genuine fear, knowing the reprimands I would receive would be real and permanent.

I was sure the flavor of the soup was wonderful since it smelled fresh and enticing, but all I could taste was bile. For a while, there were no other sounds in the room but the clink of cutlery against porcelain as we ate our soup.

I didn't fold first. Any words I had to say to Stone would've broken my cover as a slightly willing fiancée. So I waited.

My bowl emptied as I went through the motions of eating. Giovanni came in as if he sensed I was done, sweeping the empty bowl away.

"It might interest you to know," Stone dabbed at his face with a napkin, "that your sister and one of my younger lieutenants have gone missing." His jaw twitched, the only sign that this displeased him.

It took everything I had to keep a smile from my face. This was the first concrete news I had that Daisy was safe. If she wasn't, I didn't doubt that Stone would have paraded her around this table in handcuffs or with a gun to her head.

"Missing?" I repeated, reaching to take the glass of amber liquid that he had assured me was not alcoholic. I took a small sip. It tasted just as earthy and rich as I remembered wine being, so who could know if it was real or not? I decided I'd worry about the potential relapse later. This was a game I was playing, one I was learning on the fly, but one I intended to win.

"What a shame," I tutted. "Your favorite bargaining tool is gone, and now you're going to have to resort to either charming me or threatening me into staying." I took another long sip of the wine, not breaking eye contact.

Stone watched me carefully, measuring my every word, my posture. He was probing me for weaknesses, sincerity, for threats. Surely, he was smart enough to know that I had come to hurt him, not to concede. Then again, male arrogance knew no bounds.

"I don't think I'll have a problem finding ... methods to convince you that becoming my wife is in your best interests." His eyes were aglow with excitement. This was turning him on, thinking of the ways he'd bring me to heel. This wasn't his first rodeo. He was practiced at torturing, breaking women. Something instinctive told me I was not the first woman to sit here.

My spine tingled with unease, and every instinct inside of me shouted 'danger.'

The door to the dining room opened and closed before I could say anything and before Stone could threaten me further. Giovanni placed a large bowl of pasta in front of me, creamy and invitingly smelling of garlic and parsley.

"I was also made aware of your preferences when it comes to eating meat," Stone said, sipping his wine. "And I've made the necessary arrangements. Though I hope throughout our relation-ship I can coax you over to the dark side. Giovanni makes veal that will melt in your mouth."

I glanced up at Stone, plastering a smile on my face. "Why doesn't it surprise me that you revel in eating baby animals?" I snapped before I could stop myself.

Stone's face was blank for a handful of seconds before he smiled, chuckling. The sound was low and throaty and might've sounded warm to the casual observer, if you didn't know what a piece of shit he was.

"Ah, there's that fire that drew me in. I was worried you'd let it go out in your ... time with Knox." I caught the slight stiffening of his shoulders and the glazing over of his eyes as he mentioned Knox. He was forcing his composure, but I could see the rage festering underneath.

He wanted to punish me. Hurt me. I could see it. Feel it. But first he wanted to coax me into a false sense of security.

Maybe it might've worked had he just plucked me off the street, but I doubted it. I was not one to be wowed by grandeur, money, a shiny suit and smile. Not when the man who fathered me was just like him. Cruel and weak.

"It'll serve you well, having that spark." He cleared his throat, glossing over the Knox remark.

I forced myself to eat some pasta, if only to have something to do that wasn't stare at Stone. The flavor profile surpassed even my rage-filled body, and I had to suppress a moan.

"Is that what you want from me?" I asked once I swallowed. "To serve you?"

Stone's eyebrow rose, and he leaned back in his chair, eyes making a slow trail down my body. "You came here of your own free will," he said instead of answering once he was done assaulting me with his gaze. "Well aware of the lengths I would go to in order to make you mine. Do you expect anything else from a man like me than a wife who will know her place?"

I considered his words. My next move. How dangerous it would be. Every decision I made felt riskier and riskier. I still couldn't shake the certainty that Stone had no intentions of marrying me, that he was going to play with me until he wasn't amused anymore, breaking then discarding me.

If I acted how he expected me to act.

Looking longingly at the most delicious pasta I'd eaten in my life, I reached up with my napkin to dab at my mouth.

Feeling Stone's eyes on me, I pushed out of my chair, noting him tense as I rounded the table. He turned his body toward me, as if he expected me to attack at any moment.

The small knife that Elizabeth had given me was tucked into the garter belt of the exquisite lingerie I was wearing. It had been slightly weird to put on the lingerie of someone who I had just met, however nice they were, but she'd assured me that it was brand-new and had been custom-made so there was a spot for the blade so thin, I barely felt it. Except for the cold brush of steel against my inner thigh every time I crossed my legs.

It was a risky spot for the blade, not entirely easily accessible and not good in a pinch, but we'd reasoned that any other kind of weapon would've been noticed by the men who had indeed searched me for weapons when I had first arrived at the restaurant.

My hands ached for the blade, thirsting to embed it into Stone's neck. Patience... I had to be patient. I was not going to be a slave to my anger, let it push me into hasty decisions. No show of brute force would save me here. I needed a delicate touch. I reached back for the zipper of my skirt, bile replacing the aftertaste of the pasta as I shimmied it down to my ankles, revealing the garter belt, stockings, and white, lace panties.

I'd inspected myself from this angle to see if the blade was visible. It wasn't. And I was hoping that Stone might be too caught off guard to look too hard at the wrong places.

My hunch about him being a big, old pervert before he was anything else proved correct when his gaze focused in on where my panties left *nothing* to the imagination.

He pushed his chair out, splaying his legs open with the arrogance of a man who knew that the gesture itself was an invitation, an order and a threat all in one.

I licked my lips and forced a seductive smile onto my face, as if I were hungry, wanting instead of trying to fight back vomit.

I took measured steps toward him before giving away all of my pride and kneeling at his feet, my hands going to his zipper.

His hands went to my hair, fisting it and tugging it back brutally. Nothing in the pain was erotic; it was a grip meant to *hurt*.

Stone's mouth was stretched into a satisfied smile as he forced my eyes to meet his. "On your knees for me, Piper. This may be a fruitful union after all."

My scalp screamed with pain and tears filled my eyes, but I forced myself not to grimace. "I think after I'm done here, you'll understand how badly I want to serve you." It wasn't a lie. I did want to serve a man's whims. Wanted to kneel at his feet. Just not that man. And I'd serve Knox in the way he preferred. With blood.

Any moment now, I told myself. *Any moment now he's going to see through me.*

This was a ruthless, educated man, the head of a powerful crime organization. There was no way a woman baring her pussy and getting on her knees in front of him was enough to make him let down his guard, let go of all sense.

He kept hold of my hair a second longer, pulling even tighter.

This is it, he's going to hurt me now. It's over.

He let go of my hair to roughly shove his fingers in my mouth. They were hairy and large and tasted sour.

I forced myself to dutifully suck them even though I wanted to vomit. He moved them roughly, penetrating the back of my throat with a spear of pain, activating my gag reflex. Panic crawled up my throat as he made it hard to breathe. Spots danced in my vision as I fought against my instinct to bite down on his fucking sausage fingers.

Smiling with ill-gotten male satisfaction, he removed his hand in order to unzip his trousers.

My hand on his wrist stopped him. It was bold of me, breaking the sexual tension, and I instantly noted the way his body stiffened, and his eyes glowed with irritation at my action.

"Won't we be ...interrupted?" I asked, still speaking in that faux-raspy tone, eyes darting to the door that Giovanni came in and out of.

Again, I waited for Stone to get suspicious, to understand what I was doing. Ensuring no one was coming in to save *him*.

Instead, he smiled. Why wouldn't he? He didn't think he needed to be saved. He was the one who had the powerless female on her knees. "Shy? I wouldn't expect that from you."

I ran my tongue along my front teeth. "If you want me to be yours, I'm just yours." What I was doing was risky, considering the Knox-shaped elephant in the room. "I'm not a toy." I forced myself to inject agency into my tone, trying to impersonate the way in which a mob wife might speak. "If I'm yours, I'm yours. No voyeurs."

Stone smiled wider and leaned over to type into the phone that had been lying beside his plate. I waited with bated breath.

He returned to his stance, leaning back, seemingly relaxed.

With a thundering heart, I went to where his dick strained against his slacks, unzipping them then reaching into his underwear to free it completely.

I circled the base of his cock, gripping it tightly, earning a groan of pleasure from Stone. I looked up at him purposefully. "It's your power," I whispered to him. "I couldn't resist how fucking powerful you are. It makes me so hot."

My other hand was busy between my legs, finding the small, sharp blade. But from the casual observer, it could have appeared that I was touching myself.

Stone was so deluded that he believed me. Leaning down as if to wrap my mouth around him, I moved rather clumsily instead, freeing the blade and embedding it right where Lukyan had instructed me a femoral artery lay. I stuck it down deep and hard then yanked along the skin to make a long incision in case I was off by a few centimeters. If I was, then I'd almost certainly be dead.

Blood sprayed at my chest in spurts, communicating that I had in fact hit the right place.

Stone let out a muffled yell before I was catapulted out of my haze and burst up, plastering my sweaty hand over his mouth.

His body spasmed as he tried to fight me. I gritted my teeth at his strength, panicking that I was no match for it. He would overpower me. Get my hand, yell for help, then I'd be done for. I forced myself to fight against him, even though it was a losing battle. But within seconds, his grip waned, and his body was no longer stronger than mine.

My eyes were locked onto his as our bodies ended up pressed together in a horrifically intimate position. I watched as his vehemence gave way to apprehension, to realization that he was dying. Then he turned desperate. Helpless. Afraid.

Unable to look away, my heart thumped as blood pooled around us, the intense spurting from his thigh slowing as his robust struggle became weak jerks against me.

My lungs filled with lead as I watched life creep out of his eyes, like water draining from a bathtub.

It was horrifying. Unnatural. I'd never forget it. Not until the day I died.

My heart pounded against my throat as I stayed in place, transfixed, my palm still pressed against the slack mouth of a corpse.

How long did I stay like that? Seconds? Minutes? Who could know? My heartbeat was no longer thundering; it had slowed to a low thump, but it still felt high in my chest, almost in my esophagus.

I stepped away from his body as it slumped off the chair and onto the ground with a loud thump. My eyes darted to the door Giovanni had been entering and exiting from. Would he have heard that and alerted some kind of alarm?

I decided that if that happened, I would not like to be caught in nothing but lingerie, so I quickly shuffled back into my skirt.

The process took seconds, but it felt like eons, the clock in the corner ticking in the now stifling silence.

My breathing came in heavy pants as I fastened my skirt.

I'd done it.

Killed Stone De Luca. Don of the Italian mob. I'd done it. Myself. Without help.

But it turned out that was the easy part.

I still had to figure out how to get out of there alive.

TWENTY-THREE

PIPER

I was covered in blood.

I hadn't considered how messy killing someone would be.

"White was a bad choice," I muttered. Another thing I'd tell Elizabeth. *Ensure your next ward is sent off in comfortable shoes and in shades of black when planning on killing someone.*

I looked down at the lifeless man in front of me, blood everywhere, his flaccid cock hanging out of his pants like a sad worm.

I expected feelings of sickness to overwhelm me. After all, I'd just ended a life. A human life. No matter his sins, he was human. But I didn't feel any of the regret or self-hatred I expected. Instead, I felt satisfied. He was gone from my life. This man who'd felt entitled to women, to control over bodies and lives, who had likely terrorized countless people, ruined lives. His reign of terror was over.

One in the sea of many wasn't much, but it was one less. And I'd done that.

It felt good. Empowering.

That power didn't last for long though, a low pop of gunfire sounding in the hall. My gaze whipped toward the closed door.

Screwing up my face in disgust, I leaned down to search Stone's body for a gun. Surely, this guy was wearing a shoulder holster. He was a mob boss, after all. But nothing.

"A disappointment, even in death," I grumbled as more pops sounded.

I tried my best to brush the blood off me, which only served to smear it more.

My time was limited, that much I knew. Knox had obviously not gone quietly like I'd wanted, which had surprised me. It didn't surprise me that he was coming back for me, even after I'd hurt him so badly. But it did surprise me that he was signaling it. It was taking a risk with my life. He had no way of knowing I'd killed Stone, and he would've considered what Stone might've done upon hearing sounds of conflict outside.

That was, kill me.

Even though I'd gravely wounded Knox, I knew he wouldn't take such a risk with my life.

Something must've gone wrong.

Or one of Stone's other enemies had picked a really inconvenient time to attack.

It didn't matter which it was. All that mattered was that I needed more than a knife if I planned on making it out of there alive. Which I did. How horribly ironic would it have been if I made it through all that just to be killed by some nameless henchman in the end?

It would make for a good tragic love story, at least. Hadn't I thought, in my heart of hearts, that Knox and I weren't going to have a happily ever after?

"Enough of that shit, Piper," I hissed at myself.

I clutched the knife I was holding as I searched the room for a weapon. The space was expensively appointed—no handguns hanging on the walls as I'd expected for a supervillain.

Inconvenient.

The sounds came closer, then the door burst open.

I froze where I was standing, with the bloodied knife in my hand and Stone's corpse at my feet.

I didn't recognize the man in front of me, but he had a gun, and he raised it toward my head the second he understood I'd killed his boss.

Though I wasn't one to give up easily, I squeezed my eyes shut and waited. I couldn't outrun a bullet, after all.

Knox, I love you, I silently called into the ether.

I flinched at the sound of a low pop. But it wasn't followed by pain or any kind of impact.

I didn't feel anything at all.

Maybe it was a headshot. Maybe I was already dead, that it happened that quickly. But no, the afterlife wouldn't smell of coppery blood, excrement and expensive cologne.

My eyes eased open, and the man who had previously been holding a gun to my head was sprawled on the ground, red pooling underneath his head.

And the man standing there, who had obviously shot him, to my complete and utter surprise, was Lukyan.

Not a hair was out of place as his eyes flickered to Stone's corpse, and he nodded once. I supposed he was impressed, though he didn't say it.

"You ready to go?" he asked me blandly when I didn't say anything.

The request was ordinary, as if he hadn't just fought his way through however many people in an effort to ... what? Save me?

I looked around. "Um, yeah." I stepped on unsteady feet around the corpses to approach him.

"I thought you said it wasn't your job to come in and save the day?" I asked him, breathing heavily.

Lukyan didn't smile so much as grimace. "My wife convinced me to try on the hero's cape. I don't think I'll be putting it on again."

I swallowed a hysterical giggle. "You should. It suits you."

He gave me a look that could melt paint and that might've flayed the skin off my bones if I hadn't gone through everything I'd just gone through.

"I won't. Consider yourself the luckiest woman in the world. And if you see me after this, run because it means someone paid me to kill you."

I blinked at the line delivered so flawlessly that it sent cold terror clutching my throat like a vice. But I'd just killed someone. I was in love with an arguably scarier killer. I wasn't so easily afraid those days.

"Dude, someone needs to write a movie about you or something," I wiped some blood from my cheek. "You're like John Wick, but you killed your *own puppy*."

Lukyan looked at me like I had grown another head, not my question with an answer as he turned down the hall, not looking back to see if I followed.

Which I did.

I was not blindly deluding myself into the whole *femme fatale* thing. It was mostly dumb luck that had me accomplishing my goal, that and a whole lot of feminine rage. But that would only get me so far. And I wasn't so much of a feminist that I wouldn't hand the reins over to a very capable, ruthless hitman willing to do the rest of the work.

So through the horrifying maze of bodies in his wake, I followed him.

———

We made it out of Stone's place alive.

Not alone either.

I'd been surprised and delighted to meet up with Elizabeth in the foyer. She was holding a gun and had bodies of her own at her feet. Clad sensibly in black, no summery sundress to be found, her hair pulled off her face, making her look sharper, more severe. A predator. That was a *femme fatale*.

Feminine rage honed, sharpened and fashioned into a weapon.

Lukyan didn't hesitate to abandon me, walking over to his wife, capturing her in his arms and murmuring something in her ear. She replied too low for me to hear.

They were a sight, the two of them, armed and beautiful, entwined in the foyer of a grand mansion surrounded by bodies...

They brought a new meaning to the term 'power couple.'

Melancholy slammed painfully into me at the sight of them, yearning for Knox while also understanding this was not my new identity, clad in designer clothing, covered in blood. I would never be his equal.

If he even still wanted me.

With a desert in my throat and an emptiness in my heart, I'd followed Lukyan and Elizabeth to the waiting SUV. Elizabeth surveyed me with pride that felt sacred. She didn't say anything, but I somehow felt we'd been connected for life.

Not exactly girlfriends or even kindred spirits, but women who loved men on the fringes of society.

I didn't even ask where we were going. I'd guessed back to the city, hopefully to Knox. But we pulled off onto a long driveway toward a small, nondescript house.

A 'safe house' Lukyan had explained. And then they'd told me Knox was on his way, and we were to wait there for him. Elizabeth had presented me with a small bag—a change of clothes and toiletries—then Lukyan showed me to the back of the small house to a bedroom with an adjoining shower.

His sheer energy was overwhelming as he lingered in the room, taking over it with his presence. I'd expected him to leave as soon as possible, since he did not seem overly fond of me.

"You've still got a choice," he said instead of going anywhere. As always, his voice was low. Harsh.

I glanced up at him after eyeing myself in the mirror for a long time. I barely recognized myself.

"You've done things, seen things that are everyday events for people like me, Knox," his gaze skirted to the hallway. "My wife. But you are not stuck on this path. Not yet at least. You can still go back."

I stared at him, shocked at what he was saying. It felt like mercy, like he was offering empathy. A kind word from a killer. An opportunity to go back to a life that felt as if it were on another planet.

"It will be a variation of this." He motioned to my blood-soaked body. "Not every day. Not all the time. But you won't escape it. He cannot escape it. His world. You still have the chance."

Did I want to go back to my life before Knox? After seeing the horrors that human beings were capable of? The very real world operating beneath the surface? There was none of the romance popular culture injected into it. It was dangerous and vile and terrifying.

"Why are you saying this?" I asked Lukyan.

His eyes once again went to the hallway. "Because I often wish someone had said it to my wife."

I stared back at him, the tortured villain, pain clear in his words if not in his face. The sheer magnitude of love he felt for his wife was overwhelming.

"If they had, she wouldn't have taken it. Not for the world," I told him.

His head snapped up. "You don't know her."

"Don't I?" I asked, unafraid of the brutality in his tone.

We stayed like that, standing there in some sort of standoff.

That was until Knox pushed through the door so hard it came off its hinges. I flinched in shock at his entrance, my heart hammering at his presence. First relief, then fury coated his body like armor, eyes wide, nostrils flaring, hands fisted at his sides. His advance toward me was nothing short of ferocious.

"What the FUCK was that?" he roared. Right in my face.

I had envisioned somewhat of a more tender reunion.

Then again, I deserved his anger, didn't I? How quickly had I forgotten those hateful words I'd spoken to him. My brush with death had infused me with too much hope for romance, it seemed.

I was shocked at Knox's savage bellow. At his abandoning of the control I was used to seeing in him. It wasn't just the door that was unhinged, it was *him.*

My pulse thrashed in my ears as I struggled to steady my breathing.

"I was—"

He cut me off with a hand at my throat, pushing me backward so my back slammed against the wall. My body cried out in pain, still recovering from a beating ... how long ago now? Knox had been so mindful with my injuries, careful. Right then, there was no care in the way he handled me.

"You were stupid. And reckless with the only thing that matters," he snarled. "Your *life.*"

I blinked rapidly, trying to weather the sheer weight of his anger, nothing like he'd ever unleashed on me before.

"Knox."

When a voice shattered through the cloud of his ferocity, I realized that Lukyan was still in the room. I'd truly forgotten about his presence, something to note since Lukyan's presence was almost as all-encompassing as Knox's.

In a smooth move that seemed to take a single blink, one of Knox's hands left my throat as the other took the gun from the holster underneath his jacket, pointing it in Lukyan's direction.

"Say another word in a situation that involves me and my woman," he dared.

I tore my gaze away from Knox, horrified that he was threatening Lukyan after he'd helped us. And not just threatening him; I got the distinct impression that Knox wouldn't hesitate to pull the trigger. He was balanced on a knife's edge, savagery clawing at the edges of his soul. I could see it. His thirst for death.

Lukyan, for his part, did not look the least bit afraid that he was quite possibly seconds from death. In fact, he raised an eyebrow, as if amused. "The thanks I get for saving your woman?" He shook his head, then all amusement left his face. "I'll give you one pass for this." He waved toward the gun. "Once. Because I understand the pull of the underworld when your woman is in danger. But this is not a grace I will give you again." His eyes bounced to me, to the hand at my neck. "Good luck, Piper," he said before he turned his back to leave.

Arrogant or brave or delusional, to turn his back on Knox with the gun still pointed at him.

Admittedly very badass too.

I'd held my breath because I really did not need to witness another murder. Especially of Lukyan. I might not have liked the man—he was impossible to like—but I liked his wife a great deal. I felt a kinship with them, had an affinity to the intensity of the connection they shared. I understood what Knox would be obliterating if he had pulled the trigger. It would be destroying something truly sacred, and if he had shot him, I didn't doubt karma would find us—if there was an us—to return the favor one day.

Luckily, he didn't.

But he didn't lower the gun until long after Lukyan had closed the door, Knox's chest rising and falling quickly.

Nor did he let me go from where he had me pinned against the wall.

My breathing wasn't entirely obstructed, but my lungs were beginning to burn from the effort it took me to suck in air. My ribs throbbed, and my muscles groaned from the exertion I'd put them through these past few days.

I wanted to call out to him. Wanted to lift my arm to touch him, embrace him. But all of my instincts were telling me to stay still, to wait.

Slowly, Knox put the gun back in its holster then returned his attention to me.

Rage was an inferno in his eyes, but it seemed somewhat contained now. But I didn't miss the cruel, angry shine that seemed to cover him like armor.

Fair enough.

I'd shown him that he needed armor around me now. It didn't matter that I'd done it for the right reasons. With the best of intentions. The road to hell was paved with all those good intentions, after all. And that's where I walked. For Knox. Into hell. I would've lived there, as long as it was with him. A fool's hope, maybe.

Knox searched my face. Every pore. Every crevice. For what, I didn't know. Maybe marks? Bruises?

The pressure at my neck remained, but now his thumb brushed against my artery with a gentleness that was a balm to my soul.

Knox exhaled roughly and slowly as he leaned forward, his forehead resting against mine.

My frayed nerves were unable to turn off entirely, but I slumped at the touch, my body reveling in the intimacy of his touch.

"I'm sorry," I whispered. "For saying those things. Those horrific, untrue things. I didn't mean them. I know it'll take more than that for you to forgive me, but..."

Knox brought his head back up so he could regard me with a crystal-clear gaze. No hurt swam in it. "I do not need to forgive you for what you said because I knew you didn't mean it, right when you said it."

His tone was harsh, still laced with anger but not for the betrayal of using his most intimate trauma against him.

"Piper, do you believe I think so little of you that I would let words, foolish words used as an attempt at a *rescue* so much as scratch my feelings for you?" He continued rubbing my neck. "I do not devalue what we are so easily. I do not devalue *you* so easily."

"You're not mad at me?" I asked, breathy at the gravity of his words.

"Oh, I'm fucking livid at you," he gritted out, eyes glowing with that lividity. "Not for that, though. For putting yourself in the line of fire in the first place. For not trusting me to take care of you." There it was. Hurt. He was hurt that I hadn't trusted him.

"I trusted you to take care of me," I quickly countered. "I didn't want you to have to. I wanted to save *you*."

Knox didn't belittle me with an *oh, you're so cute, you're a woman who thinks you can save a man* type stare. No, his brows bunched as he searched my eyes. "You save me, Piper," he leaned forward so our lips almost brushed, "by breathing. Existing. You do not save me by giving me the abject terror of watching another man take you from me without the grace of watching that man take his last breath. You stole his death from me. Worse, you marked your soul when it is my job to keep it pristine."

He lowered his hand to my chest, which was soaked and crusted with blood. I hadn't exactly forgotten about it, but I hadn't fathomed the sheer amount of blood I was coated in. I looked like Carrie at the prom.

Knox's hand skimmed over my body, his face impenetrable. The power in which he was holding himself still made his entire form seem to vibrate. I could feel the furor.

"I should probably change, shower." I was suddenly uncomfortable, shy under his intense gaze.

"You're not leaving my sight," he growled. "I can't fucking breathe properly until my cock is inside you, Piper." I gasped as his hand skimmed down my skirt, hiking it up.

"He had you for eight hours and thirty-six minutes." He fisted my skirt, eyes locking with mine. "What did—"

"He didn't rape me," I interrupted him in order to banish the misery I saw chaining his soul.

He exhaled heavily but didn't relax. "There are other things—"

Again, I cut him off, but I didn't do it with words; I did it by taking hold of his wrist and pulling it upward to where my pussy was wet and waiting for him.

Knox let out a low snarl as he felt it.

"He didn't do anything to me," I told him. "I did it all. I killed him with my bare hands. He didn't lay a finger in any places that belong to you."

Maybe a little white lie since Stone technically had touched me, but dead men kept secrets.

Knox's gaze zoomed in on me as he searched my pussy, finding the string of my tampon I'd hid with an expert hand. Inconvenient to be on my period when I was supposed to be taking down a criminal enterprise. But I'd managed it despite men's favorite line, using our menstruation as the reason why we couldn't be trusted with power.

I did it all while wearing white too.

Knox swiftly drew my tampon out, flinging it carelessly across the room. Though I was near mad with desire, I made a mental note to retrieve it after we were done. I didn't have shame over Knox handling my used tampon, but that's where my comfortability ended.

Knox rubbed my aching clit, and I let out a strangled moan as I realized just how keyed up I was. How desperate I was for his merciless touch.

"You killed him." Knox continued rubbing.

"Yes," I rasped.

"How did you do it?"

I tilted my head at his request, asked in a guttural tone.

He stopped rubbing at my pause, stopped delving into my arousal, no longer coating me with it and blood.

"How did you do it, Petal?" he repeated, teeth grazing my lip.

"I-I ruptured h-his artery."

Knox's hand resumed its stroking.

"Which one?"

My eyes were in danger of rolling to the back of my head from this sordid, forbidden, depraved conversation happening in tandem with this overt and delicious sexual act. And I liked it.

"Femoral," I gasped, my pleasure building, the edge rapidly approaching.

Knox didn't stop his vicious assault, didn't take his gaze from mine, yet he slowed his circles, stealing my imminent climax.

"So you had to get close," he deduced, his words smoke and iron.

I nodded.

"Where were you?" He leaned forward, inhaling my neck, lips grazing the skin.

Even through my haze of feral desire, I knew answering this question was dangerous. Knox was thirsty for information that had the power to unravel him. But also, if I wasn't mistaken, it was turning him on. A whole lot. I'd never felt such unrestrained, wild hunger from him before.

And that was truly saying something.

"On my knees," I whispered, barely audible, terrified my answer would make him stop. Make him angry enough to punish me with no release to this almost painful buildup of tension.

He pulled back, jaw marble, nostrils flaring, eyes pits of wantonness. "You brought down one of the most powerful men in the country ... on your knees."

Pursing my lips, I nodded.

His lips stretched into a wicked smile. He lifted his hand to cup my jaw with his large hand.

Then his fingers were no longer working my soaked clit. One of my legs was hitched around his waist, his hand expertly freeing his cock before sending it thrusting into me in one brutal blow. My head would've thrown back to hit the wall in pleasure if he didn't have such a tight hold over me.

Our gazes remained intertwined as he plunged in hard.

"My good girl," he grunted. "My good fucking girl."

My world exploded on the next thrust, from the praise, from the expert angle, the pent-up frustration.

All I knew for certain was that against that wall, covered in blood from the inside out, we had the most life-shattering sex I'd ever had in my life.

Elizabeth was right.

Humanity was overrated.

TWENTY-FOUR

PIPER

After I was showered and changed—with Knox leaning against the sink in the bathroom watching, never taking his eyes off me, as promised—we left the safe house.

Lukyan and Elizabeth were long gone, unsurprisingly since he and Knox had exchanged death threats. It was also good that they left so they hadn't heard our loud lovemaking—if it could be called that. But I felt sad that I couldn't express my gratitude to them both.

I was also hungry for more of their story, to understand how Elizabeth came to be the way she was, how they made it work.

It felt incredibly juvenile to be wanting to talk to two hitmen— hit … people?—about the secrets to a long-lasting relationship, but with the real world rapidly approaching, I was desperate to figure out a way to make Knox and I work. And by rapidly approaching, I was being quite literal. We were driving back to Manhattan.

I'd marinated on that the entire drive back to the city. The villain was dead—one of them, at least—so I assumed I was otherwise safe. If not, Knox wouldn't have agreed to take me back home.

Regardless, our story wasn't over.

We weren't riding off into the proverbial sunset; we were driving toward real life—which I'd longed for at the beginning of my captivity, but now I just yearned for Knox to drive us back to our cabin in the mountains. Reality be damned.

But we couldn't hold off the world forever. The truth of that was searing and somehow more terrifying than the mob boss I'd just killed. And I was sure that deed would come to haunt me eventually.

The ringing of a phone ripped me out of my daze.

My phone.

I glanced at where the ringing was coming from, the center console. I hadn't even noticed it.

Knox must've gotten it for me at some point. It had been taken an age ago, when he'd apprehended me during my run. I'd assumed he'd destroyed it. Yet there it was.

Though I wanted to know the details of when and how, the name flashing on the screen silenced my questions. My eyes were on Knox as I answered.

"Daisy!" I half-yelled, delirious with worry. "Please tell me you're okay." She had been in the back of my mind the whole time, but I'd been convinced she was safe. For my own sanity more than anything else.

"*Me?*" she yelled. No halfway about it. I winced and held the phone farther from my ear. "I'm not the one who was apparently embroiled in a plot to *assassinate and overthrow an entire regime.*" I could still hear her crystal-clear from that distance, as could Knox.

His hand twitched on the steering wheel.

I wouldn't have said that I considered Stone's enterprise to be a regime, but it seemed ill-advised to interrupt Daisy. And even hysterical, my sister's voice was music to my ears.

"I know you take the older sister role very seriously, but this is too far, even for you," she continued, still shouting. "Couldn't you let go of the reins for just a moment, and let Knox save the day?"

Her tone had lowered, but it still delivered a sting. "I'm sure he was absolutely itching to. I bet you playing hero chafed his horns."

I didn't miss the underlying disdain my sister had for Knox, even still.

"Not my style, Daisy," I told her. "And what if he needed to be saved too? The hero costume is so much more flattering on women."

I didn't look at him when I said that. I assumed it was an unwise thing to say, endangering his masculinity or something.

Knox's hand went to my chin, turning it so I faced him. He didn't say anything, just cupped my face, watching me for a dangerous amount of time before his gaze returned to the road.

I guessed he wasn't angry.

My mind whirled with all that went unsaid in that gaze. He didn't appear to feel emasculated or irritated. He looked ... proud. Reverent.

"Him? Needing saving?" Daisy snorted. "Yeah, right."

"Where are you?" I demanded, cutting off the conversation. She did not need to know the finer details of just how much Knox needed saving, nor was that the right time to try to win her over and put her on Team Knox. I figured that would take a while, if he stuck around.

A stab of panic hit my midsection at the thought of him being anywhere but there. With me.

"San Francisco," Daisy answered, taking the change of subject in stride. "Well, Napa. We've got a little villa here." I didn't miss the warmth in her tone, the bashfulness.

"*We?*" I clarified. "As in you and Joey?" I'd known they were together, but the hitch in her voice told me that they were also *together.*

I got the job of seducing and killing the mafia don, and she honeymooned—for lack of a better word—in wine country with the mafia man who started all of this. Exactly how it should've been.

This was the pinnacle of me protecting Daisy from the horrors of life, the full consequences of thoughtless actions. It wasn't exactly healthy of me, but I didn't give a shit. I'd preserve my sister's hopeful naïveté for the rest of my life if I could.

"Yes, yes. I don't want to hear it," she whined, obviously expecting some kind of lecture about Joey. I wasn't going to give one, since I didn't really have a leg to stand on when it came to talking about choosing appropriate partners. It didn't mean I liked Joey, though. "He did save our lives, after all."

I pinched the bridge of my nose. It didn't serve me to point out that he was the one who put our lives in danger in the first place. Without Joey, we never would've been pulled into this world. If my sister had never met Joey, I never would've met Knox. Unthinkable. Somehow, I owed my life as I knew it to one of my sister's lovers.

Fate was a funny thing.

"You're coming back to the city?" I asked, yearning to see my sister. Despite the complicated situation that would arise with her and Knox being in the same vicinity again. I would never be able to forget his hands on her neck.

"Eventually," Daisy said, guilt soaking her tone. "As long as you're safe," she added quickly, obviously feeling strange about taking a vacation when she knew I'd been through some serious shit.

Sure, the thought of being able to see my sister again, to download all that I'd been through on someone familiar, was tempting. But I'd never tell her the full truth of it anyway. My sister was all sunshine, no clouds. I'd added a whole bunch of clouds to my persona in the past weeks. I didn't want to change the way she saw me.

I looked at Knox, my eyes catching on the ridges of his face, the glorious profile he cut. "I'm safe," I whispered. And I truly was. Knox was danger personified. Death personified. Everything I'd always protected myself from. Nevertheless, I felt safe.

"Good. We've got a lot to catch up on, huh?" Unsurprisingly,

Daisy's good nature persevered as she failed to catch all the layers to my response.

My eyes refused to look from Knox, worried about the shape of our future. "That we do."

"But we made it," Daisy's voice filtered through the phone, triumph in it.

"We made it," I agreed. Another victory for the Matthews women.

"Grandma would be proud."

My eyes squeezed shut. Sometimes my sister could be obtuse, and other times, she could be perceptive to an uncanny degree.

"She really would," I choked out, thinking of my hard yet soft grandmother. Complicated, strong, fierce and kind. A woman of multitudes.

We lingered in the silence of our grief and love for a handful of seconds before a squeal punctured the quiet.

"Joey," Daisy laughed. "Don't, I'm talking to—"

The call cut off, in true Daisy fashion. I smiled at the screen, shaking my head and feeling endlessly grateful that some things hadn't changed.

I put the phone down between me and Knox.

His hand instantly threaded with mine.

I didn't ask exactly where we were going. I didn't need to. It didn't matter. Though I had a guess—and though I'd yearned to go home—trepidation filled me at the prospect of those walls, whether I'd ever fit between them again.

My hand fit in Knox's.

I'd figure out the rest.

———

Knox was cooking in my kitchen.

In my apartment.

Within twenty-four hours of killing the head of a criminal organization. It was the early hours now. I hadn't bothered to pick up my phone again. It had once been a lifeline to the world, one I'd been unhealthily glued to. Being without it for so long had made it lose its appeal. Why in the heck would I want to mindlessly scroll right then?

Knox had asked what I'd eaten, after he'd traipsed through my apartment like an anthropologist walking through the home of a foreign tribe.

He didn't touch anything, just stared at the pictures in frames. Some art I collected from antique stores and flea markets, anything with woods or fairies or a little bit magical. Crystals were placed around various surfaces, same with candles. Photos of me with friends and of me with Daisy. I didn't look too closely at those. I was a different person in them.

The one frame he did pick up was my most treasured. Two small, beaming girls with dirt on their faces, clinging to a long-haired woman in an apron, with the backdrop of the Appalachian woods.

The last photo we had taken with my grandmother.

Knox stared at it for an impossibly long time before setting it back down with the utmost gentleness.

He was a slash of black in my colorful space. So large in it. I worried if I blinked too much, he'd disappear.

There was no food in my fridge, since I'd been gone for a month, but he'd found things in the pantry to cook. Pasta, olive oil, some fancy tinned fish I'd paid way too much for and hadn't known what to do with.

"Do you want children?" he asked as he set various ingredients out. I'd leaned on my kitchen table, watching him.

I pondered the question which had been hurled out of left field. Of all the things I'd thought he might ask me, that was not one of them.

"I can't have children, remember?" I replied carefully, though I was pretty sure he remembered. He held on to the most minute details, saving them up, storing them somewhere important. That's how intense his feelings were for me. It felt immensely world-changing to have someone want to know you that entirely. Study you that deeply.

"Yes, but do you *want* them?" he probed. "Traditional pregnancy is not the only way to become a mother."

I watched his face for a sign of where his mind was going, but he wore a mask so solid, even I couldn't find a tell. And I'd made it my business to study this man very deeply.

I tapped my finger against my thigh. "No, it's not the only journey to become a mother."

I'd thought about being a mom many times over the years, more since my thirtieth birthday had come and gone. Then my thirty-first, and so on. I might not have had a biological clock, but I felt the window of time closing in on me. If I did choose to become a mother, the process was infinitely more complicated for me—especially doing it alone. It would take a long time to even get a child, by then I'd be older, and society demonized older mothers almost more than those who didn't have children at all.

"The process is long and expensive..." I said instead of voicing the conclusion I'd come to long ago, what I'd always known in my heart of hearts.

"Money is no object, and I could get you a baby within a month, if that's what you wanted." His posture was rigid, eyes full of ice.

I stared at him. "You don't joke, and now is a *super* weird time to start."

He didn't answer me, which I assumed was his menacing way of saying he was not joking.

"You could 'get' me a baby?" I air quoted. "You're in the business of trafficking infants?" Previously, I had been certain that there was nothing Knox could do that would affect my feelings toward him, taint them. But children were a hard line. I'd been sure that he wouldn't touch them, wouldn't harm them.

He shook his head, and I sagged with relief, knowing he caught the gesture. "I know powerful people, and I have money. I'm owed a lot of favors." He filled up a pot with water. "You think the billionaires of this world wait for anything? They jump the line for healthcare, organ transplants, drugs not available to the general public, and children—if they want them."

Okay, he was serious. Deadly serious. And deadly *rich* if he was talking about having the kind of money required to procure a baby through murky 'legitimate' means.

I hadn't thought about Knox's financial situation. It hadn't really been top of the list when we first met. Or any time after. Sure, he wore very nice suits, everything about him was expensive and sophisticated, but I'd never equated that with what it might've meant in the real world.

We'd lived in a suspended sort of reality, never giving myself the luxury of thinking about us in the real world. I was suddenly clutched with panic as to what that would look like.

How it would work.

We'd made it through the entire Italian mob trying to get us and a boatload of childhood trauma just to have the mundanity of life destroy us? Surely not. That was too tragic for even a tragic love story.

I forced myself back into the present, with Knox, where he was waiting not so patiently for my response. His energy had grown even tenser, eyes clouding over with a sharpness I knew he used as a defense.

"No," I whispered. "No, I do not want to be a mother." I drew in a long breath after releasing the words that were so shameful and frowned upon even in our post-feminist society—if such a concept ever truly existed.

Who was a woman who didn't want children? There must've been something wrong with her. She must've been cold, selfish, damaged. Or simply not smart enough to know her own mind.

The few women I had told this secret to early on in my twenties had rolled their eyes, patted my arm patronizingly and assured me I'd change my mind. As if my own mind wasn't mine. Since then, I hadn't spoken of my plans not to have them, had tightly smiled whenever people raised the subject.

My eyes fixed on Knox. "Even before the cancer, I knew that's not what I wanted. I'm sure it has a whole bunch to do with the trauma I grew up with, my own mommy issues, but whatever the crux of it is, that's not what I want. Not who I want to be. I want to be the eccentric aunt to Daisy's brood."

I thought good-naturedly about my sister who, thankfully, was safe and to her eternal knowledge that she'd be the mother to break generational curses and heal generational wounds. If there was anyone who could do it, it was her.

"I love my job," I continued. "I get to be around the best of children and fill that void inside of me that nature created. And I also get to be around the worst of them, to remind me that I don't have the tools to navigate that on a full-time, never-ending basis."

I waited. For him to assure me I'd change my mind or to reject me for being horrifyingly unfeminine and wrong for not wanting to be a mother. Even if he was sure about not wanting children. Men had a funny way of doing things. They wanted women with a backbone, but they wanted to be able to bend it. Didn't want children but wanted their partner to have that nurturing instinct. Without it, she was damaged.

Though I thought better of Knox, knew better of Knox, the concrete admission sent a thread of fear through me.

"Good," was all Knox said.

Then he turned around to make dinner.

"Good?" I stepped forward, unable to let sleeping dogs lie. I had to pick and pull, see if there were any loose threads that I could tug on, that would unravel us.

He nodded, tipping pasta into boiling water before reaching for a tin of fish.

I put my hand on his wrist. "There needs to be more context as to the question and the response. Do *you* want children?"

He looked at me blankly for a moment then let out a bark of cold laughter. "No," he said soberly. "Absolutely not." His face screamed of shame I wished I could scoop right out of him.

"I'm not ... capable," he stared down at the boiling water. "I'm barely capable of loving you in a way that won't destroy you wholly." I watched his knuckles whiten as he gripped the tin he was holding.

It didn't surprise me, his stance on children. I'd have been knocked over by a feather had he said he wanted a family. But I felt relieved, nonetheless. Not relieved about the trauma he endured that made him believe he was not worthy to be a father, but that we would not be separated over such conflicting needs.

"What would you have done," I asked, stroking his hand. "If I had said yes, that I wanted a baby?"

"I would've gotten you a baby," he replied without pause.

I swallowed at the answer, the devotion with which he spoke. As if I just had to request anything in the world and he'd procure it for me, human beings included. "And where would you be in this equation?"

His gaze shuttered. "Close," he murmured. "Close enough to watch you both, to keep you safe. Ensure that your lives are long and happy. But you'd never lay eyes on me again."

My body revolted against the promise in his tone, his certainty.

"You'd l-leave m-me?" I pulled my hand back. Or attempted to, at least.

"I'd never leave you." He snatched hold of my wrist again. "I'd give you everything you deserved and ensure you kept it."

I looked over his shoulder as I digested this. "What if I met another man?" It was unfair, cruel to us both to keep the hypothetical going, but I was a woman. I couldn't help but live in the imagined future.

Knox tightened his hold on me.

"If I met another man?" I pressed, even though he was radiating deadly fury. Even though my wrist was beginning to protest with a pain I was becoming used to.

Knox's eyes darted up to me, the can clattering against the counter. He backed me against the fridge.

I gasped at the impact against my back as he caged me in. I was never complacent with him, my body never becoming accustomed to his nearness, his need. Every time was like the first time.

Knox hovered inches from me, hips pressing into mine with sublime pressure. "If you met another man, I'd imagine his death every moment of my life. But I wouldn't kill him as long as he made you happy." His eyes made a slow tour up and down my body. His gaze told me he was hungry, needful, but irate too. "Now are we done with this fucking insane conversation?"

I pursed my lips, nodding, knowing when to back down.

"Good." He pushed off the fridge and resumed cooking as if the most intense conversation I'd ever had hadn't even happened.

We'd eaten in complete silence, not speaking since the conversation about children. Knox was still stewing. I was a little angry at myself. I couldn't help but push him, strain the limits of this dynamic between us, trying to find the edges.

There was no edge.

No end.

I was scared I had hurt him, ruined something sacred between us, until the second we finished the meal when he sent all the plates clattering from the dining room table then fucked me on it. The man had never-ending stamina, as did I, despite my injuries and the general trauma of the past week. If anything, it made me more desperate for the escape he offered. The safety of our coupling, drowning out everything that wasn't connected to our bodies.

Still, we hadn't spoken, not afterward, not as we cleaned up or as he carried me to the bedroom, tugging my naked body so I lay on his chest, arms locking around me just a little too tight. Just how I liked it.

"Will we survive this?" I asked in the darkness.

Gone was the quiet the woods offered. Sirens sounded in the distance, street noise filtered in, grating against my ears.

Knox's arms might've tightened around me had they not already been as tight as humanly possible.

"The real world," I continued. "Will we survive it?"

Some of the tension in my body slackened with relief of asking the question that I'd been torturing myself with.

"Yes."

I waited for more of an explanation, even though I knew Knox well enough to know he wasn't one to offer more when he didn't feel the need to.

"Yes?" I echoed. "That's it?"

Knox shifted me so I was straddling him, the movement sending a gasp from my mouth as my tender, aching body ground against him where he was rapidly hardening against me.

His hand curled around the back of my neck, then he yanked me down so our foreheads pressed together.

"Yes, Petal. That is it. We, us, will survive whatever comes because there is no other option."

The way he said this was so concrete, so certain, it had the power to wipe all of my doubts away.

For a time, at least.

For once, Knox fell asleep before me. I heard it in the cadence of his breath, the very slight loosening of his grip. He still held me as if he were convinced I'd melt from his fingers.

Though I was exhausted in a way I'd never been in my life, I was unable to sleep. I wasn't haunted by taking another life—a subject Knox hadn't broached, interestingly. Sure, my actions rattled in my brain, promising to make a mark at some point, but as of yet, it failed to land.

Instead of lifeless eyes and spurting blood, I thought of Knox.

I thought about the choices I'd made that led me here.

In love. With a dangerous man. The one kind I'd sworn I'd stay away from ever since I was old enough to comprehend my father's role in our destruction.

But if there was anything I'd learned from the past month, from what I'd observed with Lukyan and Elizabeth, it was that there were two kinds of dangerous men. There were the ones who ensured women didn't walk home alone in the dark, who we were cautious with when rejecting them, who believed women were just objects to be owned. Then there were the dangerous men who considered us their treasure. Not theirs to own but theirs to protect. The dangerous men who would never hurt us but would protect us from a world designed to break us. The men who would commit the most heinous crimes, cover themselves with blood and gore, to keep us clean. And who would teach us to become weapons in our own right when we wanted to fight too. Men who weren't afraid of strength in their women. Who fed it like kindling to flame.

As these thoughts raced through my mind, I understood how my mother had fallen for my father. Stayed with him. Because she was looking for the latter type of man. All that violent energy... She'd hoped that he'd expend it outward to keep her safe, not inward to keep her tortured, captive.

Despite Knox's hold on my body, I felt anything but captive. I was freer than I'd ever been in my life.

And on that thought, I fell into a deep sleep.

EPILOGUE

I t's your birthday."

Knox handed me a coffee that he'd taken to making in the espresso machine, the one new addition to the apartment since he'd moved in. That and the easel in the sunroom—the jewel of the apartment. Such a rare find in a city of studio apartments with barely any windows, let alone a whole room of them, bathing in morning sunlight.

We'd created a ritual of sorts. He started the morning by fucking me. Always. Unless I was sick or overly tired or not in the mood, which was incredibly rare. On those occasions, though, he did not sulk or punish me for rejecting him; he didn't change an iota of his behavior. He respected my boundaries, which I had few of with him. That made him all the more sexy and more emotionally mature than 99 percent of the male population. Respect for boundaries. Hotter than any six-pack. Though he had one of those too.

He cooked for me—another thing that he always did. Breakfast, lunch and dinner. That was unless I was in the mood to cook too, which again was rare since he was incredibly good at it, and I liked being taken care of in that way by him. He repeatedly said he was bad and wrong and would destroy me, yet he did small, everyday things that a run-of-the-mill, suburban husband with a 'normal' upbringing failed to do to his wife daily.

He *nurtured* me.

After fucking, food and coffee, I ran.

He'd trail behind me, unseen if he sensed I needed the alone time, other times running with me. We'd had a small argument about whether the shadowing was necessary.

"I ran alone in the woods in the middle of nowhere," I reminded him that first morning, my body yearning for the crunch of detritus underneath my shoes, the smell of pine and even the scent of the cabin. Old, musty.

Brackets of lines framed his eyes with the deepness of his frown, his mouth pulled into a thin line. "Yes, and the worst you could encounter there was bears," he replied in a clipped tone. "Which you had spray for. The worst you can encounter here is a man. There's no spray for that. There's me for that."

And that was his argument. Which I couldn't counter, beyond him being over-the-top protective and possessive. Which he was. He was obsessed with my safety, nearly ripped the face off any man who looked at me too long. Life in the city was unraveling him a little. He was used to living in the shadows, killing people, only interacting with criminals in the underworld. Now that I'd brought him into the light, into Whole Foods, out to dinners with friends— he was struggling with his new identity.

Not that he'd ever admit to that.

But there were growing pains.

I could see that.

And I was too. Struggling, that was.

I'd slotted back into the life I'd made to fit me so precisely. The apartment, the job that somehow welcomed me back with few questions, and the friends who had a bit more questions about how I'd taken off for a walk across Spain with no warning and had come home with a deadly-attractive, menacing boyfriend who barely said boo to anyone and scowled his way through dinner, twirling my hair between his fingers instead of answering questions.

I found that I was a convincing liar.

I discovered that I had become a new shape that didn't fit into the life I'd so valued.

The city was too loud. Too crowded. Yet I still loved it. The chaos. The vibrancy. The shine had come off, though. After relishing the freshness of the mountains, the pristine nature of the woods. The quiet.

I felt caught, stretched between two worlds. Though I loved my job, going back to a place where I cared for toddlers was ... uncomfortable, given the fact that I was a killer. I'd seen people die. I'd killed someone.

It didn't quite haunt me the way I thought it would. I didn't wake up in the middle of the night covered in sweat, shaking off nightmares. No panic attacks, flashbacks. I just felt ... colder. Like I'd opened up a gaping canyon in me I was afraid of. Sometimes, in the middle of finger painting, my hands covered in paint, I remembered when it had been blood. Yes, that was difficult but not impossible to handle.

"It is my birthday," I answered Knox, trying to remind myself to live in the present, not to live in an existential crisis. At the time, I was holding a hot mug of coffee, and the man I loved was standing in my kitchen shirtless, his scars illuminated by the morning light, looking at me with a warmth that the sun could never produce.

"You weren't going to tell me." His eyes narrowed.

I smiled at him, unafraid of his ire. I knew that it unsettled him, that his menace bounced right off me. "I didn't think I'd need to, considering you likely rectified any lack of research you'd done." I was teasing, but also, I had assumed that he'd delved into every corner of my life, intent on finding out every benign detail about me.

"I don't need to delve into anything to learn things about you, Petal." He stepped forward. "Except here." His hand ghosted over my breasts, feathering over my peaked nipples to settle above my pounding heart. "And here." The other skimmed my stomach to cup me possessively between my legs.

Even though he had just fucked me extraordinarily well, I still hungered for more of his possessive touch.

I wondered if I'd ever satisfy my appetite for him. Ever stop needing him in a way that felt hard to weather.

I doubted it.

"I don't like making a fuss about my birthday," I told him in a gasping breath. "It falls at a rather ... odd time."

Knox loosened his grip between my legs, but he didn't let me go.

He let me bathe in the silence, sipping my coffee as he held me close. He still did that, held me whenever I was within arm's length, with a desperation that he thought I might just dissipate. Dissolve into nothing.

He wasn't trusting of our new state.

Happiness, I tried to explain it to him as if the concept were as foreign as pigs flying.

"My birthday happens in the summer," I stated the obvious. "Which meant it was celebrated with my grandmother."

I smiled as I remembered homemade cakes decorated with berries we picked ourselves. Presents wrapped in old scarves. Music blasting into the night as we stayed up past our bedtime, the summer air still balmy.

I squeezed my eyes shut. "And then we stopped going. I only had one more birthday here in New York. My mother attempted to make it special, but she wasn't practiced in that."

She'd tried to make a cake but burned it. The money for presents was spent on booze. My father had smashed the stereo the night before, and he was sleeping off a hangover, so we all had to tiptoe around.

"The next year, my father killed her then himself a month before my birthday." I squeezed my mug tighter than I needed to. "And that was when we were still in foster care while social workers tried to track down family." Eventually, they'd tracked down my aunt, the one who owned this very apartment, and we got lucky with a kind, quirky guardian willing to take us in. "The day got lost, and I never really found it again," I whispered, catching Knox's gaze. "It kind of has a gloomy shadow over it."

I didn't tell him that in my drinking days, I'd spend the day with the curtains drawn and in the bathtub with a bottle of vodka. Daisy had long given up on trying to make it special as I'd done a good job of convincing her that I didn't want the attention.

A foreign concept to her, but she'd accepted it.

Once I got sober, I drowned my sorrows in a cake I'd make every year, my grandmother's recipe. I did that alone, usually while rewatching some '90s TV shows, maybe shopping online for a pair of shoes I didn't need.

It was all the celebration I gave myself.

Knox stared at me after my admission, his hand tucking a stray hair behind my ears, nostrils flaring. "I doubt I'll do a satisfactory job of lifting the shadow from the day, since I'm not practiced, but..."

He stepped back to take an object from the kitchen counter.

I frowned at it in his outstretched palm.

It was a key. Old and rusted.

My soul skipped as I took a hopeful guess as to what it was.

"Our cabin?" I asked, not daring to breathe.

Knox nodded curtly. "It is yours, actually. Name's on the title."

My head snapped up. "Add yours. It's ours." The order was clear in my voice.

His lip twitched. He was doing more of that. Almost smiling. Being more expressive. "Yes, ma'am."

And more of that. Deferring to me. Submitting to me in a way that managed to be alpha and irresistible all at once.

I stared at the key. He was giving me something infinitely special. Something precious. A chance to revisit the past. Not just ours but the treasured past with my grandmother. The ability to relive it. Honor it. He was offering me a different future. One that already felt like the perfect fit

"About the names..." I grasped the key in my hand. It felt much heavier than it really was. Maybe because of the past and futures it contained.

"I have a birthday request," I whispered, nerves crawling up my throat, making it impossible to speak any louder.

"Anything." Knox didn't hesitate.

Though I was afraid, I didn't drop eye contact. "I'd like yours," I said quietly.

I didn't think Knox could be shocked, but I'd managed it.

His mouth was no longer twitched upward; it was slightly open, his expression entirely blank.

"My name, my heritage is not something I'm proud of," he replied in an even tone.

"I'm not asking for your name because of your past," I whispered. "I want it because of *our* future."

He didn't say anything for a long time. Didn't move. He stood as still as a statue, whereas I fidgeted with unease as I waited for his response, unable to read any of his emotions.

"You want my name?" he repeated.

I nodded, trying to keep my composure. "I would like to be your wife."

There it was. The thing I wanted more than anything.

"You're my *everything*," he growled. "You don't need a ceremony and a contract for that. A contract steeped in traditions of trading women like livestock."

I didn't even try to hide my smile at Knox's feminist argument against marriage.

I folded my arms in front of me. "Yet here I am, wanting to be yours. By law."

"I don't adhere to the laws of this country," he reminded me harshly.

"So that's a no?" I asked, trying to fight back the need to burst into tears.

He glared at me. "Of course, it's not a fucking no."

Then he kissed me. Hard.

And just like that, we were engaged.

KNOX

"I thought I said I'd kill you if I ever saw you again," I told the man who had joined me on the rooftop of Piper's apartment building.

It wasn't unusual for me to go up there without her. I regularly left her sleeping in the apartment I'd outfitted with top-of-the-line security. There were still weak spots, though. Neighbors. Shared elevator. Fire escape.

That was the only downside of living in her home—the lack of privacy and control over the environment. My penthouse encompassed an entire floor, meaning no one could access it unless they had access to the private elevator that was monitored at all times.

Giving it up was a concession, a big fucking concession, I'd made because Piper loved her home. I enjoyed being in her space immensely. Every corner of it was filled with her.

Though I felt as if I cast a shadow over those corners, unable to understand just how I'd fit into her life.

That was the reason I hadn't killed Lukyan on sight and had agreed to the meeting when he'd reached out through untraceable means.

A chuckle sounded through the night. I was surprised to hear it come from him. "Unfortunately, just like me, Knox, love has made you ... less trigger-happy."

I lifted the gun I was holding in his direction, hating that he understood my weakness. I should've killed him for that alone. "Sure about that?"

He stepped forward to join me, unfazed by the gun I was pointing at him, finger on the trigger. "I'm sure, since I promised you what I'd do if you pointed a gun at me again."

Threat was clear in his tone, one that would have most grown men shitting themselves, knowing their time in this world was approaching its end.

Lukyan wouldn't have come here to kill me, though. Not by coming announced anyway.

"What is this about?" I was not one for small talk.

"I am aware that you are not interested in keeping ties with the new leadership at Rosso." The restaurant was the hub of the mob, the central heart. Whoever controlled Rosso controlled the organization.

I stared out into the city. "Considering they are a grudge-holding lot who would kill me on sight if they knew about my involvement in Stone's demise, and worse, Piper, no." My throat constricted at the very thought. We had been extremely thorough in ensuring that everyone who knew about Piper's connection to Stone was in the ground, but I couldn't let myself lapse into a false sense of security.

Especially since I had the bad sense to keep Joey breathing. He was, apparently, out of the game and in love with Daisy, but that didn't stop me from lying awake at night, thinking of him as the weak link who one day, when Daisy inevitably cast him aside, would be mad enough to want revenge. There were numerous times I'd gotten close to ignoring Piper's wishes and my promise to her about sparing Joey's life for her sister's happiness. A broken promise was nothing compared to Piper's life. But I'd stopped every time.

Because it would hurt Piper. Wound her. That betrayal. And I couldn't gather enough strength to do that.

"So you're in need of a job," Lukyan's voice cut through my thoughts.

I ground my teeth together. "I have enough money to fund a hundred lifetimes." Which was true. Stone had paid me well, and I'd amassed plenty of funds before my tenure with him. I'd learned how to play the stock market. Money was security. I could buy anything I wanted. Except I didn't want a fucking thing beyond my woman, safe and warm and happy.

Lukyan smiled at me, white teeth shining in the moonlight. "I'm not talking about money. You're not going to retire and take up chess in the park. You can't. I speak from experience."

I'd thought about this, realizing that no matter how fundamentally Piper had changed me, she couldn't erase the past or change my nature. I'd always thirst for death, something to keep the beasts at bay.

"I won't answer to anyone," I snarled, comprehending what he was hinting at. He was offering me a fucking job. As if I'd bow down to him.

"I'm not asking you to," he replied, his tone telling me he was still amused. "I'm looking for a partner."

This surprised me. Lukyan and I had never enjoyed a cordial relationship. Actually, I'd been halfway certain he would kill me one day. He was the only one even remotely capable of that. Yet there he was, offering to be fucking partners.

"I'm a married man now, to an extraordinary woman who can hold her own in our world." His normally lifeless tone gained a richness that I didn't miss when talking about his wife. "I am unable to change myself for her, but I've found I'd like to ... adjust my business. I'd like to send those to the grave who deserve it but go untouched in our world."

My surprise was bone-deep, but I didn't show it. "You want to police the underworld?" I bit back a laugh, only because he was deadly fucking serious. That and I didn't laugh.

"Police?" He shook his head. "No judges, no jury. Just executioners.

And we'll make this a business how?" I asked, unable to not be intrigued.

He smiled, knowing he'd caught me. He'd fucking caught me. "Killing is always a business. We'll meet about the details at a later date." He buttoned his suit. "But you're agreeable. This partnership means we make a gentleman's agreement not to kill each other."

"We're not gentlemen," I reminded him.

"That we're not."

Regardless, he extended his hand.

And regardless, I shook it.

Piper

We hadn't decided on where we would live long-term. We were going through too many changes already, especially once Knox's paintings had been picked up by an incredibly prestigious gallery. Only on the provision that he remained anonymous, not in any way tied to any of the publicity surrounding the sale or promotion.

He said it was because of his enemies, which I was sure was partly true. But I knew it was also because he'd never be fully ready to come out of the shadows, even if he was baring pieces of his soul to the sunlight.

These stipulations along with the exquisite surrealism of the paintings were what made them blow up more, selling for *six figures.*

I'd known they were stunning, that they spoke to me on a cellular level, that they were magic, but I thought it was because I was unequivocally in love with the painter.

Knox hadn't even blinked at the money or the popularity, so I often questioned whether it had been the right decision to take them to a gallery and force him into a different life.

Not that he was entirely in a different life. He didn't give me a lot of details—he still wasn't a man of many words—but I knew that Knox had engaged in some kind of *partnership* with Lukyan.

He'd mentioned it in clipped tones, then I'd spoken to Elizabeth on the phone—we did that sometimes—and she'd given me a little more detail. But not much. I was on the outside. Because I wasn't one of them. That knowledge chafed at me, even as I tried to shrug it off.

I knew they weren't starting a bourbon company together. I knew that Knox left some nights, and when he came home, his energy was both heavier and lighter at the same time. He wasn't done killing. I didn't know if he'd ever be done. He couldn't be repaired just with my love and a paintbrush and an easel. Not that I thought he needed repairing. He had stopped cutting himself, though, which I took as a large victory.

No, I didn't think he'd ever leave the shadows completely, but he still stood in the sunlight with me.

And I was finding I liked to exist in the shadows too.

———

We married in the cabin.

The guest list was short. Daisy and Joey—who were somehow still together. Joey who shot uneasy glances in Knox's direction as if he was waiting for him to shoot him between the eyes at any moment.

I secretly thought Knox enjoyed torturing him just a little.

The three other guests were Kane, Avery and Mabel.

The resemblance between the brothers was uncanny yet also unsettling. They were so alike. Kane was maybe a glimpse of who Knox might've been... Easy to smile. Warm. Friendly.

Not that I wanted Knox to be any different. I just mourned the life he might've had without his trauma, even if it meant we never would've met.

Kane had hugged me within seconds of meeting me.

I returned the hug, surprised at the open affection that his brother did not possess. He squeezed me then held me at arm's length, not letting go even though I knew Knox was staring daggers at him.

I wanted to roll my eyes. It was his *brother* who was hugging me in front of his wife and daughter. I doubted he was a threat. But Knox didn't know how to turn that off.

"What do you do for a job, Piper?" Kane asked, still holding my upper arms. "Knox has been really fucking cagey about this whole thing, about you. But you're gonna be at our table for Christmas, Thanksgiving, Easter, Mabel's birthday. He's not gonna be able to keep you wrapped up in bubble wrap." He winked at me.

My skin warmed at the forgone conclusion of us being with them for the holidays. At the slight hesitation to his tone. I got the sense that Knox had not been in attendance for previous holidays. And that Kane loved his brother.

"We're not coming for fucking holidays," Knox cut in at the same time I said, "Of course, we'll be there."

He glared at me. I beamed back at him before looking at his brother again.

"To answer your earlier question, I'm a kindergarten teacher."

Kane's amiable gaze went blank for a long moment before he threw his head back and laughed. True belly laughter.

I smiled with him because I understood he wasn't laughing at me. He was laughing at the absurdity of his badass brother getting married to a kindergarten teacher with wildflowers threaded through her hair.

Kane's ice-blue eyes were shimmering as they caught hold of

mine, no longer laughing. "Thank you," he said, his voice low and rich.

"For what?" I asked, confused.

He looked at his glowering brother with a smile. "For being his sunlight. He deserves it."

I'd been in danger of bursting into tears right there and then, but luckily, with a toddler around, the tender moment was quickly interrupted with squeals of delight at discovering a butterfly and then tripping over a log. Both Kane and Knox rushed to Mabel's aid.

That was when my attention moved to his stunning wife, Avery. It took me a while to recognize her since she looked different from the photo I'd seen of her in a restaurant review. The photo had shown a striking woman, but one who was hard, severe looking. Nothing like the warm, smiling woman who gave me a hug of my own then one to Knox, even though every signal he was giving off shouted that he repelled physical contact. She wasn't scared of him.

Same with Mabel, who clawed at Knox's leg until he relented and picked her up with a grimace she didn't notice as she put two small hands to his cheeks and laid a kiss right on his lips.

He winced, but I didn't miss the softening of his features, the way he held on to that little girl like she was priceless.

It was heartwarming to watch. Precious. The love he didn't think he was capable of was staring right at me, giggling at the teddy bear that was her uncle.

Mabel was the flower girl at our small ceremony that Knox had fought tooth and nail against but quickly relented to when I told him how important it was to me.

"We don't have to do any of the traditional vows," I'd assured him. "Or mention gods or sins."

Kane had officiated with what could only be described as a shit-eating grin on his face.

"I promise to never let you go and to kill anyone who hurts you," were Knox's vows, unsurprisingly.

This had elicited a low cough from Kane, covering a chuckle.

I'd merely smiled, expecting nothing less. "I promise to be yours. Forever."

My vows were slightly less bloodthirsty but no less true.

I had no idea what our future entailed.

But it was ours.

Whatever came.

And I was more than okay with that.

A monster had brought me to this cabin in order to break me.

And instead, I'd broken the monster, splitting him apart to reveal the man inside.

ACKNOWLEDGMENTS

I never intended on writing this book. After writing *Things We Burn*, the plan was to go to the next book in the Jupiter Tides series. But Knox had other ideas.

The second I started writing his character, I felt a spark. A low whisper of his story.

And the second *Things We Burn* was done, I started writing *Captive Souls*.

I needed to. My own soul needed to. An outlet for some of the anxiety I have been feeling. I find writing dark books when I'm struggling with my own mental health to be deeply healing. I find solace in broken characters.

Writing this book with a toddler that doesn't sleep, a husband doing his Master's degree and family across the world was *hard*.

Raising a child without a village is *hard*.

Writing this book, I was overcome with guilt as I snuck away to get words in. I'd tap at my keyboard exhausted at the end of the night.

But I did it.

And just like raising a child takes a village, so to does writing every book I write. I couldn't do it without the wonderful people in my life.

Taylor. My husband. My baby daddy. My best friend. Thank you for being my biggest cheerleader, for being patient with me as I navigate through this season of our life. Thank you for taking over bedtime and naps so I could get this book done. I love you so much.

Juni. Our little June Bug. You made me a mother. You make me a better person every day. Everything I do now is to make you proud. Make you happy. I consider it my greatest honor and achievement to be your mum.

Mum. Thank you for supporting my dreams, for talking me through motherhood, for being there to cut the cord, to hold your granddaughter while we got much needed sleep. Thank you for giving me such a wonderful model of motherhood to look up to.

Dad. You never got to meet your granddaughter. I know that you would have adored her. I know you're watching from somewhere, so proud of her. Unfortunately, you are the reason I know how to write about loss. I feel lucky to have had you as my dad but I wish every day I had you for longer.

Annette. You have been there for me through so much. You help me with everything book related, everything life related. You're such a special person.

Jessica. You're such a talented author, such a great friend. Thanks for always being there to vent, to proof my blurbs, to help inspire me.

Kim. Thank you for working so hard to make this book into what it is today.

Cat Imb. Your light is so bright, your heart is so big and your talent is endless. Thank you for creating covers that make me want to write a book worthy of them. Thank you for being my friend. I adore you.

Ginny. Thank you so much for always being there. For loving my characters as much as I do. For telling me what I need to hear. You are the best.

My girls. Harriet, Polly & Emma. You're half a world away but distance means nothing. You've all gotten me through some of the hardest times of my life and I'm so so lucky to have you as friends, as sisters.

And last but not least, **you, the reader**. Without you, dear reader, I would not be here. I would not be creating stories as a job. Thank you for making my dreams come true.

About the Author

ANNE MALCOM has been an avid reader since before she can remember, her mother responsible for her love of reading. It started with magical journeys into the world of Hogwarts and Middle Earth, then as she grew up her reading tastes grew with her. Her love of reading doesn't discriminate, she reads across many genres. She can't get enough romance, especially when some possessive alpha males throw their weight around.

One day, in a reading slump, Cade and Gwen's story came to her and started taking up space in her head until she put their story into words. Now that she has started, it doesn't look like she's going to stop anytime soon, with many more characters demanding their story be told as well.

Raised in small town New Zealand, Anne had a truly special childhood, growing up in one of the most beautiful countries in the world. She has backpacked across Europe, ridden camels in the Sahara and eaten her way through Italy, loving every moment.

Now, she's living her own happy ever after in the USA with her brilliant husband, their precious daughter and their two dogs.

Want to get in touch with Anne? She loves to hear from her readers.
You can email her: annemalcomauthor@hotmail.com
Or join her reader group on Facebook.

Unquiet Mind

Echoes of Silence

Skeletons of Us

Broken Shelves

Mistake's Melody

Censored Soul

Greenstone Security

Still Waters

Shield

The Problem With Peace

Chaos Remains

Resonance of Stars

The Vein Chronicles

Fatal Harmony

Deathless

Faults in Fate

Eternity's Awakening

Buried Destiny

Retired Sinners

Splinters of You

The Klutch Duet

Lies That Sinners Tell

Truths That Saints Believe

Standalones

Birds of Paradise - Elizabeth and Lukyan's story

Doyenne

Midnight Sommelier

Hush - co-written

What Grows Dies Here

A Thousand Cuts

New Hope, Old Grudges